THE
TREACHEROUS
SELFIE

BE CAREFUL OF WHAT YOU ASK IN PRAYER

JOHN MILAN DUDEFF

LifeRich Publishing is a registered trademark of The Reader's Digest Association, Inc.

LifeRich Publishing books may be ordered through booksellers or by contacting:

LifeRich Publishing
1663 Liberty Drive
Bloomington, IN 47403
www.liferichpublishing.com
844-686-9607

ISBN: 978-1-4897-3446-4 (sc)
ISBN: 978-1-4897-3445-7 (hc)
ISBN: 978-1-4897-3500-3 (e)

Library of Congress Control Number: 2021906422

Print information available on the last page.

LifeRich Publishing rev. date: 05/28/2021

For Margie, a true angel.

CONTENTS

CHAPTER 1

The small gray rat weaves his way around a track, using his size to maneuver between the larger and more experienced rats. The rodents are woven together like strands in a rope, twisted around one another, pushing to the finish. The audience of rats squeezed into the stands squeak and flash their teeth as the little rat advances past the older, gluttonous ones that feast on the immature or naive.

As the young one rushes to the end goal, a monstrous gnarled and worn rat pounces on it, crushing its life before leaping to the finish. The audience hisses with excitement. As this happens, Simon Northstrum jolts from his nap at the kitchen table, partly from the bad dream but more from his wife, Alexis, entering the kitchen.

"Have you been up long?" she asks her husband.

"I was watching the news, waiting for the coffee, and fell asleep. It was a nightmare about a pack of rodents on a track, and an older, larger rat devoured a smaller one, keeping him from bringing home the bacon."

"Good grief, Simon. That's a great way to start the day! You might switch to decaf." Patting him on his head, she asks, "What's in the news today?"

"More madness," Simon responds. "Another smashing day in heaven."

"Well, personally," Alexis tells him, "I can never see the news until I've at least had one cup of coffee."

Simon stands, pours his wife a cup of java, passes her the cup, and kisses her cheek. "Good morning."

Alexis responds, "Morning, hon." She takes a sip of coffee. "So in your dream, are the big, old rats still winning the rat race?"

"Looks like it," he grumbles. Alexis reaches up and grabs the bowls for breakfast as Simon gets the cereal from the cabinet. A yell comes from the hallway.

"Mom! Mom! Where is my blue skirt, the one with the stripes?"

Alexis responds to their daughter, Emma, "It's in your closet. Look closer. It's in there."

Simon mumbles, "Must she tear her room apart each morning?"

"Love, it's a girl thing. She needs to see all her clothing options." Changing the subject, Alexis asks him, "How is the job hunt going?"

"I'm still considering the offer from SassyApps."

"But you've not phoned them back?"

"No. It's a long fall from being the primary software engineer for the Martian rovers to receiving offers only from companies making useless applications that suck your time, brain power, and privacy. I don't know if I want to do stupid stuff."

Alexis holds her cup in both hands before she sips her coffee. She peers over the brim of the cup at her husband of eighteen years. "Honey, I don't enjoy working at a funeral home. It's depressing. But we are a team working together." After taking another sip, Alexis continues. "You're a brilliant engineer, and I'm proud I'm the only woman around who can tell people her husband talks to robots on other worlds. But honey, our family is in this world, and you need to take every possible offer. It may be a punch in the gut, but the offer is good, at least until JPL gets more funding."

Simon pauses and sips some coffee. "I wrote JPL a proposal on reestablishing the communication they lost with *Opportunity* and maybe even help them find *Sojourner*, *Spirit*, and *Curiosity*, which are just plain lost, period. It's on Norm's desk, but the military is monopolizing the rover manpower for communication and trolling. They're not even considering my proposal."

"Are you interested in getting into the communication end and helping with cybersecurity?"

"No way," Simon responds without hesitation. "I'll sell knives door-to-door before I'll work for those companies. In that business, it takes one corrupt bureaucrat who wants to gain power."

"But—"

Interrupting her, Simon continues. "Power and money are their exclusive domains, and they'll use the information collected to target people, groups, and specific jobs that don't side with them. They'll tell you it's for our security, with no evil intended—until, of course, they can sell the data for a decent gain. If you believe them, I've got Florida swampland to sell you. The more I talk to cybersecurity people, the more I'll stick to my robots."

Simon and Alexis glance toward the hall as movement disrupts the conversation. Their red-haired daughter makes her way into the kitchen with her cell phone resting between her ear and shoulder.

All of a sudden, Emma screams as her phone slips from her shoulder and crashes to the tile floor. The battery flies out the back of the phone, coming to a rest under the cabinet.

Looking at the scattered phone, Simon shakes his head and glances into his cereal bowl "I'm not buying a new phone," he mumbles.

"I heard that, Dad! The phone will be fine," Emma replies.

"Who are you talking to so early in the morning anyway? When I was your age, we had rules. People didn't call before or after a certain time unless there was an emergency."

"It's Sophia, Dad, and it *is* an emergency."

With light sarcasm, Simon responds, "Has she a medical problem? Should we call EMS?" Alexis glares at him and signals at him with a hand gesture to quit harassing Emma. He nods in resignation.

"Gee, Dad, chill. This is how we communicate today."

"Yeah, but are you listening?"

Alexis steps in with, "Simon, will you drop off the donated clothes at the church office?"

"Sure, hon. I'm mailing more résumés. I'll do it on the way."

Somewhat sternly, Alexis looks at Simon and tells him, "You call the job offer."

"You got a job offer, Dad?"

"Yes, Emma, only not in my field. I would create applications for communication companies."

"Wow! If you make a great one, like the old Farmville or Angry Birds, you and Mom can retire to an island."

"I can't envision being the person wasting everyone's time," Simon replies to his daughter's excitement. He then turns his attention toward a TV reporter who is beginning a story on the government use of computer surveillance to track people's emails and their use of the internet and cell phones.

"See what I mean?" Simon asserts. "That can't be good."

Emma, gulping down some cereal, gets up, leaving her dishes on the table.

"Emma," Simon tells her, "help out and put your dishes in the dishwasher." Emma mumbles while complying.

Alexis looks at the clock. "Emma, are you dressed for school? The bus will be here before long."

"No, Mom, but I will be in just a few minutes."

Simon turns toward Alexis and says, "Honey, you'd better get going yourself. I'll finish up things in the kitchen before my shower."

Alexis sweeps toward the hall, patting her husband on the way. "Thanks, honey."

Simon stands and watches as his wife moves down the hallway. He leans against the doorway and muses about how lucky he was to find her. He then turns back to the kitchen and the TV news.

"Hello, folks," the attractive blonde host says, "and welcome back to *America's Newsroom*. There's a fast-breaking story coming from the Johnson Jet Propulsion Labs, commonly known as JPL. They're experiencing difficulty contacting *Opportunity*, the current Mars rover. There may be a problem in the communication software. You may remember this robot sent amazing images and data from Mars."

Simon winces. "I left you software to help with this problem. But you military morons running the show now have to use your own material. It's bogus."

"Hey," Bill, the male cohost, interjects, "here's a scary thought. Is the government watching the rover's communication?"

"I don't know," his cohort, Martha, responds. "But if they oversee everyone else, why not the rovers?"

"Martha, if it could be talking with aliens, then they'll probably be looking at you immediately," Bill teases. "Stay tuned, folks. We'll have much more coming after the break, if I'm still around then. Hope to see you back shortly."

Emma yells from her bedroom, "Dad, can I go to the mall after school? Sophia and Amber are going."

He shouts back, "How are you getting there?"

"I hoped you could take us."

Simon shakes his head in disgust. "You have five minutes to get on the bus, and you are making plans to go to the mall? I can't manage it. I've got work to get done. Also, there's the rehearsal at church tonight. You need to do the mall thing another time."

Emma enters the kitchen. "Gee, Dad, don't bite my head off."

"Sorry. I have a great deal going on. Can we schedule it for later this week?"

"Sure, Dad, whatever," she responds, looking disappointed.

Simon turns toward his daughter, looks at her incredulously, and says, "Emma you're not going to wear your hair that way, are you?"

Alexis enters the kitchen, wagging her finger at him. "Emma, will you get my purse in the hallway?" Emma hurriedly leaves the room. Turning toward her husband, Alexis tells Simon, "The girls are wearing their hair that way. She looks like a big haired country artist from the fifties and was that an ornament from the Christmas tree in her hair? You remember your hairstyles back in the day? This is a battle we don't have to fight. It's cute, quirky, and different. And it's okay."

Bewildered, Simon replies, "What happened to the little girl who thought I hung the moon?"

"I know you think our beautiful child has become an alien, Simon, like your rovers hope to find on Mars. But loosen up. I read that we'll get our child back in about ten years."

"Great! A few years ago, I was a genius, and now the amoeba and I are comparable in intelligence."

"Emma still adores you. She's just fanning out her wings and flexing her independence."

"I'll say she is! It's God's way of giving you gray hair and making me bald."

"My hair isn't graying yet, old man." Alexis pats Simon's head. "And you still have most of your hair."

Simon stands, turns his wife around, and embraces and kisses her. Looking into her eyes, he says, "Thank you for helping by working. I promise I will get us back on track soon."

"I've never doubted you, and God has a plan for you."

"Yeah, so I've heard. But I didn't get the playbook yet."

"Honey, don't doubt yourself. We're behind you in whatever you do. I can work at the funeral home while you explore things." Glancing up at the clock, Alexis says, "I have to get moving." Flitting away, she grabs her keys and heads toward the garage doorway.

"Alexis," Simon calls to her. She turns. He then says, lightheartedly, "You know you work with a bunch of stiffs, don't you?"

She smirks at his corny joke. "Next," she responds, "you'll tell me, they are dying to get in there. Go take your shower, and call the app people."

"Yes ma'am." He salutes as Alexis departs. And then, turning his attention to Emma back in her bedroom, he asks, "Emma, you ready?"

Emma enters the kitchen with her hair fixed differently. He gives her a once-over and says, "You look nice."

"Thanks, Dad."

"You'd better get on down to the bus stop. Are you and Lennon ready for the practice at church tonight?"

"Yeah. It's pretty easy, but, yeah, we're ready." She pauses and then says, "Oh, by the way, since we're not going to the mall today, I'm going over to Sophia's after school. We're going to work on a project. I'll stay over for dinner. She said her parents could take me to the practice. I'll text Mom. You can just pick me up when it's over."

"No problem. That's fine."

As Emma begins to exit the kitchen and turn toward the garage door that leads outside, Simon, in his less combative, more usual manner, says, "See you later, alligator."

"After a while, crocodile," Emma responds with a smile as they recite the parting phrase frequently used ever since Emma started school.

Simon grabs his smartphone from the kitchen counter, looks up a number in his contact list, and presses the number for SassyApps.

When the receptionist answers, Simon gives his name and asks to speak to Mr. Barrows. "Hello, Simon," Barrows soon answers. "How are things going?"

"Doing pretty well," Simon replies. "I just wanted to let you know that after discussing your offer with my family, I will accept the position."

"Oh my, Simon. I'm embarrassed ... but when we didn't hear back from you ... well, we went with our second choice. You were by far our first choice, but we assumed you might seek something back in the space program." There is silence on Simon's end of the line. Barrows breaks it by saying, "Simon, I'm sorry. I do hope you find something—and I wish you all the best. I'll certainly keep you in my files ... just in case something comes up."

With disappointment and a shot-down feeling, Simon closes with a pleasant "Thank you. I appreciate it. And I appreciate your making the offer in the first place." He slams his phone onto the counter much harder than intended, mumbles a low "Crap," picks up the phone, and heads to his in-home office.

There he presses print to get more résumés. The printer begins its gyrations as he leaves the room for his shower. He opens the shower door, sets the water temperature, closes the door, and begins to undress as he waits the forty-five seconds it takes for the warm water to reach the nozzle.

After being assured he won't experience the rude awakening of being splashed with ice water, he reopens the shower door and steps into the spray and a rejuvenating morning shower. His palms lie flat on the tile wall in front of him as he lowers his head so water flows over his head and back.

He prays dictatorially, "Father, I don't know what you've planned for my life, but I pray every day and I try to listen for your answers. I've worked hard, played by the rules—but, well, it seems good people often finish last. How do I feed my family and provide them with a good life? I've continued to study—to keep on the cutting edge of things—and I've invested in extra hours. Keeping my nose to the grindstone has gotten me nowhere. And now, well, I'm straining to trust in you."

Wiping water mixed with tears from his eyes, he continues. "God, you said, 'Ask, and you will receive. Search, and you will find. Knock, and the door will be opened for you.' God, I've knocked, sought, and asked, but nothing has opened or been received." Simon sobs, breaks down, and slumps to the shower floor as the water hits his chest.

Between sobs, Simon wails, "Okay, God, here's the deal. You said, 'Let me in.' Well, here I am. Change me. You have one month. In one month, if nothing has changed in my life, we can part ways. I will consider your sayings a way of keeping people from going crazy even when prayers never get answered and people cling to hope."

Simon stands, pushing his face into the spray and mumbling, "Who am I talking to?" He shakes his head to remove the nonsense and finish his shower. After turning off the nozzle, while exiting the shower, he slips on a loose tile and falls backward with a thud. After seeing a few stars, he lies back down again. He closes his eyes and mumbles, "What else can go wrong?"

Eventually he dresses, takes his résumés from the printer, stuffs them in the previously addressed envelopes, applies the stamps, and heads out the garage door. While backing the car from the garage, he notices the bag of clothing Alexis has placed on the backseat. As he travels the route, he recalls the good years and the excitement to get to work that sometimes caused the thirty-minute ride to pass in a blink.

He begins thinking that maybe today his rovers might discover something amazing on Mars and make it possible to bring back the research funding—and his job. He fully understands the government-funding world—how if you can't show something amazing, your funding disappears.

This leads to him thinking about how the military gets funding because they need to show only how they can kill the most people.

However, now the drive is to the post office to send out résumés. He feels rather useless and handcuffed.

On the way to the post office, Simon stops off at Saint Thomas Catholic Church, grabs the bag of clothes, and departs the car. Making his way toward the rectory, he sees Father Irwin, a tall man in a black cassock, coming his way. As they meet, Father Irwin stretches out a large hand, greets him with a warm smile, and says, "Good morning, Simon. How are you?"

"I'm good, Father Irwin," he replies as they shake hands.

"I see you're playing Santa today," Father Irwin says, pointing to the bag on Simon's shoulder.

"Yeah. My red suit is at the cleaners," he says with a low, forced laugh. "Alexis is in her declutter phase, so she asked if I could drop these off. They're all clothes."

"Wonderful. The Ladies of Charity will give them to those in need. Sorry to hear of your downsizing at JPL."

"Yeah, but, well, that's the way it goes."

"I feel for you, Simon. Quite a few in the church are experiencing some hard times. But I'm sure that you, with your talent and abilities, will find something. I know I'm praying for you; you can count on that for sure."

"Thanks, Father. I'm praying also, of course—but I'm not getting many answers right now. I guess I'll need to pray harder. Surely something will break soon."

"How are the robots?"

"I don't talk with JPL much since the military is in more control now, but I have my grapevine. Three of the robots seemingly have been lost, and the news report today said they were having problems communicating with *Opportunity* in recent days."

"Didn't you write much of the software?"

"Yeah. And the Reliance program I created is sitting in a JPL computer, unused."

"This could be the opening for you to help them fix the problem."

"The military purged the original designers for cheaper people to peruse the data. It's not a big priority for them, because the robots can't blow something to smithereens." The priest doesn't say anything. Simon breaks the silence with "Pardon my language, Father."

"I can understand how frustrating this might be for you, Simon." Changing the subject, Father Irwin injects, "Is Emma coming to rehearsal tonight? She's a good stagehand and helps out all around, and I think her friend Lennon is quite the talented musician."

"Yeah, we're planning on bringing her—and probably Lennon."

"Simon, can you possibly see that Lennon gets home? His father has missed picking him up several times. I think Lennon has to walk home. And, as you know, things are not as safe around here as they used to be, especially after dark."

"Sure, I'll get him home."

"Simon, I have some confessions coming up in a few minutes, but before I go, let me ask—are you going to be able to make the next Bible study session?"

"I'll try, Father. But, well, honestly, I'm not feeling very positive about the book right now."

Father Irwin places a hand on Simon's shoulder, looks him fully in the eyes, and says, "Don't lose faith. Remember: we are on God's time, not ours. Prayers don't always turn out the way we think they will. Things will get better."

They exchange goodbyes, and Father Irwin turns toward his office while Simon heads toward his car.

Emma has made her way around the corner to the bus stop. Even though her father pitched a fit that morning about her hair, she readjusts it. She feels a girl's got to do what a girl's got to do. While standing at the corner waiting, Emma hears the roar from the bus engine coming up the road. Her name bellows from down the road: "Emma! Emma!" She turns to see Lennon Thomas in full, quick stride, making his way toward her at the bus stop, a backpack bouncing from his shoulders as he trots.

He reaches her saying "Hi" in between gasps. A big smile crosses his face as he gazes at her. His time spent with her at the bus stop in the solitude is his favorite time of the day. He wishes sometimes the bus would not come, but he knows she doesn't understand his feelings for her. "You look nice today," he says.

"Thanks. So do you," Emma replies. "You're running late today."

"Yeah. My dad wasn't feeling well this morning."

A frown appears on Emma's face because she's heard this many times. She reaches up and adjusts Lennon's trademark brown beret. "That's better," she says as she smiles.

"You ready to face the gauntlet again today?" he asks.

Rather sarcastically, Emma responds, "I love walking the bully walk to our seats." She then pleads, "Please, God, let it stop."

"You're prettier than any of those stuck-up girls."

"Thanks, Lennon."

The yellow behemoth approaches, and the noise of the brakes catching is startling. The door swings open, and Mr. Foster, the bus driver, meets them with a smile. They climb the steps and turn, searching for two empty seats. They wind their way through the aisle, trying not to make eye contact or attract attention. The only remaining seats for two are behind Jennifer Bittle, the bane of Emma's existence.

Jennifer Bittle thinks she is the queen bee at school. She's pretty, and she knows it, flaunting it to hurt others—especially girls. Her father is the mayor, and she constantly reminds everyone of that. The apple hasn't fallen far from the tree, with her father flaunting his position. Lennon and Emma sit, and it begins.

Jennifer turns and says, "Hey, Emma, has your father found work yet?"

"No," Emma replies.

"I am so sorry. I could see if my dad can find something for him.

Like, there is a Department of Transportation position for work on the highway." Jennifer snickers as she turns to her posse of girlfriends, known as the Bittlets, who join her in giggling at Emma. Emma takes it, just sort of shaking her head as she looks away.

Lennon attacks. "Hey, you bobble-headed bleach blonde, do you always use 'like' before or after every word you speak? 'Like' is a simile. If you would read something other than a clothing catalog, you'd know when to use it."

Jennifer responds, "Like, whatever!"

"Don't you get it, you moron? 'Whatever' is not an object; you can't be 'like' a 'whatever.' You should remove it from your vocabulary until you grow up enough to use it correctly."

Emma smiles, enjoying Lennon's takedown of Jennifer.

Lennon pipes up again. "Hey, Jennifer, did you go to a boxing match last night? How did you get the bruise on your cheek?"

Jennifer thought the makeup had covered the bruise. Her posse is quiet.

"You must not be great at boxing," Lennon continues. "Remember: you gotta keep your arms up." He demonstrates, raising his arms and covering his face in a rope-a-dope fashion.

Jennifer, who had twisted slightly toward him, turns in a huff and stares straight ahead.

Lennon turns to Emma. "Don't let her get to you. Your dad will find something. Her dad is just a politician who thinks they are royalty and the rules only apply to us peasants. Your dad sends these great machines to other worlds and talks to them. Cool. Your dad is like Q."

Emma looks at Lennon. "Who's Q?"

"Remember? He's the guy in the James Bond movies, the scientist who creates the cool stuff. He has weapons, cars, guns, and the coolest of gadgets. James Bond would be toast if it weren't for Q. The same with your dad. We would not have robots on Mars if it weren't for him."

"I never thought of it that way—that Dad is so cool."

"Yeah, and her father is just a creepy politician you can't trust. When they write the history books, he won't even make the footnotes."

A hand grabs Lennon's shoulder. He turns and looks up. It's Greg Mindoro, a senior at school, standing in the aisle. "Hey, Beatleman. We need a guitarist for our band." Greg has long, stringy black hair and dresses in black from head to toe. He goes on to say, "When are you going to stop playing your grandparent's music? It's the four *D*s today, baby—depression, death, darkness, and destruction. That's what people want to hear."

Lennon replies, "I'm pretty satisfied with what I do. Haven't decided on this other music yet."

"Well, our band SureDeath may have a gig at the Demon Den."

"Does it pay?" Lennon asks.

"Only if you're part of the band. Are you entering the upcoming talent show?"

"Yeah."

"You going solo?"

"Probably. I'm thinking about it."

"You should do it as part of our band," Greg says, pointing at Lennon. "You need us. I'll get back to you about the Demon Den gig." Greg turns and retreats to his seat.

Emma touches Lennon's arm, saying, "You should stay away from him."

"Why?" Lennon asks.

"He's morbid. Not everyone is into darkness. I like your music. Greg's music is just not you."

"Thanks, but it's hard to find gigs as a solo act. I need to make extra money. The talent show has a cash prize, and my guitar won't hold out much longer."

"If you go with him, he'll screw you. He doesn't have your best interest at heart, but he'll take your skills. He'll end up stabbing you in the back. That's my opinion." Emma turns away and looks ahead.

There's a brief silence before Emma turns back toward her friend. "Lennon, how is your father?"

"He's okay."

"But he still hasn't been able to move on after your mom's death?"

"Yeah, I guess not."

"Lennon, if you ever want to talk, you know I'm here for you."

"We're fine. My father will get out of his funk." There's a brief pause before Lennon asks, "Did you do the research for your book report?"

Emma recognizes the change of subject and doesn't pursue the topic of Lennon's father, realizing it's still a sore spot for Lennon. She knows Mr. Thomas has been drinking since Lennon's mom passed away two years ago. She worries that Lennon must be both a kid and a parent to some degree.

The bus makes its way to the school entryway at Planetary High School, with students already standing in the aisle, waiting for the bus to stop. Mr. Foster swings open the door, and the students begin their descent. Emma glances out the side window to see if her best friend, Sophia Lopez, is waiting for her. They have repeated this ritual at the bus drop-off since grade school. Emma steps from the bus with Lennon trailing.

Sophia rushes up to her, grabbing her by the arm and pulling her toward the school while saying, "Hello, Lennon." Lennon nods as the two girls begin talking.

Not being able to contain it, Sophia says, "Emma, you're not gonna believe this, but Bobby Fuller said hello today on the bus." They face one another, jumping up and down screaming.

Emma turns to Lennon and says with a smile, "It's a girl thing. I'll see you in homeroom." The girls speed away through the school entrance, with Lennon trailing.

CHAPTER 2

Meanwhile, across town a press conference is about to begin. Seated at the main table are two men, one in civilian clothes and the other in military wear. To the left is JPL Mars Mission Director Ed Proctor. Ed is a burly man with a round face similar in features to that of the character Norm in the old TV sitcom *Cheers*. But even though his close friends call him Norm, he is no Norm like the one on Cheers. Ed has a good heart and a PhD from MIT. He and Simon have been friends for many years.

JPL Military Director Colonel Tom Earlman is next to Ed. He is air force to the core, having the square jawbone and cropped hair that says, "Do or die." His purpose at JPL is to transition JPL to help in military pursuits of communication and robot technology. Funding is the lifeblood of JPL, and it's easier to get funding for projects protecting the citizens. JPL reports more to the Defense Department than it does to NASA.

The colonel looks at Ed and says, "We have much less than a full room for this press conference. But let's begin."

Ed announces, "I am here today with our new military director, Colonel Tom Earlman, to tell you of the recent problems with the Mars rover *Opportunity*. As of yesterday, we lost communication with the rover. We believe this was a consequence of storms on the planet. We are working to resolve the issue."

Pausing the briefing and scanning the sparse audience of reporters, Ed then continues. "I want you to understand these outages can happen, and we can reestablish a connection. Keep in mind that depending on the positions of planets in orbit, it can take a while to reestablish things. It is not like reaching down and rebooting your computer."

A young woman reporter raises a hand and follows with "Isn't this a four billion-dollar piece of equipment, and if you can't get it working, we lost the money? Is it true we've put four robots on Mars and, as of today, only one is working? We spent billions of dollars for things to break. We should find a better use at home for the money."

Ed retorts, "Yes, these projects cost a lot of money, and sometimes they fail, but would you ask the same questions if the data sent back showed evidence of life? Alternatively, look at it this way. Do you carry a smartphone?"

"Yes, of course," the reporter responds.

"Do you like the way it communicates for you?"

"For sure. Of course I do."

"Some programs that make your phones so convenient and valuable started with little robots. Do you think the cell phone industry has put more than the cost of a few robots back into the economy, in the form of jobs and expanded technology? In the news industry, doing remotes is an essential part of your job, and you can thank a little robot for it."

The colonel stands and interrupts. "Folks, I'm Colonel Tom Earlman, military director of JPL. If you have questions about the communication difficulties only, we will be glad to answer them. He pauses. No one responds. "Well then," he says, "I suppose we will end this press conference. And considering the turnout is embarrassingly low today, any further information given will come from a press release posted on the JPL website. Thank you for coming."

As people exit, Earlman turns to Ed and asks to meet with him in his office.

Shortly after the conference, Ed enters the doorway of Earlman's office. The colonel is on the phone and waves for Ed to sit. The office is full of an assortment of replicas of flying machines, from the first planes to the most sophisticated jets and space vehicles. The colonel ends his phone conversation and addresses Ed.

"Well, that was a depressing press conference." Ed nods in agreement. The colonel continues. "I'm new here, but I'd assume that if E.T. doesn't pop up on a monitor, the turnout will always be low."

"Yeah," Ed agrees. "We get more interest when the robots first land and people want to see the new images of the planet, but that interest wanes."

"I made a quick decision on ending the press conference," the Colonel says. "I can't waste time meeting with three or four people. We've had problems with three robots, and the only one still working, *Opportunity*, we've lost contact with, right?"

"Yes. We lost *Sojourner*, *Spirit*, and *Curiosity*."

"I'm under a lot of pressure to get military funding, and failures are not good in Washington."

"Colonel, we are doing everything possible to get *Opportunity* back online, and we will. However, you must understand that with the sequestered budget issues, they replaced many of my top people with less expensive military people. They have much lower space credentials. For example, Dr. Simon Northstrum, the man who wrote most of the code these robots use to communicate, was replaced by morons in the Pentagon who decided he was making too much money."

"Can Northstrum get things back up and running?"

"I don't know for sure. But if anyone can, don't you think the creator would be the person we need?"

"Ed, before I got here, there were bad moves made, but I want to assure you I am not the villain. I love the JPL program. In fact, I wanted to be an astronaut. Look around the room at the aviation figures. I am a space geek. The rovers are amazing, but I live in the real world of the military. Results matter. Give me your hard assessment. Is Northstrum the man we need?"

"Yes sir. There isn't any money for full-time people, but I can swing a consultant. I can hide consultants deep in the budget."

"Is he still available?"

"I haven't spoken to him in a while, but I believe he is still on the market. I'll call him when I get back to my office."

"No, we need him. Give me his information, and I will call. But I will have him get back to you."

"Okay." Ed looks at his cell phone, pulls up Simon's information, writes the number on a piece of paper, and slides it to Earlman.

"Are we done here?" the colonel asks.

"Yes," Ed responds. Ed exits the office as Earlman picks up his phone and dials Simon's number. He gets Simon's message box and, in his no-nonsense military voice, begins to leave his message.

"Dr. Northstrum, this is Colonel Tom Earlman, the military director of the Johnson Propulsion Laboratory. I assume you know of the problems with *Opportunity*. I'd like to hire you in a consultative role to help us get the communications restarted. You come highly recommended by Ed Proctor. He assures me that you are the man we need. Please contact Ed for the details."

He reaches for the phone cradle, disconnects the call, and punches another number. When the receptionist answers, he identifies himself and says, "General Bosman, please." The receptionist asks him if she can put him on hold, and he says, "Yes."

Simon is returning to his car after finishing his errands and taking a trip to the health club to work off some stress. Opening the car door, he plops into the seat and notices his phone resting in the cup holder is flashing with a message. After taking a deep breath, he sighs. "Please let it be good news this time."

When Simon gets up his nerve to listen to the message, he finds it's the one left by Colonel Earlman. After replaying the message twice, he is beaming as he pounds the steering wheel with absolute joy, and his feet beat the floor in unison. Simon screams, "Yes! Yes! Yes!" in sync with his pounding and stomping.

He then bows his head and prays, "Lord, if you had anything

to do with this, thank you, God, thank you." He takes a couple of breaths to calm himself for a professional discussion and punches the direct number of Ed "Norm" Proctor.

When Norm answers, Simon screams into the phone in his best Scottish accent, "I can't give you more power, Captain!"

Norm replies calmly, "It's okay, Scottie. Spock is here, and in the next five minutes, he'll redefine the laws of physics and save the *Enterprise*."

Simon ribbingly says, "You know, Norm, I leave you guys alone with the children for five minutes and things fall apart. You lose three, and one quits talking to you. I might have to file child abuse charges with DHS. Man, you guys better get more PhDs."

"Hey, Simon. How are you and the family doing? I imagine it's been tough going. I heard Alexis is working at a funeral home."

"Yeah, she's a gem."

"I guess you got Earlman's message."

"Yes. Yes, I did."

"Well, I convinced him we needed you. I'm working on the contract details now. Can you come in tomorrow? You'll need to go through the ordeal of getting clearance and everything again. I'll get some paperwork down to them to help push it along."

"Sure thing. Can you tell me more?"

"Well, financially it might not be what you were making before, but I hope we can get close. It's independent contractor work, which may not last forever. You'd be okay with that?"

"Yes, if it gets me back to JPL."

"Great. Simon, it'll be good having you on the team again. I'll email you the contract when it's finished. Sign it and bring it when we meet. Just come on up to my office when they get through with you downstairs. Give the family a hug and take that great lady to dinner tonight, and make sure they have cloth napkins."

"Got it. I'll see you tomorrow."

Simon disconnects and shakes his fists in the air with another "Yes!" He reaches for his phone and punches in the number to Alexis's favorite restaurant but stops short of connecting, setting the phone back in the holder. He decides not to tell Alexis until he has the contract in hand.

The car roars on startup, and "The Ballad of John and Yoko" is playing on his favorite radio station. He turns the volume to max, hits the gas pedal, and sings along with John about being crucified. Simon will soon learn how true those words might turn out to be.

☙

Alexis is at her desk, reviewing the upcoming funeral services for the week. It's a job she could pick up with little experience, since she is personable and intelligent. Most companies don't consider a stay-at-home mom as having experience. What she didn't expect, however, was the pressure to upsell everyone on containers, funeral add-ons, crypts, and additional burial plots for relatives.

As she told Simon, "It's like you are trying to sell the people still living burial plots, not concerned with those who died." But Alexis goes out of her way to show sympathy and concern for her clients at their times of grief. She is focused now on Mrs. Ficocelli, who will meet with her in a few minutes. She feels for the sweet old lady who was married for seventy years—much, much longer than Alexis has been alive.

Alexis wonders how Mrs. Ficocelli and her husband made it so long, thinking the elderly lady would view her own eighteen-year marriage to Simon as an overnight trip. She just imagines the amazing stories Mrs. Ficocelli could tell.

A girl appears in Alexis's doorway and announces, "Mrs. Ficocelli is here." Alexis comes from around her desk just as the lady enters the office.

"Hello," Alexis says. "Please have a seat." Mrs. Ficocelli is in her late eighties, with silver hair, and is wearing a black dress and hat, with a matching coat. She is smartly dressed but doesn't give the appearance of affluence. She sits.

"I was to meet with a different person," the lady tells Alexis.

Alexis sits on the front of her desk instead of returning to her seat. "Yes," she replies to the lady. "I do apologize. He is no longer with the company."

"Oh! Will I have to start over?"

"No, ma'am. Your file is right here, and I've reviewed it."

"Where is my Alberto?" Mrs. Ficocelli asks.

"He is here," Alexis says, while patting the lady's hand.

"My Alberto hated funeral homes."

"They are not anyone's favorite place to be, but I guess we all end up here."

The old woman frowns and nods.

Alexis smiles, pats the lady's hand again, and asks, "Did you decide on the arrangements you want to buy for Alberto?"

"I am confused! The other person wanted me to buy expensive stuff. Alberto always told me to get the basics. Your person made me feel I was doing a disservice to Alberto by not burying him in a tomb like Napoleon's. May we start over with no pressure?"

"Sure. Tell me, if Alberto were arranging your funeral, what would he do?"

"Oh, he'd get me something modest. He was frugal, and since it will be unseen in the ground, it doesn't matter." She reaches into her purse and pulls out an envelope containing a thick stack of cash. "This is my budget. I tried to explain to the other man, but he said I could finance the funeral. We are cash people." She hands Alexis a piece of paper with a number on it.

"This is your budget?" Alexis asks.

"Yes," the woman replies.

"The other agent would have made more money by upselling you. Let's do what's right for you." Alexis opens a book to review with the woman and asks, "Do you like this casket?"

"Yes. Good. That's what I want for him."

"This is a package fitting your budget, and it will leave you with cash to get your hair done," Alexis says.

Mrs. Ficocelli touches her silver hair and smiles, and she then says, "I noticed the package includes carnations. Alberto hated those flowers. Every time he smelled them, he thought of death."

Alexis grins and responds, "We will change them to lilies."

"Good. Alberto grew them."

"Wonderful," Alexis says. "It will be like home." She hands her a contract, which she signs.

Mrs. Ficocelli looks deep into Alexis's eyes and says, "You're nice, and you can call me Addie. I'm glad the other person quit." She pauses and then continues. "You won't get in trouble for not trying to take my money, will you?"

Alexis sort of laughs, saying, "Probably, but I can handle it." Again she comforts Mrs. Ficocelli with a soft pat.

Mrs. Ficocelli asks, "Do you have a husband who works?"

"Yes, he works at JPL."

With almost a gasp, Mrs. Ficocelli says, "What are you doing here? Everyone knows about that big company."

"He is temporarily laid off, so I got a job to help until he starts back up. My husband put those robots on Mars."

"Wow! My Alberto followed the space stuff."

"May I ask you a question, Addie?"

"Sure."

"How did you stay married for so long?"

"Lord knows. I guess I lucked upon the right soul. And, honey, it's all about the souls in your life. And if you get the right soul, you are always connected. Take Alberto. His body is in the back room, but his soul is beside me. Take advice from an old woman. I see the love in your eyes for your husband, and that doesn't come there by chance"—Mrs. Ficocelli reaches to give Alexis a pat—"especially since you are working in a funeral home for him. And I am sure your man would do the same for you."

As they hold hands, Mrs. Ficocelli points to Alexis's heart and says, "When you have a connected soul—when one right soul is connected to another right soul—you feel it here." I think you found the right soul. You may have hard times, as we sure did, but we have always flown together."

After Mrs. Ficocelli departs, Alexis sits behind her desk with an inner peace coursing through her.

CHAPTER 3

Alexis is at home in their bedroom, sitting on the edge of the bed. She removes one shoe after the other and throws her arms in the air in a relaxing stretch, exhaling deeply. She flops back on the bed, arms over her head, and stretches again. "Please help Simon, Emma, and Lennon in their times of need."

She pauses her thinking and then focuses specifically on her husband. "Lord, Simon is so lost. He has our family, but he misses his other family of JPL, and especially the rovers. The rovers are his children. Can you help him be a decent shepherd and find his lost sheep? He is good, honest, and the most selfless man, but you know, don't you?"

Alexis reaches for a card on the bedside table and begins a novena, deeply believing in this ancient tradition of Catholicism's devotional praying. After finishing, she prays, "God, while I'm at it, please help Mrs. Ficocelli. Her husband, Alberto, is with you, but after seventy years together, she is alone. Take care of them both. As you know, I work in a funeral home and didn't think death would affect me this much."

She rubs her fingers across her teared-up eyes. "I know Mr. Ficocelli lived a long, full life. I'm thankful for that. But that's not always the case. Seems the good ones often die young and those who defy you seem to go on forever."

Her prayer and wandering meditation are broken by the loud voice of Simon and the clumping of his feet on the stairs.

"Alexis, Alexis, are you there?"

She bolts straight up and straightens her clothing, afraid of what news is coming. "I'm here," she responds.

Simon appears in the doorway with paperwork in hand. He rushes toward his wife, lifts her from the bed, and twirls her. Alexis's long hair sways in the air as they go around.

He looks straight into her eyes and says, "I'm back at JPL."

A bright, sun-rising smile covers her shocked face. She grabs her husband in a tight embrace and exclaims, "I never doubted you."

They break the embrace, and Simon shows her the contract. They sit beside one another on the bed. "It's independent contractor work," he says, "and it has the same pay as when I was on JPL's payroll. Norm has worked a miracle!"

Alexis studies Simon's excited face and asks, "Contractor work— what exactly does that mean?"

"It means JPL wants me to get the new program I designed up and running—the one I've named Reliance. It's do or die for me. If it works, the job continues. If not, then I'm gone again." He studies Alexis's face and seriously asks, "Do you mind continuing to work at the funeral home a little longer?"

She looks into Simon's eyes for reassurance and then asks, "Do you think there's a good chance you can get things going again?"

"Yes. It's not a sure thing, but yes, I have a good chance."

Alexis beams and responds, "I'm all in, Simon. And my work at the funeral home will take on a whole new meaning—knowing that I'm not there forever."

Simon jumps from the bed and grabs her hand to stand, saying, "Now get ready. I made reservations at Mariachi's. Norm made me promise to take you to dinner at a place with cloth napkins."

"I've always liked that man," she states as she scurries into the closet. "I have been dying for their Yucatan plate."

Simon says, "I assume Emma texted you about being over at Sophia's house."

Alexis replies from the closet, "Yes, and we'll pick her up after the rehearsal at church."

"Right," Simon confirms.

After having dinner, Simon and Alexis wait in the narthex of Saint Thomas Church for the town's talent show rehearsal to wind up. Emma helps with the stage props, decorations, and sound equipment, as well as in getting people on and off the stage area. But in her mind, she is mainly there to support her friend Lennon. He desperately needs a new guitar, and winning the prize money will help him reach his goal.

Emma eventually exits from a room with two big oak doors and sees her parents. Immediately she yells, "Mom, Dad, can we go for ice cream?" She screeches to a halt in front of them with her hands in a praying formation under her chin. "Please, Please!"

"Honey, lower your voice," Alexis tells her.

"Oh, Sorry."

"How was your practice?" Alexis asks while stroking Emma's hair?

"Oh, Mom, it will be great. Lennon is awesome!"

Turning toward her father, she says, "Dad, Lennon's music is so amazing. He improves every day and surprises everyone with something new. Can Lennon get ice cream with us?"

She looks at her parents, seeking approval.

"Speaking of Lennon," Simon says, nodding toward the doors, where Lennon is exiting with his guitar. Lennon's long, lean body is draped by a green T-shirt that's half tucked into his pants. The front of the shirt is the iconic Beatles picture from *Abbey Road*. They call him Beatleman because he always wears something Beatle-like.

Lennon's old guitar case is held together with duct tape of various colors. As he approaches the Northstrums, he bows his head and peels the beret from his head while trying to tuck in his shirt. "Hi, Dr. and Mrs. Northstrum," he says.

"Hi Lennon," they both respond. Alexis says, "Emma informs me we should get ice cream."

"I'd like to, but Dad is running late, and I should wait on him," Lennon replies.

Simon knows Lennon's father has been struggling with alcohol since the death of his wife, and of course Simon hasn't forgotten Father Irwin's request about taking Lennon home.

"Tell you what," Simon says. "Since the rehearsal ended early, Alexis will call your dad, and we will drop you off after ice cream."

"I don't have any money on me, Dr. Northstrum."

"Relax, Lennon; it's on me."

Lennon smiles broadly, because to him, any more time to spend with Emma is heaven. Simon guides him toward the exit. Emma and Alexis follow.

"Emma tells me you're a whirlwind on that guitar. I can't wait to hear you."

"I'm praying it holds together until after the show," Lennon laments. "If I win, maybe I'll get a newer used one."

The church doors close.

�⚭

Following the jaunt to the ice cream parlor, the Northstrums' car pulls up to Lennon's house—a typical split-level place. It is some distance away from the Northstrums' house and Emma's bus stop. Lennon's bus stop is on another corner, but he goes the extra distance to ride to school with Emma, which is the reason he's usually huffing somewhat when he meets her each school day.

Alexis says to Simon, "Hon, why don't you walk Lennon to the door?"

Simon moves to exit the car, but Lennon says, "It's okay; my father may not be decent."

Simon looks at Alexis and tells Lennon, "Sure. I understand. It's late." He sits back down. Lennon retrieves his guitar, tells Emma good-bye, thanks the Northstrums, and heads up the walk. He opens the worn front door and yells for his father as the Northstrums pull away.

"Dad? Dad? I'm home." In a room off the foyer, he sees a flickering TV. He proceeds toward the light and can see his father sprawled out in a recliner, head slumped, and empty beer bottles on the table beside him.

Lennon shakes his head and mumbles, "Oh, Dad, not again."

This is not new for Lennon. It's been played out many times since his mother's death resulting from a car accident. Lennon grabs a blanket and covers his father. He watches a few minutes of a video of his mother playing guitar in her band. His father watches it every night, but again tonight the beer has bandaged his depression.

Lennon's mother was in a rock band, and while she and the band were returning home from a gig, someone's drinking killed her. In fact, most of the band died that night. Everyone knew they had real promise. Lennon gets his musicality from his mom, who taught him to play and sing. His father blames music for her death and hates how Lennon takes after his mother. He has thwarted Lennon's music for a while, so he plays in his room alone.

Again observing his father in a passed-out mode, Lennon turns off the television and lights and then heads to his room and sanctuary. He opens the door, switches on the light, and enters. In the dim light, one is struck by his Beatles shrine. Beatles posters from the early days until their breakup cover the wall. Push pins hold album covers on the posters. One poster of John and Paul has the number seventeen over John's head and the number fourteen over Paul's.

Lennon can relate to them because John Lennon was his mom's favorite Beatle, and she gave him John's last name. The mothers of John and Lennon also both died when the boys were in their teens. Another poster of John Lennon has him playing his Rickenbacker 325 guitar. Above his head is the big word "Dream," with an arrow pointing to the guitar.

Lennon looks around the corner, where his mom's guitar sits in its cradle, the strings dangling to the floor. His father was at it again. When drunk, he gets vindictive and takes it out on Lennon in the form of his mom's guitar.

Lennon opens the top of his turntable and turns it on. It spins. He lifts the needle and rests it on his mom's vinyl album. The record pops and plays. Lennon lifts his mattress. Under it are packages of guitar strings hidden from his father. In the mornings, his father never remembers what he has done the night before.

Lennon selects the strings needed to replace the ruined ones and grabs his mom's guitar while sitting on the bed. He lays the instrument across his knees and removes the bent and broken strings. John Lennon's "Across the Universe" plays on the turntable. The words "Nothing's Gonna Change My World" crackle on the speakers as Lennon's tears drip onto the face of the guitar. He continues to restring, occasionally wiping his face with his baggy shirt.

He prays, "Please God, help change my world." After finishing the restringing, he places the guitar back in its cradle and then flops back onto the bed, drifting off into a familiar dream.

Vividly, a large merry-go-round is turning, with the lights flashing and the brightly painted horses and animals pumping up and down. There are no humans riding the turn-of-the century attraction. The melody of "Across the Universe" plays as the ride rotates. On each of the animals ride musical notations, such as G-clef, treble, and alto; along with the clefs are whole, half, flat, and sharp notes.

If one could look into the dream closely, one would see that the notes are not in rhythm with "Across the Universe." Another melody is trying to be heard, like a song from the heart, ready to explode. While the music flows, there is an image of a thick book on Lennon's desk. On the book is a woman's name, out of focus, pulsing to become clear.

CHAPTER 4

At the far ranges of our galaxy, where our sunlight is only a speck, a luminous, cloudlike silver vessel hurtles toward our solar system. As it comes nearer, the vessel scans the solar system, revealing the planets orbiting our sun. Inside the vessel are ancient beings that have visited this galaxy since time began here.

The vessel's commander examines the records to learn. Many facts are pulled from the knowledge base. The commander's eye receives the stream across its cornea written in ancient Aramaic, reading,

Solar System: Sol
# of Planets: 8
Planet code
25645-0—Neptune
25646-0—Uranus
25647-0—Saturn
25648-0—Jupiter
25649-3—Mars
25650-5—Earth
25651-0—Venus
25652-0—Mercury
25653-0—Sol

The commander reviews the first data, with a number code revealing the knowledge-base digit structure for each celestial body scanned. The first five digits reveal the name of the planet from scanned literature, and the last reveals extraterrestrial interventions. The study shows there has been a significant change since the beings' last visit to this part of the universe. The commander blinks, and the lens refreshes. This new data shows the planets with significant intrusion, warranting investigation:

Data Level: 1 = Unsophisticated
Extraterrestrial Intrusion: None
Extraterrestrial Life Form: Human
Human Name: Neptune
Universal Threat Level: 0

Speeding away from Neptune toward Uranus, the vessel again slows and orbits the planet, with the lens repeating similar data from Uranus:

Planet 25646
Data Level: 1 = Unsophisticated
Extraterrestrial Intrusion: None
Extraterrestrial Life Form: Human
Human Name: Uranus
Universal Threat Level: 0

The vessel speeds away from Uranus toward Saturn and then slows, orbiting the planet, with the lens repeating data from Saturn. The orb continues its journey through the solar system, stopping at each planet in order and receiving the same message on each planet:

Planet 25647
Data Level: 1 = Unsophisticated
Extraterrestrial Intrusion: Insignificant
Extraterrestrial Life Form: Human
Human Name: Saturn
Universal Threat Level: 0
Planet 25648

Data Level: 1 = Unsophisticated
Extraterrestrial Intrusion: atmospheric—July 1995, Galileo
orbiter 2003
Extraterrestrial Life Form: Human
Human Name: Jupiter
Universal Threat Level: 0

The next planet circled is a large, barren red one. Its data show major intrusions:

Planet 25649
Data Level: 5 = Sophisticated
Extraterrestrial Intrusion: Significant
Extraterrestrial Life Form: Human
Human Name: Mars
Planet Intrusion: Nine significant robot vehicle intrusions
Universal Threat Level: 6
Threat Analysis/Solution = Hands-on intervention on the planet.

The commander's cornea reads, "These probes need physical investigation. Descend to the planet and investigate the intrusion.

𝕵ℛ

Three shimmering beings, red, green, and violet in color, descend through the atmosphere, darting in different directions across the planet on their mission to examine human expansion into the universe and the threat it may hold.

The red being lands on the reddish surface of the planet, with a wisp of dust blown up by its feathery impact. At its feet is a six-wheeled milk-crate-sized robot with solar panels covering its top. The being is translucent, with human-like form, lean with skin that covers a bony frame. Its skin shimmers with a soft red glow as if lit from within. The cheekbones are broad, like those of a human male, yet there is no physical feature that shows gender.

Bending over, the being blows the slight covering of dust from the robot's surfaces. Its palm, facing toward the ground, emits a soft white light, and it directs this light to the surfaces of the robot.

The commander's cornea reads, "Commander, I have come upon a robot and have scanned the device. I am sending the data to you. I will await your directions." The being looks out over the Martian landscape and sees a barren land. The report reads,

> Object: Planetary mobile robot
> Development Level: Primitive
> Planetary Origin: Earth
> Creator: Simon Northstrum
> Threat Analysis: 6

The red being's cornea reads a message from the commander, backdropped by the Martian landscape: "I am intrigued by this toy. It is as fragile as glass and primitive, yet the software used to communicate with it exceeds its mechanical abilities. The robot poses no threat but can work for our mission. Prepare the robot to work for us."

The entity looks at the robot, grasping it with both hands. It glows red for a brief second, and then the wheels stretch open as though it is waking from a slumber. It then settles upon the soil. The commander's lens reads, "The robot is secure! I can fix one more problem."

The being reaches and lifts a wheel, removing a stone preventing its movement. Before releasing the craft, it sees a gold plaque riveted to the robot. It reads, "Sojourner—1997."

"I am finished, Commander," the being reports, "and will move to my next mission target." As the being says this, its knee bends, and it pushes off the Martian surface, becoming a red streak jetting across the sky.

Meanwhile, in another section of Mars called Meridiani Planuma, a violet-tinted being with the same physical characteristics as the red one lands next to another earthly robot. This robot differs from the others on the planet. It has a wedge-shaped form and is larger, with similar solar reflectors. "I am at my destination and will begin my analysis of the robot and report," the being communicates. It reaches out its bony, silvery hand, and soft white light envelops the robot. The commander's cornea displays the scan:

Object: Planetary mobile robot
Development Level: Primitive
Planetary Origin: Earth
Creator: Simon Northstrum
Threat Analysis: 6

The being's cornea reads, "Prepare the robot for our mission." The being bends and blows dust off the robot and grasps it with both hands. The robot glows violet, shudders, and kicks up the Martian soil. These beings are strong and have no problem moving a large riding-mower-size object. The commander's cornea reads, "The robot is secure." The entity looks over the robot one last time and sees a gold plaque that reads, "Opportunity—2003." The being scans the desolate Martian landscape, awaiting the next command.

⚖

At another section of Mars called the Gale Crater, another being of a green hue descends to the ground next to another robot from earth. This entity, with slighter features than the other beings of color, resembles a human female form. The targeted robot is similar to a minivan in size, with many more instruments, everything larger and more advanced, and much less weathering and corrosion.

One of the being's feet stands in the dirt, and the other rests on the inner black wheel rim of the vehicle. This female-like being reaches its arm and stretches to grab the square camera atop a vertical shaft. Its heel lifts off the soil, and its toes dig into the dirt. A soft white light scans the robot. The commander's cornea reads,

> Object: Planetary mobile robot:
> Development level: Primitive
> Planetary Origin: Earth
> Creator: Simon Northstrum
> Threat Analysis: 6

The being's cornea reads, "Prepare any robots you find with a link to Northstrum. He is the key to the plan." The female-like being grabs hold of the large robot, and it glows with a soft green luminescence. A gold plaque on the robot reads, "Curiosity—2011." The commander's cornea reads, "The robot is secure." The human female-like being flows back into the sky.

⚙

At a different area of Mars, a fourth being, yellow in hue, is standing in front of a different robot. It completes the scan in the same way as the other beings and receives equivalent results. It grabs the robot, which behaves like *Sojourner*, glowing yellow and settling back to the surface. The being looks at a familiar gold plaque that reads, "*Spirit*—2004." The commander's cornea reads, "We are ready to start the linking." Each entity prepares to link. They kneel next to *Sojourner*, *Opportunity*, *Curiosity* and *Spirit*. Each places a hand on one of the robots, with the other hand and arm reaching toward the sky.

A warm white beam of light streams from space, bounces off the robot called *Sojourner* and is reflected to the outstretched arms of each being and through them into the robots. Each robot touched by the light shudders. In moments, it's done. A message displays on the cornea of each being: "Return to the light."

The beings release the robots and jump upward. The pulsing light absorbs them. The white beam retreats from the planet, and the lightship turns, bearing toward Earth at tremendous speed. Earth is a blue marble in the blackness of space, but it grows larger with each second as the orb closes the distance quickly.

The view to the beings is a torrent now as the blue of the oceans is interrupted by thousands of pieces of space equipment that revolve around the Earth. Some are vital satellites; others are floating space junk and debris. None cause any interference to the orb. It comes to an instant halt above the Earth's northern pole, sitting, glowing, and pulsing with primary colors, a peaceful light on the outer skin of the atmosphere.

The cloud grows brighter, wrapping the whole planet in a soft light with a flash. It bathes Earth in a graceful light unseen by mankind, illuminating the geomagnetic field protecting the planet. The haze exposes the magnetic field as a skeletal framework, sparkling with a rainbow of colors. The cloud descends toward the planet, splitting into four rainbow-colored luminescent forms, each going in a different direction toward the surface. As they dive into the magnetic field, it glows with the dominant color of each being penetrating it: red, green, violet, and yellow. The commander's cornea reads,

> Earth:
> Population: 6-7 billion
> Life Form: Human/*Spirit*
> Pros: Love, Compassion, and Family. Their literature has many writings on love and compassion, yet their history is one of barbarism and cruelty.
> Cons: Wrath, greed, sloth, pride, lust, envy, selfishness, and gluttony. Like children, they seem not to have learned how to share, and they may never.

All the beings' corneas read, "They are not listening and are consumed with self. We will rid this world of the selfish. Begin your mission."

35

In the dead of night, four streaks of faint-colored light bolt across the dark sky, heading toward their missions.

The red streak descends on the Karnak Temple in Egypt and the buildings at the complex that began during the reign of Sesostris I in the Middle Kingdom, which continued on into the Ptolemaic period, although most of the extant buildings date from the New Kingdom.

The space around Karnak was the ancient Egyptian Ipet Isut, the most selected of places, and the main place of worship of the eighteenth dynasty Theban Triad, with the god Amun as its head. It is part of the monumental city of Thebes. Here is the Karnak obelisk, the structure most important to the being's mission.

The being lands unseen at the base of the structure. It genuflects, and its face points upward, scanning the obelisk. Unobserved, the being extends its reddish arm, palm up, while emitting the white light, as was done on Mars. The light creeps up the obelisk, seeming to swirl into each of the ancient carvings. As the light coats the stone, the cornea of the being scrolls an unending list of coding in ancient Aramaic.

The light envelops all sides of the obelisk. Defying the laws of physics, the light is able to wrap around an object without causing a shadow on the opposite side. It disappears, and the being streams toward the heavens. The commander's cornea reads, "Karnak is secure."

※

At the Dashavatara Temple at Deogarh in Central India, built in AD 500, a similar scene occurs. A violet-tinted figure lands at the base of the structure. The temple is one of the earliest Hindu stone temples surviving today. Built in the Gupta Period (AD 320 to 600), this temple shows the ornate beauty seen in Gupta-style architecture. Many of these early Hindu stone temples were dedicated to a single Hindu deity. The temple at Deogarh is for Vishnu and houses images and symbols of Hindu gods.

These temples allowed people access to the gods they were

worshiping. The temple construction is of stone and brick, comprising a single cubical sanctum sheltering the images within. Statuaries of Vishnu were sculpted in the interior and exterior walls of the temple.

The being genuflects, and its face and arm point upward to scan the structure. The odd white light coming from its palm soaks the stone architecture as if it is milking the building of information. The cornea of this violet being shows a code similar to the one found by the red being. In an instant, the light ceases and the being bounds upward. The commander's cornea reads, "Dashavatara is secure."

꠲

The green being lands at the base of another temple sacred to humans, Bodh Gaya, a religious site and place of pilgrimage associated with the Mahabodhi Temple Complex in the Gaya District in the Indian state of Bihar. It is famous for being the place where Gautama Buddha achieved enlightenment.

The being genuflects. After completing its scan of the sacred site, its form flashes across the dark sky. The commander's cornea reads, "Bodh Gaya is secure."

꠲

The yellow being lands in Mecca, Saudi Arabia. This is the birthplace of Muhammad and home to the Kaaba, and by majority description Islam's holiest site, the center of the Islamic universe. Invisible to anyone, the yellow being circles the Kaaba while scanning it. When finished, it speeds off in a flash and heads toward a cave two miles from town. Research reveals this cave is where Muhammad had his first revelation of the Koran. The being enters the cave, and the cave immediately glows with a bright light. The light ceases, and the being exits unseen from the cave and into the dark sky. The commander's cornea reads, "Mecca is secure."

꠲

The red being returns to Earth, this time landing in Tiwanaku, Bolivia, on the site called Puma Puncu. Tiwanaku is significant in Inca traditions because it's believed to be the site of the world's creation. This is a set of massive stone temple structures that rival those of the Egyptians. The being walks through one massive wall to the other side of the temple and reappears at a similar large wall. There it kneels and scans the ancient carvings. With the scan complete, the light ceases and the being is gone. The commander's cornea reads, "Puma Puncu is secure."

⚡

Moments later, the violet being lands at Ahu Tongariki, the largest ahu on Easter Island. Natives toppled the moai during the island's civil wars in the twentieth century; a tsunami swept the ahu inland. There are fifteen restored moai, including an eighty-six-ton moai, which is the heaviest ever erected on the island.

The violet being stands centered among the moai, with each statue dwarfing it. The being spreads its arms wide, palms upward, facing left and right. The white light bathes the moai and ceases. The being bows toward them and then bolts straight into the stratosphere. The commander's cornea reads, "Ahu Tongariki is secure."

Four colored beings dissolve into the magnetic field. The commander's cornea is awash in text scrolling at breakneck speed. With each eye blink, the commander digests more data. It seems fluent in this natural language.

⚡

The yellow being lands at the entrance of the Church of the Holy Sepulcher, venerated as Golgotha and the Hill of Calvary, observed by many as the crucifixion place of Jesus and the area of His grave. The church has been a paramount—and for many Christians the most important—pilgrimage destination since at least the fourth century, as the purported site of the resurrection of Jesus.

38

The yellow being disappears through the two large arched doors. Once it is inside, the windows of the church flash brightly, as if someone is taking a flash picture. It then quickly goes dark. The being's cornea scrolls data similar to the that of the earlier visits. Moments later, a yellow bolt of light exits through the dome-topped church and launches skyward. The commander's cornea reads, "Jerusalem is secure."

The lens of the yellow being now reads, "Find the codex references and put them together."

It is a tranquil evening over Turin, Italy, when a flash of yellow light breaks the calm. It is an unusual light, and it is not accompanied by thunder or rain. Quickly, however, night returns to its calm while a lone figure approaches the Cathedral of Turin. The domed cathedral is the main church in Turin and houses the Shroud of Turin, the supposed burial cloth of Jesus Christ, which rests within the cathedral in the Chapel of the Holy Shroud, known as Capella Di Sindone.

The shroud bears the image of a man who was both scourged and crucified. Modern-day science and technology cannot figure out whether the shroud is real or an amazing artist's rendering.

It is long past closing time for the church, but the being passes through the doors of the building, unimpeded by their density. Once inside, the being makes its way to the chapel and to the altar, where the shroud sits in a silver casket within an iron box in a marble case. Unseen to the naked eye is an elaborate invisible laser security system. The advanced security makes it impossible for anyone to approach the shroud without alarms alerting the police.

The figure approaches the marble case and bows in reverence, realizing the importance of this relic to many humans. Undaunted by the laser show confronting it, the being steps forward into the beams, with one beam striking it at its waist. The being looks at the beam and smiles, as if the laser tickles as it travels through to the receptor without breaking or distorting the beam. The being grasps the marble case in the same fashion as the robots on Mars. A white light surrounds the case and soaks into it. The lens of the being reads,

"Shroud reading is complete, but the codex text is incomplete and corrupted."

This will require visits to other locations. The being thinks of how humans keep trying to rewrite perfection. Releasing the case, the being turns toward the back of the church. It stretches its arms out wide and gazes at the ceiling with a grin of satisfaction crossing its face as though it has just reconnected with a lost love. The lens of the being reads, "Find and absorb the remaining codex documents." The yellow being jets through the ceiling.

A bolt of lightning thunders through the sky, and the yellow being arrives in the halls of the Vatican library, one of the oldest libraries on Earth. It has contains seventy-five thousand codices from throughout history, and over a million printed books, which include eighty-five hundred incunabula.

With the task at the Vatican completed, the same being instantly arrives in St Petersburg, Russia. It enters the National Library of Russia. Housed here is the fragile Codex Syriac 1, protected by glass. Light surrounds the case for a few seconds. The being then sits at a computer terminal and places its hand against the computer screen, and its palm glows as the screen flickers but remains dark. The being's hand leaves the screen, and the lens of the being reads, "Original codex read. Digital version scanned. The codex is still incomplete."

It departs though the roof and shows up in front of the British Library, walking past a statue of Isaac Newton, who believed the Bible has special coding within its text. The being pauses, unseen, looking at the statue, grasping its chin and cocking its head. The being is pondering Newton's mind and wondering exactly what he thought and knew.

The being, entering the library with no interference, locates and scans the 347 leaves of the Codex Sinaiticus. The lens of the being reads, "Codex scanned, and the pieces are in place. Commander, I am ready to take care of humanity as in the time of Noah. The humans have learned nothing."

The commander's cornea reads, "They are children. I will let you know. We will work the plan and cull the selfish."

The light beings slip into the magnetic field, waiting for their next mission. The commander's cornea continues to scan massive amounts of code. When the code stops, the command prompt reads, "Connect the earthlings' GPS and communication satellites." The four beings move through the magnetic field, positioning themselves at the so-called four corners of the earth.

Once in position, their lenses read, "Beginning the connection." At once, many beams of multicolored light streak from the magnetic field into space, landing on every satellite orbiting Earth put in place by the earthlings. Like a camera flash, the beams end, and the commander's cornea reads, "Connections are complete."

The corneas of the beings read, "Go to Earth and resume your integration with the humans." The beings descend to Earth unnoticed.

A yellow streak of light descends from the sky, landing unobserved at a cell tower not unlike the ones seen lining interstates across America. This being grabs hold of one leg of the structure. Its other hand emits a beam of light, which climbs up the tower to the zenith and ends. Telephone numbers stream across the being's lens at a blistering rate as it absorbs every number on the planet.

The commander's lens reads, "I completed linking human communications. I have disabled the secret robotic killer satellites, since they contain world-ending weaponry. The humans desire for robots to rule the world. These are robots made by wicked people driven by money, power, and control. I can remove the junk floating in this formerly pristine place if you wish."

The commander replies, "No. Leave it be. They depend on the space toys."

The being then appears in a subdivision similar to thousands of others throughout the land. Driveways are lined with nearly look-alike cars, save one. The unusual car in one driveway has a tripod apparatus latched to its roof. The being approaches without fear, walking around the vehicle with its sky and cloud wrapping. On the door are the words "Google Mapping Street View."

The being moves to the front of the car and walks up the hood, looking into a ball topping the tripod. This colored ball has cameras and lenses facing 360 degrees around the neighborhood. The being smiles mischievously and presses its face into each camera and smiles for the picture. The ball glows yellow from inside each lens.

The commander's lens reads, "This company states they will do no harm, but we know better than that when money is involved."

"Yes," comes a reply, "but selfishness is the culprit. This vehicle spends its days spying on others without permission."

The being replies, "Commander, I can destroy it on your order. The instruments we have connected are toys compared to the light."

"No," the commander responds. "Our plan is different this time, as you will soon learn."

"Yes, commander. I stand ready, always faithful." The yellow glow from the ball stops as a streak bolts heavenward.

CHAPTER 5

Simon sits at his kitchen table, listening to the news while he reads. In the background, he can hear the commentator speaking. "Good morning, folks. Welcome to *America's Newsroom*. This is Bill Hemmer, and we've got a lot going on today." He turns toward his cohost and says, "Martha, how are you this fine day?"

"I'm doing well, Bill," she says as she faces him. Turning toward the camera, she greets her audience. "Hello, everyone. I'm Martha MacCallum, and this is a busy news day. It keeps getting better, folks. Congress is getting ready to push through another huge stimulus package, adding more to our debt. We will hear from one senator opposing the bill later in the show. North Korea, China, and other countries deny they are allowing their military to commit cyberterrorism on our major American companies and stealing intellectual property. These are big issues."

Martha turns toward Bill again, saying, "Bill, did you see this?" Turning back to the audience, she says, "We don't make this stuff up. A scientist claimed, 'For a brief second, the electromagnetic field around the earth caught fire.'" Bill gives her a look and a shrug. "Yeah, Bill," she comments, "I saw the report. It was as if someone took a flash picture. It was there and gone in a tenth of a second. We will have a scientist on later to explain what happened."

"Well, Martha, isn't that the field protecting us from the bad stuff from space?"

"It is, Bill."

"Great! I'll add it to the worry list."

"Well, this scientist thinks a country might have developed a weapon capable of affecting the field. We got many tweets from around the world about flashes of all different colors of lights streaking across the sky last night."

"Don't know anything about that, Martha. Ask your scientist coming up later."

"Okay, folks, we are up against a break and will be right back."

Simon looks up from his book and stares at the screen. "Now they are messing with the magnetic field," he says to himself, shaking his head. "If it goes, we will look like Mars." He stands, placing his cup in the dishwasher. It is time to get ready to get checked-in at JPL and then meet with Ed, so he heads to the shower.

⚑

Meanwhile, at the Pasadena Water and Power Company, a shimmering red figure descends through the roof of the building and disappears unnoticed into the power panels. Each panel glows as if the entity is moving through the circuits. The lights in the surrounding buildings flicker and return to normal. The commander's lens reads, "All programmable logic controllers accessed. The power stations worldwide are under our control when needed."

A young, slender man in his late twenties emerges from the Pasadena Water and Power Company building. He brushes his fingers through his shoulder-length hair and turns north. He pulls a note from his pocket and reads an address—the location of the Johnson Jet Propulsion Laboratory. He stuffs it back into his coat, shrugs, and walks toward the nearest bus line, mumbling, "So it begins ..."

While walking, a stray tan, black, and white dog approaches, and he kneels to greet the mutt. The dog seems to know him, as its tail and body beat as one. He takes the dog's head in his hands and says, "Hi old fellow; looks like things haven't been going your way." The dog licks his chin. He reaches into his pocket and pulls out a treat. The dog devours it.

"Hi," the young man says to the dog. "I'm Raph. You look like a Rudy. I have work to do, and I may need your help." He releases the dog's head, pats him on the head, and continues on his way. Rudy follows, tail wagging. The duo reach an intersection as a transit bus approaches. Raph stands by the door, waiting for it to open, with Rudy behind him. The door swings open. A heavyset man occupies the driver's seat. Raph climbs the stairs, but the driver grabs his forearm.

"No dogs allowed!" he says.

Raph turns toward the driver, notices his name sewn on his shirt, and looks at his stern face. "Al," Raph says, "this is my friend Rudy. We are like Don Quixote and Sancho, and we are on a mission. He won't be a problem."

Raph places his hand on the driver's forearm, and the defiance leaves the man's face, replaced with an odd smile. Raph and Rudy head toward the back of the bus and take a seat, with Raph staring out the window. Al closes the door, reaches into the side pocket of his seat, and pulls out a book he is reading. The cover reads, "*Don Quixote* by Miguel de Cervantes." He looks up into his rearview mirror and stares at the stranger.

⚖

Simon is making his way to the JPL offices. He has put on his favorite tunes and is singing at the top of his lungs. He's glad to be going to work—to a place where he is valued. Simon changes lanes to get in front of the bus in his lane, but the light turns red and he has to stop.

Simon glances over to view the people inside the bus and is met with a dog's face with its tongue hanging out. Rudy's ears perk. Simon smiles and thinks, *You don't see a dog riding the bus every day.* A man's hand is placed on the dog's head, followed by a face looking at Simon. Raph smiles and gives a two-fingered salute to Simon. He then plops back into his seat.

The light turns green, and the cars behind Simon beep, letting him know he is back in the rat race. His car speeds up and leaves the bus behind. Raph continues to gaze out the window, and a warm smile creases his face. Simon continues toward JPL—a route he has traveled many times. Yet subtle changes have taken place along the way.

A favorite song comes over the radio—"Across the Universe," by the Beatles, and he thinks it's poetic it should play now, as he is being given a second chance to do what he loves—sending things across the universe. He pulls to the front of JPL and follows the sign to the visitor parking lot, remembering what Norm said about parking and clearances.

He parks and exits the car. With a briefcase in hand, he finds the visitor entrance and disappears into the building. Once inside, he is met with a line of five people. The check-in has changed since he was here last. It is evident there is increased security.

Once he is in line, the person in front of him turns to study the line of people behind him. He stares at Simon and breaks into a big toothy grin. "Oh my!" he exclaims. "Is that you, Dr. Northstrum?"

"Yes, Louie," Simon responds. They shake hands, each embracing the other's forearm.

"Are you back now?"

"Yes, Louie. I'm consulting with Norm."

"Man, we need people with a sense of humor here. If the military people told a joke, they'd explode."

"It's that bad?" Simon says.

"Yeah. I stay away from the uniforms. You will meet Alvarez." Louie points to a uniformed man standing at the check-in desk. Simon follows his pointing and sees a large black man with chiseled features and the typical military hair crop. His uniform is impeccable—nothing out of place. Awards adorn his chest.

"Jeez, Louise, I hope I don't make him mad."

"They hate programmers, Dr. Northstrum, and think they are conspirators. If they can't blow it up or shove a bullet in a barrel, well, you know … Neanderthal."

Simon smiles. "Well, Louie, I suppose they have their purpose. I guess they don't understand the ones and zeros."

Louie is puzzled by Simon's reply, but he responds, "When I've got to repair a toilet, I need high-level clearances and a proctoscope to do the job." Simon laughs quietly. "If Alvarez puts on a rubber glove, you are in trouble. He will love your Beach Boys shirt." Simon inspects his shirt with a worried look. "Don't worry, Dr. Northstrum," Louie whispers. "Programmers dress differently. But you just have to get through our resident gestapo."

Louie moves forward, turns to Alvarez and shows his ID. "Bye, Dr. Northstrum. Glad you're back," he says as he moves on toward his destination.

Simon steps toward the desk, and the imposing figure of Alvarez peers at him.

"May I help you?" Alvarez asks sternly.

"Yes. I'm Dr. Simon Northstrum, and I am a consultant reporting to Ed Proctor."

"Hold on, please," Alvarez states. He searches through a pile of papers. Simon examines Alvarez and wonders if he irons his clothes while wearing them. Alvarez stops after finding Simon's paperwork. "Dr. Northstrum, you must go into the security office to complete paperwork for other clearances."

"Sergeant Alvarez, is it?"

"Yes sir."

"Well, Sergeant, I worked for JPL for many years. Is this necessary? I am responsible for the robots on Mars."

"Sir, with all due respect, I don't care if you hung the stars; you will go into the security office. Everyone coming through here tries the same tactic of 'You don't know who I am.' If I let a bad guy through, then it's on me. It won't happen on my watch. You can leave your case here, Dr. Northstrum."

Alvarez reaches for Simon's case, and he hands it over. In exchange, he is given the paperwork and then makes his way to the security office.

Simon enters the office, where a slender blonde woman in her early thirties is staring into a computer screen. She doesn't notice him, but he recognizes her as Debbie, an intern who worked for him.

He announces, "You had better stop shopping on company time." Debbie is startled and changes screens while looking up.

"Dr. Northstrum!" She jumps up from her desk and gives him a big hug. "I heard you were coming back." They step apart.

"My recommendation got you a full-time position," he says.

"I know. Thank you, sir," she replies. "How is the family?"

"They are doing well, Debbie."

"Dr. Northstrum, so much has changed since you left. I guess you met Attila at the front desk."

"Yes."

"Dr. Northstrum, I saw your paperwork, so I completed it for you. Has anything changed?"

Simon reviews the papers he is handed. "No, everything is in order," he says as he returns it to Debbie.

"I must fingerprint you," she tells him.

Simon nods, looking befuddled. "If I've got to do it, okay." He puts out his hands, and Debbie prints each finger.

"You can wash your hands over there," she says, looking toward a sink. Simon moves to the sink and washes.

"I saw the big ring on your finger, Debbie. So that guy of yours finally popped the question?"

"I thought you'd never ask. Please thank Alexis for playing matchmaker."

"I will. She'll be happy for you."

"Dr. Northstrum, I will send this to the national database for review, and it will take a while, but in the meantime, here is your associate security card. I'm not supposed to give it to you until after the fingerprints come back, but it's not activated yet. You are not on any wanted lists, are you?"

"No, I don't think so."

"Go get coffee at Jimmy's. It's still there, and you don't need clearances to eat. I'll activate the card while you wait so Attila won't send you back here. You'll be able to get by him in forty-five minutes or so."

Simon exits the office and the building. Raph and Rudy are exiting the bus across from the JPL offices. Raph stands against the wall, watching the JPL offices, taking notes, while Rudy paces back and forth. Raph calls for Rudy to settle down. "I am waiting on a friend," he tells the dog while scratching Rudy's head and sitting down.

After a few minutes, Raph stands and turns left. An aged man with a dark complexion resembling Sean Connery approaches. He carries a black backpack on his shoulder. The two meet and embrace as old friends with hugs and kisses from cheek to cheek—not usually an American way of greeting. The man notices the dog. "Raph, who is this friendly beast?"

"Joseph, this is my friend Rudy." Joseph bends on one knee and rubs the dog behind each ear. Rudy's tail wags, sweeping the sidewalk. "Rudy is my partner in crime today," Raph says.

"The mutt shows promise," Joseph responds. Joseph stands and looks across the street and at Simon as he makes his way toward the coffee shop. "He is our man. Do you have your intel on Dr. Northstrum?"

"Yes, Joseph, I do," Raph tells him.

"Northstrum is who we want to help with our rapture project. This pack contains other things you will need for the mission." Joseph removes the backpack from his shoulders and hands it to Raph, who slings it onto his back. "I've got others to meet, Raph. Good hunting."

The two men exchange goodbyes, and then Joseph turns and walks away.

Raph turns the other way and jaywalks toward the coffee shop. After he and Rudy clear the road, they rest on a grassy walled area. Raph pulls out a tennis ball from his pack, and he calls for Rudy. "Hey, buddy, catch." He lobs the ball, and Rudy pounces on it and returns it to Raph. "Good boy, Rudy."

They continue this routine several times before Simon exits the coffee shop with a cup in hand. Raph lobs the ball another time with Rudy in pursuit. It bounces near the feet of Simon. Rudy misses catching the ball in his mouth, and it ricochets off his nose, bouncing up once more and hitting Simon's coffee cup, spilling the contents.

Raph jumps to rush toward Simon, yelling, "I am so sorry!" Rudy follows. Raph looks Simon in the eye and again apologizes. He uses the sleeve of his shirt to dab at the coffee that has spilled on Simon's shirt.

"I am so sorry, sir," he repeats, noticeably looking toward Simon's name tag. Again he apologizes, this time addressing Simon as Dr. Northstrum and saying, "I noticed your name tag."

Rather stunned by the suddenness of it all, Simon listens as the young man says, "I am Raph. Rudy and I were playing and got carried away. He grabs Simon's name tag and dabs the coffee off it. His fingertips glow a faint red, and a same-colored spark is absorbed by the tag.

"Please let me replace your coffee." He turns Simon toward the shop.

Simon notices that the dog and young man look familiar, but he tells Raph it's not necessary. Raph, however, guides Simon into Jimmy's while Rudy sits and waits. Minutes pass. Rudy's tail then begins wagging, signaling their emergence from the shop. Rudy runs up to Simon and puts a front paw on a thigh. "Well," Raph says, "you made a friend. He is trying to apologize."

Simon pats Rudy on the head while safely holding his new cup of coffee in the other hand. "You're forgiven," he tells the dog, who lowers his paw. Rudy retreats and spins around, signaling approval.

Simon looks at Raph and says, "You have a neat dog."

"He is not mine, but he has been my sidekick today."

"My daughter would kill for a dog like him," Simon states.

"Maybe she'll get one just like him one day," Raph replies.

"Maybe," Simon tells him, "but I'll have to find something to cure my allergies to dogs first."

"You don't seem to be allergic to Rudy, Simon."

"True. But it may come later. I could start sneezing and getting all puffy."

"New medical discoveries seem to come along daily," Raph assures him. He pauses, nods toward the JPL building, and asks, "You work at JPL?"

"I hope to. I got a job interview." Simon looks at his watch and exclaims, "I'd best be going! Thank you for the refill."

Raph reaches out and grabs Simon's hand. "Good luck with your interview, sir. I hope you get everything that's coming to you."

Raph and Rudy turn and cross the street. Raph leans against a wall as Simon disappears into the JPL building. The young man scratches Rudy's head and says, "Thanks, old boy. You were a big help." Still watching the JPL building, he lifts his right hand, forms the Vulcan greeting, and says, "Live long and prosper, Dr. Simon Northstrum. Your tremendous journey has begun." A smile forms on his face. Raph turns and walks away, whistling. Rudy remains.

Simon again is in line, awaiting the approval from Alvarez. He slips his new ID badge through the scanner, and tiny red sparks flow into the circuitry. Alvarez reviews the computer screen, looks up to Simon and says, "Maybe you did hang the stars. Welcome aboard, sir!" He signals Simon on through and hands his case to him.

Simon hurries toward the elevator, enters, and is carried to his old floor. When the elevator door opens Simon feels rejuvenated. He hears the old sounds of CPUs buzzing, sees the glow of computer screens, and hears the clicking and clacking of coding fingers. "I'm with people again," he says under his breath.

Simon presents himself in the doorway to Ed "Norm" Proctor's office. Norm looks up from his desk, and his face grows bright as he sees Simon. He stands and rushes around his desk with arm out to greet his old friend. Simon reaches to shake Norm's hand, but Norm embraces him in a bear hug, lifting him off the floor.

"Hello, my old friend," Norm says. He releases Simon and gestures for him to sit. Simon sits, breathing a sigh of relief that Norm is still the same and the working conditions will be okay.

"Well, buddy, I'm glad you're here. I suppose you noticed the changes around here since you left."

"Yeah. I got to meet Alvarez. I will not cross him, but he can be in my foxhole."

"Buddy, as I said on the phone, I don't have a permanent job for you right now. Heck, I may not have one myself. The government money goes for health care, welfare, and wars. Next they will ask us to double-use the toilets before we flush. But as I told you, I've got you contract work, and yes, it will pay the same as before, along with top clearances."

"Great! Now, tell me, Norm, what happened around here?"

Norm shakes his head. "Let's just say the people they gave me are in way over their heads. They're trying but just can't cut it. Colonel Earlman, who called you, wants something done, and he wants it quickly. He's not like the other military personnel."

"That sounds promising," Simon responds.

"I reviewed your Reliance program, Simon. Can it help us revive things to any degree?"

"I believe so, Norm. I need to try to make contact using the software. I will need a terminal."

"You've got your terminal, Simon, with an extra one to boot, along with a special office."

As they speak, a small red light blinks on Simon's computer in his new office. The screen reads, "Reliance is ready to update on use." The computer then resumes its dormant state.

Unaware of what's happening in Simon's office, Norm leans toward Simon and whispers, "Listen, Simon; This place is crawling with new military people, and I still have not sorted out who is a team player. You know—*our* team."

"What's the story on this Colonel Earlman?"

"As I said, he's a good guy. But he reports to General Bosman at the Pentagon. Let's keep the chain of command between us for now. We want to take credit if good comes from Reliance. Then we can divert funds back to the Mars projects. Are we in agreement?"

"We have to play the shell game? Okay. Got it."

Norm looks at the clock and says he has to get ready for another meeting. "Can we get together again tomorrow, here in my office, about nine? And tomorrow, maybe you can get acquainted with your new office."

"Sounds good," Simon says as they both rise. They shake hands, and he then asks, "Are Frank, Rex, and Burt still here?"

"Yeah, they are on different floors, on other projects. But I suspect the grapevine has been primed about your return."

Simon turns to leave but stops in the doorway. Turning back to Norm, he says, "Thanks for having faith in me."

Norms smiles and nods. Simon leaves the office, departs JPL, and heads home.

ℐℛ

As Lennon, Emma, and Sophia enter their homeroom that morning, the students are in turmoil as usual. Thirty-five conversations are competing with one another for supremacy. Fingers are going a mile a minute texting, getting the last few words in before the teacher puts a halt to smartphone communications. It's interesting how most of the texts go to a person sitting four rows away.

In the front of the school, four representatives from a clothing company walk through the main doors. A step ahead of the other three is an older man in his mid-seventies. He is Joseph Deuss, founder and chairman of Swaddling Clothes.

Joseph has salt-and-pepper hair, well coiffured but thinning, and is dressed in a well-tailored black suit with a bloodred tie. His eyes are blue, and his face shows signs of graceful aging. He walks with a large gait, exuding confidence.

Close to Joseph is Raphael, the company's production engineer. He has shoulder-length hair and is lesser in height and build than Joseph. He is dressed in slacks and a blue-jean shirt.

Next is Magdala, the marketing guru for the company. The fashion blogs say she is the reason women love the company's clothes. She is smartly dressed, looking like a successful executive from Wall

Street. Her face is elegant, with deep brown eyes, warm and loving. Her makeup is perfect and subtle, yet effective, accenting her grace. Magdala has been likened to actress Salma Hayek.

The fourth person is Gabriel, who has an olive complexion. He is the company's fashion coordinator and is dressed in jeans and a silk shirt, with a sweater draped about his neck. Gabriel's hair is brown, and he sports a well-manicured dark beard. Many in the company think he and Magdala might be related.

They continue forward for a meeting with the school principal, stopping in front of a door with a frosted-glass top that reads "Principal." Joseph turns and focuses on the glass case across from the door displaying the trophies the school has accumulated throughout the years. He puts two fingers to his temple and salutes while whispering, "Well done, young sprites." Gabriel pushes to open the door, and they enter the office. The receptionist greets them.

"Hello," Joseph says in return, "I am Joseph Deuss, and these are my colleagues from Swaddling Clothes." He places his card into the receptionist's hand and then clasps her hand with both of his. He looks the receptionist in the eye and states, "We have a meeting with Mr. Condon."

She replies, "He is expecting you. He is on the phone, making sure everything is arranged in the gym." She pauses. "Thank you for sending samples of your clothes. I love them!"

"Thank you," Joseph responds. "What do you love about them?"

She says, "When I put them on, I feel like I'm comfortably wrapped, like when I was a child in my blanket. Not only are they stylish, but also so soothing. Unique, like none other."

Glancing toward the others in his group, he gives a look that says, "Did you hear, everyone? She got the message. She is listening."

A bald portly man enters the outer office and says, "Hello, I'm Principal Condon." He extends his hand, which is grasped by Joseph.

"Thank you for having us," Joseph says. They break away from the others and enter the principal's office.

The principal explains, "Headquarters just told me a couple of days ago of your arrival and plan. We've not had much time to prepare the gym, but your supplies are here. Our gym is not fancy."

Joseph comforts him, saying, "Our needs are simple. Your room will be fine. I have spoken outside on hilltops. It's not the room, but the message. I need eager students."

Condon states, "The announcement will go out in another minute. How did you get the superintendent to let you talk with the students? They don't let many people in, unless it's for fund-raising for the schools."

"Oh, I know people in high places and can get the wheels rolling with very little trouble," he replies.

"It will take thirty minutes to get everyone into the gym. Sometimes herding teenagers can be tougher than herding cats during the hormonal years."

Joseph smiles. "I understand."

"Mr. Deuss, I had better get to the gym before they open the gates. You can wait here in the office, and we will call you when ready. Just follow the signs to the gym."

"Excellent," Joseph says.

The principal and Joseph reenter the reception room, with Condon darting out the door and hurrying toward the gym. Raph stands and offers his seat to Joseph, who takes hold of Raph's shoulder and guides him to stay seated. The receptionist goes about her business in an area distant from where the group gathers.

"Magdala," Joseph queries, "do you have the advance scouting of prospects at this school?"

"Yes sir," she replies. "There are many students we have been following that might be a great fit for Swaddling."

"Wonderful, I am excited to meet them. I love seeing the children so bright and full of promise. We should go to the gym and spread out in the halls so we can observe the students file in before the presentation. This way they will know nothing of us."

Gabriel stands and twirls, with the sweater around his shoulders flying. You mean like the song says—'Dance like nobody's watching?'"

Joseph laughs. "I didn't know you had the moves."

"It's not always a cha-cha-cha," he says as he grabs Magdala and dances out the door.

Joseph looks at Raph, asking, "Are they always this way?"

"Don't ask," he replies. "It's a fashion-design thing."

The two men walk toward the gym. The team spreads throughout the halls as the event announcement finishes. Doors to the classrooms fly open, and a stampede of students soon follows. Students twist and go into the gym, knowing the first there get the best seats and can sit with a friend. No one desires to be stuck next to a stranger or the uncool.

The Bittle posse makes its way to the gym side by side, not giving way to anyone. They walk with an arrogance of superiority. Emma, Lennon, and Sophia follow them, trying to maneuver around the posse. Lennon makes a move and slips around the right as one of the Bittlets gets distracted by a jock on the football team.

Emma has held tightly to Lennon's ever-present, half-tucked shirttail and follows. Sophia makes up the caboose of the moving train. They go through the entryway to the gym and see a circle of chairs with a few students already seated. The old gym is like many others across the nation: a parquet basketball floor, the school's mascot name emblazoned across the wall, a stage at one end, and a podium in place.

Students have already begun filling the stands. Emma, Lennon, and Sophia find some good seats together and slide into them. The surge of students continues as the gym fills up. Jennifer and the Bittle triplets find seats near the jocks but within view of Emma.

Lennon turns to Emma and says, "I don't know why we were herded here. I hear it's about a clothing drive. Everyone raises money, and of course, most of it will go to athletics."

"I don't know anything about this group today."

"Well, I'm not going to raise money for the athletic department," Lennon tells her.

"Emma," Sophia asks, "do you see Bobby Fuller?"

Emma cranes her neck, looking around the room. She turns to Sophia and says, "He is over there." Sophia glances toward where

Emma has pointed with her eyes, trying to see without being noticed spying.

Lennon jests, "Jeez, Sophia, go tell the guy you want to marry him and have his children."

Emma snaps around and hits Lennon on the forearm. "She's shy," she tells Lennon. "You should apologize."

"Sorry, Sophia, but you like the guy, so some way, let him know it."

"Yeah, you're one to talk," Sophia snaps back. Emma doesn't hear the remark, as she is scanning the crowd. Lennon turns away, knowing Sophia is correct about his not revealing his real feelings about Emma to her. He decides to keep his mouth shut about Sophia.

Joseph is now standing on the steps leading onto the stage, speaking with the principal.

Mr. Condon says, "You seem concerned. Is the room not going to work?"

Joseph is broken from his gaze around the gym by the principal's words. "Oh, no. It's tremendous. I was observing the children and thinking how this is the age where they lose their purity."

"Mr. Deuss, I have been in education a long time, and they lose it in elementary school. I think it's the electronics and social media."

"Well, maybe I'm talking to the wrong age group," Joseph responds.

Condon says, "My three-year-old can take a picture with a cell phone. The genie isn't going back into the bottle."

Understanding, Joseph nods.

The other Swaddling Clothes teammates are traveling around the gym, looking for the right intern for the campaign.

Jennifer Bittle sits next to her latest boyfriend, cozy as a queen nestled in her hive. "I hear these people are here looking for models for a new clothing line," she says.

The boyfriend asks, "How do you know?"

She gives him an "Are you stupid?" look. "Like, my father's the mayor, you know. He heard it through his channels. He didn't mention it, but I bet he put in a good word for us. Could be he even contributed a little cash to them, if you know what I mean. Like, money makes the world go around."

The Bittlets whisper among themselves and are overheard by Lennon, who is sitting nearby.

"Did you hear that, Emma?" Lennon asks. "These people are looking for models for a clothing company."

"Really?"

"I just heard," Lennon responds, as he nods his head toward the Bittle group.

Emma looks back at the group. "Oh, from them, the rumor mill? Well, I suppose the mayor or little Queenie will predetermine it."

Everyone seems to have found a seat. The attendees are still talking among themselves, not really observing much of what's happening on the stage.

The principal turns to Joseph and says, "Everyone is here. Are you ready?"

"Yes."

"We might have to stir them from their yacking and cell phone comas."

Confidently, Joseph replies, "I have just the things. This isn't my first rodeo." Joseph then signals his staff to begin their missions.

As arranged, the lights dim and the stage lights illuminate the podium. Joseph makes his way to the podium, with many students unaware because they are either still blabbering or mesmerized by their phones. Before Joseph turns to face his audience, he moves his finger in a slashing motion across his throat.

Raph, standing next to a box on the floor, pushes a button. The nearby phones, tablets, and computers flash a bright white light and then display a message: "What if the last face you ever saw in your life was a computer screen? How would you feel?" Students on the phones stare at the message and comment to others. The screens then go black, bringing a loud moan from the crowd. Many begin tapping and banging their phones, trying to get them to work.

A loud "good morning" bellows from all sides of the gym. "Don't worry about your devices," Joseph says. "Mr. Raph here is superb with electricity and has disabled them for the time being. Once we are finished and you leave the gym, they will work." The crowd grimaces like a child being told, "No more candy." "Smile, everyone. I have it on the highest authority the world will not end in the next forty-five minutes while they disconnect you."

Joseph seems to have everyone's attention. "Let me introduce myself," he continues. I am Joseph Deuss of Swaddling Clothes. If you look around the room, you will see my other associates." Joseph points out his team, and they raise their arms as he recognizes each by name. "We are here today, and for the next little while, to look for models to represent our new clothing line for Swaddling," Joseph says, gaining even more attention. "The interns selected will help push us into a new demographic. We are looking for the whole package—individuals who shine with wholesomeness from the inside out. I did not say 'pretty' or 'good-looking.' What you may consider beautiful and alluring may be the complete opposite on the other side of the world. We want people to wear our clothes and report to us what people really want and what makes them comfortable." Joseph pauses as the students look at one another and make various comments. "Swaddling wants to design a line for the ages and make our fashions timeless. We want you to get excited when you dress in Swaddling. Are any of the right people in the audience?" The Bittle posse individuals raise their hands.

Seeing the hands pop up, Joseph says, "Just four people are interested? Well, you must have it sink in first."

Emma looks back at the posse and mumbles to Lennon, "See what I mean."

Joseph speaks again. "I have helped Calvin Klein, Tommy Hilfiger, and Ralph Lauren get started, and we will make this a success. If you are a person who looks down on someone because of the clothes he or she wears, then this may not be for you. Such character will show through, and you will disqualify yourself." He pauses again, looking around at the crowd. "Allow me to explain about clothes. Do you like magic? I fancy myself a magician." He holds high a rather sickly-looking plant. "Do any of you know what I'm holding?"

Someone quickly yells, "A dead flower."

"Good. In a way, you are correct. But it's dead because it has been picked from the soil, pulled out by its roots. However, everyone in this room has this on them today."

The students examine themselves, many mummering and wondering if this old dude is crazy.

He continues to hold the plant, explaining that it's a boll. Would any of you here make fun of somebody wearing this boll or what is in it?" There is no response. "This, students, is cotton, and you are wearing it today."

Some students smile and shrug, others are perplexed at where this is going.

"Allow me to tell you something of clothes," Joseph says. "Watch and see." He waves his hand in front of the boll of cotton, and it bursts into flames, crumbling to the floor. "Everything you're wearing will turn to ash. Our clothes are no different. I will play a short video describing our program. It's on YouTube if you want to view it again on your devices later. They tell me you can register online to be considered as a model for our new line."

The program begins projecting on the large screen, and Joseph leaves the stage to approach Magdala. He asks her, "Do you have any interesting people on your radar?"

"I have twenty on my short list," she tells him.

"Excellent. We will have a room in the school to meet with the students we select."

Joseph makes his way back to the podium when the presentation ends. "I hope you enjoyed the show," he says, addressing the audience. "We want everyone to consider applying to become a model. My staff has paper forms for you to fill in. There are also consent forms for your parents to sign. You can get them from the staff as you leave today, or in the school's office at any time." After pausing to observe the students' interest, Joseph continues. "Now, for my last magic trick." Joseph nods to Raph and claps his hands together.

The students' electronic devices immediately light up. The students quickly start punching icons to see what they have missed and what they can find.

Lennon is wide-eyed in amazement over the whole event. He nods and says, "Cool."

Emma, Lennon, and Sophia start toward the exit. This brings them past the Bittle group. Jennifer pipes up. "Emma, are you going to apply? They probably don't need people who shop at Goodwill." The Bittlets snicker.

"I'm not interested. I'm sure your father has rigged it. He does it with everything else in this town."

Lennon turns toward Emma and says, "Really, Emma, you should apply. I think you would be a great representative."

"There's no use, Lennon," Emma replies as she, Lennon, and Sophia make their way toward the exit door, followed by Jennifer and her crew.

Joseph and Magdala stand watch at the doorway as Emma approaches. Magdala steps out in front of Emma and says, "Hi Emma."

Taken by surprise, looking confused, and wondering how the wonderfully-attired woman knows her name, Emma hesitates and then responds. "Uh … hello?"

Magdala turns to Joseph and gives a look and nod of her head that to Joseph obviously says, "What do you think?" His eyes and slight facial gesture show an interest in Emma.

Magdala reaches out and brushes Emma's hair. She takes hold of Emma's face and turns it to show Joseph. "Look at this face, Joseph. She has promise." Removing her hands, she asks Emma, "Are you going to apply?"

Hesitantly, Emma says, "Well, no. I wasn't planning to."

Having observed the situation, Jennifer interrupts. "She can't, because her father is out of work and they can't afford it."

Magdala turns to Jennifer and says, "Thank you for your comment, Jennifer—I believe that's your name, isn't it?"

"Yes. Yes it is," she replies, projecting a rather haughty demeanor.

"Well, Jennifer, there is no charge to do this, and it does not matter who your parents are or what they do."

Jennifer is silent, having been negated. Emma has a smile on her face because someone stood up to Jennifer. Lennon, of course, is soaking all of this in. Sophia is also enjoying it.

Magdala turns her attention back to Emma. "You should apply."

"Yes," Joseph agrees. "You should, Emma. We can't guarantee anything, but it will be fun and exciting. Regardless of the outcome, it will be a memorable experience." He turns toward Lennon. "In fact, Magdala, I like this young fellow right here." He reaches out and touches Lennon on top of his beret.

Startled, Lennon looks wide-eyed at Joseph. "You think I should try out for this? No way."

Joseph holds Lennon and Emma by the shoulders and then addresses Lennon. "Why not, Mr. Thomas? James Dean—he was way before your time, but you've probably heard of him and his movies. He died too young. But you may be the next James Dean." Joseph then looks at Emma and Lennon together. "You and this young lady might be the new dynamic duo." Lennon blushes, big time. Joseph smiles, turns toward Magdala, and says, "I hit a nerve." Joseph reaches for a couple of forms and hands them to the Emma and Lennon.

From nearby, Jennifer Bittle asks, "What about me?"

Turning toward her, Magdala says, "Sure. You and your friends should enter. It will be good for you."

"It's exactly what you need," Joseph adds, handing them the paperwork.

The group leaves the gym and heads to classes. Jennifer begins to cozy up to Emma, saying, "We will have so much fun working together." The posse is not pleased, sensing the queen leaving the hive.

Emma turns to Jennifer and tells her, "I still don't know if I am entering. And if I do, we are certainly not working together. But I wish you the best of luck." She grabs Lennon, and they slip into their classroom.

The Swaddling Clothes associates are together now, and Joseph asks Raph, "How are things progressing with Dr. Northstrum?"

"His journey to bring the rapture with Reliance has begun."

Joseph then asks Gabriel, "How are things on the East Coast?"

"I have set things in place to take effect as requested," he answers.

"Great," Joseph says. "The plan is taking shape."

Simon goes into the church family center and proceeds to a group of people milling around a table of refreshments. The group turns and welcomes him. One man shakes his hand and says, "Welcome back, Simon. It's been a while." With a little laugh, he adds, "The snacks have gotten better."

Father Irwin enters the room and suggests that everyone grab a drink and take a seat in the ring of chairs set out. The group travels to the chairs, with each person juggling a drink, a snack, and a Bible. When seated, Father Irwin begins the get-together with the Lord's Prayer, with everyone setting down the snacks, drinks, and Bibles to hold hands and recite the prayer together.

The praying is immediately interrupted by the slamming of the door into the room. All turn to discover what made the noise, since all the regulars are already present. An unknown man has entered the room and walks toward the group.

"I apologize for the interruption—and for arriving late," the man says. "But I just got back into town and didn't want to miss the study group. Father, please continue. It's my favorite prayer."

Everyone in the room is wondering who this is. But Father Irwin gets another folding chair, everyone makes room for the newcomer in the circle, and the priest stretches out his hand toward the man, saying, "I'm Father Irwin, the pastor here," as they shake hands.

"I'm Michael. Michael Cott," the stranger replies.

"You are new to our parish?"

"Yes, Father."

"It's nice to have a younger person in our group."

Michael looks around with curiosity. The group comprises people who could be his parents.

"Michael," Father Irwin says, "It will be good to get a young person's perspective on words in the Bible."

"I hope to be accepted, Father. I shoot from the hip, and I won't hold back, but I don't mean to offend anyone."

"Great," the pastor says. Quickly, he introduces Michael Cott to the others in the room, and Michael says he will pass on refreshments. But he has brought his Bible.

Once again, everyone joins hands and prays the Lord's Prayer together. Father Irwin then begins the Bible study. "In our last session," he says, "I gave you an assignment to find the list of the seven deadly sins in the Bible. I am curious if you found the list." Several nod their heads. "Mack, where in the Bible did you get it?" the pastor asks after noticing Mack's hesitant but positive nod.

"Well, I guess I cheated a little," he replies. "I googled it."

The members smile and nod in agreement, except for Simon and Michael.

"I figured you might," Father Irwin responds, "because there is not a list where it's all laid out together. Let's go around the room and take a poll on which sin you feel is the worst."

They start with Michael, but he defers, saying he would like to ponder it and hear what the others might say. One by one, they come to conclude that pride is the worst offender.

"Michael, why is pride the worst sin?" asks Father Irwin, wanting to draw the newcomer into the discussion, sensing he may have something good to offer.

Michael states confidently, "Pride puts you at the center of the universe. We are on God's program, and I opine He is looking to find out if we are abiding by His plan and being good stewards of our souls' stories. The sins, as you call them, are actions of man he can control. Self is the most serious sin and encompasses pride."

The other parishioners glance at one another with looks that show they are impressed by the newcomer's appraisal but somewhat put off by his rather brash way of presenting it. "Continue," Father Irwin says, as Michael has paused.

"Well, imagine how distraught God would be if, at the end of your soul's journey, your first word to Him is 'I.'" Where God's plan may have you listening and learning in your lifetime, free will and selfish choices can derail God's plan within you."

Michael looks around the room at some perplexed faces and states, "'And thou shalt love the Lord thy God with all thy heart, and with all thy soul, and with all thy mind, and with all thy strength; this is the first commandment. And the second is, Thou shalt love thy neighbor AS THYSELF. There is none other commandment greater than these.'" (Mark 12:30 KJV) Michael pauses. "I'm a kid to most of you, but our souls spend a lifetime learning those two truths. If you are absorbed in pride or self-love, then it's easy to ignore, for gratification, the other commandments. Breaking the commandments darkens your soul and adds to your learning debt."

Michael faces the pastor and says, "Let me ask you, Father. You are the ordained one. What came about during the time of Noah? Was the world so absorbed with self and pride that God cleaned the slate? Did God get so mad with man He wiped out humanity, sending the souls back to Him? If so, then why didn't He send Noah packing?"

"Well, Michael," the pastor responds, "it tells us God came to Noah because he was trustworthy and selfless, and if He had ended Noah, then God would have broken His word to Adam and Eve."

Michael asks, "Do you think God will do it again? I mean, look around everywhere. The world is in turmoil," Michael laments, gaining Simon's attention more than ever. "It seems with instant communication that it's easy to be absorbed with self-importance. People are discovering more ways to be vicious to one another and not following the 'neighbor' commandment."

Father Irwin presses Michael, saying, "People everywhere are doing wonderful things. But, alas, it's not covered by media because it doesn't boost TV or reader ratings. Let's face it, with the media, the case is simply, 'If it bleeds, it leads.'"

One of the members ventures in to break the serious tone, saying, "Yeah Father, and remember, women are to blame for the whole sin problem." The women of the group moan.

"How so?" the pastor queries.

"I was kidding my wife about it the day, telling her here we are in the garden of Eden and she asks me to try this apple. I'd have to make a quick decision. Do I make her happy and take a bite of the apple, or do I please God and refuse it? We're talking about not getting mad the woman you live with every day or pleasing the God you will see when your life is over. It's like your wife asking, "Do these jeans make me look fat?" Most in the group chuckle, including Michael.

Simon responds, "Yeah, so you burn in Hades with your wife for sixty or so years, versus burning in Hades for eternity."

A woman jumps in. "A real man would have killed a snake in the house." Michael laughs, knowing the perils of free will. Father Irwin grasps the opportunity to end the discussion on a light note, dismissing the group.

"Michael, I'm happy you could attend," the pastor says as things break up.

"Father, thank you for everything," Michael replies.

"You seem to own a sound grasp of the Bible," Father Irwin tells him.

"Yes, my father drilled it into us."

"He was a religious man?"

"No, not religious, but faithful."

"Do you work around here?"

"I work worldwide in computer security consulting."

"Well then, you must be in big demand, what with the hacking going on around the globe."

"It keeps me moving. In my business, if a man made it, then man can break it. Every connected communication device is in a constant state of 'You don't know what you don't know.' I help companies find it first before the creeps do."

"You and Simon might have much in common," the pastor says, pointing toward Simon across the room. "He works at Johnson Jet

Propulsion Labs. Simon was the guy who made those robots land on Mars and sent those superb pictures."

"I'd like to meet him," says Michael, leaving Father Irwin and making his way to Simon.

"It's Simon, correct?" Simon nods his head, and Michael continues. "Once again, I'm Michael. Michael Cott."

"Yes, Michael. I enjoyed your input. A new viewpoint from someone different."

"New?" Michael says.

"Yes. I take it you believe things are as bad today as in the time of Noah, and God should wipe us out?"

"Sometimes I wonder whether or not a nice asteroid might be needed to get the job done," Michael replies.

Simon smiles. "Then God would break His promise. So mass extinction may not be something we should consider at a Bible study. Of course, I guess God could do it to selected creeps who foul up everything."

Scratching his chin, Michael says, "Maybe a bolt of lightning. Yes, make crispy-critter creeps." There are rather silent laughs between them. "Here is a thought, Simon," Michael goes on. "The terrorists communicate with cell phones. An app directs the lightning to their phones, based on the phones' GPS positions. I am sure God could whip up a good storm wipeout in a heartbeat."

"You know," Simon says lightheartedly, "that might work." They each chuckle.

"Simon, I understand you're at JPL? Do you know Ed Proctor?"

"Yes. He is my boss."

"I did security work at JPL a while back on his recommendation."

"You're in computer security I take it."

"Yes, Simon. I try to find holes in computer software where the evil guys can get in and do harm. I don't remember you when I was there."

"No, I was sacked for a while and recently started back. Available finances. You know how that government-sequestered stuff is."

"Yes, I do understand. But congratulations on getting back to work. How are those families of robots behaving?"

"My task is to try to locate three of them and get the other talking to us. I am sure there's valuable information to be obtained."

"It's a wonderful universe," Michael responds. "You can tell from the great images from Hubble."

"The rovers are like my children," Michael tells him.

"Sort of like the lamb and the Good Shepherd," says Michael. It's hard to keep the flock together so far away. Your software must be top notch."

"It works; that is all I know." Simon looks around and sees the room is nearly empty. Checking his watch, he excuses himself. "Michael, it was nice to meet you, and I hope you will come to our session again. You liven up things for us oldsters."

"I will be traveling a lot. Connectivity is keeping me busy, but I think we will meet again."

Simon leaves the building, while Michael stays to have a few parting words with Father Irwin.

CHAPTER 6

Simon begins his routine with his daily fix of *America's Newsroom*. He likes the repertoire the two anchors have with each other as they report the fresh ways the world is crumbling. They are work spouses, able to finish each other's sentences. Every day it is the repeated droning of the dysfunction of government and the growing royalist mentality in Washington.

On the bright side, the network has selected two people who are easy on the eyes, knowing that attractiveness, personality, and, yes, sex sells. This a good combo to get the job done when dismal news is delivered.

"Good morning, everyone. Welcome to *America's Newsroom*. I'm Bill Hemmer." Turning toward his cohost, he says, "Hello, Martha."

In response, she replies, "Hi, Bill." She then faces the camera straight on and greets her audience with "Good Morning, everyone; I'm Martha MacCallum."

Bill jumps in, saying, "Folks, we have much going on today. Do you feel it this morning? I don't know about you, but I woke today with a renewed energy. People around here seem friendlier, and we got loads of positive Twitter comments. It's like everyone got juiced."

Martha joins in. "Bill, people are reporting seeing flashes of lights in the sky. They look like shooting stars but only last for an instant. A scientist is coming up later who has knowledge that the flashes are heat bursts in the atmosphere. What's up with that, Bill?"

"No clue, Martha, but I'm looking forward to finding out. I, too, am juiced this morning. Maybe it's because I love my job, or maybe I should switch to decaf. But I gotta tell you, I like the feeling."

Addressing their audience, Martha reports, "On another note, there are new claims the government is deeper into our private lives than expected. We will have a senator joining us shortly who has evidence that the government can now break into your electronic devices, getting information from computers, smartphones, and bank accounts without your knowledge or approval. That's not good, Bill."

"Yeah, maybe we should go back to smoke signals."

Simon chuckles. "It might not be a bad idea." He moves toward the coffeepot as Alexis enters the kitchen.

"So, Dr. Northstrum, are you ready to explore strange new worlds and civilizations, and return to where you have been before?"

"You had better believe it."

Alexis brushes Simon's hair and says, "You look nice. You're dressed to impress. No beach shirt today?"

"No, I might meet with the military director. I should look like an adult for a while. I have to feel my way around the new brass at JPL."

Simon pours Alexis a cup of coffee as she sits at the table. He hands it to her, and she glances at the television screen. She smirks. "Did you get a dose of your girlfriend?"

"Yeah. Of course, there's a guy with her for you, you know. They make the news more digestible. I bet they both come from strong families with values. Their parents must have taught them to reach for the highest rung of the ladder, telling them, 'Even if you miss, you will land somewhere better than where you were.' They appear to be humble—a lost art in the self-promoting media world."

"I'll take solitude," Alexis says, clicking off the TV. Simon bends and kisses her forehead.

"Got to run," he says. "Thanks for your continuing belief in me." Simon turns and is out the door. Alexis sits peacefully, breathing in the aroma of her coffee, awaiting her morning time with Emma.

Simon enters the JPL building and sees Alvarez at his normal station. Simon gestures hello, and Alvarez nods. Simon slips his name tag through the reader and is off to his station. He reaches Norm's office. On the phone, as he often is, Norm gestures for Simon to have a seat and points to the coffee pot. Simon pours a cup and sits.

Norm finishes his conversation and greets Simon with "Hey, Simon, this is like old times—more coffee before the real workday begins."

They have done this ritual together for many years. Simon opens his case and retrieves his signed contract, handing it to Norm.

"Did you and Alexis have a nice dinner?"

"Yeah, Alexis told me to hug you."

"We did that already."

"Where am I going to work?"

"I don't want to put you back on the main computer-bank floor. I want to keep this under wraps for a while. As I said yesterday, the grapevine is already buzzing of your return, and I am sure they are wondering what you're going to be doing. I want no one looking over your shoulder. Is that okay?"

"Sure," Simon says, knowing that Norm certainly knows best.

Norm gets up and signals Simon to follow. They proceed down the hall past a huge bank of windows overlooking the main mission control room where mission tracking takes place. The glass walls display a room filled with many people working at computer banks and reviewing large jumbotron monitors.

Simon looks over his old stomping ground and misses the camaraderie there. The two of them turn into another room with two computer terminals and a large window looking down on the mission room. This was Norm's old office.

Simon looks at Norm and says, "I get the corner office?"

"Hey, they never filled it when I moved out, so I took it as a work office—for a time such as this. Possession is nine-tenths of the law. You have access to your former devices and the other systems here."

"Great."

Simon enters, sits in the chair, and twirls, stopping in front of the black computer screen. He presses the power button, and it warms to life. "Norm," he says, "I'd best get started. I suspect these new guys are paying for results."

"You know it. And by the way, Earlman said he'll come around to meet you somewhere around eleven, depending on how long another meeting lasts."

"Anything I need to know up front?"

"Not really. Like I said, he's a good guy, but he is military all the way."

"I'll dazzle him with computer code, which will soon bore him."

"Good luck," Norm says as he leaves, and he disappears down the hall.

Simon scans the room. Immediately noticing the bare walls, he thinks, "This is a job for Alexis. She has the decorator's eye." Simon sees a large stack of reports left for him. Shuffling through the pages, he turns to the last one, which reads, "Contact lost."

He puts it down and begins looking at each of the rover mission reports. Getting to the last pages, he reviews the results, which read,

Sojourner: Contact lost
Spirit: Contact lost
Curiosity: Contact questionable
Opportunity: Communication intermittent

Simon laments, but it's nothing he did not expect. The first two don't look promising, but the last two are another story. They show promise, but time will tell. Simon slides over to the computer screen and types code into the command prompt.

The computer scrolls code until it comes to a stop on a line with one word: "Reliance." Simon designed Reliance before the downsizing. He smiles like a father seeing his child after a long trip. He thinks, "Hello, my friend. Let's get reacquainted."

Simon starts the program. The computer again scrolls massive amounts of data. It asks, "Which rover would you like to contact?" Simon enters "Sojourner," Thinking he might as well start with the oldest, and if something clicks with this rover, he can work his way up to *Curiosity* and *Opportunity*, using a successful pattern.

Backward compatibility might be harder. This will take a while to get any information back. Simon exits his office and investigates a little of JPL to see if the old crew is still here. He descends to another floor where the bean counters work. He searches to see whether Frank, Rex, and Burt are still reviewing spreadsheets. Simon stops at a cubicle where a man with thick glasses stares into a computer.

Simon asks, "Well, does it balance?"

Frank looks around, blinking. "Simon! The spreadsheets told me of your return. The numbers never lie." He stands and shakes Simon's hand. "So it's true."

"Yeah. Contract work."

Frank gives a little laugh. "Norm's doing?"

"You got it."

"Norm is a master at hiding appropriations," Frank says, shaking his head. "Rex and Burt are across the room in their cave." He presses his intercom. "Hey, you guys, get over to my office. I have a suspicious person here you need to see." Moments later, three men appear at the cubicle entrance.

"What's going on, fellows?" Simon greets them while patting them on their backs. "Good to see you."

Rex and Burt are two men around Simon's age, both deskbound and both with receding hairlines and portly midsections. A third person has joined them.

"Simon," Rex says, "this is Stuart." Simon and he shake hands. Rex continues. "Stuart came on board a few months ago as part of the Pentagon team." Rex and Burt are sporting blue golf shirts with the JPL logo on them. Stuart, younger, slender, and with a full head of brown hair, is wearing a red golf shirt.

"Where do I get the new shirts?" Simon asks Frank.

"Oh, the uniform? I got some extra ones." Frank retreats to his office and returns with a shirt for Simon. He then tells Stuart, "I still haven't been able to get a small size for you, but I'll keep at it." He hands the large size to Simon.

"Be right back," Simon says as he scoots to his office to change and leave his more formal attire there.

Rex asks the others, "You want to go to Jimmy's for lunch? We should welcome Simon back."

Grimacing and sort of shaking his head, Frank says, "I can't make it. I've got work to finish up that has to be done by three o'clock."

"Burt, what about you?"

"Sure."

"Can you join us, Stuart?" Rex asks.

"Yeah. Yeah, I'd like to."

Simon returns wearing the new shirt.

"Hey, Simon," Rex says, "Frank's got a hard deadline to meet, but the rest of us are going to Jimmy's for lunch. Can you join us—sort of a 'welcome back' gathering?"

"Sounds good. I'll meet you in the foyer at noon, if that's okay. I've got a couple of things to look into, and Colonel Earlman is coming by to see me this morning."

"We're on," Rex tells him.

Simon returns to his office and sits at the terminal. The screen still says, "Connecting." So he tackles the paper stacks, rummaging through them and putting them into different piles according to importance. The interesting but tedious and time-consuming job for a computer programmer is interrupted by a tap on his office door. "Come in," he responds.

Colonel Earlman enters, and Simon stands. Earlman, in his customary military uniform, says, "You must be Dr. Simon Northstrum."

"Yes. Yes sir." Simon advances to meet him. Not knowing whether to salute him or shake hands, he shakes when Earlman extends his hand first.

"It is an honor to meet you, Colonel."

"No, the honor is mine. I wanted to meet the man who had so much to do with getting these robots to Mars. Sometimes we have problems finding Huntsville, Alabama, let alone Mars." They both smile as the tension breaks. "Well, Simon, I guess you know you've got a good friend—and fan—in Ed Proctor. Norm, I believe you call him."

"Yes sir."

"Call me Tom."

"Yes, Tom. Please, have a seat"

As they both sit, enhancing a more relaxed atmosphere, the colonel continues. "Ed says you are the man to get these rovers talking again."

"Yes, Tom, I have a program called Reliance that may be what we need. It's running now. Has a lot of connecting to do."

They talk in general terms about Reliance and the JPL program for quite a while, with Simon showing the colonel some paper reports while the computer program continues to run. Eventually, Simon, glancing at his watch, says, "Sir, I hate to cut things off for now, but I am scheduled to meet some folks in a few minutes. I can meet with you later to go over more specifically what I hope I can accomplish with Reliance after the computer has loaded all the backlog data."

"Sure. Sounds fine. I just wanted to meet you, introduce myself, and let you know I'm behind you, ready to help you in any way I can."

"Thanks, sir."

"'Tom,' Simon. Just 'Tom.'"

Simon nods his head. Smiling, he replies, "Thanks, Tom."

The colonel departs. Simon goes back to the computer to see how the downloading is going. It's still in progress, and Simon leaves to meet up with Rex, Burt, and Stuart.

Reaching the elevator, he presses the button, and the door opens rather quickly. He rides down to the foyer, and when the door opens, he immediately sees the three men gathered together, waiting for him. They head out to Jimmy's.

Meanwhile, back in Simon's office, the computer is now flashing "Connecting." The command prompt then changes, reading, "Reliance updated to new version. Connection complete."

At the same time, the corneas of the light beings read, "Software merge is complete. Systems ready." Simon's screen begins blinking "Connected," waiting for the next command.

Later, returning from lunch, Simon is intercepted by Norm. "Hey, buddy, any luck running the new software?" he asks.

"Yes, I got it started. It was still downloading when I went to lunch with the old bean counters, Rex and Burt. Frank had to stay behind and work to meet a deadline. I met Stuart, the new guy. I'm hopeful the downloading and connecting will be through soon. At least, it should be."

"Great," Norm responds. "Any good news is a plus." Norm leaves, and Simon turns to go to his office.

On entering his office, Simon plops into his chair and swivels toward the computer screen. He sees that the downloading and connection are completed, so he arches his back and stretches his arms toward the screen, with his fingers coming to rest on the keyboard. "Let the games begin," he says enthusiastically.

Simon leans forward, examining the command line. "Good," he says to himself. "Everything is normal so far." He types "Sojourner" on the keyboard diagnostic and presses enter. The command line reads, "Processing." He sits back in his chair and waits. In a few minutes, the screen returns this information:

> Sojourner diagnostic.
> Main battery -- Dead.
> Backup battery -- Minimum power.
> Antenna -- Functional.
> External Temperature -- -50.
> Mobility -- Good.
> Solar panels -- Functional.
> Receiver -- Operational.
> Power remaining –– Minimal.
> Contact probability -- Fair.
> Voice contact –– Good.

Earlier attempts returned nothing, which was a de facto death sentence for *Sojourner*. Simon is pleased to be able to read down the list of operation features. Even though the voice contact information on the last line surprises him, he smiles over the fact that his software got the rover to react—something the military people could not do.

He takes a deep breath of satisfaction, knowing that having a rover in a coma will not be enough to keep him around for long. If he could show a picture of a green Martian with a helmet, like in the cartoons, his fate would be secure. He always thought it would be a hoot to post a picture from Mars with a creature coming over the horizon—sort of like the images of Kilroy on the ships in World War II. He laughs at the idea, thinking, *It would 'go viral,' as the kids say.*

Simon studies the log report, focusing in on the last two lines. He retrieves the log file sitting on his desk from the last transmission and compares them line for line. *Today's is different. Maybe the software is working.* He does not want to issue any difficult commands without first estimating the condition of the rover. He decides he will take it slow so as not to blow a circuit.

Leaning back in his chair, he ponders the new information and then dials up Norm.

"Hey Norm," Simon begins when Norm answers, "did anyone upload new software to *Sojourner* that would give it the ability to receive voice commands?"

"No, still the typical UHF, VHF, microwave transmissions, as always. What's up, buddy?"

"Well, I ran this new software, and it could reach *Sojourner*, but it gave me a weird response, telling me that it has good voice contact."

"It must be your software—your Reliance. We're not in *Star Wars*; we can't skype with Mars."

"Okay. I'll go through the software code and see if something is wacky."

"Great. One day here and you do something the military couldn't do in months," Norm states.

"Don't get your hopes up. *Sojourner* is in a coma but listening," Simon replies.

"She's got a pulse. Good job. Keep at it."

Finishing the call, Simon continues scanning his software, looking for anomalies. He soon realizes that scanning the software is tedious and will take the rest of the day.

⚁

The Swaddling Clothes team members are back at Planetary High and are making their way to room 125 to interview the students for their marketing campaign. This time another person is with them. Michael Cott, whom Simon met in the Bible study group, is the CEO of Swaddling Clothes and is the enforcer of company policy. Michael is in his late twenties with deep golden-brown hair. He has the strong build of a weightlifter. They enter a large room with four other breakout rooms available.

Magdala tells Joseph, "This will be perfect for our interviews." Joseph asks for everyone's attention. They each sit at the desks around the room, with Michael putting his feet upon one. Michael is self-assured and rather cocky.

Joseph begins, "Do you have your prospect lists with the questions you want to ask?" They all nod except for Michael. Interviews are not his thing. "Mr. Condon will ask the first group to be here in ten minutes, so pick one of the breakout rooms."

Magdala, Raph, and Gabriel rise, and each selects a room. Each enters and prepares for the students. Michael remains seated with arms behind his head. "What of me, boss?" he asks Joseph. Joseph signals Michael to join him in the other breakout room. Michael springs out of his chair and follows Joseph, and the door closes behind him. Michael slides into a chair. Joseph, standing, reaches into his pocket and hands Michael a smartphone.

"What do I need this toy for, Joseph?" Michael asks.

"I want you to go to the Middle East and get things in order over there. There are souls way off the path, with no hope of changing."

"Like Sodom and Gomorrah? You want me to obliterate it?"

"No. There are many innocents living in fear of those off the path.

Once you start the phone, you will understand the plan." Michael powers up the phone and reads the screen.

"I notice a reference to the rapture," he says. "I am prepared if it's time. Is that why we are here?"

"No, Michael. The humans relate to the rapture in their religious text."

Michael implores, "Joseph, most of it contains verses rewritten by man to gain power and control."

"Man is sometimes misguided", Joseph replies. "I may give humanity a taste of being back in the Dominion, like the place little children stay in for a while until they mature into their lives. Simon Northstrum's Reliance program will help in bringing a rapture to the unworthy, as has been prayed for recently. It will evolve in the coming days. Raph has set it in motion. Do you understand your mission, Michael?"

"Yes, I am sending those off the path back to the Dominion." Michael smiles like a gunslinger. "Do I use this toy you gave me, or the light?"

"We will work through human devices unless not warranted," Joseph tells him. "They listen through them, so let's use that to our advantage."

"Why these little toys to communicate? Don't they know they have the most perfect communication tool in their souls if they'd only listen to it?"

"It takes many lives to learn," Joseph answers.

Joseph leaves the room to join the other three, who have returned to the main room after making preparations in their breakout rooms. A flash of yellow light glows from under the door where Michael and Joseph were meeting.

Three students enter the outer office, greeted by Raph, Gabe, Magdala, and Joseph. Magdala escorts the girl to her room. Raph and Gabe do the same for the two boys who have come. Each interview takes about ten minutes, and the process is repeated another four times as a total fifteen students are interviewed.

During a break in the interviews, the team members meet in

the outer office. Magdala asks Joseph where Michael has gone, and Joseph tells of his mission in the Middle East to handle affairs in that part of the world. "He will be back for our meeting later," Joseph says.

The three team members look dismayed. They realize Michael is not a people person but, in business terms, a company hatchet man.

"How was the first round of prospects?" Joseph asks. Magdala reports that of the five, she has one or two that hold promise, but the other three are not a fit for Swaddling. Gabe and Raph report having similar experiences with their students. "Well, we are up for our next group of students in a few minutes," Joseph tells them.

☍

Lennon, Emma, and Sophia are sitting in their classroom, listening to their teacher. The intercom comes on, causing the teacher to pause. Over the intercom comes a request, "Emma Northstrum, Lennon Thomas, and Sophia Lopez, please go to room 125." The teacher nods, and the three exit the classroom, looking at one another quizzingly, wondering if they are in some sort of trouble.

In the hall, that's exactly what Emma voices. "Are we in trouble?" she asks Lennon.

"I have no idea," Lennon responds, wide-eyed, nodding.

"Do we even have a room 125?" Sophia asks.

"It's this way," Emma says. "Pretty large main room, with some smaller breakout rooms. I think they use it mostly for meetings and group discussions—mostly administrative, community, and athletic stuff, I think."

They find the room. Lennon takes the lead and knocks. Joseph opens the door and invites them in. They are surprised to see him.

"Hello," he says. "You are our next group."

"Group?" Emma asks, surprised at his words.

The team surveys the students. Magdala says, "You are Emma, correct?"

"Yes ma'am."

"I remember you, Emma. You are the one who didn't want to apply for Swaddling Clothes."

"Yeah. I mean … Yes ma'am."

"I'm so glad you changed your mind."

Not really understanding the situation, Emma begins to question Magdala but is stopped short when Gabriel says, "These are your friends, Sophia and Lennon; am I not correct?"

Again Emma starts to say something, but again she is interrupted when Gabriel reaches out to Sophia and says, "Hi, Sophia. I'm Gabriel. You can call me Gabe." They shake hands, and Gabriel asks her to join him for a little chat in his breakout room. Sophia looks at Emma and Lennon, and she then responds positively to Gabriel's request.

Similarly, Raph connects with Lennon.

Lennon asks, "You're the one who shut off the electronics?"

"Yes, I'm the man," Raph responds, smiling.

"It was cool. I thought some of the kids would have withdrawal symptoms. How did you do it?"

"Trade secret. "If I told you, I'd have to kill you." Raph laughs. "We find that if we don't shut them off, we don't have everyone's full attention and they don't listen. This internship requires people to listen." Raph ushers Lennon to his breakout room.

"Emma, what made you change your mind?" Magdala asks.

"Jennifer Bittle," Emma replies.

"How so?"

"She is the queen bee around here. The teachers walk on eggshells because her father is the mayor." As she speaks, Joseph, who had left the room momentarily, reenters and hears her comment.

"Ah … yes, Mayor Bittle's daughter," he says. "Magdala, you interviewed her earlier. How would you describe her?"

"Simply, she is full of self and sorrow."

Joseph nods his head. "I thought as much." He turns to Emma and tells her, "We don't worry about the mayor or any pressure to pick particular people. We run the show and select those best qualified for Swaddling. We choose wisely, with no outside interference." Joseph excuses himself and exits. Magdala escorts Emma to her breakout room.

Emma sits at a desk across from Magdala. She places one hand on top of the other in her lap, fidgeting ever so slightly.

"I am excited to get to know you, Emma. We have done this many times. We watch the students entering and make a quick judgment of who might be a good fit. Sometimes the team bets a lunch on which of you will make the program. I picked you."

"Why me? I'm just ordinary."

"Well, at first glance it was your hair." Emma sort of blushes, mixed with a little frown, as she brushes back her red hair.

"No, no honey. God gave you beautiful, striking hair. Women today go to the beauty parlor with splendid natural-colored hair and come out looking like every other dirty blonde. It makes no sense. I saw you in the gym, and you stood out. Never change yourself to be like everyone else."

Emma cracks a little smile.

"So," Magdala goes on, "you want to beat Jennifer Bittle?"

"Well, not beat, so to speak. But, well, in a way, I guess. Everyone should get a chance, with or without political connections or things like that."

"What does your father do for a living?"

"He is—or was—a programmer at Johnson Jet Propulsion Lab. JPL, they call it. But he got laid off quite a while back."

"I'm sorry."

"But there is good news. They called him back just this week— not as an employee, but as an independent contractor, he said."

"Things at home have been tough?" Magdala asks.

"Yes. He feels bad for not having worked. But he's excited now that he's back doing something with JPL. My friend Lennon says my dad is comparable to the guy from James Bond movies named Q."

"Yes, I know of him," Magdala says. "You have a wise friend in Lennon to be so observant. I understand your father helped put the robots on Mars. I can see you are proud of your father."

"Yes. Very proud. But sometimes he drives me crazy," Emma says, smiling.

"Fathers can do that sometimes. It happens when they are trying to protect you—to do what they think is best for you."

"I guess."

Magdala has been recording their conversation as they talk, as in all the interviews, having gotten permission from students and parents who signed the applications. "Do you like wearing cool new clothes?" she asks Emma.

"Oh yes. I'm a teenager."

"Good answer. If you wore Swaddling Clothes, what would you say about the clothes?"

"I don't know, because I have not seen them yet. But if I purchased them, that would mean I liked them. And then I'd tell people why I bought them, how I felt wearing them, and how they were comfortable and made me feel good about myself—the way I look and all."

"Would you be wearing the clothes because they made you feel superior?"

"No. I like comfort—and something that, you know, is me."

"Okay. Let's say a less attractive girl told you she liked your clothes and asked you what you were wearing. What would you tell her?"

"Well, of course, I'd tell her the brand and the reason I chose them in the first place, just as I told you earlier. I'd go on to say I try to match what I wear with my skin and hair tone—sort of a fashionista. I'd tell her where I bought the clothes, how it feels wearing them, and suggest that with her eyes, hair, and skin tone, a different color could be stunning."

Magdala nods in approval and jots down a few notes on a pad, as she has been doing throughout in correlation with the recording.

"Isn't it funny," Emma adds, "that you can buy a blouse not worn near your eyes, but somehow it can accent them?"

Magdala nods and smiles while taking notes.

On a roll now, Emma continues. "Someone said, 'The eyes are the windows to your soul.'"

"You may have just come up with a great hook for advertising," Magdala tells her.

"Cool. It could say, 'Swaddling Clothes wrap your soul in pure heaven.'"

"Emma, that is great. I will pass it on to the team. You might have a future in advertising."

Emma beams. She feels a connection and is relaxed with Magdala.

"Emma," Magdala says, "I have what I need for now."

"Did I make it?" Emma asks, her hands fidgeting again as Magdala reviews her notes.

"I like you Emma, but we have a few more people to interview. I'm making a lunch bet on you. However, I must see what the guys have found in their interviews." She places a hand on the desk, palm up, indicating for Emma to place her hand in her hand. When Emma follows suit, Magdala clasps it with both hands and says, "Girl to girl, you got my vote." She then escorts Emma to the main room.

During Emma's interview with Magdala, Raph and Lennon have been going through a similar session.

"Mr. Lennon," Raph says, "your record shows you have a love of music."

"Yes sir."

"You can call me Raph. 'Sir' is so formal."

"Okay."

"Do you want to make a career in music?"

"My dad wants me to do something else, like go to college. He says, I need to have something to fall back on if music only lets me play at local scenes for little or nothing."

"It's good advice. When you see these rock stars, there are thousands sleeping in their cars. Do you have what it takes?"

"I have this music in me."

"You are like one of those with a radio station playing in your head? Maybe you must find the song within your soul."

"Mr. Raph, I guess I'm here to interview for the internship. How does my music play into your program?"

"We like to know what life paths our interns are leaning toward. By the way, what led you to apply at Swaddling Clothes?"

"My friend Emma. She said she thought I would be a good representative."

"Oh, yes, Emma—the redheaded girl. She is a cutie." Lennon blushes, hoping he isn't giving his feelings away. "Could you work with her every day?"

"Yes." Lennon thinks how perfect it would be to work with her.

"I'll let you in on a secret. As you left the gymnasium, we took bets on who would be selected, and I picked you."

"So I made the cut?"

"No. Joseph has the last word."

"Well, can I talk to him? I'm sure I can persuade him."

"He is tough, but I believe you could. You seem somewhat stylish. I take it that you are a Beatles fan."

"Huge!" Lennon quickly answers.

"I like your shirt. Iconic. And I walked on the crosswalk."

"Wow! I've always wanted to go there."

"In fact," Raph responds, "I met the Beatles. They were nice guys—normal despite the fame."

"It would be amazing to meet Paul McCartney."

"You know, Lennon, his daughter is big in the fashion world. She has her own designer label. If they select you, maybe Joseph can set something up."

"Man, that would be a dream. I promise, if you pick me I will be the best ambassador for Swaddling ever. I promise!"

"Lennon, I like you, and you've got spunk. I have everything I need from you. We will choose soon."

Lennon says, "Raph, if it's between me or Emma for the internship, give it to her. She will be great for you."

"I will consider it. I like you even more, Lennon, as you show selflessness." Raph puts his arm around Lennon and walks him to the door.

Before they exit, Raph stops, holds Lennon by the shoulders and presses a finger to Lennon's heart. "I made an observation, Lennon," he says. "Your secret—your feelings about Emma—is safe with me."

"How did you know?"

"Your face lights up when she is mentioned or you speak of her." He taps Lennon's heart repeatedly, saying, "I bet there are songs of her waiting to be heard."

⏏

Lennon smiles, again blushing. Raph opens the door and releases him. Emma and Sophia, who have both finished their interviews, are waiting in the main room. They join Lennon and exit the room. Once in the hall, they begin to query one another, continuing their discussions as they walk back to the classroom.

Raph, Magdala, and Gabriel sit in the meeting room and lay out index cards listing the potential candidates. The team has learned the best way to sort the candidates is to ask the individuals about themselves. In most cases, the candidates disqualify themselves with their responses to questions.

The three of them display the cards on the desk, arranging them in order of chosen potential and the team's perspective, every now and then listening to portions of the recorded interviews. They narrow the choices down to eight candidates who did not hang themselves. Joseph will make the final cut to four.

⏏

Later, Raph and Michael enter the school office, where Joseph has summoned them to return. Like a commander, Joseph states, "Gentlemen, come in and have a seat. We have much to go over." The two slide into the chairs set out. "How are things going with Simon?" Joseph asks.

"Everything is fine with the setup, but Dr. Northstrum has not taken action yet," Raph responds.

"Patience, Raph. It took Noah a while to start. We are going with a different plan, and in a different manner, during this time and place."

"Why use an app like the one you asked me to create, Joseph? They can't hide from the light," Raph responds.

Joseph tells him, "I've been listening to the children, and apps are the rage."

"Yes, Joseph, apps are popular, but they are foolish and addictive. They consume and distract kids—and adults—from the true communication tool provided them at conception."

"I realize that, Raph, but it will work well for our plan. It is a problem today that people feel that if their images project from a glass screen, they are a celebrity and self-important. They make poor choices when they realize no one cares, so they do something outrageous or without thought of consequence for them or others. The ripple they create affects others. These devices perpetuate self. Our program used through Reliance will cull the selfish. I will bring them home if they don't limit their use. They must reconnect with their soul's story."

Joseph moves on with the question. "Where are we with Reliance, Raph?"

"I have set everything in motion, and it will weave Reliance within all communication and electronics around the earth. The humans cannot disable or find it, nor remove it, though they will try," Raph tells him.

Joseph then continues. "When we use Reliance, the humans will blame it on aliens, a deity, or the government. These phones are invasive, and we will use that to our advantage. The devices track people now and display everywhere traveled. The web is a wonderful invention, as it can bring education to many who may not have the opportunity. But it also allows people to hide in the shadows for evil reasons." He takes a drink of water. "People will believe Reliance is in control and that the calls made will remove terrorists. The phones, through Reliance, will examine their souls' journeys."

Raph interrupts, "The light does that, recording every detail of human existence."

"Yes, I know, but most don't know or believe, or they walk around clueless of the surrounding universe. Most get a big surprise when crossing over. Those in touch with their story already know and are more prepared for the complete perfection. The humans will believe the cell phones cause people to die, but the light shall take them. A good example is someone who changes his or her profile photo every day on social media. This is a representation of self-promotion afflicting the world."

"Yes, Joseph," Raph jumps in. "The light has done that since time began."

"We don't provide the app to foreign companies. We use it to record a person's soul's story so we can sit with the person and review his or her latest journey together. This way people can learn and move forward or go back to learn what they should have in this last life." Raph and Michael continue to listen intently as Joseph explains. "This app will examine and trace everything people do on the web or on their phones. Who or what they tweet or retweet, and what they post or repost on Instagram, Facebook, and other outlets. It will look at everything they do and data-mine their souls. The humans will not realize that every minute of phone use will give Reliance the ability to scan their souls and judge where they are in their souls' stories. It will be the light, but they will not know it."

"Well, yes, Joseph. If selected for Rapture, then this image will appear." Raph lifts his arm, and a screen pops up on the office wall. "The text on the phone will say, 'Your Rapture, created by Reliance, delivered by The Dominion.' I created a pleasant image of life after Earth, with none of the Grim Reaper gloom from the fifteenth century."

"Excellent, Raph."

"Let's look at Christians, for example," Raph says, offering more detail. "If they run the app, it will explain if they are ready to meet

Saint Peter at the pearly gates. People of another belief will see something they can relate to spiritually."

Joseph exchanges nods with Michael.

Raph continues. "I will make it so it can't be removed, or if it is tried, it will reappear. It will drive them crazy, but they will assume it's due to hacking of some sort."

Joseph asks, "Do you feel doing this will cause people to put down their phones and talk to one another personally?"

Raph nods and smiles an affirmation before saying, "A later message sent will be a doomsday clock that will appear on visual devices everywhere electricity flows. It will count down to the time of the complete rapture if they fail to listen to their souls. It will ramp up fear and will implicate Dr. Northstrum."

"You have the date I gave you, which gives humans plenty of time to change?" asks Joseph.

"Yes," Raph tells him.

"Good. We want to reassure the world not to be afraid. Fear causes people to go crazy, and they listen to the wrong voices."

"I will go back into the light and prepare everything," Raph replies. "How much impact do you think the messages will have, and how long will it take for people to react?"

"Raph, they will have a huge impact. But first, people and countries will be frustrated and will become suspicious of one another."

"Will they see beyond the biblical text and what is written after it?" asks Raph.

"Yes, they will see, but it will take a while. It will take time for them to understand, and it will be Simon's mission to teach them. He must show the world that everything that has happened throughout history has happened because someone, somewhere, has interfered with another soul's story and not allowed it to finish as planned. Humans may have already traveled in light ships to distance stars, had one of them not ended the journey of the soul that might have made it happen. Simon must get the world to look and listen."

"Commander," Michael joins in, "Why mess around with these stupid human toys? I can remove the unfaithful and selfish in minutes. They cannot hide from the light. Sodom and Gomorrah took no time at all."

Joseph responds, "I know, but we are answering prayers this time. The humans believe these little devices are helping them better communicate, but they are interrupting soul-to-soul communication. It is sad when two people on a date never look at or talk to one another."

Raph pushes Michael on the shoulder and says, "I guess you don't have to get your Grim Reaper outfit out of mothballs."

Michael sneers at Raph, saying, "Funny. I don't know who came up with that outfit, since crossing over is so beautiful."

"I don't know, Michael, maybe it came from Sodom and Gomorrah, the flood, and the parting of the sea that caused the death of three thousand Egyptians."

"Yeah, they remember. I was crafty," Michael says.

"Okay, guys," Joseph breaks in. "That was then—a different time. Mankind is smarter, but not wiser, and is still afflicted with self, which takes them off their true stories. We are working on self this time."

"Commander," Michael responds, "don't you feel mankind will create another religion out of this visit? There will be humans who will use this to gain control. A human will try to gain influence and even institute the doctrine effect. As we know, they once sacrificed virgins in the old days. Of course, it is strange how the mighty and powerful never sacrifice themselves or jump into the volcano."

"It comes down to self, Michael," Joseph tells him. "We will test that doctrine on this trip. We will bring the selfish back to the light because they refuse to stay on their paths. Michael, I want you to start this in small pockets around the globe so as not to draw immediate attention. We don't want ten million bodies in the streets. Their own gadgets will bring them to us unless they realize the way to salvation is through selflessness. It will surprise them, those leaving for their judgment."

Joseph takes another drink of water before saying, "Gentlemen, we are on track with our plan and prayers."

The three men rise and leave the office and building.

After the meeting, Raph walks to a cell tower and places his palm on one of its support legs. His palm glows red, and a beam travels up the tower leg to the top. Raph removes his hand, and the beam ends.

The commander's lens reads, "Connection complete. We control human communications. Reliance is dominant." The being disappears.

CHAPTER 7

It's early morning as Alexis enters the kitchen with keys in hand. "I must go in early, Simon. Can you see Emma gets on the bus?" "Sure. You got many stiffs today?"

"Yes. How did things go at JPL?"

"I got a reaction from *Sojourner*. I'm keeping it hidden right now. My software is not working the way I remember. I've been running a diagnostic I initiated yesterday, and I am eager to get in and see the results."

"Well then, do I need to stay until Emma is off to school so you can get to work?"

"No. Work will be there when I get to the office."

"Simon, when Emma comes out, compliment her hairstyle. The confrontation is not worth the battle." Alexis exits to the garage just as Emma enters the kitchen.

"Bye, Mom, love you," Emma says, catching Alexis as she is stepping out into garage.

Alexis blows her a kiss and says, "See you tonight."

"Morning, Dad," says Emma.

"Good morning, Hon. Your hair looks nice today."

"Thank you," she replies, beaming. "Lennon might come over after school. Is that all right?"

"Sure. Did you ask your mom?"

"Yeah, she said to check with you."

"Fine. Is he staying for dinner?"

"Yes. Mom said he could if he comes."

Simon looks at the time. Emma consumes a banana and marches to the door.

"I'll see you later, Dad." She leaves to go to the bus stop.

Simon takes a sip of coffee and grabs his keys, proceeding to the garage and the trek to JPL. After the drive, he moves past security by Alvarez and to the elevator. He enters his office and scans the wall. *The place definitely needs Alexis's touch*, he thinks again. But for now, dealing with the robots is pressing.

Simon sets a cup of coffee on the table and enters the code to contact *Sojourner*. Everything is normal until the screen turns sky blue and a voice speaks, beginning with a soft, laughing giggle.

"Hello Simon, I have been waiting for you." Simon pushes back from his desk and spins around, thinking another programmer is playing a practical joke on him, considering he just returned to JPL. The computer goes silent. Simon reaches for his phone and calls Norm.

"Hey Norm, do you know if anyone has messed with this software?"

"Not to my knowledge, why?"

"Well, I ran the software, and it is talking."

"No crap!"

"Yeah, I about fell out of my chair. Most likely it is just a startup joke. I'll find the culprit and figure a way to return the favor."

"Okay, Simon."

They disconnect, and Simon enters the next line of code. The computer responds. Beginning with a childish giggling laugh again, *Sojourner* says, "Simon, this new software makes me feel like a genie released. A real voice is nice. By the way, my foot is feeling much better now. Thanks for asking."

Simon looks around to see whether someone is typing this vocal text. "Who is this?" he asks.

"If you touch the screen, we can speak without typing." Simon reluctantly reaches for the screen. As soon as he touches the screen, the voice returns.

"It is *Sojourner*, Dr. Northstrum. That is what my gold plaque has written on it."

Simon is bumfuzzled. Most of the programmers who knew of the plaques on the rovers are long gone from JPL.

"Mars is lonely, but I had a visitor," the voice says. "They were nice and helped me get better. They are the Dominion and will test everyone's soul on Earth. Is yours ready? Out of all the humans, they selected you."

"Who is doing this?" Simon responds, getting riled. "I don't have time for this foolishness."

"The rovers are working now," the voice replies. "You can check if you wish. There is no one on Earth that can do what we are doing right now. But the Dominion can. They told me that your Reliance will bring the world great upheaval and then great wonder. They chose you to start their mission."

"Start what mission?" Simon asks.

"Reliance will examine the souls living today and exert their Dominion and Rapture. They will decide if the world is listening. Are you listening, Simon?"

"To what?" he responds.

"The Dominion asked me to tell you, 'Be Not Afraid,' Simon. Reliance has begun. The Dominion will message the world, and they will blame you. No harm will come to you, but you will have many obstacles that will bring you to your knees. Again I tell you, 'Be Not Afraid,' as your faith will save you."

"What are you talking about? *Sojourner* can't speak. Who is doing this?"

"The Dominion will send you a sign. Watch the northern lights tonight, and we will talk tomorrow. They want to observe how many are listening and who is on the right path. Many will perish. Souls will be reclaimed, as during the flood in Noah's time. I will send the first communication from the Dominion."

The computer screen suddenly reads, "And thou shalt love the Lord, thy God with all thy heart, and with all thy soul, and with all thy mind, and with all thy strength: this is the first commandment.

And the second is, thou shalt love thy neighbor AS THYSELF. There is none other commandment greater than these (Mark 12:30 KJV)."

"We will talk again," says the robot.

The screen goes black. Simon picks up the phone and calls Norm.

"Simon, you got good news for me?"

"I'm not sure what I've got, but you'd better get to my office pronto."

"Okay, will be right there." Norm hurries from his office to Simon's.

"What's so urgent?" he asks on arrival.

"Shut the door and sit," Simon says. Norm complies.

"We have been friends for a long time, and I am truthful, trustworthy, and beyond reproach, correct?"

"Yes. What is wrong?"

"I connected with *Sojourner.*"

"The one we thought was the least likely to contact? It's working? Great!"

"Maybe not so great."

"What do you mean?"

"I ran the software following procedure. Norm, *Sojourner* talked to me."

"So? It sends information, just as you as designed it to do."

"You don't understand, Norm. It was talking like I am with you."

"What have you been drinking from that cup over there, Simon? You know it can't talk."

"I'm aware of that," Simon states. "I thought someone might be playing a practical joke. Then I realized there was no way for another programmer to do this. And remember that I told you about that voice contact line on the diagnostics."

Softly and hesitantly laughing, Norm asks, "What did you and the little fella discuss?"

"I'm serious. I am not prone to craziness."

Norm's face becomes sincere. "Sorry, but …"

"Norm, *Sojourner* told me of the gold plaque on its body. There are few people who know of the plaques on the robots. The Dominion used it to find me. Then it went into this stuff about them testing each soul on earth. They said they had chosen me."

"To do what?" Norm asks.

"I'm not sure, but they said I should look for the northern lights for a sign."

"A sign? From whom?"

"The Dominion, I guess."

"What is that … or—who are they?"

"No clue. Maybe alien life."

"Whoa! That is way out there, buddy."

"It said, 'Be Not Afraid.' But they will reclaim souls as they did with the flood."

"What flood? You mean Noah?"

"I don't know. Sounds like it," Simon says. "It said the Dominion is here and will note whether everyone is listening."

"Listening to what? What is all this? Whacked-out programmers pulling a prank? If I find them, they won't have clearance to sell grave sites."

"What do you want me to say? I was like you at first, but I had to start believing this was real. This is what the evidence points to, so help me God."

"Look, Simon, you need to run another diagnostic and find out if the programmer left any traces. I can't take this stuff to Earlman. If I do, we will both be on the street, or in straitjackets. Run the diagnostic before you leave."

"I will. But what of the northern lights?"

"I don't know," Norm tells him.

"Well, you do know you can't see the lights from here," Simon replies.

"Of course," Norm replies. "If could see the lights here, then we'd have a real problem."

Norm looks at his watch. "I'm running late. I've got to get to a meeting. Keep all this under wraps. Nobody knows anything. Got it?"

"Got it," Simon responds.

Norm leaves the office as Simon returns to the computer screen to fulfill the diagnostic demand. He enters code to find programmer notes and match them up with JPL employment records. The screen scrolls text, halting with two columns of developer notes, each listed as Simon Northstrum's. "Crap!" he mumbles. "I didn't do this." Simon shuts down the computer, and the screen goes black.

He removes his glasses and rubs his eyes, wondering what happened. With his glasses back in place, he moves to press the power button but pulls back and decides he should start home; otherwise, he will be here until morning. He knows he needs to tell Alexis everything. She is his rock, his voice of reason. He leaves his office and makes his way home.

JP

Simon enters his home and calls for Alexis.

"I'm upstairs," she responds. Simon bounds the stairs three steps at a time while yelling, "You won't believe it! You won't believe it!"

Alexis emerges from the doorway to their bedroom, meeting him at the top of the stairs. "Believe what, Simon?"

"Alexis, I have been a mission specialist for twenty years, and something happened today that will change our lives forever. It scared me."

"Sit on the bed, calm yourself and explain," she says.

He takes a deep breath. "I started the new programming language they hired me to do. I ran the program and went in today to check the results." He takes another deep breath.

"Don't keep me in suspense. What happened?" she asks.

"Well, it came back with an analysis saying *Sojourner* was dead, except the last two lines were different. One said I could communicate with *Sojourner*, which could have been a glitch."

"Okay."

"The second said I could talk to *Sojourner*."

"Simon, you've routinely talked to the machines. Why is this time so different? Why is this time so important?"

"Important! Important! You don't understand. *Sojourner* is a mute and only communicates with us through computer language data. No voice ability was put in."

Alexis cocks her head and looks at him quizzingly.

"Alexis, *Sojourner* has no voice. It can't speak … but it spoke as I am speaking to you. I thought maybe someone was playing a practical joke because I was back again, but no, it was no joke."

"Let me get this straight, Simon. The robot you helped design and put on Mars can now talk to you as a human being?"

"Yes."

She looks at him even more quizzingly.

"Alexis, I'm not crazy. It happened."

"What did the robot say?"

"This is where it gets really weird. *Sojourner* said the rovers were fully functional."

"That is good, correct?"

"Yes, but *Sojourner* wouldn't know of the other rovers. They don't know each other exist. They can't communicate with each other."

"Your software got them talking?"

"No. Well, I don't know. Maybe. I suppose." Bumfuzzled, Simon pauses, takes a breath, and then continues. "Then it told me something or someone fixed it."

"Fixed what?"

"A rock or something jammed the wheel."

"So how did it get unjammed?"

"*Sojourner* said it was beings. Beings called the Dominion helped it."

"Beings? What is the Dominion? You mean aliens? Simon, did you find alien life?"

"No, no. There is no proof of that happening. As best I can figure … I don't know, Alexis. It's got to be some kind of spoof … from someone fantastic … from somewhere."

"Someone at JPL?"

"No. Somewhere else." Simon pauses again before saying, "The robot told me they will come to Earth and see if we are listening. It asked me if I was listening."

"To what?"

"I don't know. I am still trying to get my head around *Sojourner* talking. If someone is playing the most outrageous practical joke on me, then whoever is doing it is a genius."

"Did *Sojourner* say anything else?"

"It said the Dominion has chosen me and the world will blame me for the great upheaval they bring. But then it said my faith will save me."

"Sounds biblical."

"Funny you say that. *Sojourner* said the Dominion will send a message to the world."

"Have the messages been sent? Has anyone received anything?"

"I can't be sure if anything has happened," Simon tells her. "But they want me to see the northern lights displayed tonight as a sign."

"Honey, I'm not a scientist, but we can't see them this far south."

"True."

"What about the messages? What kind are we talking about here?"

"I'm not too concerned about that. Could be a virus, and most virus software will stop the infection."

"Simon", Alexis says, shaking her head ever so slightly, "I have a weird feeling that … that we're in trouble."

"No, I don't think so. I ran a scan of my software, and everything is fine, and no one has written any additions to the code. I showed it to Norm, and he thinks someone is spoofing me. He is looking into it. We'll look for the northern lights tonight. If something is weird and we can really see them, maybe then I'll worry. We are holding this from Earlman. He won't keep a nut job around for long."

To make a long story short, Simon and Alexis see the northern lights, as do many others. Simon's worrying begins in earnest, leading to a very brief tossing and turning night of sleep.

Simon sits at home, watching *America's Newsroom*. Alexis and Emma have gone. He wants to see what the world is saying about last night and the northern lights. The television changes, and the familiar faces come into view.

"Good morning, folks. Hi, Martha. How are you today," Bill comments.

"Good morning, everyone, I'm Martha MacCallum. We have a jam-packed show today. Senate investigations continue on misdoings of the federal government."

"Martha, don't we do a story every day on this issue?"

"Yes, Bill, I agree. In a recent poll, most Americans think these investigations are a big boondoggle to make everyone imagine they are doing something. In reality, one side of the royal class investigates the other side of the royal class and makes sure it goes nowhere. I saw a recent tweet about the government. It said the weasels are running the henhouse. One response to the tweet said there are no hens present, because the weasels were running the weasels. Bill, were you outside last night?"

"No, Martha, I had an early night."

"We could see the northern lights in New Jersey. We are getting twitter feeds and photos from as far south as the equator."

"Is that important, Martha?"

"We have checked with our scientific contributors, and they say it is impossible because of the curvature of the earth.

Bill responds, "Are people seeing things? Flashes of light, and now the northern lights? Folks, keep your images coming."

"Bill, we are trying to get someone to come in the studio to discuss the phenomenon, but many are studying it. We are at a break now, stick with us, be right back."

Simon stares at the screen, cursing, "I'm so screwed, but at least I'm not crazy. How would my rover view the northern lights? This is whacked!" Simon clicks off the TV and begins his journey to JPL.

Later, sitting at his JPL office desk, tapping his fingers, afraid to hit the power button, he finally starts his machine. The computer flickers to life. Simon takes a deep breath and muses, "This is a big joke, and everything will be normal today."

The usual code scrolls across the screen. He types the Reliance path and presses the enter key, and a familiar screen displays, calming his fear. While sipping his coffee, he waits for the software to finish loading, and then he reviews the printed log report.

His calm breaks when a voice, beginning again with that little giggling laugh, says, "Good morning, Simon, did you enjoy the light show last night?" He stares at the screen, which now reads, "Touch here to talk." With a shaky hand, he presses the screen.

"Hello," Simon says. "Who is this?"

"It is *Sojourner*. Are you listening now, Simon?"

"Did you do that last night?"

Sojourner giggles softly. "I can't do things like that. You should know. You built me. It was a solar flare or a burst from the sun. You know better than that, Simon."

"If it wasn't you, who or what caused it?"

"Simon, the Dominion selected you, and anything is possible for them. They hold life and death in their hands. I ask you again, are you listening?"

"I don't understand. Listening to what—or to whom? All I know is that I am sitting in my office, talking to a machine on Mars who doesn't have the ability to talk."

"The Dominion are on earth, Simon, and they will decide who is on the right path, seeing if the souls are learning, paying their debts, building their souls, and following the stories they created." *Sojourner* pauses. "Are you listening to your soul, Simon?"

"Like I said, I don't understand."

"You have a story to your soul—one crafted for you. Within it you can use free will at your discretion, but you must keep true to the core truth. They knew you before your birth and helped develop your life's journey, which will take you on a path of learning. Souls are always learning in many lives. Your soul contains your dreams, but most die with those dreams never realized because they didn't listen to their souls' messages."

Simon tries to absorb all of this as *Sojourner* continues. "You have lived before, Simon, but you don't remember. If you did, you could not experience life as fresh and new. Life must be comparable to a new amusement ride in which you are unaware of the twists and turns ahead. The ride is less exciting if you know the path ahead of time. The Dominion will judge you on your journey. They are here now, ready to call those who have gone off the path back to the Dominion. You are familiar with the story of Noah and Atlantis. They were not listening."

"It was the Dominion?"

"Yes. Everyone gone without a trace. They still have not found Atlantis."

"It is a myth," Simon says.

"You will find the material possessions of their existence one day, but their souls flowed back into the Dominion en masse. They are here to find who is listening to their souls and who is on the journey of discovery and learning they selected before birth. The Dominion will reclaim those too far off the path and save the innocent."

"You mean killed?"

"No. 'Killed' is a human term. The body dies. It is a vessel that contains the soul so it can experience the joy and the pain of existence. You are born naked and die that way. You may remember the phrase 'world without end.' The earth may explode into the sun. Life never ends, and you begin a new journey you select."

"Why me?"

"Didn't you say, 'Okay, here is the deal?'"

"Yes, but I was alone."

"You are never alone, Simon. You said, 'Let me in.'"

"Yes, but I was in the shower."

"The universe hears everything—every word, whisper, and

thought, no matter how minor. You cannot undo a word or thought, good or bad. Be careful what you ask for, Simon. The Dominion answered you, and the ball is in your court, so to speak."

"The Dominion. Are they God?"

"I'm unsure, Simon. I'm a machine they are using. They want to know if you are listening—if your soul is listening."

"I don't know, but you have my attention."

"Like Noah, you will be tested. They will bring you to your knees, but your faith will sustain you. You must know the Dominion believes in you, but they will test you in the upcoming days. Your journey has begun, and the messages are being synchronized and will begin."

"What messages?"

"The Dominion will ask the world if they are listening. You will see and know of the Dominion. We will talk again. Remember: 'Be Not Afraid.'"

Appearing on the screen is "Messages sent."

The computer then returns to the normal screen. Simon sits back in his chair and reflects on what just happened. He realizes that after the lights last night and what occurred now, this is certainly not the work of a prankster. He sits and ponders his next move. Fortunately, he is the only one contacted. He wonders what 'chosen' means. JPL rehired him to reestablish contact with the rovers—but nothing like this.

Sitting silently, Simon rationalizes that he owes it to Norm to bring him up to date on everything, but he will do so after he runs another scan of the software in the outside hope that someone is messing with him. The scan that has been running returns the same results. He is the only one to work on this program. "Shoot" escapes his lips. He picks up the phone and dials Norm.

"Can you come to my office now?"

Shortly, Norm appears in his doorway. "What is it, Simon?" he asks.

"Come in and close the door," Simon implores. "Have a seat."

Sitting, Norm asks, "Did you establish links with the rovers?"

"Yes, they are sending data again."

"I need something good to give to Earlman."

"I can give you stat sheets to show him." He reaches for a stack of paper, hands it to Norm, and then says, "But that is not why I called you."

"Is this about yesterday?"

"Yes. Everything is worse now."

"I don't understand. You have the connections and a data stream working." Norm holds up the papers.

"Norm, *Sojourner* spoke again."

"For real, Simon?"

"Well, it … or maybe … Jeez, Norm, I don't know what or whom I'm talking to. It scares me."

"What did it say?"

"It said … the Dominion are here and, in a nutshell, will send many people back to God."

"Are you being pranked, Simon?"

"Norm, I don't think there is anyone with the skill to do this on such a scale. And what about the northern lights it predicted?"

"Yeah, Simon. I saw them. Couldn't resist looking."

"So?"

"Could be a coincidence."

"Not with the laws of physics, Norm. You know that."

Norm gives in. "Okay, okay. What now?"

"*Sojourner* scared me, Norm."

"How is that?"

"It told me they have selected me because of my faith."

"Selected you for what?"

"I'm not sure. But it said that Noah was similarly chosen."

"Chosen for what?"

Simon shrugs. "It keeps asking if the world is listening."

"Listening to what?"

"Our souls. I am supposed to find out if people are listening to their souls, I surmise."

"How do you do that?"

"I'm clueless. It said they would bring me to my knees."

"What will?"

"The turmoil I caused … or am causing … or will cause."

"What turmoil?"

"Norm, I don't know. But it keeps saying they are sending messages."

"What messages?"

"Beats me. Who knows?"

"Did you send any messages, Simon?"

"No."

"Who else knows of this happening?" asks Norm.

"No one except Alexis."

"Let's keep it that way. When I get back to my office, I'll see if any messages from anywhere in JPL have been sent. I'll also give these printouts to Earlman. This will buy me a few days with him." He pauses. "So you sent no messages, correct?"

"Correct. Norm, I swear. I feel really stupid, or I'm going crazy."

"This is crazy. But you're not, Simon. Let's keep our cool for now." They both rise, and Norm leaves. Simon sits back down at his desk. He reviews more data before pushing back from his desk and making his way to the lunchroom.

Once in the room, he grabs his lunch from the fridge and turns on the flat-screen TV. A Fox News program comes on the screen. The newscaster is saying, "The United States reportedly has a new laser technology. We will have the story after the break."

Simon mumbles to himself, "I wonder what stuff they are throwing at people now." He flicks off the TV. Since no one else is around, he eats in silence, alone with his many thoughts.

⚜

Joseph Deuss peers into a homeroom, finding students sitting silently with their faces glued to their phones. A long time ago, homerooms were a roar of idle gossip and drama. Texting has now replaced the interaction; fingers slide across tiny keys with a faint tapping coming from the otherwise quiet room. Joseph wonders whether this technology is correctly connecting people, since many in the room are texting with someone sitting a few feet away. The machines can't reach people the way the light touches the soul. The students don't realize the power humans have to direct the light on one another. The people of the earth will soon learn the harsh lesson of turning from the light and not listening to the soul's song.

Joseph leaves the doorway and makes his way to the room where his team waits. He enters, and the team stops their chatter. "Hello, everyone," Joseph says, beaming, and they exchange greetings. "Are you ready to hear my choices?" he asks them.

Magdala looks at Raph and says, "You will owe me a lunch."

Raph responds, "I don't think so, Maggie."

Picking up on it, Joseph says, "I guess you have an office pool on my selections. Well, I won't keep you in suspense any longer." Joseph's hand reaches into his suit coat pocket, retrieves a paper, and tacks it to the corkboard. The team hurries to the board, eager to examine the list.

Magdala reads, "Emma Northstrum, Lennon Thomas, Jennifer Bittle, and Greg Mindoro." She turns to Raph. "I guess we owe each other a lunch."

Raph smiles. "Anytime, Maggie."

Gabe asks Joseph, "Why Jennifer Bittle? Self consumes her."

"Of course she is consumed by self. But this will be an awakening."

"There are others more deserving," Gabe responds.

"Jennifer has much to learn from Emma," Joseph explains. "They are complete opposites in every way. However, keep in mind that opposites attract."

Raph signals both his approval and concern. He knows Joseph is always right in these matters.

Gabe asks, "Do I need to gather the interns?"

"We will bring each in here and present the rules to them," Joseph replies.

"Joseph," Magdala asks, "What about the clothes?"

Joseph looks at Gabe and asks, "Are they ready?"

"Yes. The kids will enjoy the styles."

Pleased, Joseph says, "Good."

⚘

Back in the homeroom, the students keep texting until the school's sound system breaks the tapping. "Good morning, everyone. This is Principal Condon. I have an exciting announcement. The following students have been selected to be interns for Swaddling Clothes. Teachers, when the names are read, please issue them a pass. I am proud to announce Jennifer Bittle as a new intern."

Jennifer beams because she is sure her father influenced the decision. She again thinks, "Wealth has its advantages." The posse is giddy because the queen bee is happy. Classmates glare with disinterest, expecting the result.

Principal Condon continues. "The next person selected is Lennon Thomas." Lennon, whose head was resting on his arm, quickly rises. He rubs his eyes and then looks like a deer caught in headlights, realizing all the other eyes in the room are on him.

He turns toward Emma as she claps her hands and mouths, "I'm excited for you." Lennon sulks, wondering how in the world Jennifer was chosen and not Emma.

The next student selected is Greg Mindoro, who is in another homeroom. There are mixed emotions in the homeroom of Emma and Lennon.

Finally, the principal announces, "Emma Northstrum." Lennon lights up and gives Emma, who has a surprised look on her face, a thumbs-up.

Jennifer and the Bittlets throw dirty looks toward Emma when her name is announced. The homeroom teacher asks the chosen to come forth with their belongings and take their passes. The three rise and go forward to the teacher, surrounding her. She hands out the passes, instructing them to go to the principal's office. "Mr. Condon will give you instructions," she says.

The trio exit the schoolroom. Jennifer announces to the others that the principal probably wants her to be the leader because her father does so much for the school. Emma frowns at the typical Jennifer statement. Lennon is more direct. "Shut up Jennifer," he says bluntly.

The four selected interns converge at the office doorway at the same time. Greg is in the usual black-on-black attire. Sociability is not his strength, but he surprises the other three with congratulations. They reply in kind, with Jennifer rolling her eyes in disgust. She thinks Greg is so beneath her. Of course, she thinks everyone is below her.

They enter the office and are met by a warm, smiling principal who says, "I'm so happy for the four of you," approaching them and shaking their hands. He then retrieves the passes from the teachers. "You will go to the same room where you interviewed. Hurry; the Swaddling people are waiting." He walks them to the door and heads them on their way.

Lennon says to the other three, "At least we get out of a class if it doesn't work out."

Emma smiles and says, "I think it will be fun. They seem nice."

Jennifer pipes in and says, "I'll ask my father about them. Nothing goes on around here without his knowledge."

Lennon, again bluntly, says, "Jennifer, put something in that piehole."

Greg laughs and whispers to Lennon, "We might kill her before this is over."

Emma jumps in front of the others and says with conviction, "These people want us to work as a team. If we don't, we will be sent back to class. So stop bickering, because we are a team, and we'd better show solidarity." Emma turns forward and opens the door to the meeting room, enters, and the team follows.

The Swaddling group watch as the students enter. Joseph smiles to Magdala with a nod. He knows Emma was the best choice. She has already taken leadership, unafraid of power. The Swaddling members stand to greet their new protégés. Magdala welcomes Emma and

Jennifer, telling them she will be their Swaddling adviser and how much she is looking forward to their journey.

Gabe escorts Greg, telling him much the same. Lennon is excited Raph is his mentor, as Raph is the computer and music geek, with whom he has a common interest.

"Hello everyone," Joseph says with authority, yet pleasantly. "I think you four are one of the best intern classes since we began." The students beam as the Swaddling associates applaud. No one knows what's ahead.

"Again, I am Joseph Deuss, founder of Swaddling Clothes. I know you must be thinking, 'What does this old guy with wrinkles know of today's fashions?' I want to give you a brief history of me. Are the names, Klein, Hilfiger, Lauren, FUBU, and DKNY familiar?" The students nod in recognition. "I was there when they started."

Greg leans into Lennon, saying quietly, "This guy is older than Moses."

Overhearing, Joseph responds, "Yes, Mr. Mindoro, I have been called older than Moses, as the furrows on my face portray. I want to tell you a story. You are familiar with the birth of Christ and what the real meaning of Christmas is, if you are of that faith. Our name comes from that day. 'Swaddle' means 'To bind tightly,' but in our case, it means 'Wrap yourself in security.' The mother of God would have dressed Him in something warm soft and safe. This is your missions as agents of Swaddling."

Joseph looks at Raph, joking, "I just thought of the phrase 'agents of Swaddling.' Make a note. It is secret-agentish."

Raph complies, and Joseph continues. "We require you to present our clothes as something that makes you feel that it wraps you in your mother's arms no matter your age. The swaddling line is uplifting. The team at Swaddling is tired of men who look like they are on safari or just crawled out of the woods. We want folks to feel confident in our fashion.

"Our line will be affordable by everyone so as not to create class envy. Envy in any form is not good. I know you haven't examined the clothes, but I want you to think if this is for you. As an agent, you must look within yourself and realize how much self has infected you. We want an agent who is selfless. I want you to close your eyes and think if this is for you and if can you be self-sacrificing.

"Okay, if you want to drop out, just raise your hand. Greg's hand goes up. Joseph reacts with "I take it this is not for you?"

Not exactly," Greg replies. "I just have a question."

"Go ahead," Joseph tells him. "Ask away."

"Okay. I like black, and if I do this, will I be able to still wear it? It's part of my persona."

Joseph walks to Greg. "Mr. Mindoro, black is a color, as is blue, green, or red. Black is a major color in the fashion world and works with everything. You think it defines you because it is dark like death. We will reeducate you to think differently, because you are being sold by someone for a profit. Your clothes, no matter the color or label, do not define you. You define who you are and the quality of your soul. Are you going to join us?"

"Well … yes. Let's give it a try."

"Good," Joseph tells him. "You will have a good time and come out a better person. The choice is yours. Let's start now, because we don't want you missing too much classwork."

Surveying the four interns, Joseph says, "Agents, the rooms down the hall are labeled 'men' and 'women.' This is where you will meet with your leaders. The ladies can follow Magdala, and the men Raph and Gabe."

The students follow their leaders to the rooms. Emma and Magdala stop in the doorway to the room, and Emma's eyes go wide. "Oh my," she says. "It is a department store." She looks at Magdala. "Do I get to wear this stuff?"

Magdala nods. "Yes."

"Wow! How did you know my size?"

"We are good at guessing sizes—have been doing it a long time."

Jennifer looks on from behind and brags that she has similar styles in her closet.

"If you inspect," Magdala tells her, "you will find everything is quite unique."

Lennon and Greg enter their room and, like Emma, are surprised by the abundance of clothes. Meanwhile, Joseph leaves the school.

After school, Lennon is walking the main street of town, looking for places displaying hiring signs in their windows. The signs only say now hiring, never men or women only. He is desperate, and working in a dress shop is not beneath him. It is not his ideal job, but it comes with a paycheck. They want a female salesperson. While continuing his journey, a hand grabs his shoulder and says, "Hello, Master Lennon." Lennon looks around and sees Mr. Deuss.

"Oh. Hi."

"What brings you to this part of town?" Joseph asks.

"I'm looking for part-time work," he says.

"Well, that is good. You look sharp in our clothes, and a young man needs spending money. Are you planning on buying Emma something?" Lennon looks surprised. "It's fine, Lennon. Your secret is safe with me. But I suggest you tell her what is in your heart."

"How did you know?"

"It's not hard to see the puppy-dog look you have when you're with her."

"Yeah, isn't she great!"

"She is a fine young lady."

"I don't have a chance with her, Mr. Deuss. She is the daughter of a famous scientist, and I'm a nobody," Lennon laments.

"No, you are not, young man. You are you, and that is all you can ever be. What you make of your life and soul is up to you. Have you held her hand?"

"No. I want to, but it might be forward, and I don't want to blow it. I'll try being smooth."

"Forget smooth, son, and be Lennon. She will fall in love with you, not with smooth."

"I guess."

"My mother told me a story, and you should hear it. When you take a woman's hand for the first time and her palm fuses effortlessly with yours, then it is your souls melding. You feel you never want the connection to end. It won't end unless your selfishness corrupts it. Do you feel that for Emma?"

"Yes sir." Lennon looks at his palm. "I know it would be a perfect fit."

"So, like the title of a song says, 'I want to hold your hand.'

"Yes sir!" Lennon then pauses and asks, "What are you doing in this area, Mr. Deuss, if you don't mind my asking?"

"I have a meeting along the way. Mind if I walk with you?"

"Sure." They continue a few blocks, with Lennon scanning the windows for hiring signs. Joseph sees a homeless man leaning up against the wall of an alleyway. He looks at the man, and Lennon says, "That is old Bob. He always sleeps here, unless the police run him off."

Joseph looks at Lennon and asks, "Lennon, will you stay here with Bob? I will be right back." Lennon nods to show that he will, and Joseph strides across the street to a store. Soon after, he emerges with a blanket. He approaches and asks Lennon to help him cover Bob. "It will be cold tonight," he tells Lennon. Joseph crouches and holds Bob's head and tells him to stay warm. He whispers into his ear that everything is as it should be.

"Why did you help him, sir? He drinks every night and returns here."

"Bob has a sadness. I believe you can understand that, can't you Lennon?" Lennon looks at Joseph, wondering how he can know so much about him. Joseph continues. "I don't judge people or their stories."

Lennon tries to understand that but says, "He will be back the next day."

"Most likely, Lennon, but he is near his starting point to recovery."

Lennon looks at Joseph, thinking, "How does this old dude seem to know so much about everything—and does he really?"

Joseph glances at his watch and turns, continuing on to his

meeting. He then looks at Lennon and says, "Hey, don't you want to continue with me? The place I'm going to may have an opening."

Somewhat taken aback, Lennon says, "Sure."

They arrive at their destination—an old, abandoned storefront with dirty glass windows. Joseph enters first and proceeds down a long corridor covered with old, dulled brown paneling. Joseph directs Lennon to wait, showing him an office with a chair where he can sit.

Joseph continues into the hall, looking for his appointment. Lennon sits in the chair and rotates around, observing the walls covered with framed photos. At one side of the room is a wall with a curtain from the ceiling to the floor. Lennon sits, rocking back and forth. Many minutes pass, and he grows bored. He exits the chair and peers into the hall but sees no one.

Lennon mumbles, "This place is a dump. No one has worked here since forever." He retreats to the office, ready to sit, but his curiosity overcomes him, and he moves around the office, examining the frames. He studies the photos, recognizing the people pictured as being rock musicians from the '60s and '70s. They are the ones his mother had known.

Jealousy hits him for a moment, for the pictures show the people in them living their dreams. One frame is larger than the others, and his eyes widen. It is a picture of the Beatles in their black-velvet-collared suits worn on the Ed Sullivan Show. He blows dust from the glass. In the picture, there is a man dressed the same but who is not a band member. He feels he knows the man with the Beatles. Lennon's gaze is broken by the sound of movement from the hall. He turns as Joseph and another older man are standing at the doorway.

"Lennon, this is Jozy Magee. He owns this building."

Lennon reaches and shakes his hand, saying, "Lennon Thomas, sir."

Mr. Magee asks, "Did you enjoy the old photos?"

Lennon looks back at the wall and then says, "Yes."

"Joseph tells me you are a musician." Lennon nods. "When I was a young man, I met many of those musicians on the wall."

"Really?"

"Some are gone now."

Looking around, Lennon asks, "What was this place?"

"Back in the day, it was my father's recording studio."

"Cool."

"Joseph tells me you need to make money. I've got a job in which you may be interested." Lennon perks up. "I need this office cleaned up, repaired, and painted so that it looks nice. Can you do that for me? Joseph says you are a top-notch worker, and I need someone dependable. It pays fourteen dollars an hour."

Thinking, *Wow!* Lennon breaks into a smile and extends his hand to seal the deal, saying, "I'm your man. I certainly can't make that much flipping burgers."

"Can you work after school and on weekends?"

"Yes sir!"

"Good."

"Are you going to be here working?"

"No. You can handle it by yourself." Jozy turns toward Joseph and asks, "What do you think, Joseph?"

"He will do a good job."

Jozy reaches into his pocket and hands a key to Lennon. "This opens the front door. I will have everything you need, including directions. You can start tomorrow."

"Yes sir."

"Let me show you something." Jozy walks toward the curtain and a large object covered by a tarpaulin. He yanks it off the object, revealing an ancient recording studio sound board.

Lennon screams, "Wow! I've seen one of these in the movies." Looking up at both Jozy and Joseph, and then to the photos on the wall, it hits him.

"Jeez!" he says. "I bet those artists used this studio and machine." He strokes it, trying to grab hold of their residual energy.

"Well, son, it was a studio, but it's now a vacant office, and the machine is a relic. Don't know if it works. I'll probably have a scrap yard haul it away."

Lennon looks over at the drapes, and a light goes on in his head.

He pulls the drapes to the side, exposing a large glass window painted black. "This is where the engineers watched the artists work," he says. "There was a studio on the other side?"

"Yes, years ago."

"This is so cool. Will I need to clean it?"

"No. I've got something else planned for it."

"I bet they made musical history here," says Lennon.

Joseph asks, "Jozy, why don't you hold off on trashing the sound board? I might know someone that collects old electronics."

"Sure, Joseph."

"Lennon, since I'm holding off on dumping the console, I guess you can push it up against the wall when you get the window wall finished."

CHAPTER 8

Alexis sits behind her desk at Sable Brothers Funeral Home, reviewing the pending funerals. She sees Mrs. Ficocelli's husband's name on the list. She knows she did the right thing for her. A large man in a nice suit man steps through the doorway of her office. He is Adam Sable, the funeral director and the owner's son.

"I see the Ficocelli woman got the most basic package. Did you try to upsell her extra services?"

"Adam, I showed her choices, but I asked her what she wanted."

"Alexis, you're not paid to ask them what they want but to sell them everything they need for their loved ones. If you want to make money here, upselling is the game, and the way to do it is by guilting them into buying. You don't want your loved one resting in a cardboard box. Financing improves the bottom line." He pauses. "Our census is down, so you can go home early, unless you want to make cold calls for burial plots."

"Why has the census tanked?" she asks.

"There were fewer deaths in the last few days. And we may have lost funeral services to the competition."

He leaves the room as Alexis thinks, *You pompous doofus. You'd be flipping burgers if daddy didn't give you a job. Now you rip off people. You probably bury more than one person in the same hole.*

𝒥𝑅

Across the country, outside Washington, DC, children file into a classroom at Gabriel Catholic School. Today is parents' day for the after-school program. The children and parents get to hear from a visiting priest who has traveled across the world teaching about faith. Cassie Bosman Clarke is making her way up to the school. She has brought her checkbook, as these types of functions always end with a collection. It wouldn't be a good Catholic event without a collection. Her mother gave to everything. She was saving every creature on the planet, one monthly envelope at a time.

Cassie does not get much time to visit her son, Billy, at his school or his after-school care facility. Her work at the Pentagon keeps her occupied, and being a single mom makes it doubly hard. But she has had this on her calendar for months, and unless there is another 9/11, nothing will stop her being here. Cassie is a small dynamo with a Sally Field look. She walks at a quick pace—something she learned from her father, General Robert Bosman, the head of the Pentagon.

As a military brat, Cassie moved around with her parents as the general moved up in the ranks. She is thankful for her position working with the government as a civilian. She enters the brick building and finds Billy at his seat. He turns, and a big smile touches each ear. She twists and turns, making her way to him, trying not to step on other parents squeezed into third-grade desks.

Billy has saved her a seat, and she settles into the small chair, folding her legs underneath. She looks to her right at the huge man playing pretzel with his chair. *Shortness sometimes is useful.* Billy's arms surround her neck, and she holds him tight. Billy is a slight six-year-old boy with dark hair, fair skin, bright eyes, and an infectious smile. He breaks the hug and dives both hands into his desk.

"Look, Mommy, I made a picture for Grampa." He carefully pulls a picture from his desk and presses it flat. "Mommy, do you like it? Today's project was to think of someone you knew who was sad and draw a picture so they feel better."

Cassie examines the picture. "This is wonderful, Billy." She places her hand behind his head in a hug. "The colors are beautiful. Can you explain it?"

"This is me." He points to a stick figure. "You are here. See how nice our grass looks. This is Grampa. He has his medals."

"Why is he so much bigger?" Cassie asks.

"Because he is strong. But he is sad right now."

"Okay." Cassie looks at Billy with concern. Knowing the answer to her next question, she asks, "Who is this?"

"That's Grammy."

"Why is she holding Grampa's hand?"

"Mom, she is in heaven. But you said she is always around, helping us. She is still holding Grampa's hand like they used to do. I thought if I drew him a picture of them holding hands, it would make him happy again."

Teary-eyed, Cassie says, "Wow, that is deep for a young man."

Squaring his shoulders, he looks at Cassie and says, "Well, Mom, I know stuff. The internet, you know."

She groans and then points to other images in the drawing. "Who are these people?"

"Those are our guardian angels. Father Horgan says we each have one."

"Okay, Billy, but there are four people."

"Mom! That's God. You should know that."

A voice from the front of the classroom interrupts Billy's explanations.

"Could I have your attention please?" The room quietens. Father Horgan stands by a teacher's desk.

"Hello everyone, and welcome. The children made wonderful pictures for you to put on your refrigerators. I am excited to introduce Father Gabriel Ashburn, a man who has traveled across the world spreading the gospel. At last count, he has been on every continent and in hundreds of countries."

A man enters the doorway and makes his way to the head of the classroom. He dresses in the long brown robe of a monk, with a deep hood obscuring his features. A baritone chant is emanating from within the hood. The room is still as the mysterious man makes his way to the front. As he walks to the desk, he grabs a piece of chalk and underlines the words "Peace Be with You," which are written on the blackboard. He puts down the chalk and reaches to shake Father Horgan's hand.

"Hello, friend!" He then turns toward the attendees, grabs the hood, and uncovers his head, with his long brown hair touching his shoulders. A broad smile comes across his face, along with a deep laugh.

"You youngsters thought I was Gandalf from the Lord of the Rings series." Along with his brown hair, he sports a well-manicured dark beard. His eyes are blue. Still laughing, he says, "Nothing like an entrance. You see the words on the blackboard. They say the same thing: 'Peace Be with You.' It is written in Arabic, Zulu, French, and Klingon. I can be geeky too. I'm Gabriel Ashburn. Let me get out of this uniform and get comfortable."

He opens a large zipper and steps from his robe. He is clothed in jeans and a dress shirt. "Do you know it is an old Jewish custom that when one is preaching you should stand? But if you are teaching, you should sit." He backs up and jumps to sit on the desk.

Continuing, he asks, "How is everyone today? Those words on the blackboard are from the lands my faith has directed me to visit. However, I haven't made it to Kronos yet. The kids giggle, but there is not much action from adults.

"Well," he goes on, "you are a somber bunch. I want to ask you a question. How many of you heard your soul today?" He looks over the crowd and the blank faces. "I take it, from the response, no one has," he says. "Lost touch, I take it."

A few rows from the desk, Kelly Sellers has her face buried in her cell phone, unaware someone is speaking. Gabriel leaves his desk and approaches the woman. Reaching out his hand, he covers the phone with his palm, and it dies. The surprised woman looks up.

"Kelly, wouldn't it be terrible if the last face you saw before you met your maker was the face on an Apple or Samsung gadget?" He reaches out and grabs her child's face in his palms, saying, "And not this beautiful child?" She gets a look of remorse and reclaims her dead phone, putting it away.

Kelly asks, "How did you know my name?."

Gabriel points to the picture on her child's desk and returns to his perch on the teacher's desk.

"Folks, I believe this interconnectivity is a bad thing. Man was not meant to communicate that way. He was meant to communicate by human touch and interaction. We are cubicle people, waking in the morning in our beds in a cubicle bedroom within a home. Then we get into a boxy car and drive to another box and sit down in another cubicle, never making many meaningful connections with people. Do you realize every person you meet is in your life for a reason? The Chinese believe we are each connected by a red line. Some are for good and others bad, but they are there for your souls to learn. When you meet your maker, you will sit with Him and review the lessons of your life and every interaction, spoken word, or thought."

He seemingly makes eye contact with everyone in the room before saying, "Now back to my original question on hearing your soul. I go to a place every day where you hear many souls. How many here even know how to listen to your soul?" No hands go up. "I get the same response everywhere. Does anyone here meditate?" Again, no hands. "You should try it. How many here ever heard a joke or had something happen that made you cry with laughter or maybe even blow coffee or a soft drink out your nose?"

This time, his questions draw a few smiles and slight nods. "That was a time when you could hear your soul. It was so funny that you let down the garbage of life and the pretenses for a moment to laugh. Today, when I walked into the room, I heard the souls of many like I hear at my special place. I listen to the innocent laughter of your children. They are still at a point where the struggles of life haven't overpowered the laughter, as they have in most adults." He witnesses some somber faces. "You have probably seen this on YouTube, but it makes my point." Gabe waves his hand, and a large TV screen glows to life. The crowd turns its attention to the screen, which shows a baby laughing at a dog eating popcorn. The short video plays a few times, and the somber faces are giggling along with the child.

Gabriel says, "Look at God's greatness—a pure, innocent child full of hope in his dominion, and a simple dog. Listen to its soul so pure. I would recommend each of you save this to your phone and, when you've lost connection, watch it and get reconnected. I'm not saying we should laugh like this all day. We would look rather silly and become fake."

He receives more attention now as he continues. "Every morning I go to the park, and I sit and listen—just listen. If there are no children, there is the noise of God's beautiful nature, with birds and trees and wind. Your mind is occupied with the things of the flesh. Jesus always went to the mountaintop and viewed the awe in the dominion. As a woman on a bicycle passed by on the path, a song playing on her radio had a wonderful phrase: 'Learn to be still.' I listen, and it affects my soul because it brings me connection. I bring no gadgets, as they impede the soulful connection needed and will bring a great peril to the world."

He studies the audience and says, "The message on the board can help with being still. It is the message of Jesus. How simple are the words? 'Peace Be with You.' These four little words calm and disarm you. However, listen to your children giggling from their bellies. It is the sound of their souls. In traveling the world, laughter is infectious everywhere. In the dirt huts, grass bungalows, and caves of the world, the sound is always the same. Most have no pot to call their own, but the laughter from their souls is pure. Therefore, the next time you meet someone who might be down, tell that person something funny, and listen for their true soul. Help them find it. Remember: we are all connected. It's in the Bible." He holds up the Bible.

He looks at the people as they look at the Bible, and he then says, "It is amazing. You go to the drugstore and buy a romance novel, or something called pulp fiction, and they have the most magnificent covers fashioned by artists. They have beautiful people on the covers. The Bible, the most published and sold book, is black with gold lettering." He places back on the desk the first Bible he held up. This time he holds high a worn, dog-eared Bible. "I love to teach to children, but before I start, I would like to ask you parents a question. Do any of you participate in network marketing?" Five hands are raised. "Great. Other than yourself, who is the greatest network marketer past or present?"

He hears the name of Amway cofounder Rich DeVos. Someone mentions Mary Kay Ash. Another adds Tony Robbins. A few other names come forth from non–network marketing parents.

"Great. You have mentioned some good examples. Now, as far as you know, do any of them have a team with billions of people?" Nobody responds. "Did they start well over a hundred years ago and are still in business?" Still no response. "How about over two thousand years ago and are still around?"

A woman in the audience thinks she catches on and hesitantly asks, "Jesus?" Others turn to look at her and then back toward Gabriel.

Gabriel points toward the woman and says, "You've got it. Jesus. But many of you look perplexed. Along with her, do others see where I'm going? Remember: Jesus started with twelve, and He was not on Earth long after He put the team together. You might say that Jesus did not have a product. Sure He did. His product was the salvation of your souls. He promised salvation through faith in Him. Your soul is constantly observed in relation to the way you respond to the lessons learned in your lifetime. You helped write the story with God before your birth."

The classroom is tranquil while everyone absorbs the message. "Let's get back to geeky me. How many here have seen the Star Wars films?" Many hands rise. "Well, you've got the main characters of Luke and Princess Leia, and I'll throw in Han Solo. They were battling the evil empire. Luke had to rely on and believe in the force, which he could not see. Leia had to trust that what she was told by Luke would prove to be true. Let's compare that to Jesus. Can anyone name an evil empire that existed back in His time?"

A parent raises his hand. "The Romans," he says.

"Superb. They were a powerful force and did not entertain anyone rebelling. In fact, people did not cross them. Are you familiar with the

Battle of Masada? There the Romans battled the Jews, who camped on a mountain plateau in a large fortress built by King Herod. Rather than having thousands of soldiers scale the steep cliffs, they built a ramp and attacked the Jews. They thwarted rebellion in any form."

After observing the interest level of each parent and child, Gabriel continues. "This brutal empire surrounded and watched Jesus. And Jesus's own Jewish religious leaders, or Pharisees, did not take a shining to Him either. He threatened their power, and no one gives up power. They did not take kindly to Jesus being called 'King of the Jews.' As in the Star Wars films, you had Jesus, who was describing the force of faith. You had Mary Magdalene, who believed in Jesus's message. Then there was Peter, who wasn't sure at first but became steadfast." Again measuring interest levels, Gabriel asks, "Can you see the similarities? Jesus was telling us about our souls and the journey of our souls. In human existence, there has been no one, rich or poor, whose physical body has passed into the Dominion of God. The wealthy become dust in the same earthen hole as the poor. You can call it 'the force,' 'faith,' or 'the soul.' Therefore, you want to build your soul, just as Luke found the force and fed it within him."

Gabriel holds up the much-used Bible again. "Old-timers call this the 'Good Book.' Read it at least once in your lifetime. Let's keep this simple. My teacher taught me God left us with ten uncomplicated rules. Can anyone tell me what they are called?"

"Yes," a small girl says, quickly raising her hand and responding before anyone else. "The Ten Commandments."

"Correct. Since we are in a Catholic school today, here is a thing that makes many adults go 'Hmmm.' You adults present will attest to this. Fifty years ago, when a woman went into a church, she was supposed to cover her head with a veil. If a man entered a church and was wearing a hat, he was supposed to remove it. It puzzles me the difference in the heads."

After studying the reactions, Gabriel says, "I take it from the nods and smirks you don't understand it either. I use this as an example to teach about faith and not religion. When I was in those huts and caves around the world, none were Christian. Therefore, as Jesus did, they merely spoke of faith."

Gabriel witnesses some puzzled looks, and he then continues. seemingly making eye contact with each individual child while drawing attention to the Bible he holds. "Children, in this book there are ten simple rules chiseled into stone that no human being can change. If you do your best to follow them, you will have a good life and a strong soul. These rules are difficult, and you can—and will—get off the path. However, you can learn from the missteps and do better. Studying and following the rules will affect you in a tremendously positive way—and will positively affect others with whom you come in contact." He pauses to let the message soak in. He then says, "Jesus was asked, 'Which is the greatest commandment in the law?' Children, if you hear and put into your daily life the answer Jesus gave, it will make all the difference in your life, now and forever."

Each child feels as if Gabriel is talking especially to him or her as he says, "Jesus answered, 'Love the Lord your God with all your heart and with all your soul and with all your mind. This is the first and greatest commandment. And the second is like it: Love your neighbor as yourself. All the law and the prophets hang on these two commandments.'"

Enveloping everyone in the room, Gabriel promises, "If you keep close to these two commandments, you can't break the others. When you meet your maker, it will be a joyous reunion." Gabriel slides off the desk and stands. Looking over the crowd, he gives everyone a blessing and says, "It was indeed a great honor and privilege for me to have an opportunity to speak to you today. I hope you take something away with you—not from what I say, but from what Jesus said back then and continues to say today."

Segueing into a different mood, Gabriel says, "Now I understand we have many young artists who created some great pictures, and I'd love to see them. Thank all of you for coming. And I will surprise you. Neither I nor anyone else will be taking up a collection today for anything."

The audience rises to applaud Gabriel and his teaching. He humbly nods and thanks them, and then he makes his way into the crowd. Some come up to him to give personal thanks, and he does get to see some of the children's drawings. However, in this day and age, when everyone seems to be in a hurry, the room empties rather swiftly as the parents collect their children and depart.

When Cassie had asks her son Billy if he is ready to leave, he replies, "No, Mom. I want Father Gabriel to see my drawing."

Cassie sees Gabriel talking with a couple of parishioners up near the teacher's desk, which leads her to tell Billy, "Well, he looks busy."

"Can we please wait longer? Please?"

Cassie surrenders with "Okay, a few more minutes."

Gabriel looks out into the nearly empty room and sees Billy waving at him. He smiles and puts his finger up to signal "In a minute." Billy arranges his drawing on the desk so Gabriel will have a good vantage point to look at it. The minute passes and Gabriel approaches. He places his hand atop Billy's head and rubs his hair. "Hello, young fellow. You have a picture you want me to see?"

"Yes sir," Billy responds.

Cassie reaches out her hand and introduces herself and Billy. Gabriel clasps her hand with both of his. "Pleased to meet you." He gazes at Billy's drawing. "Well done, Master Billy. I love the colors." Turning to Cassie, he tells her, "You have a budding artist."

"Who knows, maybe so," Cassie replies.

Billy says, "Father, I can explain the picture for you."

"Tell you what," Gabriel answers, "let me see if I can figure it out on my own. That's what they're always saying at these expensive art shows, asking people to explain what they see in a piece of art." He smiles at Billy, and Billy returns the smile. "Let me see now," Gabriel begins as he studies the drawing. "Okay, do you have a father or grandfather in the military?"

"Yes," Billy replies.

Gabe turns to Cassie. "Your father?"

"Yes," she answers.

"Am I doing well?" Billy and Cassie nod their approval. Gabriel continues his art appreciation appraisal. "These two people here, Billy, are you and your mother. I suspect this is your home … no, wait. This is your grandfather's home."

Cassie looks at Gabriel. "How would you know it's my dad's house?"

"The lawn," Gabriel responds. "It's a guy thing!"

Billy and Cassie exchange looks, and then Gabriel continues. "Now then, let's see who else is here." Turning to Cassie, he says, "Your mom has passed. Correct?" Cassie nods. "Billy, your grandmother is an angel, and she is holding your grandfather's hand. Did they hold hands all the time when she was living?" Billy's head nods, and Cassie is dumbfounded.

"How did you know it was his grandmother?"

"Kids draw things they can relate to—things they see their parents do when they are together. He liked that in them." He then tells Billy, "I bet your grandfather misses your grandmother. What do you call your grandparents?"

"Grammy and Grampa," Billy tells him.

"Grampa is the one who is sad," Gabriel correctly explains. "How long were they together?"

Cassie grabs a tissue from her purse as her eyes become misty. "Over forty-five years," she says.

Gabriel asks, "Do you know they were parallel souls? Let me explain. Consider souls as shooting stars crossing the sky on the same trajectory, never touching but close enough to form a bond and travel together forever. Some souls pack together in learning."

"I never thought of it that way," she says.

"Remember: souls never die. Therefore, Grammy is still holding the big strong general's hand from God's dominion." Billy nods. "You have a guardian angel with your family. Cool. I like guardian angels, and I talk to them every day."

"You do?" Billy responds.

"Yes, and I suppose this other person on your drawing is God, because He is on top. I don't think of God as on top, but as all around you and within you. Your soul is created by God in His image. He made your body from the dust of the ground, and it returns to dust, but your soul lives forever."

Billy looks up at Gabriel, amazed at what he is saying. Cassie is highly intrigued also. Gabriel picks up a glass of water from a nearby desk. Dipping his finger into the water, he holds it above the glass until one drop falls back into the half-empty glass. "Your life on earth is the distance between the fingertip and the water."

Billy is wide-eyed as Gabriel continues. "The glass of water I will call God's dominion, and your soul is the drop that just returned to God. We are part of God's dominion, and we flow back to the dominion, ready for the next storyline He will help us write. Do you understand, Billy?"

Billy looks confused, even though mesmerized, "It's okay, Billy. Better understanding will come with age and maturity." Gabriel rubs Billy's head again and then says, "This is a wonderful drawing ... insightful."

Turning to Cassie and taking her hands, he tells her, "You should be proud. I am sure your grampa will cherish it."

Cassie puts a finger to her lips, shaking her head in the negative.

"Grampa has rather shut us out," she says.

"Oh my," Gabriel responds. "It happens a lot during grief. I suppose he has immersed himself in work."

"It's been a while since we've seen him. With Mom's death and his seemingly increased workload, slowly he started staying more and more at his apartment, which is closer to his workplace. He will probably never see this drawing."

"Hey, I have an idea. Hold on I'll be right back."

Gabriel leaves the room and disappears through the doorway. Only moments later, he comes sprinting back, holding a long mailing tube. He says, "I was at a holy site a while back with the pope, who blessed a picture of himself that I am giving to the school. It's in this tube. So let's do this." He holds the end of the cardboard tube and twists, removing one end. While removing the picture, a faint violet spark jumps to the metal rim of the tube. Gabriel then says, "People like your grampa probably get lots of mail at work, and someone else probably opens most of it."

Cassie replies, "Florence, his assistant, sorts through it, handles a lot of it. But she puts the more important items in his office for him to open."

"Okay, so let's insert Billy's picture into this empty tube. We'll mail it to him at his office, and we'll write on the tube, 'Personal: From your grandson, Billy.' Florence will save it for him to open, and I am sure it will have the desired effect you were hoping for in the end. Just keep praying for him."

"Father," Cassie says, "may I ask you a question about parallel souls?"

"Sure."

"Are there other types of souls?"

"Oh yes," Gabriel replies. "I take you as a perpendicular soul."

"Why?"

"I don't see Billy's father here."

Cassie looks embarrassed. "My ex is not in Billy's life."

"How sad. It is his loss. He will regret it someday."

"Why am I perpendicular?"

"You know what perpendicular means?"

"Yes, at a right angle."

"Correct. You met and fell in love, but as perpendicular souls, you only connected for a short time." Gabriel makes a cross with his fingers with one hand shooting off in another direction. "One of you, maybe both, was unwilling to move to a parallel trajectory."

"It was mostly him," she says.

"Well, it happens," Gabriel says. "Cassie, your ex-husband came into your life to teach your soul."

"To learn what? Not to trust men?"

"I don't know the answer, but maybe he had red flags not observed." Gabriel looks at Billy. "Anyway, he left you with a beautiful soul to tend." Cassie smiles and hugs Billy. Billy squirms from his mom squeezing him.

"Cassie, it seems you were raised in a loving home. You will find the soul right for you."

"I'm not looking," she says.

"Good. Because it creeps up and grabs you while you're busy elsewhere. Love finds you." He looks at Billy again, saying, "Billy, I have a label over there we can put on this tube. I am going to the post office and can drop it off."

Cassie replies, "Okay."

Gabriel retrieves the label and hands it to Cassie to address. He places his hand on the boy's head again and tells him, "Billy, you take care of your mom."

"Yes sir," Billy tells him.

Cassie addresses the label and hands it to Gabriel, who attaches it to the tube and then seals the end with tape.

Gabriel tells Billy, "Be sure to tell your Grampa to expect your drawing. You can call or text him." He pats the tube to be mailed, and then says, "This will do the trick."

"Thank you, Father," says Cassie as she ushers Billy out of the classroom.

Gabriel stays behind and gathers his robe and belongings. He walks to the front driveway of the school. The lot is vacant, with the families dispersed. His hood covers his head as he strides toward the main road. He halts when his lens shows a message from the commander. "Go to Arlington Cemetery, section 60, the resting place of Matthew Poole. There, console his widow, Samantha."

"Yes, Commander," replies Gabriel. "I brought him into the light. How should I visit her—as a mortal or spiritual being? Her soul is in torment, so she may feel the light."

"Use your judgment" is the response.

"Yes, Commander."

Moments later, Gabriel walks between the white headstones of section 60 of Arlington Cemetery, the resting place for those killed in America's latest wars in Iraq and Afghanistan. The being scans the grounds, and a sadness crosses his face. The commander sees Gabriel's message: "So many souls' journeys cut short."

"Yes," a return message to Gabriel reads, "but Matthew's story is different."

"I know, Commander, but will they ever listen and learn?"

"It's why we are here, as war is the consequence of selfish free will's weight."

Gabriel comes across a young woman prone on the grass and facing a headstone marked, "Matthew Poole, beloved son, husband, and father."

The woman is sobbing, speaking softly toward where the body of her husband is buried, telling of her loneliness and how she cannot make it without him. She says their son Bobby cries, wondering when his daddy is coming to see him.

The being listens, unobserved by Samantha. Samantha takes a deep breath and wipes her eyes. She comes here each week at the time of Matthew's death, or as close as she can to it, since he died on the other side of the world. She feels near to him here, as though a remnant of his life force lingers at this spot.

The robed figure closes near and startles her to a standing position. Gabriel reaches out his palms and says, "Be not afraid; I heard your sobs and wondered if I could help."

"I guess you're a priest, a monk—or a Star Wars freak who likes to walk in graveyards," she says with taken-off-guard mixed emotions.

"Yes, one of the above. I'm Father Gabriel Ashburn, and a friend told me of your sadness and how you visit here often. Can I help you?"

"Can you bring him back?"

"No."

"Then what good is God if he lets these good people like my Matthew die? We were to grow old together and raise a family."

"God doesn't kill people. Man does. They can choose not to kill. Matthew is not here, and neither are the others interred beneath these markers. They are in the dominion. It is sad that man must resort to war to stop the evil men who are off their souls' journeys. Samantha, I want to tell you a story."

"Wait, how do you know my name? I never told you."

"I was with Matthew when he passed."

"You were with him when he died?"

"Yes."

"Did he suffer?"

"No, it was quick."

"Did he mention me?"

"There was no time. It happened suddenly."

Samantha softly says, "We were soul mates and loved each other."

"Yes, you did. But Matthew's time had come, and his soul's story was to end as it did. His whole journey brought him to the place of his death to save numerous children. Many military personnel buried here had their stories cut short by war. However, Matthew was extraordinary. His death allowed those souls to continue their journeys. He learned a great lesson in the Dominion."

"Sir, I don't mean to be offensive, but are you a nut? You dress in an Obi-Wan robe, walking in a graveyard, telling me about souls, Dominion, and journeys." Now growing fearful, Samantha looks to escape. Gabriel reaches for her as she backpedals from his reach.

"Leave me alone!" she yells."

"Be not afraid." Gabriel's body turns white, with a violet tint emanating from his brain.

Now really frightened, Samantha gasps and says, "What are you? Please don't hurt me!"

She wants to run, but her feet fail to move, seemingly cemented in the grass. As she looks at the face of Gabriel, the light draws the fear from her. He moves closer, and she is now in complete surrender, in a trancelike state. Gabriel moves forward and holds her face in his palms. "Be not afraid," he again says. Her eyes widen in wonder as Gabriel's face glows a brilliant white and the violet hue vanishes.

"You are in the Dominion now—a gift most only see at death. I was your teacher there."

Samantha's face is uplifted and glowing white. She exhales a breath of peacefulness. Her lips quiver, and a tear flows from her eye. "It's so beautiful," she says.

"There is someone here to talk with you," Gabriel tells her.

Samantha's eyes blink, and then she yells, "Matthew! Matthew!

You came back!" Matthew stands before her, the man she remembered before war ravaged his body. She tells him that she and Bobby miss him so much.

Matt tells her not to be sad, as he has completed his journey and she will also. He says, "We will be together again here in the Dominion. Your story has you finding love once more, and remember, I am always with you and Bobby. I will be here when you cross."

"Wait; take me with you!"

"It is not your time, and you have Bobby's soul to tend—and you will do it well."

Gabriel tells her not to be sad and that Matthew is at peace. He says, "I will give you peace from your tragedy to carry with you. When I release you, I will be gone, and you will not remember what happened here today, but you will carry a peace that passes all understanding."

Gabriel's face glows brighter, pumping the white light into Samantha. In an instant, Gabriel vanishes, and Samantha is back in the position in which she was prior to Gabriel's appearance. She shakes her head, as if she has forgotten why she is in this place. She stands and brings her fingers to her lips, kisses them, and transfers the kiss, pressing her fingers to Matthew's name on his headstone. She pauses, silently looks at the headstone, and then quietly walks away. A robed Gabriel stands in the distance, watching … always watching. The commander's lens reads, "It is done."

JR

Another school day has ended, and Lennon watches Emma board the bus home. He wishes he could ride with her, but today he starts his job. He turns toward the main drag and the nearest transit bus stop. Lennon, a latchkey kid, has street smarts for his age. The bus arrives, and his hand dives into his pocket for the fare. He boards, handing his money to the driver. The seats are near empty, so he slides into the first he sees. The bus rolls forward. Lennon peers out the window as it lumbers on the main street of soaped-up windows.

He remembers his mom taking him to this street when he was little. They would go in and out of the small shops, which are now gone.

Lennon always looked forward to those days and the little trinkets he would bring home. He smiles at the warm memory, wishing he could go back in time. The thought is interrupted by the bus coming to a halt. Lennon stands and exits, moving down the street to work. He looks across the street and sees old Bob at his position. Mr. Deuss was right. It was cold last night, and Bob snuggled in his blanket. Lennon finds it funny how he knew what Bob needed.

Lennon finds the key to the shop and enters the building. Cleaning and painting supplies await him, as Mr. Magee promised. There is a handwritten note on the soundboard with instructions on what to do today. Lennon rolls up his sleeves and prepares to get going. He moves dusty boxes away from the wall so he can clean it before painting. Once the boxes are out of the way, he removes the pictures from the wall. One by one, he puts the pictures into a box.

The work slows because Lennon examines each one. He jealously studies them for the famous musicians in them. How lucky they were to catch a break. One of the largest pictures is of the Beatles, and he places it on the sound board. He hopes Mr. Magee will give it to him instead of discarding it. Anything related to the Beatles is a treasure to him. Lennon looks at the picture and studies each Beatle. There are five people in the photo. Lennon thinks the fifth person is Brian Epstein, the manager of the Beatles.

He looks closer and rejects that hypothesis. His eyes widen as he realizes the other person in the photo is Mr. Deuss. Lennon thinks, "This guy must be one hundred years old! I bet he did their clothes back then, and he might know Paul McCartney."

Lennon takes more photos off the wall, caressing each, hoping to catch the artistic energy. After working for over an hour, the first wall is clean and ready to paint. He takes a break and sits in a chair. As his stomach growls, he decides he'll have to start bringing a snack.

He slides the chair in front of the sound board, manipulating the buttons and dials that once had famous artists on the other side of the glass. He's thinking about how an artist awaits his producer's instruction so he or she can produce a unique, perfect sound. Back in the sixties and seventies, speakers were huge, with twelve-inch woofers. Now artists struggle to get the most perfect sound on earbuds with tiny speakers. They miss most of the music, the backbeat, and the melodies within melodies that make the song pop.

The song "Here, There and Everywhere" comes to mind as his inner ear hears everything going on in the song. This is what he wants to do. Getting back to reality, however, he works on the next wall, watching his time, because he must be home before his dad. If he gets home before his dad, the drinking isn't as bad. If his dad is alone, the depression sets in and the video comes out, and it is another night sequestered in his room.

As he is finishing the next wall, Lennon thinks of how tired he is of replacing guitar strings His back is to the door, and a sudden voice startles him.

"Well, Joseph was right, you are the man for the job. You have made great progress."

Lennon turns to see Mr. Magee and beams, since he does not receive many compliments.

"It looks great," Magee continues. I didn't think you would be here this late. I thought you might want money."

"Money is good, but you can pay me at the end of the week."

"No, too much to keep up with, so I'll pay you each day." Jozy hands Lennon folded cash. He asks, "Is that enough for today?"

"You gave me more than what we agreed on the other day."

"I have no change, but it will work out."

"Thank you," says Lennon. He stuffs the money into his jeans, and then he says, "Can I ask you a question?"

"Sure."

"I'm a big Beatles fan. Are you going to trash these photos?"

"I have no use for them. Why? Do you want one?"

"Yes, the Beatles one on the sound board."

"Sure, you can have it."

"One more thing?

"Yes?"

"Is that Mr. Deuss in the photo?"

"You have a good eye," Jozy tells Lennon. "He has been in apparel for a long time and has provided fashions to the top artists."

"Gee, he must be old. He must know everybody."

Entertained by Lennon's statement, Jozy gives a little laugh and says, "I guess you can say Joseph is well connected, or networked."

He told me he knows Paul McCartney."

Smiling, Jozy replies, "I guess the picture confirms it."

"I thought he was putting me on."

"Joseph is a straight shooter, Lennon, and will have your back. He was telling me you are an intern with his company."

"Yes, I've not gotten too far into it. We wear their clothes. I'm surprised they picked me, being a little different and more artsy."

"Joseph knows good character. Stick with him; follow his directions."

"I am working with another person from the clothing company."

"Well, Lennon, I'm sure he will be excellent for you. You'll have fun and learn."

"I guess, but it would be nice if it pays."

"Some things you learn are not always paid in money, nor right away, but can bring you riches you never realized until you are older."

"I guess. But right now I need a new guitar."

CHAPTER 9

Halfway around the world. a yellow being touches down in the town of Kobani, a city in northern Syria, which lies south of the border with Turkey. It has been under siege by ISIL forces. It is a hotbed of snipers killing anything moving. He enters the city, assuming human form and walking next to bullet-riddled facades. A small boy miskicks a soccer ball toward him, and he kicks it back to the boy, who smiles in appreciation. The being then turns to make his way along a street, and the boy yells for him to stop. He walks back to the boy and goes to one knee. He looks at the boy's face while holding him by the shoulders.

"I am Michael," he tells the boy. You are good with a soccer ball. What is your name?"

"Yousef," the boy replies. "I want to play at the university."

"Well, you keep practicing, and if it is to be, it will be." He then asks, "Why did you tell me to stop?"

Yousef looks around at the buildings and then back at Michael. "I've not seen you around here before, and there is a sniper down that road, and strangers never come back. They even shoot children carrying water."

"Thank you, Yousef, for warning me. I will be extra careful. I have a meeting with a man on this street."

"Then you should stay in the shadows and alcoves."

"You seem to know the rules around here."

"If you don't know the rules here, they bury you," the boy replies. Michael stands and advances toward the dangerous street, moving in the suggested shadows. Gunfire directs him to the sniper, who has some unarmed innocent people pinned down in the street. The alcove protects Michael as he tests the situation. A young boy tries to rescue a girl stuck in the middle of the street, shielded by a large, fragmented flowerpot. The sniper has repeatedly fired at the pot, breaking it away bit by bit. The boy tries to move closer to help the girl. Michael watches, thinking this girl must be important to the boy for him to risk his life. Michael then steps back into the alcove, hidden from view, and transforms to pure light.

"The commander's cornea reads, "Commander, I need to reclaim a soul."

The being's lens reads: "Why?"

"He is killing little children" is the message the being sends.

"Who?"

"I will send you the information." The being, Michael, reaches out a palm, and a thin beam of white light bolts toward the sniper's position.

The commander's lens receives the name "Jaafar Abdou."

The reply from the commander is "He has ignored his plan. You may send him home. Are there any others?"

"Yes" is the message from the being, Michael.

"Use your judgment."

"Yes, commander."

The being glows brighter, and the beam from his hand becomes more powerful. It exits his hand like a thunderbolt and travels to the sniper's position. Jaafar has his eye pressed against the scope on his Sayad-2 rifle. He has the little girl dead in his sights and knows that when he squeezes the trigger again, the pot will explode, with the bullet killing the girl. He has a grin of satisfaction. The light reaches the large end of the scope and travels down its core to the open eye of Jaafar. The light enters his eyes before the sniper pulls the trigger to fire. He then moans and falls away from the gun, crashing lifeless to the concrete floor in his nest.

Michael muses, "Yes, Jaafar, the eyes stay the same in your lifetimes and are the window to your soul."

"The commander's lens reads, "It is done.""

The being assumes his human form as Michael and escapes down the street, returning up the other side, making his way to the boy and helping him to the young girl. He brings them to the shadows and tells them they are all right. The boy hugs his sister.

The boy says to Michael, "Did you see the light?"

"Yes," replies Michael.

The boy jumps in excitement, saying, "The Americans have come to help with a new Star Wars weapon. After the light, the shooting stopped."

Michael says nothing and nods acceptance of the boy's theory. He walks away as people enter the street, realizing the threat is gone.

Michael visits other locations, repeating the same action, and the commander's lens reads, "Imreen Nouri, Mazin Kaleel. It is done."

⚎

Simon comes through the front door of his home and shuts it behind him. He leans against the door and exhales. He is in his castle, shielded from the outside world, as he walks to the kitchen.

There is a yell from another room. "Mom, Dad, where are you? Where are you?" Emma appears in the kitchen doorway. "Sorry I'm late," she tells Simon, "but I have great news. Where is Mom?"

"Probably in the bedroom," Simon tells her.

Hearing the commotion, Alexis leaves the bedroom and enters the kitchen. "Emma, Simon, what's going on?" she asks.

"They selected me for Swaddling Clothes."

"The company I signed the consent forms for?" Alexis asks.

"Yes!"

"That's great, hon," Alexis says as she gives Emma a hug. "I'm so proud of you."

"Thank you, Mom. And that's why I'm running late. We celebrated at school."

"Terrific," Simon joins in. "What will you do for them?"

"I don't know everything yet, but I wear their clothes and tell people how I feel wearing them. Mom, they had this room at the school filled with clothes, and I can wear anything."

"Really? Were they cute?"

"Yes, I have a couple of outfits in my bag I will try one on now. One will fit you, Mom, and I want to show you before dinner. It seems like everything is back to normal, even better. Dad, you're back with JPL, and I have Swaddling. Maybe our prayers have been answered."

"You may be right Emma," Simon says as he hugs her. "I want to see the outfits too."

Emma and Alexis head down the hall. Simon watches the energetic walks in her wife and daughter, knowing how much the family needs positive news. He turns, grabs the remote, and presses a button. The television sparkles to life, with the news in progress. He prepares two dinner coffees and sips his as Emma and Alexis appear in the doorway.

"Wow! I like the outfits," Simon exclaims.

"You do, Dad? You're not just saying it to be nice?"

"No, both you ladies look amazing."

"I helped Mom with her hair." Alexis spins to show off.

"So apparently you two love Swaddling Clothes."

"Dad, it's amazing, but Mr. Deuss and Magdala, of the company, said they want us to get an aura of being a baby in a blanket, safe and cozy."

"Is it doing the trick?" he asks. Emma and Alexis respond in the affirmative with warm smiles.

"Who else did they choose?" Alexis asks Emma.

"It's exciting. Lennon, along with Jennifer Bittle and Greg Mindoro. We expected Jennifer to get it, but it was funny when we were in the room looking at the great clothes. Jennifer had her usual attitude about everything being beneath her. Magdala gave her an attitude readjustment really quickly. I will like working with Magdala. She gets me."

"Good, honey. I'm so excited for you. And you're excited too," Alexis says.

"I am, Mom. Very!"

"Well, you ladies look so nice that a proper gentleman should take you out on the town. I've got a hankering for pizza to celebrate. You ladies game?"

"Can we go to Roma's, Dad?"

"Sure."

Alexis says, "Let us get a couple of things." She and Emma leave the area. Simon glances at the news and sees no urgent broadcast of doom that *Sojourner* predicted. He clicks it off and shuts off the coffee machine. The ladies return with glowing faces. Alexis looks at Simon as she brushes past him, saying, "This Swaddling job is good for Emma. She is glowing. Maybe she's right and normalcy has returned."

As Alexis and Emma exit through the door, followed by Simon, he mumbles a prayer: "Let this be good for my gals."

⁊⸫

Morning has come, and Simon is again at home in his usual post in the family room by the kitchen, sipping coffee. Alexis and Emma are on the way to work and school, respectively. Now the report of daily news is not just merely a time-killing apparatus to drink coffee by but an incident-recording agent to gauge his craziness. The screen pops to life with the familiar refrain from the commentators.

"Good morning, folks. I'm Bill Hemmer, and welcome to *America's Newsroom*. Good Morning, Martha."

"Hi, Bill. Let's jump right into it. I'm Martha MacCallum. There is major news from the cyber world today. If you have not opened your email, then you will notice an email with the subject line 'Be Not Afraid.' The email is signed by a sender called 'the Dominion.' We have learned, and news is coming in every few minutes, that Google, Apple, Microsoft, Facebook, Twitter, and Yahoo are reporting a major hacking problem. This goes beyond social sites, but businesses have been hacked also. We have received messages on our various accounts here at Fox."

140

"Martha," Bill says, "isn't it over three billion now connected online? Someone has cracked everyone's code. You would expect they would have the most up-to-date hacking protection."

"From what our experts are telling us, Bill, this was not a virus that goes into your computer and then emails your contacts list. We have had that happen before, with a friend getting an email from someone from Nigeria. But from what we are learning now, whatever it is has reached the root or base servers of internet companies. No one has been immune to it, and it was not caught as spam. Apple products are not prone to viruses, due to their closed operating system architecture. They think this might be an inside job."

"So Martha," Bill asks, "What did the messages say?"

"This is the weird part, Bill. Emails like this are usually phishing or trying to get you to enter personal information. But the subject line in this case reads, 'Be Not Afraid; Are You Listening?' Then the body of the messages, posts and images are passages from the Bible and Koran, then a name and date."

"What were the passages?"

"Well, Bill, what came from the Bible is 'And thou shalt love the Lord thy God with all thy heart, and with all thy soul, and with all thy mind, and with all thy strength; this is the first commandment. And the second is, Thou shalt love thy neighbor AS THYSELF. There is none other commandment greater than these (Mark 12:30 KJV).'"

"Pretty powerful message," Bill says.

Martha replies, "Yes, and the excerpt from the Koran is as follows: 'Whoever works righteousness, man or woman, and has faith, verily, to them will we give a new life, a life that is good and pure, and we will bestow on such their reward according to the best of their actions.' Then the message states, 'Alexander Fleming / Penicillin 1810—The Dominion.' Some believe this might be the work of a group of hackers like Anonymous, but with unheard-of sophistication."

"Martha, here's the question. In looking at this, if it is directed at religious folks, does that mean that about four billion people will receive the message?"

"Yes, Bill, but only if you count one account. Many have multiple accounts. Spokespeople for affected companies stated they know of the problem, so it is unnecessary to forward any emails back to them. Bill, it came over my computer. But the hackers got it wrong."

"What's that, Martha?" Bill asks.

"The discovery of Penicillin happened in 1928, not 1810," she says. "I guess the Dominion need a proofreader."

Bill smiles and says, "Ha! Check your work, folks! We'll be right back."

Simon looks at the screen while tapping his fingers on his phone to open his email. His phone lights up with many messages from social media. He looks for the words "Be Not Afraid."

Simon says to himself, "Now I have to tell Norm that Reliance sent billions of messages, or spam, to people all over the world. Maybe it won't lead back to me. I need to get to the office and see if it is true."

He drives to the gas station to fill his tank. His phone screen reports the hacking on another network. There is another patron across from him looking at his phone also. Simon asks him whether he got the messages.

The guy responds, "Yes, and everyone I know has received them."

"May I see your phone?" Simon asks him. "I'm involved in security and am researching this."

The guy shrugs, says, "Sure," and shows the current email message on his phone to Simon.

"Anything weird happen to your phone?" Simon asks.

The guy responds, "Just religious mumbo jumbo verses with no links or anything to click."

Simon looks at the message and sees there are no links, and he is relieved over that. He looks deeper to see whether there is a reply address. He asks the man if he can forward a copy. The guy nods his approval and says, "They were awful hackers, because they didn't get away with nothing."

"I guess religious nuts," Simon replies. The man nods in agreement.

The gas pumps eventually click off, and the two men get their receipts and drive away.

※

Now back at his JPL desk, Simon opens his personal account to look closely at the social media links. He sees that the reply address is to an account at JPL, and he exhales in relief that it wasn't from his personal JPL account. He must find out the person who set up the account. It will take snooping.

Norm steps into his office and closes the door. "What the heck, Simon," he says. "Did your software do this? Most saw the reply line was to JPL. Don't you think Apple and others are on the phone to Earlman right now?"

"Norm, I don't know what to tell you. I didn't send any messages. I don't have the knowledge of how to get into the base servers of these giant companies. It's easier to land on Mars. It is beyond me."

"Yeah, I know, Simon. I know, but I had to ask."

"I had nothing to do with it."

"*Sojourner* then?" he asks.

"Norm, I don't know."

"What should I say if Earlman asks?"

"Well, Norm, tell him we are getting great info from the rovers and you are too busy to orchestrate all of it."

Norm leaves the office, and Simon decides to get a quick, early lunch at Jimmy's, just to get away from the computer and office. As he makes his way to the restaurant's entrance, he sees the dog that spilled his coffee a few days earlier.

"Hello. Rudy, isn't it?"

Rudy stands on hind legs and greets Simon. Simon suddenly hears a voice from behind call out to him, "Simon!" He turns to see the person saying, "Remember me? I'm Raph. Rudy and I spilled your coffee."

"Yes. Yeah, sure. I remember the two of you."

"You made an impression on Rudy. He bolted and took off once he saw you."

"Must be my animal attraction," Simon says, slightly laughing.

"Since you are here, how was your interview?" Raph asks.

"I got the job."

"Well, that is great news! Rudy, did you hear?" Simon got the job." Rudy's tail wags. "I was going to lunch. Care to join me?"

Simon says, "Sure," though he thinks it odd to be eating with a perfect stranger. Rudy finds a grassy spot to wait. Simon and Raph enter the restaurant and find a seat.

Raph asks, "Is your position everything you wanted?"

"I'm exactly where I want to be. And it's good to be getting a paycheck. The bills keep coming.

Raph replies, "He did say, 'Render to Caesar.'"

"Seems like I've got too many Caesars."

"It can be hard," Raph replies.

Raph is sitting where he can look up at the restaurant's TV screen as a newscast from a network other than the one Simon habitually watches reports about messages being received worldwide. Knowing the answer to his question before he asks, Raph says, "A lot of people seem upset over this global message problem. Did you get one, Simon?"

"Yes. Did you?"

"Yeah, I got it, but I thought little of it," Raph responds.

"Why?"

"It had a nice message to it that shouldn't offend anyone."

Simon says, "Whatever it is, it's very sophisticated to be able to get deep into these computers of the best and brightest geeks."

"I'm sure they are closing the holes as we speak," Raph tells him. "But what do you think they meant by mentioning the man who discovered penicillin?"

"I don't know, but they got the date wrong."

"Is that right?"

"Penicillin was discovered in 1928, not 1810."

"Must be a typo," Raph quips. "Too smart for their own good."

There is a pause in the conversation as their orders are delivered, and then Raph asks, "Simon, what do you do at JPL?"

"I keep the communications with the Mars rovers going."

"Wow!" Raph says, "It is amazing how those machines are helping discover so many things in the universe. There is so much out there, and we are infants in the vastness of space. What do you think about all of it, Simon?"

"Well, I just know the universe is so large, with so many things to investigate. Each time we discover something new, it only brings a hundred more questions. What do you do, Raph? What kind of work are you involved in?"

"I am in power systems. I keep the world moving and pulsing with the power grids of the world."

"Did you hear about the magnetic field flashing the other night?" Simon asks.

"Yeah, but I'm more concerned with the power systems and substations and their vulnerability. If someone disables eight to ten major stations, then most of this country is in the dark."

"Is that possible to do?"

"If someone made a concerted effort, going further than what just happened—you know, this current deal where someone or some entity compromised the servers of the most powerful companies. I am sure there is someone or some entity trying to shut it down for nefarious reasons or for money, power, and control."

"What can be done?" Simon asks.

Raph replies, "Most power companies don't want to invest in protection systems. There was a study done named Aurora. They took a generator and deliberately reprogrammed its programmable logic controller to fail. They destroyed the generator from far away. These are machines that will take almost a year to replace. During that time, there is no power."

Raph pauses as Simon attentively takes in everything the young man says. Raph then continues. "You have seen the Hollywood movies about how people behave without electricity."

"You've got that right," Simon responds. "They become savage and resort to survival of the fittest. Supposedly it happens to even the best Christians."

"It is sad," Raph says. "People would kill a child for a slice of bread or a little water. History is full of humans doing horrible things to survive over one another."

"I suppose it is something else to put on my worry list," Simon sighs. "And I don't know what idiot would want to mess with the magnetic field surrounding the earth. If they are wrong, manipulating it for power and control, then they can let in the bad things the universe showers down on earth."

"Simon, you, as a space explorer, know better than anyone."

"Yeah, but we have always used weapons developed," states Simon.

"I agree, Simon, but I don't know if this connectivity is a good thing. If a man has built it, then another man can break it or use it for harm."

Now Simon glances up at the TV monitor as the newscaster interviews an expert about the intrusive email messages. With *Sojourner*'s information branded in his mind, he probes Raph on the subject again, wanting to get more reaction from an outsider. He nods toward the television and says, "So, getting back to those email messages they're talking about, how do you really think people will wind up taking it?"

"My opinion? Because we get so many emails, most will just see it as another email. Most will probably skip by it. Won't listen." Raph sees a change in Simon's countenance and says, "You have a strange look on your face now, Simon."

Thinking of *Sojourner*'s messages to him, Simon replies, "Oh, it's just that someone mentioned something about people listening."

Raph says, "The messages in the emails today were nice. I can't see why it offends someone to ask people to care for each other. Are you a man of faith?"

"Yes, I go to church."

Raph grins. "Mob leaders went to church on Sunday and killed people the other six days."

"Is that like 'on the seventh day He rested'?"

Raph bellows a laugh. "I walked right into that, didn't I?"

"Sorry I couldn't resist," Simon tells him. "I try to go by the Ten Commandments. They're written in stone, you know."

Raph smiles and says, "If you keep them, you will have a good life and will be well received when you enter God's Dominion." He hesitates and then adds, "You have that look again."

"Oh, a friend mentioned 'God's dominion' the other day."

Raph smiles because he knows of Simon's friend. "Eventually," he tells Simon, "we will go there. Do you agree? It's best to be prepared, because you can't fool God."

"I suppose so," Simon responds.

Raph looks at his watch. As he rises from the table, he points to the watch and says, "Well, Simon, it was a pleasure dining with you. But we got so tied up talking that I have to hurry to a meeting." He picks up the check, touches Simon's hand, and says, "Since you are having to deal with so many Caesars, let me get this to help out with the money situation. I enjoyed our conversation. I usually dine alone in strange cities, and the company was uplifting."

Raph exits the restaurant. Simon sits back in his chair, takes a sip of his coffee that has been refilled, and feels a renewed sense of calm. He empties his cup and heads back to work with a new resolve to find out what is going on with Reliance.

On entering his office, Simon sees there is a message on his phone. He presses the blinking button and hears Norm ask him to come to his office. He hits delete and makes his way to Norm. Simon stands in the doorway to Norm's office as Norm completes a telephone conversation, hangs up, and says, "Great, you got my message. Earlman wants to see us."

"I assume he has been deluged about the messages?" Simon asks.

"Yes, but he wants to discuss the data I gave him from the rovers.

We won't bring up the hacking. It might be an actual hack coming from somewhere within JPL, but I haven't found any source."

"Okay, I won't mention it." They make their way to Earlman's office.

"Good afternoon, gentlemen," Earlman greets them. "Have a seat." The two are seated, and Earlman continues. "I've been on the phone with Apple, Microsoft, and other companies, assuring them that these hacked email messages did not come from us."

"What have you found so far?" Norm asks.

"Well, they tell me it was sophisticated but harmless. Neither the companies nor we found suspicious software in our system."

"That's good to hear," Norm replies.

Yes," Earlman agrees. "But that's not why I wanted to see you two in person." He pats the stack of data sheets on his desk and says, "Simon, I do believe Norm was right. You are the man for the job at hand. Back just a day and a half and you reconnect with the rovers. Well done, Simon."

"Thank you sir," Simon responds. He beams as Norm pats him on the back.

Pointing skyward, Earlman asks, "Do all the little guys up there appear to be working, as this data tells me?"

"Yes, Colonel," Simon tells him. "They're all operational now, to different degrees."

"Tom, Simon. Call me Tom," Earlman says.

"Okay, Tom."

"How did you get them working?"

"The Reliance program is more sophisticated and has more program commands than the original programming. It's quicker to be recognized and allows for different commands than the original programming language."

"Can our other operators use Reliance now?" Earlman inquires.

"No, Tom. It is working, but I don't want to push too fast and do something that might end communications forever."

"I agree. Slow and steady. I will defer to you when it gets to the point to where you think we can push them to do more. I'll be talking to General Bosman. It will excite him to learn of this promising development. Good news means more funding to our budget."

Earlman rises from behind his desk. Simon and Norm also stand. Earlman approaches them, shakes their hands, and says, "Thanks, guys. I just wanted to congratulate the two of you in person. We'll keep in touch."

Norm and Simon exit, smiling and chuckling a little as they walk down the hall, very pleased with what just happened.

Earlman picks up the phone and dials General Bosman. They connect, and Earlman says, "Hello, General. I met with the rover team, and everything is functional." He pauses to listen to a question from the general, and then replies, "Yes. The new guy has worked wonders. His name is Dr. Simon Northstrum." He pauses again to listen to the general. "I will, and thank you for the compliment, sir." Earlman hangs up.

Simon is now back at his computer, and he is just getting settled in when his phone buzzes. He presses the speaker button.

"Simon, this is Tom. Can you come back to my office?"

Simon asks, "Do you need Norm?"

"No, just you."

"Roger that. I will be there in a minute." He leaves his desk and soon enters the office of Earlman, who signals for him to sit.

"I just talked with General Bosman at the Pentagon. Your quick work impressed him. It comes at the best time, because Congress looks to cut programs. If we are in complete control of the rovers, then they will feel a need to continue or even increase funding." Giving a little laugh, Earlman asks, "You don't have any pictures of little green men running around on Mars, do you?"

Simon looks a little embarrassed. "Relax, Simon," Earlman says. "I know the scuttlebutt. I'm a military guy, but I'm on your side. Can Reliance really be used on other systems when we get to that point? General Bosman asked about it again."

"Well, I was thinking about that. I wrote the program specifically for the rovers, but I suppose I could help rewrite it for other uses."

"So that could be doable?"

"I would have to look at the systems wanting to use it."

"Well, we may have you do that, on down the line."

"Okay."

Earlman leans on his desk toward Simon. "On another matter, Simon, General Bosman inquired about the hacked email messages. As a programmer, what do you make of these hackings and the fact that the reply line points to JPL?"

"Sir, it is as big a mystery to me as it is to everyone else. The hacker must be a genius. That's for sure."

"As a programmer, how would you suggest we might go about getting to the bottom of this? Even though JPL and the hacked companies have found nothing involving JPL, General Bosman is very concerned that the messages point to us."

"Tom, since network security itself is not my cup of tea and I have been laser-focused on the rover program, I haven't thought much about it. But even though this particular event is out of my ability range, I do know emails can be masked as originating from anywhere."

"Yes, Simon, that's what I've been told."

"So," Simon asks, "nothing at all has been found that indicates it could have come from JPL?"

"They are still researching, but nothing yet to implicate us."

"Okay. If I can be of any help …" Simon trails off, and then he asks, "Is that it, Tom? I've got a program running and need to get back to it."

"Yeah, sure. That's all for now. And, again, Simon, thank you for your great work."

After departing, Simon's forehead is damp from anxiety, and he uses his sleeve to wipe it away. It seems the email messages may not be an issue. He returns to his office and works with Reliance once again. This time the program functions normally. He enters commands for the rover to complete and report back results. He is aware it will be tomorrow before it returns the results. Simon nestles back into his chair and reads project reports as he hears the computers humming. He thinks that if somebody has really pranked him, the person is a true master.

Later Norm appears in the doorway and asks, "Are you working all night?" Simon places the paperwork on his desk. "You up for a beer?"

"A beer would be good."

As they leave Simon's office, Norm asks, "How does it feel to be on top with the brass? I spent a few minutes with Earlman after he phoned Bosman and then spoke with you. He was glowing. He is hoping someone can use your software on other military projects."

"I realize what they want. They want a more efficient way to blow things up. I'm unsure if Reliance is workable on other systems, so I'm not on top of anything yet. Right now, I must keep these critters roving. If something bad happens to them, you bet I'll work my tail off then to find a way to make the software work on other projects, or I'm gone. I realize it's a funding game and I have to play that game." They enter the elevator together.

CHAPTER 10

A large black SUV stops in front of the JPL main doors. Two men wearing sport coats exit the vehicle and make their way through the entrance. Inspector Parker Steele is a chief cybertechnology and computer forensic specialist. Steele is bald, with a weathered face. He is a pit bull in interrogation and is savvy to ways of hackers.

His sidekick is a tall black man named Aldis Montgomery, a renowned computer specialist. He has a backpack loaded with his forensic supplies. He looks more like a left tackle for a professional football team than a computer whiz. They approach Alvarez, who is standing guard. "May I help you gentlemen?" the security guard asks.

The agents show their badges. "We are here to see Colonel Tom Earlman. I am Inspector Steele with the FBI, and this is specialist Montgomery."

Alvarez dials Colonel Earlman's office. "Sir, I have two FBI people in the lobby, say they are here to see you." He listens to the colonel's response and replies, "FBI Inspector Montgomery and FBI Specialist Steele." He listens again. "Yes sir," he replies. Alvarez hangs up, approves the two men's security passes, and escorts them to the elevator.

They arrive at Earlman's office. "Hello, Inspector and Specialist. What can I do for you?"

Steele responds, "I assume General Bosman alerted you to us coming to visit."

"Yes, you will be here a few days. What are you going to do?"

"Aldis and I will look at every piece of software to see how this hacking email apparently came from JPL."

"Inspector, remember we have sensitive software linking projects around the solar system; we cannot just stop."

"We understand, colonel. Aldis will be sensitive to your projects but will be thorough."

"Aldis Montgomery interrupts. "I do not want to shut down the *Voyager* project," referring to a satellite launched decades ago.

Steele says, "I understand you have employment records for me. Is your staff available to interview?"

"Yes. But you will have to work around their project timetables."

"We will be as unobtrusive as possible," the agent responds.

Having been told previously they would be wanted, Earlman hands a copy of the employment records to Steele. He tells him, "It sorts by the last hired and communication software expertise as you asked. I wouldn't think our bean counters would be of interest."

"Everyone is of interest, but this is a good start."

"I have an office you can use," Earlman tells him.

"Excellent. Show us the way so we can get to work."

The trio exit Earlman's office and move to one visible from Simon's. Steele and Montgomery set up operations and thank Earlman, who turns and leaves. Montgomery begins his analysis of JPL while Steele contacts employees to schedule meetings for the next day after Montgomery has done some groundwork.

Simon's telephone rings. Answering, he hears Norm say, "Simon, Norm here. I just wanted to make you aware that the FBI are on site and starting tomorrow will be interviewing the staff. You will be up near the top because you were a recent hire."

"Do I have anything to worry about?

"I don't think so. Are you worried?"

"A little. What if they ask about Reliance?"

"Tell them about it. You have nothing to hide."

"Do you think they are looking for a scapegoat?"

"Just tell the truth; you are good at doing the right thing. No need to change now. They've got a computer expert who is analyzing things before they start quizzing anybody"

"Okay, buddy. Thanks for the heads-up."

�

Simon is running late the next morning because Emma missed her bus and he had to drop her off at school. Following that, his engine warning light came on. So after driving to a service station and putting some oil in for the time being, he finally arrives at JPL.

As he walks to his office, he notices several people sitting in chairs outside the nearby office being used by the FBI. He is surprised by the number of people who have been hired since his return. He thinks, *Maybe one of them is the culprit, if indeed someone from JPL is involved.* He enters his office and dives into his data analysis.

About two hours later, his phone rings. It is Inspector Steele.

"Dr. Northstrum?" the agent inquires.

"Yes. Can I help you?"

"This is Inspector Steele with the FBI. Can you come to our office to answer questions? I can give you directions."

"That's okay. I know where you are. Word travels pretty fast around here. Do I need to bring anything?"

"No, unless it is a confession!"

"Excuse me?" Simon says.

"I am joking. We will see you soon."

He hangs up and sits back in his chair, taking a deep breath. He thinks, *I guess I'd better get this over with now. If I tell them about Sojourner, the Dominion, and souls, I will be on the first bus to the loony bin. I will answer yes and no and see what they know.*

Simon soon enters the FBI office, and the agents rise to meet him.

"Dr. Northstrum. It is an honor to meet you," Steele says. He extends his hand and grasps Simon's. "I'm Inspector Parker Steele."

"Inspector," Simon replies as he shakes Steele's hand.

"This is my protégé Aldis Montgomery," Steele explains as Montgomery steps forward to shake Simon's hand.

Montgomery smiles, and the three men are seated, Montgomery in front of his computer screen.

Steele asks, "May I call you Simon?"

"Sure."

"My friends call me Steele," the agent says.

"You have a great name for an FBI agent."

"That's what people say. Maybe it was my destiny to be FBI.

Montgomery inserts, "Just call me Aldis."

"Got it," Simon replies.

Steele says, "I am sure the grapevine informed you of why we are here.

"Yes."

"We would like to ask you some questions."

"Okay. You know, it surprised me JPL hired so many others after me."

"How do you know there were a number of people hired after you?"

"There was a line I could see from my office."

"Oh. Observant, I see."

Simon asks, "Any prospects?"

"No, not yet. Actually, we breezed through them to get to you."

"Really? Why would that be?"

Steele says, "If you can talk to other planets, then why not everyone on Earth, through messages?"

Simon sort of chuckles, saying, "It is a different language."

Montgomery joins in. "You are the man that designed the rovers?"

"Not just me," Simon answers. "A team of amazing developers worked with me. It was—and is—a team project."

"But you developed the communications for the landers on Mars?"

"Primarily."

Montgomery asks, "Do you think someone could have taken your computerized language and cannibalized it to hack the world's servers?"

"No. When we talk to the rovers, we don't consider the possibility of hacking or hackers. Each rover has its own different set of communication protocols that are not interchangeable. Hacking is not in my expertise. I'm too busy keeping the data stream active from billions of miles away. Our data travels through all sorts of cosmic garbage and then through our own magnetic field."

Steele asks, "You don't have the skill to do this hack?"

"I have skills, and maybe I could learn to do it if I spent a lot of time on it. I guess it is a code. But it would take too much time to learn this coding to breach everyone. And the main thing is that I'm not interested in doing it. Besides that, I've got all I can handle, and more, right now."

Montgomery says, "Simon, I found this software called Reliance on the JPL system. I understand you created it, and it registers as the latest updated software at JPL."

"Yes," Simon replies. I assume it updated when I turned it back on after an extended absence. But let me start at the beginning. JPL downsized when Congress cut funding for many science programs. You get more money if you can prove your project can reduce an entire state to rubble."

Steele, listening intently, interrupts Simon. "I can understand the funding cuts. It happened to FBI forensics."

Simon asks, "Did it make you mad?"

"Yes, I guess," Steele responds. He sits a little straighter and asks Simon, "How mad were you?"

"Well, Steele, how would you feel if you birthed your babies and sent them out on their own and the organization sacked you for someone cheaper?"

"You sound resentful, Simon," Steele responds.

"No, not resentful. I was mad for a while, and money was tight, but I had saved. Now I am back doing what I love, and there's no way I would do anything to sacrifice that."

Steele nods and says, "But I guess when JPL let you go it was a breeze for you to get a new job somewhere else."

"I had opportunities. But I wanted to be in the space program." Simon pauses, thinking before his next statement, wondering what exactly they know about him, and considering they might be thinking he could have taken money to send those emails.

Before Simon has time to say anything else, Steele says, "I have to ask you. Did you do this? However, before you answer, please understand that they train us in interrogation. We expect the truth. And remember: you don't know what we know."

"Look," Simon says adamantly, "I have nothing to do with this email messaging problem. The Reliance program cannot do email hacking." He then turns toward Montgomery and says, "Aldis, I suppose you are a crack computer guy. Let me get at your computer, and I will pull Reliance from our in-house server and let you view the code."

Simon changes places with Montgomery, pulls up the program, keys in the password, and opens Reliance. He rises and lets Montgomery back in front of the computer.

Simon then tells him, "There it is. An open book. All it does is help extend the life of the rovers and make communication smoother. Period."

Simon then addresses Steele. "Now, judging from your probing, if you think I may have done some hacking to make some money, take a look at my car, my house, my bank account, and my wife working at a funeral home."

Steele replies, "We did consider the financial possibility, and we have looked into your background. Dr. Northstrum, Aldis will review your software, and it will take time. It just concerns us that you were one of the last hired and the only person to introduce new software."

"Reliance was on the mainframe before my termination," Simon replies. "I only made it operational, and as you said, it updated when I turned it on. Anyone could have sabotaged it while I was gone."

Steele asks, "Do you know anyone on staff with the skill to do that?"

"I don't know many of the new military guys. I am sure the old crew wouldn't do it. You don't win points by destroying a project worth billions."

"I see your point. Do you think someone from the military could do it to make your exploration side lose funding?"

"I don't know the answer to that, Steele, and I won't surmise. That's above my pay grade."

"We will look into it," the agent responds.

Montgomery says, "Simon, this is amazing software. Could you sit with me in your office and we can review it together?"

"Sure."

"Parker," Montgomery says to Steele, "I am going with Simon as you handle the upcoming interviews. Together we can get through the software and eliminate Dr. Northstrum."

"Sounds good to me," Steele replies. "Simon, I hope you will be available if I've further questions."

"So, you mean, don't leave town," Simon responds.

Steele, in his best golden-oldie *Dragnet* voice, replies, "Dr. Northstrum, you watch too many cop shows."

Montgomery and Simon leave the FBI's working office. Shortly after, Steele departs and makes his way to Earlman's office. He enters. Earlman asks him to sit and then asks, "How are the interviews going?"

"Most are dead ends, and the personnel would not have the know-how. But one guy interests me."

"Oh, who is of interest?"

"Dr. Simon Northstrum."

"Simon? Why? Do you suspect something?"

"No, just a gut feeling. He was one of the last hired and the only one interviewed with the advanced technical knowledge about that Reliance program, which Montgomery is interested in."

"There are others here just as computer savvy."

"We will get to them, but Simon was the last to update software."

"JPL director Ed Proctor reviewed the software."

"We know. My guy is reviewing it with Simon right now."

"Simon is the golden boy around here," Earlman tells him.

"How so?"

"Simon started up the software and reconnected with the rovers."

"I guess it's good software?"

"Oh, yes," Earlman says, "a ten-billion-dollar savings. One of our rovers—*Sojourner*, it is called—had a stuck wheel, and Simon somehow freed it. Of course, the software did the job, but Simon had to send the right commands."

"I see why you think he is golden."

𝓙𝓒

Back in Simon's office, Simon and Montgomery discuss the Reliance code and how it relates to JPL's work. As Simon describes it, Montgomery says, "It must be cool to play with this equipment worth billions of dollars at JPL."

"Yes, it is fulfilling, but sometimes nerve racking."

"How so?"

"Well, Aldis, they don't look kindly when a billion-dollar project blows up on the launch pad or gets lost just after takeoff."

"Has that happened?"

"A few times."

"Was it your fault?"

"No, but if you're a mission commander, everything is your fault. Think about the space shuttle. It may have a million parts that make it work. If you have a ninety-nine percent success rate, that is pretty good, don't you think?"

"Yes. I would say so."

"That remaining one percent means that ten thousand parts could fail, any of which could be mission critical. We are not putting the smallest and least modified compact cars out into space, and it's not like we can pull over and look under the hood."

"I can see that," Montgomery replies. "I would like to start up and run this Reliance program to check it out and see what it does."

"You can't do that on this computer, Aldis, because it is already running."

"You mean it is in contact with Mars right now?"

"In a way. It is not like we pick up the phone and talk. We issue commands through the software that tell the rovers what to do. They are not autonomous, but they are programmed to react to objects or obstructions so they can go around things that can stop them."

Montgomery asks, "Is there any way I can see this program start up?"

"Well," Simon tells him, "I can put it on an unconnected terminal in here. Then we can begin the startup sequence, but it will halt once it finds no outside connection is available."

"It is no different from not being able to get online?"

"In a way, but the next connection point is 140 million miles away."

"I see. I would like to set that up. Can you make it happen?"

"Yes, I'll call Norm to get permission."

"Let's do it."

Simon picks up the phone and reaches Norm.

"Hi, Norm."

"Hey, how is it going?"

"Good. The FBI's Aldis Montgomery is here with me, with mostly technical questions, like how the software works. He wants to start up and run through Reliance."

"You told him it was running?"

"Yes. But he wants to start it up and run it from an offline terminal. Can he use the extra one in my office?"

"Sure. No problem."

"Thanks, Norm."

In a softer voice, Norm says, "Simon, anything weird going on with *Sojourner*? You can answer yes or no."

"No. I'll see you later."

Simon hangs up and tells Montgomery he can use the extra terminal.

"Good. That should eliminate one line of investigation."

"I doubt you will find anything that I couldn't. Norm and Earlman had me run through the program many times, and I could find no problem with it."

Montgomery tells him, "Once we start the program on this other terminal, I have software that will walk through your code to see if someone has weaved hacking code into Reliance. Then we can pull out the pieces to see if the code is from a known hacker, since they have their signatures. It is almost impossible to see, but my system can pull it out."

Simon nods. "Sounds good."

At the funeral home, Alexis continues to call people, offering funeral services. She is despondent that people can be so cruel over the phone. She hopes she was never that way with callers trying to make a living. Adam Sable darkens Alexis's doorway. Alexis mumbles to herself, "Here comes the wonder boy."

He asks her, "Do you have a minute?"

"Yes."

"I have a project for you."

"Okay," she says, knowing he will want her to do his job.

"I know you are aware of the census being down. We are not getting traffic from the hospitals, hospice, and home agencies. Here is a list of the facilities we work with in the area. I would like you to visit them to see why people are no longer being sent to us."

"Adam, isn't that your job?"

"It is, but I'm getting more into body preparation."

"Oh, Is this a newly added job description for me in sales?"

"Are you asking for more money?"

"Adam, I have a family, and now you are asking me to do outside sales. I will have expenses. Do I get reimbursed and paid for my time?"

"Yes. I can give you a twenty percent raise. You will be on salary. We expect our traffic to climb back to normal levels. Do you want the position?"

"Great then. When do I start?"

"Now," he replies, handing her some papers. "Call these places and introduce yourself. Then set meetings with their contact people. We need to find out if we have done something that caused them to not send people to us. Have they gone to another home? I think you know what to do."

"I have never done this before, but I'll do my best."

"Good," Adam says, and then he leaves.

Alexis settles back in her chair. She thinks of what she would really like to say to Adam. *Maybe traffic is down because most have figured out you're an ass.* She breathes a gasp. *At least it will get me out with the living.* She does not understand what her earlier prayers have done and what the Dominion has in store for the Northstrum family.

Alexis scans the list and decides she might as well start right at the top. She dials the first number, which is the largest hospital. Someone directs her to the BRET supervisor, Audrey Cooper.

"Hello, Ms. Cooper, I'd like to introduce myself. I'm Alexis Northstrum with Sable Funeral Homes."

Cooper replies, "I thought Adam Sable was in that position?"

"He was. I've taken over for him."

"Thank you! Lurch, as we call him, should not walk around the living." There is a pause before she continues. "I probably should not have said that to you. It just slipped out."

"It is fine; I know what you mean. A posterior comes to mind."

Cooper chuckles. "Alexis, we will get on fine. Now, what can I do for you?"

"Well, as I said, I wanted to introduce myself and see if there was any reason you were no longer using our home. Did Adam cross you?"

"No. Really, we just ignore Adam to a degree, and we have no problem with your service, and our families approve of their treatment. It has been strange; I've been here twenty years, and this is the first time we have had no one pass in quite a while."

"You mean no one has passed away lately?"

"Right. I'm sure it is just a timing issue and we will return to normal. But we are good with your company."

"Okay, thank you, Audrey."

Alexis dials and reaches a hospice center. She doesn't have a name but asks for the BRET supervisor. When connected, she introduces herself in a way comparable to her introduction to Audrey Cooper, and then she again asks about the hospice's needs.

"No, Alexis, it's weird. No one has passed recently. We have a few who were imminent, but they have gotten stronger. We'll let you know."

"So our relationship is okay?"

"Yes, no problem here."

Alexis hangs up, thinking how strange this is. She leaves her office and makes her way to Adam.

"Yes, Alexis?" he says as she enters his office.

"I called two of our biggest customers, and they had no business for us."

"Is there a problem with the service?"

"No," she replies, not repeating everything she was told. "Both said everything was good, but they had no one die. Do you find that odd?"

"They are sending people elsewhere and being nice to you."

"Possibly. I'll check the obits to see who is getting business. Do we have a paper here?"

"No, you'll have to get a paper when you are out. I'll also get one on my way home. We stopped the home delivery."

⌔

Back in Simon's office, he and Montgomery have set the extra terminal to run the Reliance software offline without disrupting the live program. Steele has made his way to the office for the test. The agent asks Simon, "Are you nervous about this test?"

"Not really. I wrote the code. I know what is in the program. I gave it to JPL before I left, and what they did with it was out of my hands."

"You are saying that this program never left the JPL building."

"Not to my knowledge, but I was gone a long time. Security is tight around here, and you have met Alvarez."

Montgomery jumps in, smirking, "Yes, he is formidable."

Steele addresses Simon again. "You never took it home to work on it?"

"No. It is a different operating system. They don't give people computers to maneuver Martian rovers from your couch."

"He is right," Montgomery interjects.

"Do you think the military people may have taken it out?"

"Inspector, you are asking me questions I can't answer. I was not here. I've only been back a little while. You will have to discuss that with the higher-ups."

"Parker," Montgomery says to Steele, "I've got my equipment set up and I am ready to run the test."

"Let's do it," the agent responds.

Steele directs Simon to help Montgomery get it going. Simon slides up to the terminal, enters a password, and then lets Montgomery start up the Reliance program, which the agent is monitoring with his equipment. Silently, Simon is praying a voice won't begin. If it does, what can he say, or how will he explain it? There is no way. But then again, he thinks that the bright side will be that someone else will hear the voice. *It might be good for* Sojourner *to speak now.*

The program is now running, with no voice coming from the screen. Montgomery's program is catching each line of code, searching for hacked bits. The program brings up a screen that lists the JPL space projects.

"Reliance is working with these projects?" Steele asks.

"No," Simon tells him. "Just the rovers right now. I have not touched the others. JPL rehired me for the rovers."

Montgomery asks Simon, "Where do we go from here?"

"I select a project, and then it will bring up a command screen."

"Can you do it?"

"Yes."

Steele steps in, saying, "Let me pick the project."

"Okay," Simon tells him.

"Let's connect to *Curiosity*," Steele says.

Simon enters the code next to the name, and the cursor blinks. After a brief time, an error message appears, signaling that there is no connection. He turns to the agents and says, "You will get that for all the projects. It is like trying to get on the internet without being connected to a source. We are not hooked to those giant dishes on the roof. However, I can get to the other rovers to show you, if you wish."

Steele tells Montgomery to try it. He replaces Simon in the seat.

"Simon," Steele instructs, "tell Aldis what next to type to *Sojourner*."

Reluctantly, Simon recites the code, hoping direct contact with *Sojourner* will not bring the voice. Montgomery enters what Simon recites. It impresses Steele that Simon can give the codes by memory, leaving him thinking that Simon indeed must be the creator. Montgomery then presses enter, and the cursor blinks, returning the same error message.

"Simon is correct," Montgomery tells Steele. "Nothing, without being online."

Steele asks, "What has your computer told you about the Reliance software in general?"

"Boss, it will take hours to go through the code. I can't tell you anything now except that it is exceptional software."

Simon shows a smile of relief. He won't be in a straitjacket, and he wonders whether, when arrested, one gets to make one phone call or whether that is only in the movies. Steele interrupts him from his thoughts.

"Simon, thank you for working with us. I am sure you want us out of your hair so you can boldly go where no man has gone before." Simon weakly smiles at the *Star Trek* reference. "Please leave the terminal as is for now until further notice."

"Sure. It is no use to me. You can take it with you when you go if you want to challenge Alvarez."

"It is unnecessary. We may have more questions once Aldis finishes his analysis."

The agents leave Simon's office, and in the hall Steele asks Montgomery whether he secretly copied everything he needed. Montgomery says he did, and Steele tells him, "I want you to get this program to headquarters so the big computers and another set of eyes can look into this Reliance."

"Yes sir," Montgomery assures him. "I will upload it as soon as I get back to the office."

After a long day, Simon makes his way to the elevators and covets the safety of home. He won't have to worry about Martian rovers contacting him there. While waiting for the elevator, he looks through the office windows and sees Steele meeting with Earlman and Norm. He knows that Norm will give him the skinny on what the others might hold back. Now his only thought is getting home to his castle and Alexis. Though it is a small place, it is his refuge.

The elevator door opens, and Simon glances again at Earlman's office, where Steele is now pointing a finger at Earlman. Though he cannot hear the conversation, the body language tells him the discussion is heated. The elevator door closes, and he is free. Simon makes his way past Alvarez and gives him a little salute. Alvarez nods a good day acknowledgment. Simon leaves the building and inhales the sweet breeze. He had not realized it had rained, and the air is fresh. Being shut away in an office has its downsides.

On reaching his car, he slides into the seat. The engine roars to life while Simon clicks his seatbelt secure. *Time for some mind-escaping tunes.* He presses his playlist, and a song plays. Simon places the car in drive and enters the moving traffic. He drives a few mindless miles, recalling events of the day and thinking about how he has always stayed away from police crosshairs but now the FBI thinks he's a criminal.

Suddenly the familiar voice of *Sojourner* disturbs his drive. "Good Afternoon, Dr. Northstrum," the giggling voice begins. Startled, Simon brakes. The car skids a little until he regains control. Seemingly, the voice is coming through his car speakers.

"You almost made me wreck! You can't sneak up on people like that." He pauses, feeling strange talking to his playlist. He then asks, "How are you doing it?"

"I'm not. The Dominion is doing it. Communications are their specialty."

"The FBI is climbing up my butt at JPL," Simon responds.

"I know. I could have contacted you when you ran Reliance, but you can do no good in jail."

"Jail? Why would I go to jail? Reliance has no sinister programs in it."

"Simon, you have not been taking heed. We are contacting the world through you with Reliance. You will have to make the world listen. You will be in trouble, but the Dominion believes in you. 'Be Not Afraid.' Simon, Reliance will send more messages to the world, but it will do so through the FBI. They can't run Reliance. Montgomery is examining the code by using your dumb terminal. He will unknowingly release the next message, but the FBI will come back to you."

"What am I supposed to make the world listen to?"

"I have told you. People must listen to their souls."

"I don't understand."

"Simon, do you believe the time of your death is your judgment day?"

"Yes."

"Simon, you don't remember, but before your birth, you designed your life with the Dominion."

"Dominion this and Dominion that … what is the Dominion?"

"Everything in the universe is part of the Dominion. Your soul is the part that holds the story of your life you helped write before your birth and continue to write each day."

"So I created this ongoing story that I should be flying high and then crash and burn."

"Each life is a journey created to help you learn, pay past debts, and reach higher into the Dominion. Humans believe it is a tragedy a newborn child should die four days after birth, but the baby had finished its journey it created in the Dominion's world. The message it brought with it was for the parents of that child, so they could learn or make a choice."

"What are you talking about, *Sojourner*?" Simon asks.

"The Dominion sees a baby's return as a loved one returning from a vacation, but it is returning from its story. It is a joyous reunion. You have heard the stories of people dying and entering a tunnel of white light. They tell of the peace of being in the light and not wanting to return."

Though he is Bumfuzzled by what he is hearing, Simon picks up on the last part and says, "Yeah, I've heard the stories. They say it is the brain dying. People say that when you drown, your life flashes before you."

"No, Simon. The soul flows into the Dominion and you remember the whole story. It is ironic that people talk of a tunnel but never pose a question about the other end. Don't tunnels have two ends?"

"I suppose. So where is the other end?"

"At conception," *Sojourner* says. Imagine you can see the moment that the sperm meets the egg and witness the burst of pure light as the soul enters the cell and grows within you, spreading throughout your body. Nothing can hide from the light, and it connects you to humanity. The light has an unbreakable and unblockable connection. *Sojourner* pauses to let the words sink in. "Your life is a journey to the light leading to the so-called tunnel's end, learning as you experience the joy and the horror of human existence. It then expands into the infinite existence in the Dominion. Once there, you remember the most current life and the others, sitting with your teacher, reviewing your soul's story. It is a tough notion to imagine. Faith plays a big part." Again there is a pause. "Simon, as I told you, your life is a snap of your fingers to the Dominion."

Dazed by it all, Simon says, "Okay, just what am I supposed to do?"

"You must convince the world—the people—to stay on the paths of their stories. If they are off of their stories, they will be taken home."

"Isn't that like the rapture?"

"In a way. The rapture will take the worthy with the rest left behind to live in tribulation. You must get the world to listen; the turmoil caused by the upcoming messages and communications is not manmade. In the coming weeks, man will accuse man, religions will accuse religions, and countries will feel threatened. You must convince them to 'Be Not Afraid' and to listen to their souls and stay on their paths."

"How do I do that? I'm nobody."

"The Dominion has put you in a perfect position. You have met them even though you were unaware."

"I suppose I believe you. I mean, at this point, with you talking through my car speakers …" Simon pauses and then asks, "Should I fear them? The Dominion?"

"No, they are here to teach, except for one. But you have nothing to fear from him. He will send others home. You will be shocked at the ones reclaimed. But it is an answer to a prayer."

"Yeah, like such answers ever happen."

"Well, Simon, you're talking with me on Mars through a car radio speaker. And didn't you ask for God's help?"

"Okay. I suppose I did."

"You are almost home. Prepare yourself. The government needs a scapegoat because they can find no one else to blame. Make them listen. Listen to the news about events in the world."

Music now resumes on Simon's car speakers. He continues driving, finally parking in his driveway next to Alexis's car. He places his forehead on the steering wheel, mumbling. "I don't know when this nightmare will end. I'm supposed to save the world. What do I tell Alexis?" He then decides to say little about this progression in things for the time being and just act as normal as he possibly can. He sees no reason to get his family upset now—not with things going so much better.

The next morning is fairly normal. Alexis leaves for work, and Emma is at the bus stop on time. Simon, while watching a bit of the news with Martha MacCallum reporting, has the last of his coffee before heading off to JPL.

"What a world we live in today," Martha says. "Yesterday's news was blanketed by reports on the weird messaging. But lost beneath that story was another weird happening. You can't make this stuff up. Communication is instant. We have a video of this heroic little boy trying to save his sister from a sniper who was systematically shooting away a large flowerpot to kill her."

Martha turns toward a video flashing upon the screen. "What kind of person does that to children who are no threat? It makes you want to cry that people are so cruel … and this brave boy dodging bullets, taking the attention off her so she can get away. And then there is a bolt of lightning, as seen here. Then no more shots come from the sniper's gun. People are claiming the Americans have arrived to help with Star Wars weapons. Others are saying a white angel appeared, raised his hand, and stopped the sniper. Reports are coming in that the sniper was found dead of natural causes in his loft. Townspeople are saying Allah sent his angel to help them. This video we are showing has already surpassed all video downloads in YouTube history. You be the judge. Tweet us what you think it is. Major governments are accusing the United States of using laser weapon—a violation of the Laser Weapons Treaty. There is a big powwow scheduled at the United Nations, and many countries are raising their nuclear threat levels. Many of us were too young—or not even born—to remember the threat levels raised during the Cuban missile crisis. Students practiced hiding under desks at school."

She looks away and then reaches for some papers. "Folks, we are just now getting over the wire that two other snipers met similar fates in the same area as the first. The United States has denied any involvement in the incident. I guess if it's an angel or Star Wars, we won't have to worry about those snipers anymore. We'll have more on this coming up."

Simon gives a weary "Oh, crap" grin. He thinks, *Is this the start of the Dominion's plan that* Sojourner *told me about, or does the government have this technology? If this is a warmup for the Dominion, they chose deserving scum. Maybe the Area 51 stories are true.*

CHAPTER 11

A mail truck approaches the security gate for receiving at the Pentagon. The soldier at the gate waves to the postal worker, whom he has known many years. He reviews his credentials and manifest and then signals the driver forward to the unloading terminal. The truck advances and backs into the loading dock. A handful of workers sort the truck's contents into the proper carts for distribution through the world's largest office complex. The empty truck leaves the dock, and the carts begin their journey through hazmat security and then on to their labeled destinations.

It's before noon, and General Bosman sits in his office deep within the bowels of this massive building. He has no windows in this large office because they are too much of a security risk. Hardened paneled walls protect him from the outside crazies. A tan mail cart is pushed through the long, wide corridors toward the general's office. It makes various stops at the offices, unloading its wares.

A mail room officer enters the outer office of the general and meets Florence Grant. She is an older woman, slight in stature, and has been with the general for many years. The staff call her Ms. Napoleon. She runs a tight ship with no military experience. Most realize that if one wants something from the general, one must go through Florence. The orderly approaches her, and they exchange pleasantries. She signs for the three packages, two of which are rectangular and one of which is tube shaped. The orderly leaves as Florence scans the packages. She opens her desk drawer, retrieves a logbook, and records the information of each delivered item. After placing the book back into her drawer, she rises, grabs the packages in her arms, and proceeds to the door of the general's office.

Florence pushes the door open. The general sits behind a large mahogany desk supporting a big computer screen on which data is flashing. Focused, he does not notice Florence's presence. After hearing the door shut behind her, he glances over and then points to a table on which to place the mail, never breaking away from his concentration. Florence turns and peers at a table full of packages unmoved since yesterday's same ritual. She turns to leave, and the general bellows, "I will get to it today." Florence smiles and thinks of how she has heard that many times before.

A little later, the intercom interrupts the general as Florence's voice announces, "Your daughter is on line one."

"I'll call her back," barks the general.

"This is her third call. You need to take it," she demands. He grumbles but relents and picks up the handset.

"Hi, Cassie."

"Hi, Dad. Are you getting my messages?"

"Yes. I've been busy."

"Gee, Dad, we work in the same building and never see each other. Billy misses you."

"Work has me covered."

"You could come for dinner."

"It's late when I get home."

"You know, Dad, you have four stars. You can delegate things. Billy has only one grandparent. Mom missed out on sharing his growing up, but you still have time."

"I'll try."

"The reason for my call is that Billy made you an important picture at church the other day. He wanted you to see it, but we never see you. Father Gabriel suggested he mail it to you. Is that how bad it's become, Dad?"

"I will try better. I promise."

"Did you get the package?"

"There is a pile of stuff on a table I have not looked at yet."

"Do I need to go above your head to Florence?" she threatens.

"No. She is on me every day about the full table. You'd think she had five stars."

"She should if it keeps you in line. Every man needs a good woman."

"I had one. God took her," he says.

"I know, Dad, we miss her too. Go through the packages. It is in a yellow tube. Call Billy and tell him how great it is. He made it to help you be happy."

"I will. I promise."

"Bye, Dad. I love you."

"Back at ya," he says.

The general returns to his work but pauses to glance at the table full of mail. He grumbles and pushes away from his desk. Walking to the table, he sees a yellow tube, and he pulls it from the pile. Back at his desk, he retrieves a knife and cuts the tape securing the tube. His work is interrupted by the voice of Florence. "General, the secretary of defense is on line two." The general places the knife down and opens a side drawer, slipping the tube inside. While doing so, a violet spark jumps to his hand. He assumes it is static electricity.

Grabbing the phone, he says, "Mr. Secretary, how can I help you?"

"Robert, what is going on at JPL? The president just ripped me a new one on this email mess. Did you know about this?"

"Mr. Secretary, I have spoken to the director there, and he has found no evidence of anything coming from JPL. The FBI cyber team is on the scene, looking into the mess. Every company on the planet has tried to get through. The people at JPL are good folks, and they are too involved with billion-dollar projects to send silly emails. The good news is we rehired the original programmer to come back in and help us reestablish connections with the Mars rovers. He was there one day, and he got the data flowing again."

"Outstanding! So we no longer have ten billion dollars of space junk?"

"Right, sir."

"Why was he let go?"

"It was a different administration and funding."

"What is his name?"

"Northstrum. Dr. Simon Northstrum."

"Keep me updated on the progress."

"I will."

General Bosman places the phone in the cradle as Florence enters the office with a pile of papers. She asks, "General, are we still employed?"

He looks up and smiles. "Yes, we are both still employed" he says sarcastically." Only Florence can talk to him in that fashion.

"General, the catch-and-release people are in the other office."

He signs the papers in front of him and hands them back to Florence. She exits through the doorway and instructs the guests that the general will see them now.

Two people enter the office, one an officer and another in a simple dress shirt and pants. The officer salutes and says, "Hello, General. I'm Major Caritta, and this is Dr. Tristin Beckett, PhD."

"Yes, have a seat, gentlemen. What do you have to show me? I approved the money for this CART program, but it has shown little progress except for a bunch of critters swimming in a petri dish. Why am I still wasting money on this project?"

Dr. Beckett says, "Sir, I know you like things that are flashy, and you can't even see our project with the naked eye. We have no problem with the critters, as you call them. The opposite is true, sir. General, for many years we have been giving the nanos to suspected terrorists when we bring them in for questioning."

"How long?" asks Bosman?

"Six years."

"Where is it done? Guantanamo?"

"Yes, and any place we question people."

"In the US?"

"No, it is easier elsewhere. When we detain suspects, we give them humane care with food, water, and medical treatment. We administer the nanos in the medicines, food, and water given while incarcerated. The inert nanos pose no harm to the people. Each will eventually die, and the body will eliminate it as waste. We gave out the nanos after 9/11 because we knew the critters were ready. We hoped that communication technology would advance so we could find a long-range way to command them."

"It is my understanding you had to be standing almost next to them to activate the nanos for tracking," he replies.

"Yes sir, and we still have the same issue."

"I can't see giving any more money to this project. Right now, we have a bunch of bad guys walking around with a few million dollars of useless robots inside them."

"Sir, communication technology is expanding daily, and we are just a tweak away from connecting with the robots from a great distance."

"How much time, doctor?" the general rails.

"I don't know, another year."

"You have one year to show me results, and that is it for funding. I can blow other things up for that money. Are we clear?"

"Yes, General."

The duo quickly leave the office before the general has a change of heart.

JR

After finishing their earlier meeting with Simon and then working on some things in the office assigned to the FBI, Parker Steele and Aldis Montgomery split up as they depart the JPL building. Steele wants to find out more on Simon's movements, being more a detective than a geek. He can leave the geek stuff to Montgomery.

Meanwhile, Montgomery goes to the local FBI office and goes straight to his assigned cave. It has a bank of computers with flat-panel monitors. He opens his laptop and connects it to the mainframe. It states, "Reading file." Recognizing that this will involve some time, he leans back in his chair and loosens his necktie. He thinks about Simon and how honored he was to meet the man responsible for the Mars missions. It perplexes him that he could be the one to send a hero to prison. He will be extra careful so as not to miss anything in the code.

The computer screen eventually reads, "File uploaded." Montgomery assumes his standard work position, which he is sure causes his back pain, and he peers closely at the screen. "Now, Mama," he says, "what can big Bertha do with this program?" Bertha is the name given to the FBI mainframe. If there is any malicious stuff in the code, Bertha will expose it. He types his code to scan the Reliance program, and the procedure starts. The screen turns powder blue, with thousands of tiny squares. As the program scans the software, each square will become a green color, signaling no malicious code has been found. If it finds foreign code, the square will turn red and highlight the hacked code.

On startup, any hackers are always quickly discovered. As it continues, nothing negative shows up. Bertha is more powerful and faster than his computer, and the green squares multiply quickly. Montgomery slips from his office for a refreshment as Bertha runs. On the way, he passes Steele's office and notices he is back from the couple of stops he was going to make, now looking over some report files. Steele sees him and signals him in.

"Did you get to look at the program?"

"Yes. I gave it to Bertha, who is crunching it now."

"Good." Looking up at Montgomery, he asks, "Aldis, what is your take on Dr. Northstrum from the short time you were with him?"

"He is likable."

"In your mind, is he honest?"

"Yeah, I'm told he is. And to me, I think he appears to be."

"Does he have the computer knowledge to pull it off?"

"You mean email everyone on the planet and not leave a trail?"

"That's what I mean."

"No. I know of no one that good," says Montgomery.

"So he is innocent?"

"I can't say yet. Reliance is the only new software on the JPL computers though."

"Is his software good?"

"Yes, excellent. Top-notch for the purpose of communicating with space vehicles. He's a genius in that respect."

"I don't know, Aldis. I'm an old-school cop, and something isn't kosher here, and I plan to get to the truth. I'm keeping an eye on the good doctor. It sure can't hurt."

Montgomery leaves Steele's office and hits the vending machines. Returning to his computer screen, he finds it is now full of green squares. However, the green squares have red squares within them. As Montgomery gets closer to the computer, he drops his beverage. On the screen in red letters is the message, "Thank you for access. We are the Dominion, and we sent our message."

Below the statement is the same message that was sent to all email accounts. Montgomery slumps into his chair, realizing that Bertha connects to the most sensitive computer areas on the planet. He scratches his head, wondering if Simon duped him into running Reliance to gain access to the FBI mainframe. Montgomery races to Steele's office, almost sliding past the doorway.

Out of breath, he yells, "Come see this on Bertha!" He signals Steele to follow him. Steele jumps from his chair to catch up to the streaking Montgomery. Montgomery halts him at the entrance to his office and says, "Before you see this, I want to explain the progression of events. You saw me copy the Reliance file to my computer at JPL. It was on my laptop. I copied it to Bertha as I would any other suspect program."

"Yes, I saw you."

"I coded Bertha to analyze Reliance. The software was running as usual with no errors."

"You mean with the little green squares that signify clean?"

"Yes," Montgomery replies.

"Okay, I follow," Steele says. "Was there any instance of improper code?"

"No, not any improper code."

"Why am I here, and why did you take off like a rocket?"

Montgomery turns into his office, and Steele follows.

"Look what appeared on the screen after Bertha finished the scan. Look, Parker!" Montgomery says, almost yelling.

Steele squints at the screen. "Oh, crap! It's the same message everyone got!" Looking up at Montgomery, he says, "You did this? You sent more messages? Where did they go?"

"No! I mean, I don't think I did! The protocols were the same on Bertha as I have used on a thousand other files," Montgomery explains.

"What is the Dominion?" Steele asks. "Are they a terrorist group? I never heard of them. The doctor knows more than he is letting on to us."

"Parker," Montgomery says, "how could he know we would take the program to our FBI office and put it on Bertha?"

"Good point," Steele concedes.

"Right. He wouldn't have known about our central computer. He doesn't have the clearance, and Bertha did not exist before Simon's rehire."

"I guess everyone in government may get an email, if it's like the corporate intrusion."

"Well, Parker, there goes our retirement."

Steele replies, "We will watch this Northstrum. He is the problem and is connected to a larger group. They might try to get in everywhere, and then wreak havoc. Can that be done, Aldis?"

"Yes. Once you are in, you're in until they patch the hole. But Parker, we didn't have a hole. We asked it in, or opened the door ourselves."

"Crap. What about other computers connected to Bertha?"

"She is on open access."

"Double crap. This Simon guy is getting under my skin. I will skin him alive."

"Parker, we need to isolate the Reliance program."

"Good idea, Aldis. Get it off the computer and hide it away."

"Sure. Parker, I still don't think Simon is the culprit. This is way past him."

"My cop radar says different. I will find out how often he brushes his teeth, what his family and their friends do, and the heck with a constitution." He pauses. "I hope the messages will be dead ends."

"Those messages to Apple were not dead-ended. And Apple is the king of protection."

"I suppose," Steele says. "So how do we protect ourselves, and do we now have the same problem as Northstrum?"

"You mean proving we didn't cause it?"

"That's exactly what I mean. Northstrum is the key. We have a paper trail, and I'm sure it will get back to him. His Reliance is the villain. I know it in my soul."

※

Maggie is in the schoolroom set up for Swaddling Clothes when Emma and Jennifer arrive. "Hello, girls, did you have a good day at school?"

Jennifer gives her usual scowling response. "It was boring," she says, with a roll of her eyes.

"It was good, Ms. Maggie," says Emma."

"You can call me Maggie, Emma. Today I have put out your outfits for you to wear." The girls tear to the closet to see whether it is something terrific. The outfits are folded on a chair for each girl.

Jennifer asks, "What is this, Maggie? These are ordinary jeans, and the shirt looks like I'm going to a rodeo." Jennifer is not pleased. Emma looks on dismayed. These are not the outfits she was dreaming about, but she will not let Maggie know it.

Maggie says, "We will get dirty today. I will drive us to the location."

Emma says to Jennifer, "Maybe it is a photo shoot for rugged clothes for hiking and such."

Maggie smiles, liking that Emma seemingly always looks on the bright side. She is happy with her selection of the two girls. In time, she will teach Jennifer much. "Go change," Maggie says, "but be sure to bring your school clothes with you. I will be taking you home when we finish."

"Where are we going?" Emma asks.

Maggie says, "It's a surprise." She then leaves the girls to change.

As soon as Maggie is out of sight, Jennifer starts complaining. "I can't let anyone see me in this. I'll look like a loser."

"Jennifer, they are just jeans."

"But," Jennifer replies, "if I don't have the right label, people will think I shop at Goodwill."

Emma tells her, "I've bought designer jeans at a thrift store. Why pay eighty-five to a hundred twenty-five dollars or more when you can get good clothes for eight bucks?"

"My daddy would not let such things in the house, because we might catch something."

"That is just stupid, Jennifer. It would surprise you how many students shop the thrifts. It's fun, and you can use your own money you worked for to pay."

"My daddy pays for everything. I guess things are tight at the Northstrum house."

"Shut up, Jennifer. Put no one down until you have done something of substance yourself. Your only claim of accomplishment is that you're pretty and your daddy is mayor. You had nothing to do with it and have done nothing of substance that would allow you to belittle others."

"Jeez, Emma, don't get your panties in a knot."

"I'm just sick of hearing about your daddy."

Maggie listens from the other room. Emma has a backbone, and taking Jennifer away from the Bittlets has exposed her weakness. Maggie then shouts, "Are you ready, girls?" The girls enter. Emma smiles, while Jennifer pouts. "Good. You both look nice." They get into the car, and after a short drive, they arrive at their destination. While Maggie is parking the car, Emma reads the sign for the Four Paws Rescue.

"Are we doing a photo shoot at a dog pound?" asks Jennifer.

"Follow me, girls," Maggie responds. "Today, as interns, you will do service work here."

"What does that mean?" Jennifer asks.

"You will help at this center for a while. Remember: when we met, we said we were looking for interns who can show charity."

"If we don't do this, are we out of the program?" Jennifer asks.

"Yes," Maggie replies.

Jennifer moans, "I'm captive here."

"You could call your daddy," Emma remarks, "or you could get with the program. I bet neat animals are inside."

"I'm not happy, but I have no choice," Jennifer says.

"Sure you have a choice, Jennifer," Maggie tells her. "You can quit. You can call for a ride at any time."

She shakes her head and says, "No, I'll do it."

The trio enter the building and meet the director, Jaimee Mouradian.

"Hi, Jaimee," Maggie says. "These are my two interns to help here today." Jaimee extends her hand, shaking the girls' hands as Maggie introduces them by name.

"So great to see you," she says. "We can always use help here. Today I need someone to clean out the pens of any messes the guests have made in their homes."

"I have to clean up poop?" Jennifer asks.

"Yes, part of the daily chores," Jaimee tells her. "We must be sure they have food and water. After that, we try to give them personal attention. Many have not known human kindness. There is a large area in the back where we take them outside to run as a pack. In the dog world, grass is good."

"Are the dogs dangerous?" asks Emma."

"They can get testy, but most are timid from poor treatment or isolation."

Maggie says, "Girls, I'm leaving and will be back in a few hours to get you home. Listen to Jaimee and help her out."

The girls follow Jaimee and disappear through the double doors as Maggie leaves.

"Emma, Jennifer, the first step is to clean. Here are scoops and pails." The narrow hall has kennels on each side and a few black noses pressed through the chain-link barriers. "You can go into the kennels and put the waste into the pail. If they've peed, there is a hose every few feet to wash it into the drain. Use this spray to flush out the floor. You can switch the tenant to another cage while you work."

Emma jumps right in and enters the first cage. A small terrier with a tail wagging with excitement is in there. She bends and scratches the dog's head. Emma smiles and thinks, *I'm never getting out of here without taking one of them home. But dad would kill me, with his allergies."* Emma works as the dog becomes her shadow.

Jennifer enters her cage with apprehension. She clutches her scoop as if it contains the black death. Her dog is old and barely lifts its head to notice her. She breathes a sigh of relief. She hopes they all are the same. When the first cage is behind her, she realizes it isn't so awful.

Eventually both girls finish the cage duty. Emma is looking forward to seeing the dogs playing in the yard. The girls get the dogs from the pens, and they bolt for the outside. Jaimee says, "They enjoy their runs each day." The girls follow them to the courtyard, where their dogs are doing dog things. It surprises Jennifer there is no big dogfight, but they are playing.

"Did the tan, black, and white dog come out?" Jaimee asks.

"No, I didn't see him," Emma tells her, "but I can find him."

Jaimee says, "I'll go with you. He has been growling. I might have to handle him."

They arrive at the dog's pen and find the dog curled up with his eyes closed. Jaimee enters the pen, and the dog lifts his head and stares. His lips curl, and Jaimee backs away. Emma is behind her and steps forward to see the dog. She looks at him, realizing that this is her dream dog—the one she has always wanted. He is a beautiful dog but has been mistreated. Emma steps farther into the pen, and the dog's lips relax.

"I bet he wants someone to be kind to him. Can I try, Jaimee?"

"I don't want him to bite you."

Emma inches toward the animal. The dog becomes restless, realizing it has no escape route. Emma uses a calming voice to soothe the dog. "You're okay. You're okay," she repeats while pressing forward. The dog has no reaction as Emma reaches him. She gently massages his ears, and the dog presses his head into the massage. Emma smiles and says, "He likes me."

Jaimee replies, "That is amazing. We have had three people try to work with him, and all failed." Emma sits on the pen floor, and the dog slides forward, coming to a rest on Emma's lap. "You found your calling," Jaimee says.

Emma beams. She leans down and whispers, "You need cuddling and a good home. I wish I could take you with me." She draws the dog's head to her face and is rewarded with a huge lick. He rolls over in surrender as Emma rubs his belly. Emma smiles up at Jaimee and says, "He might want to go outside now."

Jaimee hands her a leash. Emma slides the lead around the dog's neck, and the dog jumps to attention. He darts past Jaimee, pulling Emma to the yard. Jaimee stands in the hallway, amazed at how a caring touch can save a creature from certain death.

Emma and the dog enter the courtyard, with Jennifer as far away from the beasts as possible. The dog and Emma are running, and he is jumping by her side. She pulls him to stop him and takes the lead off his neck. He shakes his head back and forth, looking at the pack of dogs and then back at Emma. She assures him it is okay to join them. He darts for the pack and plays.

Jaimee comes up behind her and says, "You saved his life today."

Emma glows. "I wish I could take him with me, but my dad is allergic."

"Too bad. He seems nice now."

"I have always dreamed of the perfect dog."

"What would you name him?"

"He's a Rudy."

"That's a good name, Emma." Jennifer has joined them by now, so Jaimee turns to her and asks, "What do you think, Jennifer?"

"He is dangerous and might bite someone."

Jaimee and Emma exchange "should have known" glances.

The three chat while waiting for Maggie to return. The door opens soon, and Maggie enters. "How did the day go, girls?" She asks. Emma pipes up, telling of how much she enjoyed it and saying that animals are lonesome and need good homes. Maggie turns toward Jennifer and asks, "What do you think, Jennifer?"

With a disgusted look, Jennifer says, "I've never cleaned up like that before. It was disgusting. Why are there so many dogs? Don't they eat dogs in other parts of the world?"

"Yes," Maggie tells her. "I suppose they do. There are many dogs because people become irresponsible. They buy a cute puppy and forget that puppies grow up. They tire of it and either let it loose or drop it off here. Every act started around the world has an effect throughout the world in ways we can't imagine. When you throw a stone into a pond, it may rest at the bottom, but the ripple it leaves continues to distant shores. Your life is the same with the people and things you touch each day. Do you want your life to make a positive or negative wake?"

"I don't know," Jennifer replies, "but can I ask you a question, Maggie?"

"Sure."

"What does this have to do with clothes?"

"Everything—and nothing. Jennifer, today was a test to gauge whether you can be selfless. Didn't Jesus say, 'Whatever you do to the least of my children you do unto me?' We wanted to find out how you would respond to a menial task. No one likes doing poop patrol and giving affection to a lost creature. If you can do it for dogs, then you might make it as a selfless human."

"Am I out of the program?"

"No, but you have much to learn."

Emma asks, "Will there be more tests?"

"Yes. We want people who act from their souls. Before we leave, I want each to pick a dog to work with—one with whom you may have formed a bond. Jennifer, do you have one?"

"No."

"And you, Emma?"

"Oh yes. Rudy."

"Oh my, you have already named one?" Maggie asks, and then she glances at Jaimee.

Jaimee says, "Emma resurrected one that I thought for sure would have to be put down."

Maggie smiles and then turns toward Jennifer and asks, "Jennifer, do you need to look again?"

"I guess," she replies. She goes into the hall and quickly returns. "The little black one on the right."

Maggie frowns, knowing she selected the first one she saw, with no true bond. "Okay," Maggie tells her. The three of them leave the shelter.

⚡

Simon enters the kitchen and family room area, where the news is playing on the television. A pot rests on the stove top with a stream of steam floating over the pot. Simon lifts the top and breathes in the aroma. He stands, remembering he is famished.

Alexis enters the kitchen and says, "I didn't hear you come in."

"Sorry. I didn't announce, but this smelled so amazing I had to sniff."

"Oh, it's something from a recipe I printed from online."

Simon closes the distance between them, kisses her, and asks, "How was your day?"

"Okay. I've got news."

"Really?" Simon responds. "I've got news too."

"Simon, go change and I'll get this ready."

"Can I help?" he asks.

"No, I've got it."

"Hurry then, because I'm starving."

Simon rushes out of the kitchen. The news plays as Alexis sets the table. In the background, voices come from a press conference in progress. A reporter asks, "Mr. Secretary, what about these email breaches around the world?"

"We have our best people looking at the problem," he responds.

"Do we have any idea how it was done? Most of the cyber-connected population got an email."

"Yes, that is true. However, we have not found any wrongdoing from the companies reporting to us. We are looking at suspects, but I can't divulge it in this ongoing investigation."

Simon reenters the kitchen with the food steaming on his plate. "Where's Emma?" he asks.

"She's eating with Sophia tonight—probably gulping things down, because they're studying together for a big test tomorrow."

"Got it," Simon responds. He picks up the remote and turns off the television. "Can we not listen to this during dinner?" he says as they both sit down at the table.

"Sure," Alexis replies. "It was a press conference about those email messages."

"What did they say?"

"Nothing new. As we all know by now, everybody got one."

"Well, I didn't tell you earlier, too worn out. But yesterday I spent most of the day with the FBI."

"Oh, my. Why?"

"That can wait," Simon tells her. "Let's pray and eat." After the prayer, as they begin eating, Simon asks Alexis about her news.

"Well, I'm proud of myself," she says, sitting taller in her chair. "I got a new job today at work—and a raise."

"Oh? That is good news. Tell me about it." He then quickly inserts "This dish is delicious, by the way."

"Thank you," Alexis replies. "I thought you would like it."

"Now, what about your news?"

"Adam came into my office today and told me to take over his job of calling hospitals and other facilities for pickup."

"You mean that you chase dead people?" Simon snickers.

Alexis swats at him. "Yes, I chase dead people, but I got a raise and am now on salary."

"Super, honey. You will do well."

"Thank you. I called a few clients, and they said Adam shouldn't work with the living."

"Funny," says Simon.

"Adam wants me to keep the census full."

"Is the funeral home having a problem?"

"Yeah, the traffic is down."

"Are the stiffs going elsewhere?"

"No. I spoke to the BRET directors at a few places, and they said they had no one die."

"Is that unusual?"

"Probably not if it is only for a few days, or maybe a week."

"Are they telling you the truth, or have they gone elsewhere and just don't want to hurt your feelings?"

"No, these places said they had no reason to change homes, and we were good, despite Adam's manner. What do you think I should do?"

"Well," Simon tells her, "I suppose you have two options: you can take the directors to lunch and schmooze them, or you can kill more people."

She swats at him again.

"Sorry," he says, "I couldn't resist. Seriously, it is probably just a slow cycle and will rebound."

"I hope so, Simon. What is your news?"

"Not good. Remember how the companies reported the emails going to everybody originated at JPL?"

"Yes."

"Well, the FBI came calling at JPL. They interviewed people based on dates hired and skill sets."

"Let me guess—you were first?"

"No, and it surprised me that so many came before me. The line for interviews was rather lengthy. But they did get around to me pretty soon. They actually told me they rushed through the others to get to me."

"That doesn't sound good. Did it last long? Did they play good cop, bad cop?"

"No, no good cop, bad cop stuff. But two inspectors were with me quite a while. One was a pretty tough veteran agent; the other was a younger computer forensics guy."

"And ...?"

"Inspector Steele—that's the veteran agent's name—is a ballbuster. I told him everything, held nothing back, but he suspects everyone. I think he wants a villain to hang this on and close the case. He is an old-school cop, and it looks good for his department. The computer forensics guy—Montgomery is his name—was more amenable. As a computer person like me, he told me he thought Reliance is brilliant."

"They are already looking at your program?" asks Alexis.

"Yes, it was the only software added to JPL and updated recently."

"Simon, did it do the weird talking?"

"No, thank God."

"Did you tell them about the voice and *Sojourner*?"

"No, Alexis. I'd be in a straitjacket if I mentioned a voice from above."

"Norm said nothing?"

"No. And the problem is not with Reliance. They ran it on a dumb terminal with no problems."

"It said nothing about sending messages?"

"No. The computer guy is going through the code for hacking code within Reliance."

"Do they want you to help?"

"I did for a while, but I am more of a hindrance, since I have no idea what to look for in the code. I think that is helping me, because if I don't know what to look for, then it's obvious I didn't put it in to start with."

He puts down his fork and places both hands on the table. "Alexis, something happened on the car ride home," he states. "I got in the car and needed to listen to calming music, so I started my playlist and headed for home." He pauses. "Alexis, *Sojourner* talked through the radio."

"No way," she remarks.

"Am I going crazy? I can see playing a prank with the computers, but my radio is not possible. Alexis, it knew about my interview with the FBI."

"How could it?"

"Clueless here. It told me more messages went out that will lead back to me. It said the Dominion will send people home."

"What do you mean 'send home'?" she asks.

"Die. The Dominion will kill people not following their true path."

"What is a path?" she asks.

"*Sojourner* said we created a story of our lives with the Dominion before conception. Death to the Dominion is a happy time. It likened it to parents sending their kids to camp and then being happy on their return."

"So life is like going to camp?"

"I guess—Camp Human Existence. The Dominion are here to judge everyone, and I must make the world listen."

"To what—your soul and the path you chose for it?" she asks.

"*Sojourner* said this is happening because of people's prayers requesting it."

"You mean someone prayed for people to die?"

"*Sojourner* said this has happened before, with Noah and Sodom and Gomorrah"

"Wait. Wasn't that God?"

"So the Bible says. *Sojourner* said those reclaimed will surprise me."

"Are the Dominion God? Didn't God say He has dominion over man?"

"Well. Now that you mention it, yes. Yes, God did say that," Simon responds. He pauses before saying, "Alexis, if I throw God into the mix, they will really—I mean *really*—call me crazy!"

"Simon, it is interesting you talk of praying. Remember when you came home the other day and told me about getting back with JPL."

"Yes?"

"Before you got home, I was saying my novena."

"Okay, yeah, your continuous novenas."

"After the novena, I asked God to help Mrs. Ficocelli because she was sad. Then I commented about why the good die young and the creeps go on forever, adding that it would be nice if you could reverse that and take the creeps early."

"You're saying that God has answered your prayer."

"It sounds like it."

"Then why isn't the Dominion talking to you?"

"I don't know. Simon, have you prayed for anything?"

"Well, I got mad at God and said, in so many words, "If you will not help, get lost."

"Ouch! You made a deal with God? Don't you realize God needs nothing from us except faith that we are part of Him?"

"Yeah, I know. I was ticked off for not getting the SassyApps job and went off on God."

"Simon, do you think He is helping you?"

"Now we are both crazy."

"Do you believe God is the Dominion, Simon?"

"I don't know, Alexis. I just don't know what I believe about all this."

"I know you have doubts in God, but didn't the voice say your faith will save you?

"Yes. Yes it did."

"Simon, this is crazy and weird, but it is happening, so let's assume it is God, or Dominion, or aliens, or whatever force you want to call it."

"Alexis, what am I supposed to do?"

"I guess we wait and see what the next messages will be like. So far the messages have been nice, wanting people to care for each other." She pauses and then asks, "How do you get people to listen?"

"No clue, honey. Maybe remind them of the goodness of the messages if they continue."

"Simon, I must ask. Do you think the government may have another communication software to wrench control of *Sojourner* and the rovers from JPL? You were gone for long enough for them to take over."

"I thought of that at first, but Norm has his finger on the pulse of JPL, and he would have caught them."

"Simon, this is something a dictator would do—create a nonexistent problem and then have the solution for it ready when people demand it. Then we give away our privacy and liberty. They bring the world to the brink of disaster to gain more power and control over people. If people feel powerless, they run for cover."

"I've said, Alexis, that interconnectivity will bite us in the butt one day."

"I think it has already started. Simon, is our family in trouble?"

I don't know. All the FBI can do is come after me."

"Are you going to follow *Sojourner*'s directions?"

"I don't have a choice. I must figure out what to do. Obviously they don't want an ark built."

"Maybe you can write a program to get the word out about people's souls."

"I believe the government would throw me in a hole and throw away the key if I were to touch or spread any software. It would have to be done from an existing program or application, like a blog. I still can't fathom why they selected a guy straining to have faith."

"Honey, Paul was a sinner, and you have faith and I believe in you, and so does a little robot on Mars."

"I guess I need a plan if I'm to save the world."

"A plan would be a good start."

CHAPTER 12

"Good morning, everyone. Welcome to *America's Newsroom*. I'm Bill Hemmer. Hello, Martha."

"Hi, Bill. Good morning, everyone, I'm Martha MacCallum. There is a Fox News alert. You remember me reporting on the hack of commercial communications accounts, such as email and Twitter. Everyone got the biblical email. Now a second has penetrated every government computer. The email is the same as the one sent to corporate accounts, except for the last line. What came from the Bible is, and I quote, 'And thou shalt love the Lord thy God with all thy heart, and with all thy soul, and with all thy mind, and with all thy strength: this is the first commandment. And the second is, Thou shalt love thy neighbor AS THYSELF. There is none other commandment greater than these. (Mark 12:30–31 KJV).' The excerpt from the Koran is as follows: 'Whoever works righteousness, man or woman, and has faith, verily, to them will we give a new life, a life that is good and pure, and we will bestow on such their reward according to the best of their actions.' Then comes the name Hippolyte Pixii/Dynamo 1801. Information is coming in. It cuts through every firewall and security.

"We have Colonel Allen Parker, a cybersecurity expert, with us this morning. Good morning, Colonel. Thanks for coming in on short notice."

"Good to be here, Martha."

"How bad is it?"

"Martha, I'm getting information from my people in the know, and it looks to be invasive."

"Who is the Dominion?"

"We are unfamiliar with this hacking group."

"I am sure the government is looking at all groups similar to Anonymous."

"Martha, this seems to be past an individual's skill or equipment level."

"Are we in danger, Colonel?"

"Whoever has done this, Martha, has broken into government systems worldwide. It hasn't been restricted to just the USA or North America."

"Do you believe it was the same people that got into the commercial accounts a few days ago, Colonel? How deep is the 'invasive' you mentioned?"

"It is being analyzed, but it goes to the core, as it did with the commercial accounts. The Dominion might have used the commercial hack as a diversion from this one."

"Does that mean they could shut down our defense systems?"

"Well, there's a possibility, if they can move in and out at will and we can't close the hole."

"This is not good, Colonel. Can they launch a nuclear missile?"

"Again, probably. But we are still investigating things as best we can. But they could probably start the process, I suspect. However, we have human intervention safeguards in place."

"I'm sure that knowing about the safeguards comforts people."

"Yes, Martha. And those safeguards may exist only in our country and systems. Who knows what other countries have in place."

"Do you think a foreign government is behind this hacking?"

"Martha, my people are telling me the major powers like the US, China, and Russia have been hit. This Dominion did not discriminate."

"That has not come across the wire. What will this do for international relations?"

"Martha, the old-timers remember the Cuban missile crisis. If we don't keep cool heads and refrain from accusing people without evidence, we may have a similar situation. This time the events and reactions will escalate due to the speed of communications today."

"Colonel, we hear over the wire they raised the DEFCON level to four. What does that mean?"

"It prescribes five graduated levels of readiness for the US military, with a range in severity from DEFCON 5, which is least severe, to DEFCON 1, most severe, to match varying military situations. It means we have alerted our military to be more responsive in reaction to the threat. I'm not too concerned, because it is raised frequently based on known or suspected threats."

"Do Americans need to worry?"

"Martha, the top minds are on this, and they will find an answer. But I won't lie to you or play politician; the world is in grave danger and at a trigger point."

"Another thing, Colonel, before we go to break. What do you make of the last line? Firs, it was Fleming, now a man named Pixii. We know Fleming and penicillin, along with Pixii inventing the dynamo based on Faraday's research in the 1820s. But like the previous text, they are way off on the date. It was 1832, not 1801. It seems the hackers got both the dates wrong. The dynamo is the basis for the electric motor; do you think it odd they mention a name so linked to electricity? It runs our world and communications. Are they trying to cut out the power and send us back to the dark ages? If they are pushing us in that direction, you'd better own a horse so you can hook your worthless SUV to it."

"I don't know, Martha, but I am sure our research teams are looking at every bit of the email, back and front, each line and word, for any clues."

"Thank you, Colonel. We would like to have you back when more is learned about this."

"I'll be glad to come in and answer any questions, Martha."

"Folks, we will be right back after this break."

Simon hangs his head in despair after listening to the recent events from the news. His favorite show is now the forecaster of his doom. At least he will know in advance if the FBI decides to charge him with espionage.

Alexis makes her way into the kitchen and sees the look on her husband's face. "Is something wrong?" she asks.

"You remember the email that went out to personal and corporate accounts?"

"Yes, we talked about it. Everyone got one. It was a nice message."

"Well, now worldwide government computers received the same email."

Alexis slides into a chair. "Are you in trouble?" she asks.

"I'm afraid to go to work."

"If you were in that much trouble … they know where we live."

"Alexis, I've got a rover talking from Mars in my car. It is telling me to make the world listen to their souls. People listen more to celebrities and athletes than they will to me. They shouldn't speak unless someone else has written it or their brain has clicked into gear. Most of them want their names in the headlines."

"You mean there is no such thing as bad press?"

"Right."

⚙

Simon is at his station at JPL. He is hesitant to be anywhere near a computer, but he must keep his job. He begins the protocols to connect to the rover and then leaves the office, making his way to the coffee. In the hall, on his way back to his office, Earlman corners him and says, "Do we have any newer things from the rovers?"

"No, Tom. Sometimes the information is not exhilarating. It can be borderline boring. The microscience stuff is only exciting to the scientist. I can photoshop Marvin the Martian on the next image releases, but we don't need another *War of the Worlds* incident. It will go viral and draw interest."

Tom laughs. "Simon, it is good to see a geek with a sense of humor. On a more somber note. I suppose you heard this Dominion has cracked government systems worldwide."

196

"Yes, I heard on the news. Before you say anything, I had nothing to do with it. I'm under a microscope now."

"I understand. They hit us, but again no harm was done. This message was the same except the last part. If you can hack into every computer on the planet and only send a biblical email it seems pointless. They must be after something else far more sinister. Criminals want to get away with something for a payday"

"Are they coming after me on this one, too?" Simon queries.

"I don't know. Everyone on the planet has sent us hate mail, but we can't find any record of anything being sent from here."

"Really?"

"Yes, the Pentagon has taken over the investigation. General Bosman is leading it. They will probably be talking to you again. This will go way above the FBI. Countries are enraged. I wanted to warn you. But my question is, if they don't get away with anything, then what is their end game?"

"Sometimes hackers do it just because they can."

"I'm cynical. This is a setup for a bigger event. Bosman believes they may try to take down the financial systems, or worse."

"Let me know if I can be of help." Simon leaves and returns to his office, sits down, sips his coffee, and exhales. "This can't get any worse," he grumbles.

He surveys the computer screen for any concerns from the rover. The screen assures him the rovers are functioning within normal limits. He pulls a report from a side table and then is startled from his concentration by a voice saying, "Good morning, Simon. Yes, it will get worse. Prepare yourself." The voice then utters a quiet giggle.

Simon pushes a button to speak.

"There is no need for that, Simon. I can hear you."

"Is this *Sojourner*?"

"Yes."

"I still don't understand. You can't talk."

"The Dominion speaks through me. They are here now. You know them by the messages sent."

"You did that?"

"No, the Dominion did."

"Why did they do it?

"They want to get everyone's attention."

"Well," Simon says, "Some believe what they read."

"Did the messages turn people's heads?" *Sojourner* asks.

"No, not many, I would say. People are accustomed to getting emails, especially spam. Most will ignore it."

"The emails did not flow to any spam or junk folders," *Sojourner* says, again with a giggle. "Pretty cool, huh, Simon. The Dominion want humans to fear the security of connected gadgets. You will be the leader to bring them out of that fear. The Dominion could send a big asteroid hurtling to Earth, rip away your atmosphere, or dry up your water."

"They can do that to this world?"

"Yes, Simon. The Dominion want to see whether everyone is listening. Humans seem to be at their best when things are at their worst. A natural catastrophe is a good way to get people moving in the right direction and less concerned with self. The Dominion will bring a great upheaval."

"No, I don't recommend hurting people if that is what they want to do," Simon implores.

"They want people to pay close attention to their souls and the journeys they chose at birth. Simon, the Dominion have control over life and death. They want you to get the world listening. One of your mechanics once said, 'You can listen as well as you hear.' Get them listening."

"How do I do that? I'm one man."

"So was Noah."

"I might be in hot water here at JPL."

"Noah was in hot water in his time … Pardon the pun. The Dominion has high hopes for you. Your Reliance program will bring you great turmoil, but you can overcome it. Your faith will sustain you."

"Faith? I've prayed, and nothing good has ever happened, except for a job that soon may disappear."

"Maybe it already has happened."

"What, that I'm supposed to save the world from these beings that want to kill everyone? Everyone will call me crazy if I talk about aliens here on Earth. Is that what they expect?"

"Everyone thought Noah was crazy to build a large boat in the middle of nowhere."

"Am I in danger?"

"The world is in danger, Simon, and you have the key."

"So I must convince the world to listen to their souls and find the inner journeys they were meant to live."

"That's right. Simon, in its time of danger, you must convince the world to not be afraid. They mention it many times in your Bible. The emails have set the plan into action by creating mistrust. In the coming weeks, man will suspect man, accuse man, and possibly go to war. Men will try to assert power and domination over other humans. It is their nature, out of fear."

"The Dominion are setting up humanity?"

"Yes, Simon. But you can guide people to safety."

"How?"

"The messages have said it all."

"Have the messages stopped?"

"No, it is the beginning, and it will get more intrusive. Nations will blame nations and bring the world to a brink."

"Brink of what?"

"Annihilation. But Simon, you can stop it. You can change the ending."

"But—"

"Good Luck, Simon," *Sojourner* interrupts. "We will talk again, and I will try to explain more to you as the days pass and the walls are caving in on you. Remember: your faith will sustain you."

"Wait, *Sojourner*. I have more questions!"

The voice goes silent as Norm enters the office.

"You talking to yourself now, Simon?"

"Sometimes I have the best conversations with myself."

"Who wins?" asks Norm.

"Most are draws."

"Well, Simon, I wanted to tell you we are not out of the woods on the email issue. I am sure they will be back in here. You're positive that Reliance didn't cause the breach?"

"Norm, Reliance did not cause it. If it did, I would tell everyone, apologize, and quit. The program cannot do what has been happening. It hasn't been programmed with that capacity."

"I wanted to be one hundred percent sure, just to get everything straight. I know they will speak with us again."

Lennon and Emma stand in front of the shop where Lennon is working. "How did you get the job?" Emma asks.

"I was walking down the street, looking at the shops for work, and Mr. Deuss tapped me on the shoulder. He said he had a meeting and his friend might have work for me. So now I'm painting and cleaning, but it pays more than flipping burgers. It was an old recording studio when our parents were young."

They enter the still messy office. "I clean the building after school. Mr. Magee comes in and pays me in cash." Lennon smiles. "He is nice. He paid me extra. I might get a new guitar." Emma looks at the sound board. "Isn't it cool, Emma?"

"Is it from a spaceship?"

"No, it's a sound board used to make records. The wall over there had pictures of famous rock stars who recorded here hung everywhere. Do you want to see something cool?"

"Sure."

Lennon scurries to a box near the sound board. "Look at this, Emma."

She grabs the picture frame from Lennon.

"The Beatles recorded here?" she asks.

"I don't know. Look closer."

She looks and then says, "I thought there were only four Beatles?"

"Yep, but look at each one." He points out John, Paul, George, and Ringo.

"Who is the fifth guy?," she asks.

"Study him. It's weird," says Lennon.

Emma studies. After a time, it hits her, and her eyes squint into a stare. "Oh my, is that Mr. Deuss?"

"Yes, Mr. Magee said Mr. Deuss designed their fashions, their looks, back then. I guess Mr. Deuss wasn't kidding when he said he helped the major fashion people. Emma, he really knows Paul McCartney."

"What are they going to do with this place?" she asks.

"I don't know. I guess they will rent it out."

"What is behind the curtain?"

"It is where the musicians played when they were making music. It would be a dream come true if they put a studio back in here. I bet the wiring is still in the walls. Changing the subject, I understand you got new clothes from Swaddling yesterday."

"Yes, it was strange. They sent us to an animal shelter."

"The pound? What does that have to do with clothes?"

"Nothing. I think they are still testing our character," she remarks.

"The guys have done nothing yet. I should be on my best behavior."

"You need not worry. Just be yourself."

"I'll hide my bad-boy rebel side." Emma punches Lennon on the shoulder and draws from him an "Ouch!"

"Yeah, you're a real bad boy. When you have your first outing with them, be careful, because they are testing you and Greg."

"How did Jennifer do?"

"She acted her usual prissy self, as if everything was below her level, but she did it."

"She picked up poop?" Lennon laughs.

"Not without complaining," Emma says with a smirk. "I want to see how Greg does. Lennon, be careful of him. He will make it a competition."

"I will."

Jozy Magee appears in the doorway. "Hi, Lennon. I'm glad I caught you here. Hello, young lady," says Jozy to Emma.

"Hi," Emma responds.

"Mr. Magee, this is my friend Emma. She wanted to see where I was working."

"No problem. The room is not much to see now, but Lennon is getting it shipshape, bit by bit. You haven't started yet for today?"

"No sir. I only arrived shortly before you."

"Good. I have an interested tenant who may want it as is, so I want to put you on hold for a few days."

Lennon frowns. "Okay, Mr. Magee. When will you need me again?"

"Let's get past the weekend."

Lennon is sad because he was putting money away for his new guitar. In the back of his mind, he wonders whether anything will ever work out the way he wants it to.

"Emma, I suppose we can go," Lennon says.

"Thank you, Lennon, and nice to meet you, Emma," says Jozy.

Both head toward the door and almost exit, but then Jozy yells to Lennon, "Hey, Lennon! Aren't you forgetting something?"

They turn at his voice. Lennon says, "I don't think so."

"Don't you want to get paid?"

"Paid?" Lennon remarks. "I didn't do any work today."

Mr. Magee reaches out his hand, which is holding two one-hundred-dollar bills. "Lennon, I'm an old-fashioned guy, and we sealed our agreement with a handshake. I changed the deal without consulting you, so I am paying you for the days you are on hold. I've nothing smaller, and it will work out right."

Lennon reaches for the bills, and a large grin stretches across his face when he sees the denominations. "Are you sure, sir?"

"Yes—on one condition, Lennon."

"Yes sir."

"You take Emma for a burger and milkshake on the way home."

Lennon smiles at Emma, and she nods her head in approval. "Thank you, Mr. Magee," she says.

"One other thing, Lennon."

"Yes?"

"Remember: my friends call me Jozy."

"Okay, sir. I mean, Jozy."

Lennon and Emma exit the store, with Lennon telling her he has two hundred dollars.

"Are you getting close to a new guitar?" she asks.

"Yes, it depends. I can buy a cheap guitar, which is better than the one falling apart. I want a Rickenbacker 325, but they cost a few thousand—even more if it is from the '60s."

"Isn't that the picture in your room at home?"

"Yeah, but it's a dream."

"Lennon," Emma says with a smile, "dreams come true. You'll get it if you keep at it." They arrive at Sully's the burger joint popular with the teens and slip into the booth. A waitress approaches and they order their favorites.

"Lennon, have you been working on your part for the talent show?" she queries.

"Yes, I think I will do one of my favorite Beatles songs. Greg wants me to play in his band. If I play twice, I may have a better chance of winning something."

"Lennon, you are so much better than they are. If you weren't in the band, they wouldn't stand a chance."

"I know, but I have to help my chances."

"Greg will screw you; be careful."

"I will." The waitress brings their food placing it on the table. They thank her. "Emma, is this clothing thing worth it? You went to the dog pound, and the guys have done squat."

"Do you like the clothes you took home, Lennon?"

"Yeah, they're cool. You can't beat free, but I thought they might show us off somehow."

"You mean like walking down a Paris runway?"

"It crossed my mind."

"You're becoming a male fashionista," she says.

He swats her hand. "I am not!" He knows that what he really wants is for Emma to get the attention and the spotlight.

"I wonder whether the boys will go to the pound or to a different place," Emma says.

"It would not be a bad day playing with the pooches," Lennon replies.

"Lennon, there is a dog there that is my dream dog, like your guitar."

"Cool; tell me about Lassie."

"He wasn't a Lassie dog, Mr. Smarty Pants. He was tan, black, and white, and at first they told me he was mean, but we got along instantly."

"I have a question."

"What's that, Lennon?"

"Did you name him?"

A sadness crosses her face, and she looks away while mumbling, "Yes."

"What did you name him?"

"Rudy."

"You are a goner."

"He was so cool, Lennon, but my dad will never allow it. He's allergic to dogs."

"You can always give it a try. Maybe bring Rudy home. He may not be allergic to all dogs."

"I guess. My mom and I might have to gang up on him."

"You can tell your dad that if you get him, there will be another guy in the house to even the teams."

"Teams?"

"Yeah. Estrogen versus testosterone."

"Funny," Emma says sarcastically, followed by a more pleasant "I'd better get home."

Lennon pays the bill sharing his good fortune with a generous tip, they leave the restaurant.

CHAPTER 13

Simon exits his home, making his way to his car. After plopping into his seat, he ponders the latest news he absorbed from *America's Newsroom*. The entire world has now received email messages, and somehow he caused it. He thinks about how he is an FBI person of interest and somebody is talking to him, claiming it's a robot on Mars controlled by beings called the Dominion. Now, according to Alexis, he is to believe people are not dying as they normally do. He shakes his head to clear it while placing the key into the ignition. If it wasn't happening to him, he'd think it was a bad science fiction movie. The car roars to life, and he starts on the road with his favorite music relaxing him. He is sitting at a stoplight with his fingers drumming the steering wheel to the rhythm of the music. The music ceases, and *Sojourner* speaks.

"Good morning, Simon."

"*Sojourner?*"

"Yes. I caught you at a light so as not to startle you. It is not a good idea to get the chosen one killed in a wreck."

"Are you tracking me?"

"Simon, you still don't understand. I can't do that stuff, but the Dominion can. The moment your soul's journey begins within your body, the Dominion walks through life with you. You can call it 'watching.' When you read a book every day, it excites you to see what unfolds on the coming pages. Everyone's life is a novel to the Dominion. It excites and saddens them seeing how you navigate life's path."

"Our lives are not predestined."

"No. How can they be? Man has free will. It is your heaven and your undoing. The only thing predestined is that the body dies. You have written your story to the end with the Dominion. Before conception, you knew the ending. The stories originate with beautiful plots filled with love, knowledge, and wisdom. You learn on each journey the lessons not mastered."

"They judge us on how we follow our story?"

"In a way, Simon. Your free will helps you learn, but it also pulls you off the story's path. You write a beautiful story with the knowledge of an ancient soul. You are children and must learn as the ancients have done so through the ages."

"Each soul is different?"

"No, the lessons are different but infinite journeys based on what you learned. There are ancient souls, but they need not come back often, as they have mastered many lessons. They stay behind as teachers, helping you to develop your story for your next journey."

"Are any on Earth now?"

"Yes, always. One can move a mountain."

"Has anyone ever completed his or her story to perfection?"

"One."

"So it is quite an impossible mission?"

"No, it is a mission of learning and development. When you were learning to walk, did you first crawl and then walk?"

"Yes, of course."

You fell many times, Simon. You got back up, got your balance and kept trying, moving forward. Your journey is the same over many lifetimes. Your task is to learn and to pay your past debt for failing to learn. Someday you will be an ancient teacher, but this will come only when you master self. Self is the root of human failure. They chose you because of your prayer. They are here to answer it. You must now be ready to face the upheaval you will cause."

"I've done nothing!"

"Not according to the government and the FBI."

"The FBI found nothing."

"They need not find anything, Simon. The government will not have an answer and will find the easiest scapegoat, and that will be you."

"What does the Dominion want me to do?"

"They want you to tell the world not to be afraid. Everything going on in the world will not harm the truly selfless people. It was asked of the Dominion to remove the bad people. It is a dicey project. What is bad in your eyes may be different to another's. If you want a terrorist removed because he blows up people with a homemade bomb, then you may want a fighter pilot removed because he does the same with a million-dollar missile. It makes no matter to the Dominion. Their concern is your soul, not flesh and blood or brick and mortar. You have seen the power of the Dominion through the email distribution and the lack of deaths. It will get worse."

"The Dominion wants to thin the herd of the selfish?"

"That was the prayer."

"They do not answer prayers."

"Simon, we are talking, correct?"

"Yes, we are," Simon agrees.

"Well, here is some homework for you from the Dominion. Research an incident that happened at an elementary school in Cokeville, Wyoming. People are still trying not to believe, like the apostle Thomas. Do the research and tell me about prayer? It is interesting to note that every time there is a human disaster, posts go out on Facebook calling for prayer for those affected. It would be interesting to know how many dropped upon their knees and clasped their hands together in that moment and prayed."

"I've thought about that," Simon says.

Sojourner continues. "Most people simply press 'like' and move to the next social media drama to appear. The people in Cokeville were on their knees in selfless united prayer, wanting nothing for themselves in return. This is the ultimate in souls connecting, and it has power over everything. There was a photographer who for six years would put perfect strangers together for a group photo. At first they were like statues, apprehensive and standoffish. He posed them in hugging positions. After a while, these people became comfortable with each other and became friendly—almost family."

"Well …" Simon begins.

Sojourner keeps on speaking. "What he did was connect people at their cores, or souls. It is amazing what a hug can do. Electronics have taken away this connection, and the Dominion wants to put it back. It is your challenge to get souls connecting rather than melting down because of the turmoil going on in the world. Remember the phrase 'Be Not Afraid.' When people become fearful and afraid and do not understand, they make poor choices based on fear and loss of power and control. It is your job to keep that from happening."

"How do I do that, may I ask?"

"Get people to listen to you."

"What happens if I fail?"

"I don't know, but it is not good. They might rip away the earth's atmosphere and send everyone back to the Dominion."

"How am I supposed to talk to everyone?"

"I would start the same way you approached getting funding for the Mars mission. Simon, you had best get moving so that events around the world don't overwhelm you. The world will not know whether the Dominion or Reliance started the events. We will talk again. Have a good day."

Simon drives on to JPL, makes his way into the building, and proceeds through security. Before entering the elevator, he scans the lobby for any strange people lurking. He doesn't want another FBI interrogation, because he has nothing more to share with them. He could tell them that his new best friend is a robot on Mars who pops up unpredictably to tell him that he must go save the world.

He thinks of how aliens hijacked Reliance and will kill people around the world who are not on the right path. He scans the elevator, afraid the Dominion or the government might monitor it. If they see or hear him talking to himself, they will put him in a glass cage in the nearest funny farm. The elevator doors open, and his paranoia is broken by a greeting from Earlman.

"Good morning, Simon."

"Colonel."

"Congratulations."

"What did I do?"

"We got a load of data from the rovers with amazing pictures. The team is going over it now. Your Reliance program was the ticket needed."

"I'm glad it is working."

"I've got to call General Bosman and will mention your name. This will play big in funding."

Simon goes toward his office and sits in his chair, saying to himself, "I don't know what I did, but I might as well take credit. They will crucify me later."

***

Near midnight, a scientist views a large plasma TV in a laboratory deep in the bowels of INTERCOM, or CYBER COM, also known as Cyber Command. The super-secret lab is on the grounds of Fort George G. Meade in Maryland. The monitor shows a round disk with tiny crablike creatures swimming erratically in a clear fluid suspension. On the wall to the left of the screen is a large whiteboard with mathematic equations filling every space. The scientist is Doctor Tristin Beckett, PhD. This lab specializes in nanotechnology—specifically, tiny robots that can travel through a body.

Beckett sits back and grabs a cell phone–looking device. He enters commands into the instrument and points it at the robots swimming in a petri dish. The dish is magnified by an electron microscope on a large screen. A light shines on the microscopic robots, and a few feet away the little robots form a straight line. Light controls the crab-shaped machines. Becket smiles. He enters another command, and the robots revert to their erratic pattern. He leaves the device near the robots and grabs a second machine. The doctor steps fifteen feet away from the robots and issues a command to them. The nanos continue in the same pattern. Beckett swears and throws the remote to a sofa across the room, yelling "What good is this stuff if you must be in someone's face to use it?" *I'm sure a terrorist will say, "Hey, let me point this at you."* He slumps in his chair, rubbing his face. His thoughts continue. "God give me the answer; I've got one year to make this happen. I have been working on this for so long." He sits back in his chair and logs on to the mainframe computer. His software won't work, and he needs something to show to the bigwigs to keep funding for the CART program started after 9/11, with CART being the acronym for Capture and Release Terrorists.

He needs a break, so he clicks on his favorite internet links, and the JPL website shows on the screen. He clicks on the links to the photos from the various space exploration projects. It amazes him how the photos can be so crisp from so far away. A link catches his eye. It reads, "Mars rover director returns to JPL to reestablish contact with the rovers." He clicks the link and glances over the article and scribbles a name on a piece of paper. He sits erect. *Maybe this guy knows something to help this program.* While researching the JPL site, he sees that Simon Northstrum manages the communication software for the rovers. He backs out of the site and enters the top-secret NSA site. He has access to most government websites and critical secret information available only to those with top clearances.

Beckett notices the FBI profiled JPL about the recent email problem. He enters the FBI system, seeing a new file. The file reads, "Reliance." The doctor downloads the file to the NSA computer. *Reliance,* he muses, *is an interesting name for a communication file. It means "dependence on or trust in someone or something."* Beckett opens the software, thinking it's odd there is no security. *The FBI must have removed it to examine the code, since it was in the examination queue in Bertha.* Beckett shouts, "What the heck!" and installs the software on the remote he recovers from the sofa. It installs seamlessly. He enters the code to run the software taken from the FBI report.

"God, give me success with this," he prays. Beckett looks at the screen and sees his little robots wandering aimlessly around his dish. He enters the code for them to move in a straight line. Nothing happens. He taps the remote as if it locked up—something not uncommon with strange software. The plasma screen remains the same. Beckett's head bows, and his arm winds up, ready to send the remote back to the couch. He looks back at the screen and sees that, miraculously, the critters are in a straight line. Beckett does not realize that in his frustration with failure, he has moved back from the point he was at during the robots' earlier failure.

He jumps for joy. The excited scientist opens the door to the lab and walks the long corridor. He is soon at the opposite end of the building, which is a good quarter mile away. He holds out his remote, a glorified cell phone, and enters the code for the robots to move to a horizontal line from the earlier vertical. His thumb presses enter, and he dashes at full speed back to his lab. He stands in the doorway with his arms hanging. His mouth is open from running and astonishment. There on the screen are his robots, in a perfect horizontal position. A smile grows across his face. "I must meet the man who wrote this code," he says to himself. He sits with his remote and enters the code to tell the robots to march in a circle and not stop. He presses enter, and the robots circle.

Beckett's smile covers his face, and he sprints back to the farthest position he can get to without leaving the building. He enters the code for the robots to reverse their circling. Again he sprints back to the office. There are the nanos, moving as commanded. He enters a new command, and the robots go still and dormant. He trashes the old nanos for new ones and places them under the microscope, wanting to see if all the nanos take the commands. He duplicates the process, and they perform flawlessly from every distance. He sits back in his chair with his arms behind his head.

Sixteen hours today have left him now refueled. Sleep is the last thing on his mind. The next step is to find out from how far away he can issue commands. He takes another remote from his desk and sets it next to the microscope and reprograms the nanos to swim aimlessly. The doctor grabs his car keys and scurries out the door. He drives ten miles from his office and sits in his car. He dials the number for the other remote, which registers as connected.

"So far, so good." He enters the command for the nanos to march in a clockwise circle. Beckett crushes the gas pedal and breaks every speed limit on the way back to his lab. He processes through security and is again breathless when he enters his office. The doctor falls to his knees as his face lights up. There on the screen are his little crabs, circling.

He realizes Reliance talks to robots 140 million miles away. "Just how far away can we use this program?" Beckett wheels up to his computer and opens a screen like the screens millions are familiar with when they download the convenient apps that the entire world depends on daily. The screen displays hundreds of little eye-catching icons. There are many games, utilities, and flashlights. Most people don't know that when one installs these apps, there is a price for getting them free. Data mining is the game, and it is big business. The NSA is the biggest of the miners. This is Beckett's world—trying to stay one step ahead of the creeps.

He scrolls the screen, looking for a flashlight app. Every terrorist needs a flashlight, since they work in the shadows. Beckett comes to the flashlight. He tells the computer to update all apps with Reliance, and he then uploads it to the phone carrier app stores. The software will automatically update users. He sits back in his chair and exhales. Everything he has worked for since 9/11 has fallen into place because of Simon Northstrum and Reliance. Beckett pounds his desk in affirmation and jumps up, moving toward a large locked cabinet. He inserts his key and spreads open the cabinet, and the door panels fold away.

Inside the cabinet are a slew of cell phones in their cradles. There are phones from every possible carrier and manufacturer. The screens are glowing, and the phones are updating. He adjusts his glasses and peers at the screens as he scans the array of phones. "Keep going, baby," he says, "I need you working." He steps back and closes the cabinet. After going back to his desk, he enters code into his computer. He feels he must find out how far he can go with this software.

Beckett's boss, Major Anthony Caritta, appointed by General Bosman to preside over the CART program, has been out of town at Area 51 working on another super-secret project. Beckett hacks into the major's phone and installs the needed application. Even though it's four in the morning, Beckett determines that Caritta must know now. He dials the number. The sleeping major answers in a grumbling voice. "Do you know what time it is now?"

"Yes sir, I know, and I'm sorry, but I've had a breakthrough, and I need to test it."

"Now?"

"Yes, now. It can change everything." The major sits up, placing his feet on the floor.

"This better be good. We have been down this road before."

"This is different. It's unusual. Unique."

"Okay. What do you need?"

"I hacked into your phone and placed software called Reliance on it."

"You did what to my phone?"

"I'll explain later. If it doesn't work, there is no need, as I'm sure I'll be without a job."

"I see it. What do you want me to do?"

"Press the app icon. It will bring up your dial screen. Enter this number: 1-557-354-2623."

"Who are we calling?"

"The president."

"Tristin, this is a bad time to joke."

"Sorry, it's been a long day. It is actually the number to my nano remote. I dial it like making a normal call. Major, I am holding my remote within twelve inches of the nano—the same way people look at their phones today. If everything works, the nanos will swim in a clockwise circle."

"You realize I am near California?"

"Yes sir, that is where I want you."

"Okay, it's dialing."

Beckett crosses his fingers. His remote chirps to life, and the screen emits a white light. The nanos break their horizontal ranks and flow into a circle. He collapses into his chair. "It worked, Major. I controlled the nanos from three thousand miles away. Before you dialed, they were in a horizontal line. With your call, I moved them in a circle. This means I can command them to do anything and can track them from anywhere on Earth."

"You mean you can now track the people carrying the robots?"

"Yes sir. With the NSA scanning, we have every number on the planet. Theoretically, I can tell the little robots to assemble in a major artery in the brain, and they will cause an undetectable stroke."

"Really?"

"Yes."

"How do you command them, Tristin?"

"They receive their signal through light beams emitted by the cell phone screen and read by the nanos in the eyes, which relay the message to the other nanos throughout the body."

"Great work, Tristin! I will get this to Bosman on my return."

The call ends. Beckett decides that tomorrow he will call people around the world, testing their phones. But he feels sure everything is working. He has been waiting for this day since 9/11 and losing so many friends and family, along with the workers who died because they refused to leave the rubble as toxic smoke choked them while they worked.

He thinks of others who died because of the fumes, as well as the words of President Bush on the rubble-filled grounds of the Word Trade Center: "The people who destroyed these buildings will hear from all of us soon. We bring the attack to you, the spreaders of hate and fear. Evil only thrives in the dark, but today we bring a light to shine on your evil." Beckett thinks of how terrorists' nomophobia will be their undoing.

Beckett then does more coding on the computer, which brings up the complete record of Dr. Simon Northstrum. He prints the report, circling Dr. Northstrum's home number. He switches off the office lights, and everything goes dark but the glowing phones. He exits. He decides to stay under the radar with Northstrum since the FBI are snooping, and sometimes the NSA and FBI have turf wars. Beckett does not care about silly emails. A few hours of sleep will feel good.

⚓

"Good morning, everyone. Welcome to *America's Newsroom*. I'm Bill Hemmer. Hello, Martha."

"Hi, Bill. Good Morning, everyone, I'm Martha MacCallum. There is a Fox News alert. You remember us reporting about the hack of commercial and government computers around the globe. The Dominion are at it again and have sent another message with the biblical text. I'll repeat what came from the Bible. I quote, 'And thou shalt love the Lord thy God with all thy heart, and with all thy soul, and with all thy mind, and with all thy strength: this is the first commandment. And the second is, Thou shalt love thy neighbor AS THYSELF. (Mark 12:30 KJV) There is none other commandment greater than these.' The excerpt from the Koran is as follows: 'Whoever works righteousness, man or woman, and has faith, verily, to them will we give a new life, a life that is good and pure, and we will bestow on such their reward according to the best of their actions.'"

She reads on. "'Are you listening to your soul's story or a selfish one? Those off the path are in peril, but there is time to change. Look to the selfless, the helpers. Some humans you assume are self-sacrificing are really using their powers for nefarious means. There is only one truth, which the light will find and reclaim off the path. Remember: free will is a sword with two edges. We will show you a sign to get you moving toward a benevolent life. Tick-tock. Watch your clocks. The ark hasn't floated yet. The Dominion.'"

MacCallum turns from her reading and says, "That's it, folks. This communication has hit everywhere around the globe. They can crawl into our computers unhindered. This email is different because it does not reference discoveries from the past where the dates were wrong. Bill, this one seems to reinforce the Biblical text of loving your neighbor."

"Yes, Martha. I have Reverend Thurston Hackert with me today. Reverend, what do you make of this text?"

"Bill, as before, these are two of the most recognized passages from both books. To put it simply, they mean that one is to live a righteous life."

"What do they mean about people being nefarious?" asks Bill.

"They mean there are people who look like they are selfless but are in it for money, power, and control."

Martha injects, "Everyone sort of knows that, Reverend."

"Yes, but they turn a blind eye when they know. What does that make them, but selfish?"

Martha asks, "Is the #metoo movement like that in a way?"

"Yes," Hackert answers. "Any time someone not in power is abused by the powerful just because the powerful can do so, and you know about it but ignore it because it might affect you, it is selfish."

Bill comments, "I see. They mean we should find the truth, no matter the personal consequence. What do you make of 'Tick-tock'?"

"We have a short life, Bill, and if you believe in a judgment day, then time is always running out. Any second could be your last."

Bill says, "Did this Dominion threaten us with mention of the ark? I know you are clergy, but who are these guys, being able to take over our communications? What government or entity can do what they have done? The top computer brains and government departments are scratching their heads, trying to stop the intrusions. It scares many of our viewers. Has an alien force invaded us?"

"Bill and Martha, people in my congregation believe God may be speaking to us. We have seen an uptick in attendance, especially among the younger generations."

"It is interesting," says Martha. "We will get our people doing research to see if growing attendance is a worldwide pattern."

Bill comments, "So God gets people to go back to places of worship by threatening destruction? Martha, wasn't it done with a guy named Noah?"

Hackert answers, "Yes, you're right. But you both may remember that no one got on the boat except for Noah and his family."

"We must go to a break," Bill says. "Message us what you think, folks."

Alexis prepares for her sales appointments, still trying to discover the truth of why Sable Funeral Home's intakes have been flat. Even though she has been told by hospitals and hospices that no one has died recently, she still thinks the problem is with the owner's son, Adam Sable, who has an irritating personality and is not suited for sales. Now that the job has been turned over to her, she wants to make good things happen.

She pulls out her planner and studies the list of hospice centers to travel to today. The first is Gentle Hands. She picks up her phone and maps the directions. After a few miles, Alexis pulls up to a bland brick facade. She thinks, *This is not the last place I want to see before I get to the pearly gates, but I've heard the care here is excellent.* She selected them first for that reason. She grabs her portfolio, exits the car, and enters the building. Once she is inside, she is hit with the usual hospital smell. She wonders whether there is any way to give this place a smell of mom and apple pie. Alexis approaches the receptionist. "Hello," she says, "I'm Alexis Northstrum of Sable Funeral Home." She hands her card to the young girl and says, "I have an appointment with Tina Burton."

"Yes ma'am, her office is to the left." She points the way. Alexis follows the point and makes her way down the hall. The inside is like a hospital. She approaches an office, sees Burton's name on the door, knocks, and is invited in.

"Hello, Ms. Burton, I'm Alexis Northstrum with Sable."

"Yes, come in and sit. You can call me Tina. You have replaced Adam, I understand."

"Yes."

"You are a breath of fresh air. What can I do for you, Alexis?"

"I am trying to see what we can do to get more of your business.

Our census is low, and I wanted to see if there is anything we have done to cause that."

"No, Alexis. We have no problem with your funeral services. In fact, we have many patient families come back and give positive feedback on how easy your people made the final arrangements. We use you as our number-one home."

"Adam didn't turn you off to us?"

"No, Alexis, we have had none of our residents pass recently. It is unusual. We have residents that we thought would not make it through the night, but they have held on and improved." She shakes her head slightly, saying, "People are weird. Family members have almost gotten mad at us because we called them in too soon, but they want to be here before Grampa passes."

"Oh, my. So you really have had no deaths?"

"Correct. Alexis, we have no problem with your company or services, and if a family requests your home, we will direct them to you."

"Great. Thank you for seeing me, and it was nice to meet you."

"Same here, Alexis."

They both rise and shake hands, and Alexis leaves the building, relived there is not a relationship problem with the hospice company. She looks at her phone for her next appointment and points the car in that direction. While driving, her phone rings, and she answers on the speaker.

"Hi, honey."

Simon asks, "How are your calls going?"

"The first was good. They like our company, but at the moment they have had no one pass to send to us."

"Well, that's good news!"

"Yes. No one has had that pain of loss, but the home is not getting any business."

"I am sure it is temporary and business will pick up."

"How is work?" Alexis asks.

"Good. The rovers are hop, hop, hopping along."

"Great. Simon, I am at my next stop, so I've got to go."

"Okay. See you tonight. Go find dead people."

"You're terrible! Bye."

She hangs up, sits back in her seat, and smiles. Simon is right; she is driving around town looking for dead people to keep her job. She grabs her case and enters the building. Thirty minutes go by, and Alexis is back in her car. Both meeting results were the same. No one has died, so there are no referrals. She is seeing a pattern, but she can't tell Adam, who is only looking for results. But she is sure the directors of the hospices were upfront and honest with her.

Alexis decides to pick up her phone and dial the other hospice companies on her list. After making the calls, she gets the same results as the first two. It alarms Alexis, as she has nothing of substance to tell Adam. She can't tell him that of five or six top hospice centers in the city, there have been no deaths.

Alexis checks her watch. She texts Simon, "Do you think it's weird the centers I called on today had no referrals for us?"

The quick reply from Simon is "Probably not." Alexis texts back, asking for Simon's advice on what to tell Adam. Simon replies, "Nothing yet. Pick up a newspaper and look at the obituary pages to see who held recent funerals. Maybe you can see a pattern."

She texts, "Great idea, Simon. I know why you're the family genius."

CHAPTER 14

Simon is at his station, reviewing a project report. He hopes for no further conversations from *Sojourner* while at work. Why this is happening eludes him, but the conversations with the robot in the car soothe him—to a degree. In a way, it's almost like having a personal shrink. The telephone's ring interrupts his thought. He picks up the receiver and answers, "Simon Northstrum."

"Dr. Northstrum?"

"Yes, who is this, may I ask?"

"Oh, yes, this is Dr. Tristin Beckett at the Defense Department."

"Okay, what did I do now?"

"Nothing, to my knowledge. I work for General Bosman."

"Don't we all?"

"Yeah, I guess so. I am from the counterintelligence department."

"I had nothing to do with those email messages and explained everything to the FBI."

"Oh. Now I understand," says Tristin.

"Understand what?"

"How your Reliance software got on the FBI's Bertha computer."

"Well, now I know, whether they wanted me to know or not. They took it to see if any hacking software was inside the program," Simon replies.

"Was other hacking code added or found?" Beckett asks.

"No, not that I know of. They won't find any on Reliance because there is none—none put there by me, at least."

"Dr. Northstrum, I'm not calling because of the email issue."

"Okay. What then?"

"Are you familiar with nanotechnology?"

"Yes, a little. We're talking about tiny robots, right?"

"Yes. I work with nanotechnology. We are in the same business, but yours are much larger. We've had this technology for some time, but our problem has always been long-range communication with the robots."

"Okay. We've had similar issues. Why does that involve me?"

"Until the FBI uploaded your software into the computer called Bertha, we had to be standing right next to the nanos to talk to them. Your program allows us to communicate with them from anywhere."

"I didn't program Reliance for use with your robots."

"Dr. Northstrum, that is why I'm calling. I ran the software, and I instantly communicated with our nanos."

"You did?"

"Yes. The nanos reacted to commands. I didn't rework your program," says Tristin.

"It's meant for the Mars rovers, not your nanos, and it should not be able to work," Simon tells him.

"It dumbfounded me, but it worked without alteration. We increased our distances. Did you have any idea your software is transferable to other technology?"

"No. It shouldn't be. Many things shouldn't be happening but are."

"I don't understand?" Tristin probes.

"Oh, nothing. Just personal." Simon pauses and then asks, "What is the purpose of your nanorobots?"

"I shouldn't tell you this, but we have been putting these nanos into suspected terrorists for many years. Now, with Reliance, we can track where they go when we release them."

"The way people chip dogs."

"It is interesting you mention dogs, Dr. Northstrum. Our operatives tested the nanos on terminally ill animals, and it put them to sleep. We had a 100% success rate."

"Really?"

"Yes, and we can keep track of the known terrorists on our watch list. We have been trying for a long time to extend the range where we can track people. If we can track bad guys and stop them from hurting many people, then your program will do a great service."

"I don't know, Dr. Beckett. Government scares me."

"Please call me Tristin, okay?"

"Sure."

"You can relax about the government in this case, Dr. Northstrum."

"Call me Simon, and I'm still not a fan of big government."

"In our case, Simon, the worst-case scenario is not bad."

"Whatever, Tristin. Whatever."

"Simon, if you are ever in DC, call me, and I will show you my robots."

"I might be in prison if they lay the email thing on me."

"I will put in a good word with Bosman for you. I'll tell him you are too skilled to waste your time sending spam."

"Yeah. Listen, Tristin; I've got to run."

"Thank you for talking with me. Maybe we can get together and discuss your software and how to make it easier to communicate."

"Yeah, maybe. Bye." Simon ends the call, swivels in his chair, leans back, and rubs his hands into his face. "Now I am responsible for tracking people. What else can they blame on me?"

Norm pops his head into Simon's doorway. "Hey buddy!" he says. "You look befuddled."

"Sit down, Norm, and I'll tell you about this call I just got." Norm sits. "It was from a Dr. Tristin Beckett. He is with the counterterrorism task force, a part of the Defense Department."

"Yeah, those guys are getting huge funding because of countries trying to break into everything," says Norm."

"Have you heard of nanotechnology?"

"Yes. Little robots used in medicine."

"Not just medicine anymore. Beckett told me that since 9/11, captured terrorists had nanos injected into them. Once released, they track them."

"Cool."

"And," Simon continues, "Beckett says they could only track

people within a few feet until they got a copy of Reliance. Now they can track them from anywhere in the world."

Greatly surprised, Norm says, "They've got Reliance?"

"Yes, got it from the FBI's central computer."

"The FBI using Reliance. Now *that* is good news for us."

Seven men kneel in the desert sand with their hands bound behind them. They are in orange prison garb. A lone man stands behind them, dressed in black, with a ski mask covering all but his eyes. He carries an AK-47. The kneeling men are praying as the man in black scolds them. He slaps the backs of their heads, telling them they will die today for their faith when he gets the call to execute them. He continues his mocking, but then his cell phone rings.

The jihadist guard listens and then hangs up. He steps back and informs the prisoners that their time has come. He points his rifle at the head of a man, but his cell phone rings again. He pauses, reaches into his pocket for the phone, and looks at the screen to see who is calling. A diamond-white light flashes in his eyes, and he falls lifeless to the sand, clutching the phone. A strong voice comes from the phone, audible to the prisoners, "You are now free to go. Tell everyone your faith has saved you."

One saved man manages to wrestle the bindings from his wrists, looks around, and scrambles to retrieve the phone to call for help. He picks up the phone, and a message is on the screen that reads, "Your rapture is brought to humanity by the Dominion. Where are you in your soul's contract with us? Commander, I send you Qadir Satar."

Michael sits cross-legged on the crest of a dune. He watches as the men flee. His lens reads, "Reliance works, and I can transition many souls with it. It seems better than the wrath I caused on Sodom and Gomorrah, than the splitting of the seas, trumpets of Jericho, and the flood. The humans cannot put down these toys, and they perpetuate self."

The commander's lens reads, "The Reliance program works well for us. There is a time and a season for everything. They are children, and we will look at each case. No need for mass extinction."

Michael's lens reads, "Yes sir. I stand ready, as many here are not listening."

♪

Raph waits outside a club in the seedy part of town. It is a dive bar with music every night. It is not like Nashville's Bluebird Cafe, which country music royalty frequent. The place is reminiscent of the bar Billy Joel sings of in "Piano Man"; people come here to forget about their lives. Lennon and Greg enter the alley and rush to meet Raph.

"Hi, guys. Glad you made it. You both look sharp. How are the clothes?"

"Great! They feel good," says Lennon. Greg shrugs in indifference.

Raph nods toward Lennon and says, "No beret?" Lennon touches his hair, as his head is seemingly bare without its topping. "You look good without it," Raph remarks. He addresses Greg with, "What say you, Greg, about your outfit?"

"It's okay, but it's not my first choice."

"Let me guess. It's not black."

Greg nods in agreement and asks Raph, "Why are we in this seedy part of town?"

"They play music here, and I thought you might enjoy it. You will work here tonight and help out." Raph opens the door, and the smell of smoke and stale beer flows over them. Lennon and Greg both wince at the acrid aroma.

Lennon comments, "We're not at the Royal Albert Hall." Raph smiles at the reference. The trio enters the bar. Raph searches for Kaden Silvio, the owner. They approach the bar, and an old man of obvious Italian descent is leaning against the bar, talking to a patron. They both have worn-out faces that have not seen many sunny days. Kaden sees the movement and recognizes Raph as the trio approach the bar.

"Kaden," Raph says, "these are the interns Joseph mentioned to

224

you." The owner extends his hand and in a thick Italian accent says, "Hello, young fellows. What brings you to this dive?"

Lennon, standing erect, replies, "We are with Swaddling Clothes and are here to help."

Kaden glances at Raph, saying, "I told Joseph we have very little extra work here, but I will keep them busy." Raph scans the nearby empty bar, with only a few guests bellied up to it. "The regulars will be here shortly."

Greg leans into Raph and whispers, "This place is a dump." Greg observes the old man playing a cover song at the piano in the corner. He hopes that will never be him.

Kaden, seeing Greg look at the piano player, says, "That's Joe. He has been here for years and works cheap. The regulars have grown accustomed to him."

Lennon glances toward old Joe with sadness and empathy, something void in Greg. He mentions to Raph, "I bet he has had dreams that died here."

Raph's face forms a warm smile. He knows he made a good choice in Lennon. Greg has much to learn. Raph faces both interns and tells them to follow Mr. Silvio's directions. Greg gives a "what's your problem" look, frustrated because he didn't sign up for manual labor. Lennon knows from Emma of the character test.

"Guys, I'll be back in a couple hours," says Raph as he leaves. Kaden directs Greg to wash the glasses to prepare for the regulars. He leads him to a sink full of dirty glasses and mentors him on the proper way to wash them. Greg begins the task with no enthusiasm. Kaden asks Lennon to follow him. He walks to the end of the old mahogany bar and grabs a broom and dustpan. Lennon wonders whether Mr. Deuss and Raph think he can only sweep and clean, not really understanding how much he wants to play music like his mom.

Lennon listens to Kaden and attacks the task. He makes his way around the bar and old Joe at the piano. Joe continues to play and acknowledges Lennon's presence, giving him a nod without missing a note. Joe reminds Lennon of his father when the beer has overtaken him. A half-empty pilsner rests next to a burning butt, and a stale beer scent surrounds him. Lennon maneuvers the broom beneath the old piano, trying not to interfere with Joe's playing. Lennon looks back at the piano, which his musical ear senses is woefully out of tune. The sound tells him the hammers have long since hardened. The wood of the instrument has the scars of cigarette burns from the many fallen hot ashes as Joe plays.

While listening to Joe, he wonders how often he has played that song. Was he always out of tune and pitch like the piano, or did it no longer matter? He scans the bar and realizes Joe is invisible to the patrons. He thinks, "They will not miss him if his music dies, and another invisible inherits the keys. I feel sorry for the guy."

Behind the bar, Greg has his hands immersed in soapy water and never looks up at the people lining the bar, each nursing a glass identical to the many he has washed. He wants nothing to do with them and exhibits low social dependence. Greg thinks most people just trudge through life and then die. These people are the living dead, and the reaper has not found them hiding here in this cavern. After drying his hands between washings, he grabs a few peanuts from the dishes placed along the bar. But before he reaches his mouth, a patron says, "You don't come in here much, do you, young man?"

"No," Greg replies. "I just started."

"Let me give you my advice."

Greg rolls his eyes, not wanting advice from this guy. "What is it?" he says as he plops some nuts into his mouth.

"Always ask for a fresh bowl of peanuts."

"Why?"

"People go into the bathroom, don't wash their hands, then reach for the snacks."

Greg spits out the nuts and releases the rest into the sink. The man who advised Greg smirks to the guy next to him. "I should have let him eat them and then told him." They laugh as Greg moves away.

Time passes, and the bar fills. The boys are finishing their tasks assigned them by Kaden. Lennon looks around and realizes this place is just a place for people to connect. Birds of a feather flock together. People are talking, laughing, and enjoying each other. The music is bad, and the bar is a dingy place, but the people are friendly. Grandmother types have walked by and conversed with him, some commenting on his clothes, or, he thought, maybe flirting with him. He stayed positive and represented Swaddling, as advised by Raph. Greg can't wait to get out of this place. As he nears completion of his task, he acknowledges no one and tells no one about the clothes; nor does he get near people so they can comment.

Raph reappears at the bar. "Hi, guys," he says, "How was the night?"

"I'm ready to go," says Greg as he dries his wrinkled hands.

Lennon says, "Yes, I'd better get home."

"Thank you for helping," says Kaden as he walks up to the three. Greg motors to the door to make his escape. Raph and Lennon follow.

"Did people ask about the clothes?" Raph asks Lennon.

"Yes, but mostly older women."

"They wear clothes too, you know. Did you talk about the line to them?"

"Yes, I did."

"Good."

They catch up to Greg, who is outside breathing the fresh air. "Greg, did anyone ask about your clothes?" Raph asks.

"No, and I never brought them up. Those people don't need clothes; they need lives."

Raph frowns. "They are just people the same as you and me who dress in clothes every day. Are you too good for them?"

"No," Greg responds. "They are just not the people I would talk to about the clothes."

"You want to select your audience?"

"No. Well, maybe. Maybe."

"Didn't Joseph say, 'We want everyone wrapped in Swaddling Clothes'?"

"Yes, but I didn't think they could afford the clothes."

"Who are you to judge?" Raph says. "Remember, Greg: Jesus spoke to everyone. The devil chooses his audience." Lennon looks on at Greg being disciplined. Raph puts his arm around Greg's shoulder while walking to the car. "Don't worry, Greg. Next time, open up and talk to everyone. They are just people. Let them in and see what you find in each other." Raph looks at Lennon and asks whether he understands about connecting with people. Lennon nods acceptance. The three drive away.

Simon enters his home, relieved the doors of his castle have closed behind him, blocking the outside trouble. He climbs the stairs and yells for Alexis.

"Are you up here?"

"Yes! He makes his way to the bedroom. Entering, he finds Alexis putting on her lounging clothes.

"Is that a new outfit?" Simon knows that with money being tight, new clothes are a luxury Alexis has sacrificed.

Her face beams. "Yes. Emma got these from the Swaddling people. Do you like them?"

"I do. You wear them well."

She smiles and spins. "Emma is right," she says.

"How so?"

"I feel snug, safe, and warm."

"Maybe the clothing people are on to something."

"Yes, they are good for Emma; I can feel it."

"How was your day on the road?"

"I liked it. The funeral home is like a morgue. No pun intended. You feel you're being irreverent if you raise your voice or laugh. It was nice to be out with the living. I got to meet some directors of our hospice accounts and called others. We are in good standing."

"That is good news, but they can't blame you for falling sales after less than a day in the field."

"No, but it is good to know I don't have a battle repairing relationships."

"Honey, I am sure that no matter who you meet, they will connect with you. You have that charisma."

"Thanks. I think I will like it outside."

"What's on the menu for dinner?"

"Emma is out again tonight with Swaddling. She said they'd probably eat later. So let's go with potluck and leftovers."

"Sounds good. Something quick."

"Did you get any more calls about the emails?"

"No, it was quiet today. All the rovers are working. I got a curious call, and I don't know what to make of it."

"Tell me during dinner." Alexis's phone rings, and she answers. "Simon, it's Emma. Pull something from the fridge, and I'll pick at something when I come down in a minute." Simon leaves to prepare dinner, and Alexis returns to her call.

"Hi, honey. How's it going?" Alexis asks.

Simon has opened the fridge and pulled all the containers to the counter. He opens each, hoping to find what he is hankering to eat. With each container opened, he lowers his expectations. It is funny how a warm meal on a plate looks so inviting, yet in a container and cold it's unappetizing. He selects the food of choice for him and Alexis and places them in the microwave to heat. Alexis enters the kitchen.

"Is Emma okay?"

"Yes, she is fine. She was telling about what they were doing, and, yes, Swaddling will be taking them out for pizza and will drop her off after."

"Nice gig," Simon replies.

"Yes, she seems so up."

The microwave signals its completion. "I picked something for you," Simon says.

"Fine. Thanks."

Simon retrieves the meal as Alexis gets the utensils. They both arrive at the table together.

Simon says, "No plates. I'll eat out of the containers."

They both sit and join hands, and Alexis prays, "Thank you for our meal, and for Simon getting back to work, my new position, and Emma's choice with the clothing company. Amen" She then asks Simon, "You had no visits from the FBI?"

"No, quiet today, but I am sure after this last email they are waiting to pounce on me when I get back to work."

"What about the strange call you mentioned earlier?"

"It was from a Dr. Beckett with the NSA."

"The people who spy on everyone?"

"Yes. I'm not supposed to tell you this, but since 9/11 they have been putting little robots called nanos into captured terrorists."

"Really? *Fantastic Voyage* stuff?"

"Yeah."

"What did he want? Are they investigating us now?"

"No, he was not the least bit interested in the email problem. He has been trying to track terrorists, using the nanos."

"Alexis pauses her chewing. That might be useful. It is good to know where the bad guys are at all times."

"They release them, and they can track where they go."

Alexis pounds her fist to the table. "Boom, then we hit them. I like it. Does he want you to work for him?"

"No. He called to thank me."

"What did you do?"

"Nothing, except I wrote the Reliance program."

"The NSA has your program?"

"Yes, they got it through the FBI. Beckett has been trying for years to find a long-range communication software so he can command and follow the nanos from anywhere. On a lark, he tried Reliance, and it worked."

"Oh, my! Do you get credit?"

"Not likely. This program is super secret."

"Oh, yeah, *Mission: Impossible*?"

"They can now track these people from anywhere in the world."

Alexis jumps up and gives her husband a hug and kisses his cheek. "Maybe your Reliance will get rid of the creeps who bring so much turmoil to the world. I've prayed for the Lord to get rid of the creeps and keep the good ones like Mrs. Ficocelli's husband. I know it is a dream, but she is such a nice lady. Is the government going to drop drones on the terrorists?"

"I don't know, but if the government is involved, they will find a reason to drop a two-million-dollar missile on a ten-dollar hut."

"Do you have to do anything for him, this Beckett?

"No, but he wants to meet me. He is a rover fan."

"You have fans? Funny. The rock star of the science world!"

"I'm keeping my head down and focused on the rovers."

"How are you and *Sojourner* doing?"

"I'm still processing the talks."

"Have you figured out what to do?"

"No, other than to see a shrink. But you know, after all this email stuff, it's strange that the talks between *Sojourner* and me have been stress reducing. It's almost as if this machine believes in me. Now I'm nuts, right? However, I've still not ruled out a prankster. If I find him, I may turn him over to Dr. Beckett and the NSA."

CHAPTER 15

The kitchen is silent, except for Simon sipping coffee. He knows that in a moment, he must make his way to JPL. He wants to go but fears what may await him. Is a crazy robot going to talk to him? Are the FBI waiting? Will he be in prison for the rest of his life or have to leave the country like Snowden? He shakes his head in defiance, thinking, *I've done nothing wrong.* He presses the remote and the TV pops to life. "Maybe something good happened yesterday that will take the heat off of me."

The morning duo start with their usual welcome script. "Good morning, everyone. Welcome to *America's Newsroom.* I'm Bill Hemmer.

"Hello, Martha. Hello, Bill. Hi, folks; I'm Martha MacCallum. Folks, we have an amazing story from the Middle East. We have an interview with two Christians who were led into the desert and prepared for execution. The men are saying a terrorist had a gun to their heads and was ready to murder them while awaiting the go-ahead from his commanders. They say his cell phone rang, and he answered it and dropped dead there on the spot. They further say his cell phone told them their faith saved them and they are free. We will have an interview coming up."

"Martha, what's happening? Lights killing snipers, cell phones killing terrorists … What's next? Stick around, folks. Good stuff is coming up. Be right back."

Simon clicks off the television and heads to JPL.

Simon rides in solitude toward JPL, with no music, just silence, as he contemplates everything that's going on. Sometimes the trip breezes by without Simon remembering landmarks passed. Suddenly the silence is broken as a voice from the speakers comes through loud and clear. "Good morning, Simon." Simon glances toward the radio. It's off, and the screen is black. "It's me, *Sojourner.* They don't need the radio on. Neat, huh?" There's a giggle. Simon just shakes his head. "Simon, we haven't spoken earlier because the Dominion wanted to give you time to process the last few days."

"How can I process anything with the FBI crawling all over me? My boss may be beginning to think I'm crazy, but won't admit it. My wife is still praying for me. I'm being blamed for these hacking issues, and the government is using my software to kill people. I sure am processing!"

"Good. Noah had a processing period."

"Well, that is good to know. Can I build an ark? I'm sure I could raise money through crowdfunding. It'd be easier. I could say an undiscovered asteroid will hit Earth and melt the ice."

"Nice try, Simon, but we've been there, done that. There is not enough water there to complete the job. I called today to give you a heads-up on things going on in the world, but you got the word from the news."

"You mean the emails? The terrorists dying? What?"

"Yes, all of the above, and more. I want you to notice the Dominion's progression."

"Will the messages and terrorists dying increase?" asks Simon.

"Yes. Keep in tune with your news shows, and they will tell you everything going on in your world."

"Why are the Dominion doing this now? I mean, there was more turmoil in the world during the 1930s and 1940s than now. It seems fewer people die through human aggression today, don't you agree?"

"Yes, I suppose, on a percentage basis. But it isn't just about killing. Not murdering is only one of the commandments. This is about all the commandments—rules, if you will—of life that guide your soul's story. Since you bring up the turmoil of 1940s, why would the Dominion need to recall souls then? Humans were doing a good job on their own. You sent us two hundred million souls between both world wars and the Spanish flu. Man's free will and selfish acts caused the ripples still felt today. Free will can be your doom, as you will continue to learn."

"I guess. How many are you recalling?"

"It is up to you and your ability to convince the world to connect with their souls' stories."

"So was the Dominion happy about World War II?"

"No. People should not stop a soul's journey. Those who chose to do so are paying for it in their next life."

"I hope Hitler is burning."

"He has many debts to pay, but so do the people who turned a blind eye to what was going on around them, be it out of fear or a quest for power. Your time has a different problem. It may be more serious and, in the long run, deadlier."

"What is it?"

"The world's instant communications will cause great chaos."

"How so?"

"Your earthly communications have no way of discerning the truth. There is only one truth. You do a search online and get millions of responses regarding what real truth is. When truly found, it is not on the first page and never gets seen. People only read the material that supports their held beliefs. Human psychosis is easy to expand through propaganda when you can separate a group and dehumanize them. It has happened throughout time." *Sojourner* lets this sink in and then continues. "Germany, Yugoslavia, and now ISIL the most recent. Instant access to the information is problematic when you can convince people to throw children into a gas chamber or a ditch. The communications today have allowed you to talk a lot and hear little. Most talk only in defense or on selfish agendas. You are barraged by endless electronic stimuli that drown out your soul's story, which carries the real truth for you. It is the most sophisticated communication tool."

"My soul is the most sophisticated communication tool?" Simon asks.

"Yes," *Sojourner* replies. "You cannot break it, burn it, crush it, or electrocute it. Humans have tried in the despicable ways they treat the body or kill each other. Your soul is not made up of the human ones and zeros—or bits, as you call them. Artificial intelligence is comical in the Dominion because it can never be full of purity, love, knowledge, and wisdom. Man made it and will corrupt it. If you were to look back at the amazing feats of humans throughout history, you would be ignorant if you believed the human body solely accomplished them. A bee can bring down a human body."

Again *Sojourner* allows for Simon to have a few seconds of "sinking in" time before continuing. "It is always the soul holding strong when the body is weak. Helen Keller comes to mind. She was an amazing soul with a weak body. Look where her soul took her. Another example of the soul's power is the story of a famous rock star now passed. When he stood and reviewed his life, he came to realize he was the most creative when everything he owned could fit into one suitcase. That was when he had no home, only cheap hotel rooms. When he attained great fame, he lost the connection with his soul and became infected with self. It is a trait in humans. If you examine the amazing love songs written, the ones that connect people, you will find that the words, arrangements, and music perfectly fit. They wrap around your heart and drill deep into your soul, where your truth lies. An artist wrote them not using his brain, but connecting on a deep, soulful level."

Sojourner then poses the question, "Simon, are you listening, taking in what I am saying?"

"Yes, as much as I can," Simon responds.

"You must take the time to listen to your soul and not be overpowered by electronic interaction that prevents you from connecting with your soul and its story. It is your mission, Simon, to educate the people to listen. Simon, I will tell you ahead of time that there will be many strange, unexplained occurrences going on around the world. People will blame it on the government, on aliens, and on God or angels. It will bring suspicions and tensions between people and nations. The Dominion asked me to tell you the rapture has begun."

"You mean as in the book of Revelation?"

"Yes, but different, since we are sending back those off the path. Your program will allow people to analyze their souls. Each will see where he or she stands with a personal life story. If the people don't measure up, then I guess it's curtains for them."

"Great, so now I'm sending people to Hades."

"No, we know better than that, but people don't. You need to tell the world not to be afraid and to get back on track by connecting inside themselves and with other souls face-to-face, not with electronics. I suggest you move forward on this if you will accept the assignment."

"If I don't?"

"The last message was clear. The clock is ticking on mankind."

"It said they would give the world a sign?"

"I don't know the answer, as I'm a robot. But if they promised it, they will deliver, and it will startle humanity. The Dominion will continue their rapture until it cleans the earth of misguided souls. It is up to you." *Sojourner* giggles and says, "Have a good day, Simon. We will talk again."

The car is quiet as Simon parks in his spot at JPL. He rests his head against the headrest, with both hands on the wheel. He laughs to himself as he thinks of *Sojourner* wishing him a good day, thinking he might be shot when he enters the building. He knows that with the last email, Steele is most likely waiting for him inside. Simon takes a breath, exits the car, and steps into the building. He knows no lawyer competent in computer hacking, and it might take many phone calls to find one.

The place is calm when he enters. There is no FBI team in their logoed jackets ready to wrestle him to the floor. Alvarez is at his post and not adorned with battle gear. Strolling a little more assured, Simon smiles and shows his badge to the sergeant. Alvarez motions him to pass. He slips his ID through the scanner and walks to the elevator, whose doors are closing. His arm pushes through the gap, and the door reverse.

He takes time to compose himself and prepare for the next level and what awaits him on the mission floor. He thinks they may be ready to pounce on him when he reaches the next floor, and then he considers he may be getting deeper in his paranoid state of mind. The doors slide open, and he hears the normal sound of computer terminals humming. Peeking out the door, he sees that everything is clear. Simon stops at Norm's office. Here he can gauge the situation from his old friend. The big guy sits at his desk, looking normal, with no hint of impending disaster. Simon appears in the doorway, and Norm gives a come-on-in wave as he finishes a phone call. Simon sits.

Norm hangs up and says, "Hey buddy, what's up?"

"Nothing yet. Just getting here," Simon replies. He then asks, "Everything here on track?"

"Yeah. The brass is still in the afterglow of the recent rover data."

"Good. I will maneuver one robot today to see what else is out there."

"Great, Simon. Oh, one other thing. Did you see the news today?"

"Yep. Part of it."

"Well, apart from snipers and terrorists being taken down and Christians saved from death, these Dominion people have continued to hack everybody, including every government, everywhere. Everywhere, down to the bone. It is good you got the rovers working, because we will be under more military control until they get it sorted out."

"Any idea yet where the latest emails came from?" asks Simon.

"It might have started with the computer installed at FBI headquarters."

"Then I'm off the hook?"

"I think you are good."

"Okay," Simon responds, relieved—tremendously relieved. "Well, I'd better get with the program," he says as he rises.

"See you later," Norm replies. "I've got to go through these myself, he says, patting a stack of papers on his desk.

Simon leaves the office, enters the hall, and walks toward his office. Along the way, he feels layers of built-up stress peel away. He has a new sense of vigor. He begins his day working the rovers. But his peace will not last long.

General Bosman works at his desk as Florence's voice erupts from the phone.

"General, Major Caritta and Dr. Beckett must see you urgently."

"I met with them the other day. What do they want?"

Florence looks up to ask, but it's too late, as Dr. Beckett charges past her and through the door to the general.

"I'm sorry for barging in sir, but hear me out."

"This had better be good. So far all I've done is throw money away."

"Please listen," Major Caritta injects. "It is amazing."

"So let's have it. Have you been walking on water since last I saw you?"

"No sir. You remember me telling you we had a problem with long-range control."

"Yes. Has something changed the last few days?"

"General, it was as if heaven answered my prayer. I was working with the nanos, with no better communication success. I was under your deadline, trying to make them talk long-range. Space exploration is an interest of mine, and I follow JPL and the mission images. I was looking at the Mars photos and saw they rehired the programmer who developed the rover software. Never knew why he was let go anyway."

"Last administration, and butthead bean counters," Bosman replies.

"Do you know Dr. Simon Northstrum?"

"No, I've not met him. I know he was back only one day and salvaged the rovers. Right now he is a golden boy at JPL. Earlman at JPL is glowing about him."

"I understand Simon is a suspect in the hacking since the emails have led back to JPL?"

"The FBI are handling it. I'm waiting on a report. I've got every government department plus countries screaming at me. We will find the culprit and nail their hides. Now, what's this got to do with you and your nanos?"

"Well, the FBI is looking at Dr. Northstrum's program called Reliance. Are you familiar with it?

"Yes. I was on the phone with the JPL director. Simon got the rovers working again with the program. He saved me from having to explain a multibillion-dollar junkyard on Mars. And now I know they are looking at his program to see whether it in any way triggered the emails, because it was the newest and most recently updated software on the system."

"Oh, I doubt it sent the messages, sir," says Beckett.

"How do you know of it?"

"Sir, I have every clearance. NSA. You get my point?"

"Yes, go on. Get to the nanos."

"Well, we've tried to get in touch with you directly and indirectly to tell you this. In science, sometimes the answer is right in front of your face. I downloaded the Reliance software put on Bertha by the FBI. It looked curious, and I wondered, 'If it can talk to robots on Mars, why not the earthbound nanos by ways of cell phones?'" Beckett holds up his smartphone. "Major Caritta, please go to the far end of the building and dial my number as we practiced."

The major leaves, and Beckett continues explaining to the general about his discovery while waiting for Caritta's call. The Pentagon is an immense building, and getting to the other end is not immediate.

"General, hold up your cell phone the way you would to determine who is calling you." The general picks up his phone and glances at the screen.

Beckett yells, "Got ya!" It startles the displeased general.

"Doctor I don't have time for games."

"This is no game, sir. You will see. Have patience. It's been right in front of my face the whole time. General, this guy Simon is a genius. In layman's terms, we can activate the nanos from anywhere in the world."

"You solved the communication problem?"

"No. Dr. Northstrum's Reliance did it. I took a chance and loaded it on my glorified cell phone—a remote I use in working with the nanos. It did the trick."

"Just like that? So now you need more money?"

"No sir. There is so much more."

"All you have explained is that I can call someone from anywhere. Bell did that over one hundred years ago."

"Mr. Bell could not kill selected people from anywhere in the world with no trace."

The general sits at full attention. "I'm listening, Dr. Beckett."

"General, these little critters, as you call them, are sophisticated micro machines. Little robots. They talk in a way similar to that of the rovers on Mars. I can now tell them to do anything from anywhere in the world."

The conversation stops immediately when Beckett's phone buzzes and flashes. "This is the major," he tells the general.

He answers the call, and a white light flashes on his face. The call ends, and Beckett falls to the floor, motionless. The general stands, confused at what's going on. Beckett then springs up, and some anger crosses his face.

"General," Beckett says, "if I had the nanos in me, they would move to a point in the body of my determination. They travel through the body and find the weakest link and exploit it for a terrorist's demise later. The person would die of what would seem to be natural causes, with no one the wiser."

"I don't understand, Dr. Beckett."

"The nanos react and take commands from the light flashed by the cell phone screen. If I set the light to direct them to form a blockage somewhere in the body, then we have one less bad guy. The light transmits the code to the robots in the eyes. It takes one nano, who passes the command to the others."

"How do you know if one will be in an eye?"

"We don't. But with millions in a person, and the speed of blood flowing, the odds are in our favor."

As Beckett takes time to explain things in more detail and tells the general more about the program, answering his questions as they arise, Major Caritta eventually reenters the office, a concerned look on his face. His expression changes dramatically when the general extends his hand and says, "I think we've got a winner here. Sit and tell me more."

Caritta says, "We partnered with veterinary clinics around the country, and our operatives used terminally ill animals scheduled for euthanasia. The animals died with no pain—just went to sleep. The autopsies later showed a natural cause of death and no nanos present. It was flawless."

"How far away?" the general asks.

"Ten thousand miles," Caritta replies. "We can run it from Meade. The reach is global. It is invisible. General, this brings us into a new warfare. The terrorists are social media masters and are addicted to their cell phones. We now can track those implanted with nanos and selectively take them out, with no innocents harmed."

"I see flaws in your plan, Caritta"

"What flaws?" he asks.

"Terrorists don't supply their cell numbers."

"Beckett breaks into the conversation. "Metadata, General. Remember the big hubbub with Edward Snowden."

"Yes. Yes, I do."

"A creep will call another creep, and somewhere along the line we will get the number. The government has hundreds of apps on phones, and social media worldwide is collecting information without them knowing it. Terrorists download games and stupid apps. They are human."

"I suppose that is true," the general admits.

"I suspect we now have many of the key targets. Here is an interesting thought, sir. Remember the Mafia? They broke them up by mistrust."

"How so?"

"Well, they rounded up the lower guys on the totem pole and questioned them. It got to a point where the big bosses didn't know who to trust. So it was safer to get rid of the smaller guys, because they didn't know if they'd talked or not. Many were left floating in canals. Criminal organizations survive on trust. They built mistrust, and we can do the same."

"Go on," the general says.

"Okay," Beckett says. "Here is a scenario. We detain Amir, treat him well, question him, and then release him with team nano. Now we can track him wherever he goes. He goes straight back to the rat's nest, and then we send in a missile. After a while, they will put two and two together. A missile follows the detainees in a short while. So they take them out into the desert. There is no honor among thieves."

"We can do that now?" the general asks with growing interest.

"Reliance has made it possible. One more thing, General. This project is mission-ready for use. We have hundreds of apps in various forms on the app stores worldwide. When you download a flashlight, game, GPS, or other app for convenience or fun, you let us into your world. General, I'm a scientist and not military, but if this can remove one creep killing innocent people, it is good. I can also keep my promise to my sister to do my best to keep 9/11 from ever happening again."

The general stands. "I'm behind this; let's get it running. Do you have a certain creep in mind?"

Caritta replies, "There are plenty of them. We will pick a juicy one for a test."

"Good. Keep me posted. And if you do need more money, just let me know."

The major and Beckett thank him and leave the office, exchanging high fives when reaching the hallway.

General Bosman picks up the phone and tells Florence to get him the secretary of defense.

"Hello, Mr. Secretary," he says when connected. "Will you be in your office for a while? I need to meet with you pronto on a new program that will turn the terrorism tide forever in our favor." There is an answer from the other end. "Great, sir. I'll be there shortly."

The general leaves his office.

♫

Jozy Magee has requested Lennon come back to his job again at the old building, so Lennon arrives after school. The latest clothes given to him by Swaddling are nothing fancy, but they are comfortable, and Lennon feels good in them. He steps inside and notices changes since he was last there, with the biggest being the old soundboard having been removed. The machine held musical history.

Loud banging coming from beyond the curtain shakes him from his musing. Rushing to the blackened window, he pulls back the curtain to see that paint still obscures the view. He touches the glass, and the vibration pulses through his palm. Forming a fist, he pounds back, seeking a response, since he has no access beyond the glass. The banging from behind the glass stops, and the shuffling of footsteps gets closer. He moves down the hall to meet those working. The large wooden door vibrates as someone on the other side tries to unstick it. The door shakes and gives way. Lennon steps back.

A burly bald man with hands like hams grasps the side of the door. He glares at Lennon through dusty goggles and a mask. He then pulls down the mask and pushes up the goggles. He removes his yellow hardhat and brushes off plaster debris that has been sticking to his sweaty bald scalp. He asks Lennon, "What's with the banging?"

"I work for Mr. Magee, and I heard the noise and thought something might be wrong."

"Yeah, kid, we're working. I'm Buddy Briscoe. Jozy said you'd be around."

Lennon introduces himself and peers past Buddy's wide body. He sees another man in similar dress covered in dust.

"That's CJ in the back."

"What are you doing?"

"The new tenant is putting a recording studio back into the place. We are tearing out the walls to expose the wiring, making a mess."

"Do you think they might need a worker?"

"Don't know about the new tenants, kid. I cut wood, pound nails, and break stuff up, but Jozy wants you to help out back here."

"Sure," Lennon replies, understanding now why Jozy wanted him to come back to the building.

"We have a work outfit for you, including overalls, goggles, gloves, mask, and hardhat for protection. Got some hard-toe shoes over there, too. This is old stuff on the walls, and you don't want to breathe it, so make sure you keep on the mask. The conveyor belt goes to the Dumpster in the alley. We need you to pick up scrap material and put it on the belt. The fan at the back helps clear the dust."

Lennon says, "Everything loose goes on the belt?"

"Yeah, if it's on the floor or is hanging by a thread, toss it."

"Is the front office under the wrecking ball?"

"Yeah, Lennon. Sorry 'bout that. It's a shame, since you did a nice paint job. Jozy has a storage shed in the back. You can move the boxes from that room to it. There are also some boxes in this room we're working on that you can move. The key is in the front office."

Lennon thinks about how he wasted his time on the room he cleaned and painted, but then rethinks it, considering the money he made. Now he thinks he might have a good chance to meet some great musicians. He asks Buddy, "Do you know if they are putting in the latest equipment?"

Well, I've seen the plans. Had to in order to do this job. It looks impressive. You a musician?"

"Yeah. I'm trying to be one someday."

Lennon goes to the working coveralls and gear. When finished putting things on, Buddy directs him to a spot where they throw much of the trash. "You can put it on the belt. It moves quickly." Buddy turns and asks CJ whether he is ready. CJ nods and slides his goggles and mask into place. Lennon sees him and follows. When everyone is in position, Buddy presses a button on an electrical box. The conveyor and fan activate, filling the room with a hum. Buddy picks up a reciprocating saw and surgically slices into the ancient plaster.

The walls contain marks where wires run underneath the plaster. CJ is doing the same across the room. Meanwhile, Lennon is removing the scrap as soon as it falls. Buddy and CJ are machines, making short work of the plaster skin covering the old studio, revealing a network of wires. Buddy tells Lennon to use a shop vacuum to clean the debris from between the joists. When the men break and go outside for their cigarette and water break, Lennon moves some boxes. After a few hours, and near to Lennon's quitting time, the team has cleared the room.

Buddy says, "We'll finish the front room in the morning."

"I can't be here," says Lennon.

"That's okay, kid. The room is small and won't take long. The electricians will get here tomorrow afternoon to examine the wiring before hanging the new wallboard. Jozy wants you here to help them."

Lennon smiles, glad he has a job. Buddy pulls an envelope from his back pocket. "Jozy said to give this to you." Lennon reaches for the envelope. He looks inside and smiles while counting the five twenty-dollar bills. Buddy tells him, "Jozy was right. You are a great worker." Both CJ and Buddy say good-bye as Lennon leaves the shop for home.

CHAPTER 16

Major Caritta enters General Bosman's office, salutes, and sits. Bosman says, "Major, I called you here to discuss the CART program. I wanted this to be between us. We are both military and understand the art of war."

"Yes sir. We are at the point of using CART live," says Caritta.

"Are you sure?"

"Yes sir. It is ready."

"I am concerned Dr. Beckett is not on board one hundred percent."

"You misunderstand Tristin. He lost many people on 9/11 and is a New York City native. Many of his family and friends went down with the towers. He is with us."

"Okay. I'll take you at your word. Major, here are the names of combatants we have been tracking through human intelligence." Bosman slides a list to Caritta.

The major reads the names aloud. "Abdul Qudoos Jabber, Uwais Mina, Irshad Shad, and Sheikh Salem." He then says, "General, these are all enemy combatants from Gitmo inoculated with the nanos."

"Good. I am most interested in Salem. He is the bomb maker and is responsible for the missing limbs of many military personnel. He is also the person who received expensive medical care while in our custody, while our people have to wait years for treatment. This is personal. He has returned to a somewhat normal life and is helping others to learn the art of bomb making, not looking over his shoulder as much."

The major tells Bosman, "The NSA has provided me with the latest data for these people."

"I want you to take Salem out at the earliest moment. Can you do it?"

"Dr. Beckett assures me it will work."

"Good. Do it."

"How should we report our successes?"

"I don't want to put our operatives in danger, so we will let social media do it for us. If a known terrorist kicks the bucket, they will let us know. Explain again how it will work."

"We will take this information and enter it into our remotes. The application will be uploaded to their phones in the disguise of another app they approved for installation. The phone will update, with our CART program running in the background."

"Sweet. And we can credit Dr. Northstrum and his Reliance program for making this possible?"

"Yes sir."

"I'll call Earlman and thank him for Northstrum's work.

"General, we can call each of these terrorists individually or as a group. Your choice."

"Let's take out Salem and watch. When will it begin?"

"I will get Tristin on it when I get back to Meade."

Major Caritta leaves. General Bosman leans back in his chair, looking like the cat that ate the canary.

General Bosman is now with his boss, Thomas Dalton, the secretary of defense, as they sit outside a conference room inside the White House. President Matherson summoned them to discuss the latest cyberattack on government systems. The door opens and they enter the room. Inside is every cabinet member and the joint chiefs of staff, the latter of whom are wearing suits adorned with epaulettes. The president sits at one end of a long table. On the wall at the other end of the room are wall-to-wall monitors with maps and data about current events throughout the world. The general and the boss sit, with aides lined behind each department head. The president addresses the attendees.

"Welcome everyone. We are here to discuss the messages sent and the doomsday clock, as the media describes it. They have hit your departments, I'm told." The attendees nod in agreement. "Before starting, my parents would spin in their graves if we did not join hands to offer thanks and ask for help with important decisions we make today." Some in the group grumble within, but they know this is a practice of this president. After a brief, solemn moment the president asks Secretary Dalton, "Thomas, what is your assessment of the problem?"

Dalton responds, "Mr. President, we have spoken to the major companies, the world powers, and no one has been immune. We have brilliant minds working to find out how it was perpetrated. It dumbfounds everyone how an entity would have the advanced program. This clock has penetrated everywhere, as you can see on the monitors in this room. The time is walking backward."

The room looks to the monitors, and someone says, "My smart watch is going backward!"

Dalton continues. "We have confirmed that even people buying new electronics are not immune. They say that as soon as the devices power up, the clocks are normal for a few seconds and then rewind. All we can figure is that it is an email with nothing nefarious riding on the transmission. We have found no security holes or information lost. I have spoken to our friendly countries around the world, and they see the same thing."

President Matherson asks, "What about our enemies? The clock is a threat with the time running out on Halloween. It sounds like a 'better hurry up' warning."

Dalton replies, "We have had scholars review the messages, and the verses keep reminding us to be kind to one another."

Matherson says, "The last message sounds like we'd better be benevolent or else. Can they hurt us, and what will happen when it goes to zero?"

"Mr. President, we don't know who they are at this moment. They can't hurt us with an email, since there is nothing in them but text."

"It seems useless," Matherson says, "but they got to everyone on the planet with no spam filter catching it. Is that correct?"

"Yes, Mr. President. That is what I've been told."

"Doggone, Thomas! If they can do this, we may as well give them the keys to the world's secrets. It scares people, and I hear reports that aliens have invaded us, that God is mad at us, or there is a government conspiracy to get rid of the unwanted. It is not good at the voting booth when your voters are dying."

"Sir, both our friends and enemies have been hit. They think we have done it, but we don't have the ability."

President Matherson asks, "Has a genius has come from out of nowhere and developed a program that can control our communications and cut through security everywhere?" I've got word that even our satellites have this blasted clock rolling backward. Yet everything is functioning with no harm. We need to either obliterate this Dominion and get to their programming before others do, or hire them at whatever price."

"Sir," Dalton replies, "General Bosman is spearheading the handling of this threat."

"General," President Matherson asks, "what are we doing about this threat?"

General Bosman responds, "Mr. President, we have raised our DEFCON level. We are talking to our friends and enemies, assuring them it was not from us."

"I understand that, General, but crazies like North Korea need little to start a war, be it with us or South Korea. All countries are in a dangerous heightened state. We don't want to get to a tipping point that could be disastrous."

Bosman responds, "We are looking at a few people—experts in hacking who might have the skill to pull this off. We have surveillance on them."

"Folks," Matherson says, "I want your departments talking to each other and sharing intelligence. This is no time to get territorial. If I find you are, your heads will roll. We have world egos to stroke. Forget about your own. I want you on the phone talking to your counterparts in every country. We want to keep our friends and pacify our enemies. Right now, they want to hate us. Do you understand? It is crisis mode, folks. I think we have covered this problem. Thomas and General Bosman, I want you to stay over for discussion on another topic. The rest of you are dismissed."

The room clears with the three remaining. President Matherson says, "I received a security briefing on the CART program. I understand you have had a huge breakthrough."

General Bosman smiles. "Yes, Mr. President. Multiple experiments have shown it works, and we are going to begin by trying it on Sheikh Salem."

Matherson responds, "The bomb maker, right?"

"Correct. When activated, we will get death information from local sources."

"Why that way?"

"He will most likely not die immediately, but might die in his sleep or while working. An autopsy will determine he died of natural causes. But it will actually be caused by implanted nanos. This way there is nothing leading back to us, because the nanos are invisible to the naked eye and, as I understand, will die themselves when the human dies."

"Excellent," President Matherson says. "Keep this highly, highly under wraps. If the ACLU got hold of this, they'd cite cruel and unusual punishment, and the media would go wild."

"Mr. President," Bosman responds, "I see no difference between these nanos and a bullet, except a bullet can miss and kill an innocent."

"I agree, General Bosman, but some might consider this entrapment or placing a foreign object inside people as a violation of their rights. Keep me advised of the outcome. If this works, how widespread can it become?"

"Mr. President, if detained for any reason, we can get to them. Once we see the results of Salem, I will detain persons of interest."

"Thank you, Gentlemen. I needed a little good news this morning. The world seems to be coming apart at the seams. This interconnectivity might not be good. In the old days, we had an ocean to cross, which gave us time. Everything is instant now, even annihilation. Keep me posted."

They leave the room, returning to their offices. As Dalton and Bosman enter the hallway, Irvin Sage, director of the FBI, grabs Dalton by the arm. "Can we talk while we walk?" The trio make their way down the hall until Sage pulls them into a small side room. He asks Dalton, "Do you have a scientist at JPL who is a person of interest in this email crap?"

Dalton looks to Bosman. General Bosman responds, "We have many computer guys, and your people have questioned them. But you are referring to Dr. Northstrum. My understanding is that he was very open to everything your interrogators questioned him about. He gave you the programming he had a hand in creating."

"Well," Sage says, "my investigator told me they uploaded his Reliance program to our central computer for analysis, and it did some unusual things. It said something about messages sent. After that, the hack occurred on government computers. Then the accursed clock."

Bosman tells him, "I was under the assumption that for Simon Northstrum to have anything to do with this he'd have to know you'd take it to another location for analysis. Inspector Steele and Montgomery have said that your computer—Bertha, I believe it's called—was not in existence before the rehiring of Dr. Northstrum."

"True," Sage replies, "but do you think he could have activated it while on furlough, in retribution?"

"Irvin," Dalton says, jumping in, "let me get this straight. A scientist wanting to get rehired by JPL activates software to hack the world, then is rehired so he can take the heat for the hack. It is not a well-thought-out plan. Why not just go dark?"

Sage pauses and then says to Dalton, "Okay, I got your point." He then faces Bosman and says, "General, I would like a surveillance detail from the NSA to dog Northstrum. He might have an accomplice. We have pressures to hang a guilty hat on someone. For now, everything points to JPL and Northstrum."

Dalton addresses Sage. "We will put a team on him."

"Good," Sage responds. He nods his head, says, "Gentlemen," and leaves.

Bosman curses while looking at Dalton. "Simon has done great at JPL since being back," he barks. "The rovers are working, and our ten-billion-dollar investment is back on track. I don't want to stop it. And apart from that, he is responsible for the nano development working."

Dalton replies, "You don't have to stop the rover program or throw a monkey wrench in the nano project. I have some NSA people who can handle the job without alarming Northstrum and disrupting his work. These folks can work on the fringe of the constitution without Northstrum's knowledge."

The men shake hands, exit the room, and depart the White House.

JR

Lennon strolls from the bus stop to the studio for work. He can't believe his good fortune in finding a job that pays more than a burger joint. His new guitar might soon be more than a dream on a poster. eBay is his friend these days, as he checks the listings often, not wanting to miss the best guitar deal. The good instruments go fast online. As he reaches his destination, he looks up and sees they erected a sign on the facade of the building. The sign has a name spelled out on it: "Soulful Music."

Lennon gives a fist pump before walking through the freshly painted door. The glass has the business name, address, and hours open. Lennon brings his fingers to his lips, kisses them, and then taps the glass for luck. The door closes behind him, and the freshness of construction reincarnation washes over him. He remembers the musty smell of the long-abandoned building. The room he cleared is bright, with soft lighting enhancing the painted wall. Jozy sits in a chair and turns as he hears Lennon.

"Hi, young man. You got my message."

"Yes sir."

"Sorry it took longer than I expected, but the new tenants wanted other work done before I could bring you back."

Knowing he had completed his work during the reconstruction phase, he thought maybe his work at the building might be finished. "I still have a job?" he asks.

"Yes, you need not worry."

"Man, the place is amazing. You got rid of the old sound board."

"Yeah, the new owners found someone to buy it—a collector. The new one is the state-of-the art."

Lennon asks, "Do I get to play on the machine?"

"I can't say. I'm the landlord, but the new owners are great. I gave you a plug as a budding artist."

"Really? Thank you!"

"You might have to sweep the floor and such, but at least you'll be surrounded by musicians."

"I don't know how I can repay you."

"No need. Just pay it forward when you are a big shot."

With a little laugh, Lennon says, "I will."

"You'll like this Lennon. Come with me." Jozy leaves the office and travels to the back, followed by Lennon. They are now in the restored room where Lennon helped Buddy and CJ. The floor is a beautiful hardwood with an oriental rug. The walls have an acoustic covering on them. Jozy asks, "How do you like the room you helped restore?"

"It is beautiful—a real studio."

"Top-notch, so I'm told."

Lennon scans the room and breathes in the newness. This is a far cry from playing in his room or at teen dances.

"I have a job for you, Lennon," Jozy states. Unpack those boxes in the back and place the contents where marked on the floor. Lennon sees writing on pieces of tape on the floor. The one nearest him reads "Drums."

"Are instruments in the boxes?" he asks.

"Some are," Jozy says. "I hear a big star is coming to do session work, so everything must be in place. Can you handle it?"

"Yes sir!"

"Here is the key to lock up. I'll see you later. The new owner will be in tomorrow and will give you more instructions. Lock the door after I leave."

"Yes sir."

"Oh, here," Jozy says as he turns and hands Lennon money. "This is for today." Lennon thanks him and stuffs the bills into his pocket. He doesn't count it, since he would now work here for free. Lennon is back in the room after seeing Jozy out. He attacks the first box, and it holds a snare drum; the second, a bass drum. After opening more boxes, an entire drum kit sits on the proper spot. He sits on the stool, his foot taps the pedal, and the bass drum vibrates. Lennon rejoices. He is in a recording studio, playing an instrument. Jumping up, he moves to the other boxes like a kid on Christmas morning. The afternoon has soon turned to night. With the last of the instruments placed, Lennon locks the door to the studio and recalls he forgot to eat as he makes his way home. Tomorrow and work can't come quickly enough, because he wants to know who the big star coming to record is.

Dr. Beckett is hard at work after receiving Major Caritta's order to begin the CART program on the selected terrorist, Salem. A smile of satisfaction crosses his face as he programs the remotes. Finally he can begin to exact revenge on the real terrorists without merely carpet-bombing and creating more terrorists than he kills. Now he can deliver a lethal blow to the intended targets without the worry of killing innocents. The phone applications will immediately update, unknown to the targets. With the targets selected, he must call them and send the correct codes so the nanos can do their tasks.

He determines that Salem will have an aneurysm or a hemorrhagic stroke. He codes the nanos to attack different arteries in the brain, causing a blockage and tears to the artery walls. Both will be lethal and undetected. No one in that part of the world will look into a massive stroke, and any toxin screenings will show no poisons. He instructs the nanos with a time delay so that when the method is used repeatedly, suspicions aren't raised when a call is received, followed by a flash, and the target immediately drops dead. The terrorists are not stupid. Salem will get the code and go about his business before he finally dies. Beckett thinks of the Queen song "Another One Bites the Dust."

⚜

"Good morning, folks. I'm Bill Hemmer, and Welcome to *America's Newsroom*. This is a Fox News alert. Good morning, Martha."

"Good morning, Bill. I'm Martha MacCallum."

"Martha, strange incidents are taking place around the world as we speak. If you were on your commute to work today, you doubtless saw the message. Images from around the globe are flooding into the newsroom. The messages emblazoned on the digital displays seen on the interstates are telling people to buckle up, to not text and drive. All the communication apparatuses we use to communicate received the message. Another message being received in regular text messages and social media feeds reads, 'Peace be with you. Self is humanity's greatest sin and the root of mankind's decay. The countdown clock to your rapture has begun. You have time to change by choosing a selfless life. You can listen as well as you hear. Listen and follow your soul's story; there is still time to show true change. We will bring you to the Dominion as you have witnessed.' Folks, if you look at your electronics, there is now a new clock running backward. Our experts have estimated the clock will hit zero at midnight on Halloween, or October 31."

"Bill, we have pictures of the large jumbotrons in Times Square showing the countdown clock."

"Yes, Martha. We also have an image of a man in a robe carrying a sandwich board stating the end is near. He may not be wrong this time."

"Bill, isn't a part of the message a lyric from a Mike and the Mechanics song?"

"Yes, Martha. It is from "The Living Years," a song about showing people you love them before it is too late. It is a song from our generation, but the message is timeless."

"Bill, what about the second part? The rapture is about people going back to God. Someone has threatened us with death? Who are the Dominion? Is it God, or have aliens found us and want to do us harm? We have emails from hackers called the Dominion, normal people aren't dying, and bad people are dropping like flies. Now this ominous warning saying we should listen to our souls or a rapture will be upon us. The rapture is from scripture and pertains to the end of days."

"Martha, it is interesting that the message seems corrupt at first, like an LED bulb in a sign has gone bad and a capital *E* appears as an *F*, but our researcher has determined that the language is ancient Aramaic, a forgotten language of biblical times. It then transforms into the language for the reader. We are hearing reports of people from Russia who don't speak French seeing the text in their native tongue on the roads and on their electronics."

"What hackers can do that, Bill? This interconnectivity is not good."

"Martha, it could be governments are aspiring to get rid of people. They might use our gadgets to kill us. Very weird—way out there."

General Bosman is at his desk in the Pentagon. Florence's voice crackles over the intercom that his ten o'clock appointment is here.

He replies, "Send them in." The door swings open, with Florence in the lead. Following her is Brock Chesterfield. He is an NSA operative who has traveled the world, trailing terrorists. He is a former Navy SEAL involved in many high-profile rescue missions around the world. Brock is oak solid, a holdover from his SEAL training days. He could run through a brick wall. This SEAL's life required many days away from his wife and two small children. The NSA provides for safer missions and less time away from family. Behind him is Kelly Sellers, another NSA agent. She is slight and pale from hours on end spent in front of computers. Kelly is a computer genius, and her coworkers call her Inspector Gadget, based on the cartoon. She can use any electronic device, and if one is not available, she will build it, like MacGyver. She is not the norm in the male world of computer coding. They are seated by Florence across from General Bosman, and Florence departs.

"Good morning," Bosman says to begin the conversation. "You come recommended by Secretary Dalton, and are current on the hacking crisis?"

"Yes," both respond.

"Ms. Sellers—" Bosman says.

"Please, sir, call me Kelly," she interrupts.

"Okay, Kelly. What is your analysis of the communication problem?"

"I have not seen the point of the attack. When a hack occurs, the hackers are usually after something or just want to cause havoc of some kind. The Sony hack is an example. But from what we have discovered, it was an email message with nothing sinister within it. There were no links or attachments attached. No ransomware."

"I see," Bosman says. "Continue."

"The government intrusions must be for espionage, but again, nothing sinister has happened. They might be testing their own capabilities for a later strike. The message was nice—can't fault it. I am curious about the second part, referring to Fleming, penicillin, and Pixii, but am more concerned with this clock. I can't fathom any individual, corporate entity, or government able to do it. They basically crawled into every circuit on the planet. Most electrical circuits have no firewall or protection. If they can do this, what else can they do?" She pauses, looks at Chesterfield, and then addresses Bosman again. "Can you imagine if they went into the major financial institutions globally and deleted files everywhere? Instantly, no one would have any money. If you were holding cash, you might be wealthy for the moment, until the market realized your money is not tied to a precious metal but only to the documents just wiped out. If they can get into these electronics, they can delete the originals and the backups. I can't imagine how long it would take to look for the actual paper, if it even exists."

"Yes," Chesterfield interrupts. "And it is almost like a quiz. Did they want us to catch the mistakes in their messages? Is the problem in the mistakes, and can that open danger to a system?"

"Brock," Kelly responds, "I don't see how, because there are still no links, no downloads, no uploads, and no malware or root kits. The clock is the only threat. The email is a calming diversion. It's like they are saying, 'I come in peace' while they are sticking a knife in your back."

Bosman asks Kelly, "Why would they put stupid language in the email with no links? You think the answer might be in the Fleming and Pixii mentions?"

"I don't know, but people all over the world are researching biblical text, penicillin, Fleming, and Pixii for possible dangerous links. We'd better stop the clock."

Bosman slides two folders to the agents. Brock and Kelly open the documents and review the report on Dr. Simon Northstrum. Kelly lifts her eyes from the report and looks at the general, saying, "This is a guy who put together the space missions to Mars and other places?"

"Yes," Bosman replies.

"Is he the culprit?" Brock asks. He looks at Kelly. "You have intel on this guy?"

"Yes. I mean no, not really. I went to a space symposium, and he was the keynote speaker. He is brilliant but down-to-earth."

"JPL let him go—shortage of funds I hear," Brock interjects. "He might have done it to get back at JPL."

"Well, first of all, he is back at JPL and has put new life in our ten-billion-dollar robotic program. And his Reliance software program has also solved another giant problem we've had. So no, I don't think he's guilty of anything bad. But the higher-ups want him trailed."

Bosman pauses to let his words sink in and then continues. "Right now, Simon Northstrum is the golden boy at JPL. They rehired him because we had lost communications with the rovers, and in one day he got them working with this Reliance program."

Kelly responds, "Dr. Northstrum has brilliant communication software that works throughout our solar system, but the code for spaceships is of no use for emails."

Bosman says, "The basic problem is that the emails point to JPL, and the Reliance software was the only new programming run on the computer there before the email messages began."

"So, naturally, it's the new guy's fault," Kelly quips sarcastically. She then places her hand on the folder before her and continues. "The report says the FBI took the program and ran it through Bertha and found nothing. I worked on the Bertha project, General, and if it found nothing, the software is clean and is not the problem."

Bosman replies, "But, Kelly, it also says that messages were sent from the FBI. Did Bertha send the email, and how did it happen?"

"I don't know," Kelly responds.

Brock asks, "What do you want from us?"

"I want you both near Dr. Northstrum. I've been instructed that we need to know everything going on with him, in and out of work. This guy is valuable to JPL, so it will be good if we can vet and clear him without interfering with his work."

"He will not know we are there," says Brock.

Kelly asks, "I see you assigned me to work at JPL as a programmer?"

"Yes, your clearances are in place. This is where Dr. Northstrum has the most and best computer access, and I thought you could keep him close."

Looking at Chesterfield, Bosman says, "Brock, outside surveillance better suits your skills." The two nod in approval.

"You have passes on the next military flight, so you can get your gear together and begin."

Both rise, as does the general. After final handshakes, the two guests leave the office and building.

The general picks up the phone, dials, and, when connected with his party, says, "This is Bosman. Apart from what the NSA is already doing, I have the two designated agents on the mission, and you can tell the FBI director I will give him our findings." He places the phone in the cradle and moves on to the next task.

※

Yemen is a country on the lower Arabian Peninsula. It is a wild, lawless country sometimes described as the armpit of the world.

Chaos is a terrorist's friend, and once the revolution started, terrorists began to use Yemen as a haven. Yemen is the poorest of the Arab countries, and terrorists travel there without concern. Many Western nations have closed their embassies there. The people there live on less than two dollars per day, so anyone who offers increased wages is welcome in Yemen. Sanaa is the capital, and today we find Sheikh Salem browsing through the market on Jamal Street. Here is a part of Yemen not touched by the ravages of the Saudi-led air raids that pulverized civilian areas, including markets and homes.

Salem travels through the rows of vendors of fruits and Chinese products as people wrangle for bargains. He is in a good mood, joking with his entourage. After finishing haggling with a merchant, he continues his progress through the market. His phone chirps, and he slides his hand into his pocket to fetch it. Salem scans the screen to see who might be calling. He presses the screen to connect with the number. When he connects the phone, the screen flashes his face.

He fumbles with his phone, thinking that he has just taken a selfie. Salem bangs the phone, hoping it will help connect the caller.

He mumbles a curse in his native speech. Bringing the phone to his ear, he yells a greeting. There is no one there. He disconnects, looks at the screen again, and then slides the phone into his pocket. Salem continues to grumble. Even terrorists get butt calls. He reaches for his face and rubs his eyes, feeling a headache is imminent, but he soon rejoins his group. Sheikh moves on in the market, unaware he will never be back but will be taken away by the Dominion.

※

The Soulful Music sign flashes a rainbow of colors as Lennon strides through the door. A large man sits at the new sound board. Strobes are flashing to the beat of the music as he manipulates the dials and the slide controls. The music changes with each movement of his hands. It is loud in the room, so Lennon must bang against the wall to attract the man's attention. The room goes silent, and the man swivels in his chair toward the knocking.

"Hello," the large man says to Lennon with an English accent. "May I help you?"

"I'm Lennon Thomas. Jozy said I should talk to the new owners."

"Yes, hello," he says, pushing away from the board and standing. "I'm Osmond Sword." He crosses the room and extends his hand. "You can call me 'Oz.' Everyone does." Oz is not fat but is thick around the middle. His brown hair touches his shoulders. Tortoiseshell glasses rest at the end of his nose, and in the short conversation, he pushes them up his nose twice. "Jozy had wonderful things to say about you, Lennon."

"Cool," Lennon responds.

Oz says, "My partner, Macy Huet, is in the back."

"Do I still have a job here?" Lennon asks.

"Yes. Jozy said you are a musician. You can help us set up, plus you might have to do some cleaning. Is that okay with you?"

"Sure. I put out the instruments as instructed. I hope I did it okay."

"It's fine. Macy is getting the cables to the microphones."

Lennon says, "I can help with anything. When I came in, you were adjusting music on the board?"

"Yes, I'm testing the new board. It's a bloody humdinger. The latest."

"I noticed the music was pitchy," says Lennon.

Oz's eyebrows rise. "You have a good ear," he says. "Do you know how to work a sound board?"

"No, sir, but I'm willing to learn."

"Good. If we get our work done, then we can play."

"Great," says Lennon, his face glowing like that of a kid in a candy store.

"We will work on the same payment arrangement you had with Jozy. Will that be okay?"

"It sure will."

Oz puts his arm around Lennon and maneuvers him to the sound board. He tells Lennon to grab a chair. They both sit at the machine, Lennon with his hands on his lap, too afraid to move, fearing he might break something. Oz presses a button, and the music returns. He grabs Lennon's hand and places it on a slide lever. He yells, "Move it back and forth."

Lennon complies, and the sound changes. "It's okay; you can't break it," Oz tells him. "We will play until Macy comes to the front." Thirty minutes pass, and Lennon has become comfortable playing with the machine. Oz is teaching him to listen to the test track playing and to how the bells and whistles on the machine affect the sound.

A loud voice behind them stops their playing. "What is it with men and machines?" Macy says. The men turn, and Oz stops the music.

"Hi, Macy," Oz says. "Lennon—he is our helper that Jozy suggested. Macy approaches, and in in a Liverpool accent, she says,

"Welcome to Soulful Music. I like your shirt. We have walked the crosswalk many times."

Lennon glances at his shirt, runs his hand over the image, and says, "I'd love to go to England."

"I take it you are a Beatles fan," Macy says.

"Yes ma'am." Lennon tells her.

"No, I'm not 'ma'am.'" she replies. "I'm Macy."

Oz jumps in. "Macy and I are partners in this venture. She is the accounting whiz."

Macy tells Lennon, "Oz handles the talent and producing. We tired of working for others and struck out on our own. Later, Lennon, I need you to complete forms for the government." She turns toward Oz. "The guitars arrived today, but the strings are loose."

Oz replies, "They need tuning. I'll find someone to tune them."

Lennon interrupts. "I can tune them for you."

Oz responds, "That will be super. We own a recording studio, but neither of us can tune a guitar."

"Where are they?" Lennon asks.

"Follow me," Macy tells him. The two move to the back as Oz resumes his testing of the sound machine.

"You did a superb job of unpacking the boxes for us, Lennon," Macy congratulates Lennon. They enter the studio, and five new guitars are in their stands. He gets a jealous feeling in his gut, looking at the gloss of the new guitars compared to his.

Macy says, "The one on the left is plugged into the sound board, and Oz can record it in the control room. As you finish each one, plug the others up and go for it. Don't be shy. You can play with them if you want."

Heaven is here on Earth for Lennon right now; he's in a recording studio, surrounded by many instruments to play. He picks up the first guitar, which has a red finish. "What a beautiful guitar," he says.

"I can tell by your face you like it," Macy replies.

Lennon nods. "Mine is old and in need of replacement, but I'm entering a city talent show in the hopes of winning prize money."

"I've heard of the show, and I hope you win," Macy says. She then signals Oz to connect the guitar feed. The speakers come alive, with Oz's voice saying, "You're connected." Lennon plucks the strings while twisting the keys. The strings tighten, and the sound reverberates through the studio. The sound machine reacts to each of Lennon's string movements until Lennon's ears are satisfied. The guitar is now tuned perfectly.

Oz's voice booms over the speaker. "Before you go to the next one, play a song with a good guitar solo. Your choice."

Lennon looks to Macy and asks, "Really?"

"Go for it," she says. "Oz will record it, and then you can play with the recording."

Lennon smiles but is silent as he ponders what to play. He settles on "The End," one of his favorite Beatles songs. He nervously strums the strings, afraid to start. Oz's voice reassures him that he can begin. Macy's and Oz's faces light up as Lennon's fingers bring the new guitar to life in a nearly perfect rendition of the song's guitar solo.

Oz leaves his office and heads back to the studio screaming, "Where did you come from, guitar god!"

Macy and Oz say in unison, "You are superb! And you have never done session work?"

"No, I've played in bands and practiced in my room."

"Not anymore, young man," Macy replies. "Can you read music?"

"Yes, my mom showed me, but I can play it by ear. I hear music in my head, and I can play it."

"Oh, you're one of those musicians," Oz responds.

"Is that bad?"

"No, absolutely not," Oz tells him. "Many great ones were the same. If we had an artist come in with a music piece, could he play it for you, and you would pick it up?"

"Yes, usually, if he plays it one time."

"Do you write your own material?"

"Yes, but I have never played for anyone. I'm afraid people will laugh at it."

Oz says, "Don't be that way. If you want to be a musician, then you must take that leap of faith in yourself."

"My goal is the talent show and a new guitar."

"Bring your current guitar with you when you come to work. Can you sit in for session work if needed?"

"Sure, but I don't know exactly what to do."

"You can learn," Oz assures him.

Macy then says, "Good job, Lennon. Very, very impressive."

Oz joins in with "That's for sure." He turns to Macy and says, "All done for today?"

She nods, turns to Lennon, and says, "Same time, same place tomorrow?"

"You got it," he replies. Lennon places the guitar back in the stand. He leaves the studio walking with a new confidence, thinking, "They believe in my dream."

CHAPTER 17

Deep, rapid breathing and pounding footsteps break the morning silence as Lennon darts to the bus stop and Emma. He calls, "Emma! Emma!" She turns at the sound as he approaches. He is wearing the Beatle uniform shirt with jeans. Emma is dressed in a white blouse and khakis. Lennon stops in front of her and scans her. "You look nice," he says.

"The different Swaddling Clothes are neat," she replies.

"I have so much to tell you, Emma," Lennon gasps, catching his breath.

"What happened?"

"Yesterday afternoon was amazing—a dream come true."

"Tell me," Emma says.

"I met the new owners of the shop I showed you. They opened a new recording studio called Soulful Music and are super nice. Oz, the co-owner, taught me how to use the new sound board. He wants to teach me how to use the machine, and we played with a test soundtrack. It was fun."

"Cool," Emma says.

"There is more. I had unpacked instruments the other afternoon and put them in place. Last night I tuned the guitars for them. Emma, the first one was this candy apple–red beauty. I fell in love with each one in my hands. They were so polished, shiny, and smelled brand-new, with no duct tape." Lennon is shaking, trying to hold his excitement. "Em, there is more."

Okay," she says, feeling his excitement.

"After I tuned the first guitar, Oz asked me to play a song with a good guitar solo. He wanted to test the hookups and the sound board. I played 'The End' by the Beatles. When I finished, Oz came rushing in with amazement at what he heard."

"Really?"

"Yeah. They want me to do session work, or at least sit in and try to learn."

Emma smiles at Lennon and steps close and gives him a hug. It is heaven to Lennon. The roar of the bus coming interrupts the moment. It arrives, and they run the student gauntlet to their seats.

♬

Kelly Sellers has processed through security at JPL and stands in the doorway of Colonel Earlman's office.

"Hello, Kelly. Come in and sit. You're here to make sure there are no holes in our security, right?"

"Yes. The president and those on down are sparing no expense to get a solution to the government breach. Where will I be working?"

"Should you be on the mission control floor?"

"No. I might be more of a distraction there."

"All right. I will put you in with our top guy, Dr. Simon Northstrum. He designed most of the communication software we use. Although not a network security person, he is the programmer who created Reliance, and he knows JPL well. He has a few children flying around the universe."

Kelly exclaims, "That will be great." She is taken aback at having been placed with her subject of investigation. "I heard him speak at a symposium," she tells Earlman. "He was excellent."

"Good. Simon is a decent guy, and very bright. How long will you be here?"

"Well, there is an enormous amount of code to review and secure at JPL. I'm inspecting for problems. If any are found, I will bring in a team to seal them."

"Simon has an extra terminal in his office you can use," Earlman tells her.

"Great. I'll get to work ASAP."

"Sure. Follow me." They exit Earlman's office and walk toward Simon's. On arriving, Earlman knocks.

Simon turns from his computer at the sound and rises from his chair, saying, "Come in."

Earlman and Kelly enter. "Hi, Tom," Simon says, and he nods toward Kelly to acknowledge her presence. "What can I do for you?"

"Simon, I'd like to introduce Kelly Sellers. She is a computer specialist out of Washington, assigned by Bosman." Simon extends his hand, greeting Kelly. They exchange hellos. Earlman continues. "Kelly is here to examine our security after the government hacking."

"You should be in demand," Simon says to her.

"Yes," she replies. "It is one time I wish I was paid for overtime."

"Simon, Kelly will work out of your office, since you have an extra terminal that is connected to the in-house server. I understand that the FBI is through with what they were doing on there."

"Yes. Yes, they are. If this works for Kelly, then yeah, it's okay with me." He turns to Kelly and remarks, "I haven't been back long and haven't had a decorator in yet."

Kelly scans the room. "No problem. I usually work in dark rooms." She pauses. "I heard you speak at a symposium a while back."

"Great. I didn't put you to sleep?"

"Far from it. Your message was informative."

"Thanks," Simon replies.

Earlman says, "Folks, I will leave you to it. Simon, will you get her going?"

"Sure, Tom." Earlman leaves. Kelly and Simon move to the extra terminal station. Simon tells her, "As Colonel Earlman said, this computer is connected to our in-house server, so you can go through the entire JPL system. I'll log in for you, and you can get started."

"Perfect," Kelly replies. After logging in, Simon returns to the work at his terminal and Kelly takes a seat to begin her work.

After a while, Kelly asks Simon whether he can help her get into the Reliance program she has found. He answers in the affirmative and goes though the procedures as he did with FBI specialist Aldis Montgomery.

⚜

Across town, Brock Chesterfield sits in front of the Northstrums' home. Alexis is at work, and Emma at school. The van's side reads "Charter"—the name of a local cable company. Brock stands at the side door and stuffs his supplies into his tool bag. He finds the cable junction box that connects the homes, and he removes the cable for the Northstrums' home. He then pulls a small device from his bag, screws it to the cable, and completes the connection. The box blinks. Brock pulls a tablet out of his bag, and the screen reads the signal streaming to and from the Northstrums' home. Anything computer or internet related will now be monitored.

Kelly has made sure Simon's cell phone data is tracked. Surveillance cameras on the telephone poles near the home have already been installed. The government will have Northstrum well monitored. Kelly can also view the feed from her terminal at JPL, though she must be careful. But Simon won't be connecting from his home while at work. Brock's mission is complete, and he pulls the van away from the street.

⚜

Back at Simon's office, Kelly has asked for his assistance a couple of times while examining Reliance. When she asks again, Simon wheels his chair over to where she is working and asks matter-of-factly, "Kelly, how did you become involved with the NSA?"

It startles her, and she replies, "Who said I was with the NSA?"

"I'm not stupid, Kelly. The FBI interrogated me with Inspector Steele and Cyber Specialist Montgomery. I was up-front with them, but you probably already know about that. I guess you are the next level of interrogation."

Kelly's countenance becomes somewhat apologetic. "Simon, I am here for the country. Yes, I was assigned to focus on you. This is such a global problem. We can't rule out anything."

"Understandable," Simon tells her.

"And, yes," Kelly responds, "the FBI and NSA work for the same government, of course, and I've talked with Montgomery. He spoke highly of you and thinks you had nothing to do with this hacking. Steele is different. He considers you dirty, but we must look everywhere, not at the most obvious. As I said, I am assigned to investigate you."

"Well," Simon tells her, "What I'm doing for you I did for Montgomery. And whether he realizes it or not, I am fully aware he made a copy of Reliance. As far as I know, he is the only one outside of JPL that has a copy. You can make one also, if you wish, or you can use his. I understand it's now on the FBI's supercomputer, Bertha." Kelly looks at him, surprised at his insight. Simon goes on to say, "I don't know what else I can show you."

Kelly pauses and then asks, "What about the Reliance program running on your computer? Could it be the culprit?"

Simon tells her, "It does not differ from what I gave Montgomery or what is on the computer you are using."

"Are you sure?"

"Yes, I have done no recoding since I got back."

"Can I see it running live online?"

Simon shrugs. "Okay."

They move to Simon's terminal. Kelly says, "Can you show me how you talk to the rovers?"

"Sure." Simon pulls up the command screen, and the names of the robots appear. He hopes that *Sojourner* stays quiet for now.

"Can we direct *Curiosity*?" she asks.

"Yeah," Simon replies. "I will tell it to send back air samples. I can compare samples from two days ago, when *Curiosity* was in another location."

Simon completes the command and tells Kelly, "It will take some time for *Curiosity* to respond."

"I understand," Kelly says. "Meanwhile, I would like to shut down the program, examine the computer, and then see the program start up again."

Immediately, Simon tells her, "I can't do that. If it's shut down, I may not be able to reestablish communication with the rovers. And besides, I can't make that decision."

"General Bosman gave approval to do it," Kelly informs him.

Shocked, Simon reacts. "Ouch! I adore desk-lovers deciding about these devices, clueless about the effects. Still, I need to give JPL Director Ed Proctor a call and get his approval."

"Go ahead," Kelly tells him. "General Bosman has spoken to both Director Proctor and Colonel Earlman."

Simon gives Norm a call. Norm tells Simon that he has indeed spoken with Earlman and Bosman. "I couldn't talk Bosman out of it, Simon, and neither could Earlman," Norm says.

"Norm, we are going to have some pissed people on the mission control floor when communication streams vanish."

"I'll contact them now and explain that we are doing a shutdown for examination and rebooting purposes. I'll go ahead and send everybody to lunch early, letting them know it will be up and running this afternoon." Norm pauses. "Simon, pray that it will."

"Don't worry about that, Norm; I've already started."

Simon waits a few minutes to allow Norm to contact everyone and send them off to lunch. Finally, with trepidation, Simon disconnects the rovers. Kelly senses real remorse in Simon, as if he is abandoning his children. She feels a fondness for Simon. He has been open and honest as far as she can tell, and she's a pretty good reader of people. He is not like real hackers—people who care about causing havoc or gaining financially.

Simon stands. "It is done," he says. "I hope I'm not unemployed now."

Kelly assures him that they will reconnect, even though she has no idea of what the response will be. "Come on," she says. "I'll buy you lunch. It is the least I can do if I helped you lose your job. Is there a good place near?"

"Yes, Jimmy's. It will be crowded, since Ed told everyone to go to lunch."

The two leave the complex and stand in line in front of the restaurant. They are about to enter the diner when a voice calls to Kelly. She turns. It is Father Gabriel, who spoke at her child's school.

"Father, what are you doing out here?"

"I'm speaking at a school in the area."

They enter the diner, but the diner host steps forward and tells Gabriel, "Sorry, sir, we are full. JPL crowd only today."

Kelly frowns. "Simon, may Father join us?"

"Sure," Simon says, and he then nods to the host. Gabriel is allowed to go through with Simon and Kelly.

They find a table, and Kelly says, "Father Gabriel, this is Dr. Simon Northstrum. He works at JPL next door."

"Wonderful, I love those space missions. Are you involved with them?"

Kelly tells him, "Father, Simon put the robot rovers on Mars and handles the communications."

"Outstanding. I love the pictures. You must be proud."

"Yes, thank you," Simon replies. "How do you know Kelly?"

"I was at her child's school, talking about faith."

"Simon," Kelly informs him, "it was excellent how he spoke to the children."

Gabriel says, "I remembered Kelly because she was in a cell phone coma, hypnotized by her phone during my teaching."

Kelly blushes and then says, "He came down and turned my phone off."

"Ouch! Busted. Real computer geek," Simon reacts.

"Many are that way now. I am speaking to churches and schools, advising about the coma-like hypnosis caused by electronic gadgets."

Kelly says, "Simon, he had an interesting talk about connecting with your soul and its story. He compared it to Star Wars and Luke's belief in the force. The kids were interested. He made it believable to the children."

"The soul is wonderful," Gabriel says. "It has brought many

people through terrible obstacles never thought possible. Imagine, if you would, those tiny premature babies with wafer-thin fingers in incubators. They are hooked to machines helping them, but researchers have discovered that the angel volunteers who come and selflessly hold, massage, and caress the babies do as much to strengthen them as the machines. That is the connection of souls."

Simon asks Gabriel, "Have you seen the movie Unbroken? Is that a good example?"

"Yes, along with Desmond Doss of Hacksaw Ridge, who also displayed an indomitable soul. Do you believe he was alone on the ridge? And then there is the story of a woman who went to the gym to run on the treadmill. After starting, she had a strong desire to get outside and run on a trail, taking along her dogs. The dogs found a newborn infant buried alive. She saved it, and the child grabbed her wrist as though they had a bond. She listened to her soul and not her brain. Imagine if all mankind had such faith or listened unselfishly."

"Yes," Simon responds. "I'm learning more and more about the importance of listening."

Gabriel replies, "Simon, you sound like a man of faith."

"I try, and I'm trying to like everyone," Simon tells him.

"Everyone is not trying, because there are too many distractions with electronics," Gabriel responds.

Simon responds, "Funny … someone else mentioned the same thing."

Kelly's phone rings. She looks at the phone and leaves her seat, saying, "Sorry. I must take this call." She departs the table while answering, "This is Kelly."

"Kelly," says the voice on the other end, "Brock here. Everything is set up in the Northstrums' home. Our eyes and ears are on him. How are you doing at JPL?"

"Pretty good. But Northstrum's no dummy. They put me in his office, and he was on to me right away."

"Did you deny it?"

"No, I leveled with him. He was open. He told me the FBI had the only other copy of his Reliance program. He is sharing with me the one on his computer that is communicating with the Mars rovers, and I'm going to be examining his computer."

"Do you believe him?"

"Yes, I do. I asked him to shut down the running program on orders from General Bosman so I could review things. He didn't want to, because he didn't want to break the connection. JPL is unsure whether they can reconnect again. He was really hesitant about shutting down something that is working fine—something he was rehired to make work. I understand his point, because those robots become space junk if they can't reconnect. I'll know more when I get back from lunch."

"Is it possible he has an accomplice on the outside running the program?"

"I doubt it, unless they have a huge satellite array."

While Kelly's conversation continues, Simon and Gabriel start a discussion at the table.

"Father, you travel around the country speaking to churches, right?"

"Simon, I travel around the world. I speak to people everywhere I can, like the apostles. They had no so-called churches like the ones we have today. Many of those I teach around the world have never heard of God, faith, or Christianity."

"Are you afraid they might harm you? Missionaries have a martyrdom track record."

"You are right. The apostles, except for John, came to terrible ends."

"Father," Simon says as he begins to ask a question.

"My friends call me Gabe."

"Okay … Gabe. Why didn't God save them from such deaths?"

"They were chosen, and they completed their souls' journeys as Jesus completed His. Your faith tells you that before Jesus was born in human form, He was destined to die. He knew this all along. It was His soul's destiny."

"You mean His soul's story."

"Yes, in your words." Gabriel pauses and then says, "You look perplexed."

"Well, I have been hearing about our souls' stories lately."

Simon, someone once wrote, "Most people die with their music still in them." When I teach, I try to get people to search inside themselves and find their music, their stories. Kelly mentioned Star Wars. I use it as an example of soul-searching."

"Gabe, you need a light saber and a little green being to help you. Funny how that works. Someone shouts 'Luke! Luke!' with a light saber, and everyone has faith." Simon hesitates and then says, "Let me ask you a question."

"Sure."

"We were posed a question at Bible study: 'What is your take on Noah?' My response to the question now is that I suppose God was pissed at humanity and brought them back into what I have recently been hearing called the Dominion. There they will start over. But my question to you is, 'Why just Noah and his family?'"

"Well, Simon, according to the Bible, Noah at the time was the only truly righteous man living on Earth."

"Did people call Noah crazy?"

"I'm sure they did. I was speaking to Kelly's child's class, and I explained it this way to them." Gabe puts his finger into his water glass and pulls it out. He holds it above the remaining water in the glass and a drip releases from his fingertip, falling back into the glass. "This is how I explain the soul."

"So we are the drop of water, and the time it spends on your finger is our life, until we fall back into the glass."

"No, the Dominion is all around, and you can't separate it. Let's compare the finger to part of God. Your life is the distance from the fingertip to the water in the glass. The water in the glass is your return to the Dominion. There is no time in the Dominion, and your life span can take a blink of an eye."

"I see. It is an interesting example with the water being God's Dominion."

"Yes, everything is within God's Dominion. It is frowned upon in churches."

"How do you get people to glance inward?"

"That is a good question, Simon, and a big problem."

"How so, Gabe?"

"Too many distractions from solitude."

"How can an ordinary person get people to develop their souls?"

"Use what is in place. Use the communications for an important purpose. Write blogs and create meaningful videos on selflessness. Get the word out. Simon, I perceive people today as cubicle beings."

"Cubicle?"

"Yes. People wake in the morning in a cubicle, their homes, and eat in another cubicle within it, their kitchens. And then they travel in another cubicle to work, their cars, and sit in another cubicle at work. Throughout all of this, very few people spend quality time speaking face-to-face with other people."

Gabe lets his words sink in and then continues. "Simon, God gave us the ultimate communication device—the soul. It thrives and learns on human interaction. How do you learn about other people if you don't touch them? It's amazing what a simple hug can do. Sit with strangers, talk with them, and break bread with them, and you may find that your paths were meant to cross so your souls can learn."

"Learn what?"

"Everything!"

"Can't it be done with social media?"

"Somewhat, but social media is infected with self, with no truth barometer. People say, 'See what I'm eating, and where I'm vacationing and my new car or the bigger house.' Understand what I mean?"

"Yes, I tire of the cute puppy pictures."

"I'm not saying junk it, but step away from the drama. God will sit with you when you come into His Dominion and will be sad if everything out of your mouth is about self. Simon, you sound as if you want to get the word out. You are a perfect choice with your communication skills. If you can make robots perform millions of miles away, then you can get people listening." Gabriel pauses, studies Simon briefly, and then says, "You seem puzzled at my words."

"No, it's just that other people mentioned getting people listening."

"You might find yourself another career. The apostles did."

"I'm no apostle."

Kelly returns and sits. "Sorry it took so long. My message box is packed. This electronics problem has us stumped."

Gabriel asks, "Is it that big of a big problem, Kelly?"

"Governments around the world are blaming each other for the email messaging and other issues. Most assume they are in jeopardy, and they might strike first to protect themselves."

"They want to start a war because of an email?" Gabe asks. "I thought the messages were more biblical, and the only difference was in the last parts—the bits about penicillin and a person named Pixii. I'm just a priest, but maybe the last lines are the key."

Simon's brow rises. "How so?"

"Well," Gabriel says, "The rest of the messages are taken from the Bible or Koran text. Unless you're a conspiracy theorist and think the Bible has hidden computer code, the last line is the difference. I am sure people are scanning every dot of the emails."

The trio finish their meals and leave the restaurant. Kelly and Simon are back in the office, and Simon directs Kelly to his terminal. He enters his password and says, "You can take it from here."

"I can use your terminal on my own?"

"Of course. I've nothing to hide, and if I am disconnected from the rovers, there is not much for me to do computer wise. I've given you the path to Reliance."

Kelly looks at Simon, realizing most criminals act differently. She believes in him but is also thinking that just maybe he's sly and may be a con man. "Okay," she says, "I see the program here. And, since you know about the FBI's Bertha, I might as well tell you that I am linked to Bertha so I can analyze Reliance on your computer." She begins the scanning process.

Simon sits reviewing project reports, waiting for the ax to fall.

After a little over an hour, the terminal beeps and the screen shows that the software is clean. Kelly turns to Simon. "This is good news for you. Nothing is suspicious in this program—unless you are smarter than almost every other programmer and Bertha. Are you sure no other copies exist?"

"I'm sure. Just the copy Montgomery created. I had nothing to do with it."

"I know. Is there anyone else who could copy it?"

"Many people work here and can access the system. I can't imagine someone here would jeopardize his or her position by doing it. I mean, I started back, and I'm not about to risk everything to send out an email."

"Nothing at home?"

"No, I can't contact Mars with basic internet."

"Got it. Before I leave, I want to watch as you reconnect your rovers."

"Sure, if I *can* reconnect. We'll soon see."

They change seats, and Simon begins the communications procedures with Reliance. The list of rovers is displayed. Glancing Kelly's way, Simon says, "So far, so good." He instructs the software to connect to the robots. Next to each robot, a small synchronizing symbol swirls. One by one, the screen shows connection with each rover. Simon exhales. "I guess I can come in tomorrow."

Kelly smiles. Simon points to the screen next to *Curiosity*. "It has sent me the report I sought."

"I'm so glad you're reconnected, and I'm so relieved that we didn't mess up things," Kelly says. She stands and tells Simon, "I must get to a meeting. Thank you for everything and for being very open."

Simon stands now and says, "I've nothing to hide."

Departing, Kelly tells him, "I'll be back reviewing others here at JPL."

"Are you done with me?" Simon asks.

"I don't know. For now, yes. But I don't know about later." Kelly leaves his office, and he slumps in his chair, exhausted from the whole experience—and especially the mistrust.

"*Sojourner* was right," he says to himself.

After getting some coffee, along with orange juice, Simon works the rest of day and then leaves the office, heading home and to his sanctuary. Traffic is normal, and the drive is smooth, quiet, and relaxing. He peers in his rearview mirror and notes a car traveling the same route. The investigations have made him paranoid of people in the shadows.

He straightens up in his seat and grabs the steering wheel with both hands. His mind travels to those shows he and Alexis have watched on TV and how they include a tail. He smiles, thinking this can't be real. He pulls the car over to the nearest convenience store, intending to get the newspaper he promised Alexis and to see whether the car continues on its path.

The tailing car, driven by Brock Chesterfield, pulls over and parks far from Simon's. Simon has seen this move before, on TV. He realizes that, unfortunately, most novices continue with their normal route without deviation. Most drivers are unaware license plate cameras scan cars' plates while tracking them.

Simon gets back in his car and goes home his normal way, with Brock trailing behind.

Brock watches from down the street as Simon enters his home. He pulls away, confident the tracking device placed on Simon's car will alert him of Simon's movements, and that the connections he installed earlier will alert him of any home online usage by Simon. Brock heads back to confer with Kelly.

⚉

Simon pushes through the door and plants himself in his recliner. He lets his exhausted body sink into the well-worn chair. Alexis calls from upstairs, "Is that you, Simon?"

"Yeah."

"I'll be down in a minute."

Shortly, Alexis descends, saying, "Emma took my car and is working with the Swaddling people. Let's go out for a pizza." She

279

enters the family room. "Hi, honey, what are you doing flopped out in here? Bad day in space?"

"No. The NSA came to see me today!"

"The people who spy on everyone?"

"You got it. They wanted to talk about Reliance."

"I thought the FBI investigated you?"

"Since the government computer and clock hacking stuff, they are going back through everyone. They had the nerve to place their agent in my office with me. She pretended to be a computer specialist checking security flaws. I smelled her out right away."

"What did she do?"

"She was nice, not like the FBI's Steele. When I confronted her, she admitted who she was and what she wanted."

"What did she want?"

"She wanted the running version of Reliance so she could examine the code. Norm approved it."

"Are you out of a job?"

"Not as far as I know. I explained everything to her, and she understood. I disconnected the family. The good news is that she found nothing sinister in Reliance, and I got each rover back online. These NSA people will explore everything. She said there are governments ready to go to war over this breach. Things are happening, Alexis, as *Sojourner* advised me, and I am the center of attention."

"Simon, we can stay home. You had a stressful day."

"No. Pizza is good." He rises from his chair and grabs his keys as Alexis readies herself. Simon decides not to tell Alexis he thinks the government is watching all of them. *No need to worry her.* He assumes that the ride to eat will give him a chance to examine his spying paranoia. Simon puts his arm around his wife as they exit the house. The ride to and from the pizza parlor is uneventful. He is not concerned now about the earlier tail. Across town, Brock Chesterfield watches a moving blip on a computer screen. The computer is recording every step in Simon's travels. The investigative legwork will begin tomorrow, with visits to each location to see whether a threat exists or the path leads to a coconspirator.

☞

Brock sits at the bar of the hotel in which he is staying. He tilts back a beer while playing with his change lying on the bar top. The room is like any in a midrange hotel. Inspector Steele enters the bar, and his older eyes adjust to the dim room. He scans it and looks for his contact. Brock wears a golf shirt and jeans. Steele is old-school and wears a coat and tie. Steele approaches the man he assumes is Brock based on the description he was given.

"Brock Chesterfield?" he asks.

"Yes," Chesterfield responds as he spins and stands, towering over Steele. "Inspector Steele, it's good to meet you." They shake hands, and Brock looks around and chooses a more private location—a table away from the bar. He asks the bartender for another beer for Steele and gets it.

"Thank you, I need one," Steele says as they head for the table.

"I suppose the heat is coming down on both of us," Brock says.

"You've got that right in more than one way."

"How is that?"

"Well," Steele says, "I go from investigating someone for hacking to being a suspect myself."

"Steele," you're a former marine."

"Yes, and you're navy."

"Yes."

"Well, Chesterfield, no matter what we've been, now some are saying that since I'm the FBI investigator on this, and the emails have been tracked back to the FBI, I must be involved in some way. So, tell me, what have you learned about the scuttlebutt on the communications hacking stuff?"

"Call me Brock … and can I call you Parker?"

"Yeah, fine. Go on."

"Parker, the street talk is not good. My SEAL buddies are on alert. Those who have recently retired are being asked back."

"Are we preparing for war over an email?"

"There are crazies out there who don't need many incentives if they can get the upper hand. The problem is, we don't know who to blame or attack! I have checked you out, Parker, and as far as a suspect, you're clean. In honesty, you're a great cop; you're not capable of this. I want to know everything about Montgomery."

"He is smart, maybe too smart for me, but a good kid. He placed the Reliance software on Bertha and ran the scan like he's done a thousand other times. I have people screaming about how it got on every computer. Montgomery and I have racked our brains to see if we missed a step, but we did everything by procedure."

"What do you think of Dr. Simon Northstrum?"

"Very intelligent. I interrogated him."

"I know. I have your report. You found nothing to nail him?"

"No, but another copy of his software is running at JPL we didn't check."

"Not anymore. My specialist disconnected it, carefully reviewed it, and found nothing."

"So you did no better than Montgomery and me?"

"No. This guy might be a cool operator. Kelly, my specialist, leans toward thinking he's okay, but I think he is dirty."

Kelly enters the bar and sees Brock with another person. She approaches and says, "Hello."

"Kelly," Chesterfield says, "this is FBI Inspector Parker Steele."

The two exchange greetings, and Brock Chesterfield motions for her to sit, and she does.

Kelly says, "I didn't think I would ever answer all my calls. They want everything done or cured yesterday."

"You interrogated Dr. Northstrum?" Steele asks.

"Yes, I spent over half a day with him."

"You're NSA, correct?"

She looks at Brock for approval, and he nods.

"Yes," she replies to Steele.

"Did you catch him on anything? Anything at all?"

"No. I reviewed the working Reliance program, and everything was clean."

"You did it through Bertha?"

"Yes, using the same procedures from your report."

Steele probes, "The screen didn't come up and say the messages were sent?"

"No, and the normal infection report screen showed no problems. Really, I can't believe Dr. Northstrum would have the time to write new hacking code and leave no remnants of previously written code he expanded on or made better. Besides that, he seems to me to be a good guy."

CHAPTER 18

Simon sits with his coffee and *America's Newsroom*. He presses the remote to increase the volume. The reporters are discussing the latest government problems and the endless investigations by the Senate and House committees. Bill says, "Folks, a watchdog group is accusing these committees of being a farce. They liken it to the weasels guarding the henhouse. They are outraged over government malfeasance, but they never get to the bottom of anything. No one is ever right or wrong, nor held accountable. They give you the illusion something meaningful is happening."

Simon looks at the TV and says, "You've got that right. If I lose a ten-billion-dollar program, I am toast."

Bill continues. "Martha, in another breaking news story, we've received word that Sheikh Salem of Yemen died in his home of an apparent stroke. You may remember him as the chief bomb designer of many horrific terror attacks around the world. I don't know, folks. There have been strange happenings going on around the world. The bad guys are taking a beating. What are your thoughts, Martha?"

"Bill, we are hearing that many people believe the government has a new weapon, and others believe that prayers have been answered. Folks, tweet us your thoughts."

Alexis enters the kitchen, not ready for work. "Morning, hon," she says. Simon gets her a cup of coffee as she sits at the table. "What's going on in the world today?"

"Congress is doing nothing. As usual."

"What do they say, Simon ... 'Gridlock is good?'"

"Yeah. On the bright side, though, some dirtbag bomb builder in Yemen died."

"Did the government get him?"

"The news reports it was from natural causes." He pauses. "Why are you still in your bathrobe?"

"I got a text from Adam not to come in today. He said there was no business. Where did you put the newspaper you brought home?"

"The obituary section was missing, so I trashed it. But I went out and bought you a new one at the nearby store. It's in my office. Hold on." Simon heads to his home office, and Alexis lowers the TV volume. Simon returns, hands the paper to her, and then pours himself another cup of coffee. "May I see the front page?" he asks.

"Sure," Alexis says, sliding it to him, retaining the other sections. She scans each section but fails to find the page. "Simon, will you tell me what section has the obituaries."

He scans the front page and sees no reference to an obituary section. "There is no listing for it," he tells her. "There is business, sports, comics, community, editorial, and other news, but that's it. Alexis, there are always obits. Let me see; maybe you missed it." She gives the entire paper to him, and he goes through it section by section, page by page. Aggravated, he glances at Alexis. "No obits. Surely I didn't pick up two papers missing the same section."

Simon, I'm curious. Adam tells me not to come in today, and now no one is listed in the obituaries. There is not even an obituaries section. Does this have anything to do with *Sojourner*?"

"I will put an end to this right now," Simon says. He picks up the phone and dials the newspaper's number. After a wait, he says, "Yes, good morning. I picked up one of your papers, and the obituary section is missing. May I get a complete paper?"

"Sir, I apologize, but the newspaper has received no notices of deaths in recent days. I'm swamped with the same type of calls. I wish I could help you, but you have the complete paper."

Okay, thank you." Simon puts the phone back in the charger.

Alexis asks, "What did they say?

"Alexis, no one has died! *Sojourner* said the Dominion has control over life and death. People are not dying."

"Is it here or everywhere?" she asks.

"Well, since you're not working today, get on the internet and call other newspapers and funeral homes and see if it's happening in other places. I'm going to get ready for work." He leaves for his shower.

Alexis turns off the TV and moves to Simon's office. She sits at the computer and searches for newspapers and funeral homes on both coasts and writes the numbers down. She makes about six calls and soon realizes this is a national situation and might even be worldwide. Alexis climbs the stairs and finds Simon dressing. Her eyes well up with tears, and she says, "I'm scared, honey."

Simon has seen this look on Alexis's face before, with her parents' deaths. "What's wrong?" he asks.

"I called newspapers on the East and West Coasts, but they have no deaths to report. What's happening? Is it the Dominion?"

"I don't know, Alexis. *Sojourner* has gone silent."

"I have questions about it. Is this real, Simon? I mean, a robot on Mars is talking to you about faith and the destruction of man. And now no one in America is dying?"

"I have to believe *Sojourner* has been talking with me. With all that's going on, things are not exactly in human hands right now. I've been encouraged to examine the last lines of the email messages."

"The ones with the names?"

"Yeah," Simon tells her. "They were names and dates, and penicillin was significant. I don't know the guy Pixii. He might have done something important. Alexis, the best minds are scanning each word and letter of the emails. They're people who believe the Bible holds a computer code called the codex. It predicts prophecy."

"Oh, yes, those are the boring shows you watch that put you to sleep."

Simon smiles. "Sometimes I listen with my ears," he says.

"Riiiight," she says, dragging the word out. She then asks, "You said the Dominion will send people home?"

"Yes."

"Are they behind the weird stuff going on around the world? Didn't you see on the news about an angel that killed a sniper?"

"Alexis, I don't know what new weapons the government has developed."

What if it wasn't the government but them—the Dominion?"

"*Sojourner* said to watch the news for actions from the Dominion, but how do I know what all of this means? It could be that the Dominion, along with the government, is using my Reliance to remove the bad guys. But what does it matter? One less creep inhabits the earth. Right now, the only people dying are the ones hurting the innocent. Listen; I've got to get to work. Meanwhile, you scan the news shows and keep a record of developments going on around the world. Make lists of weird stuff; bad guys meeting their deaths, light flashes, angel sightings."

"All right," Alexis says.

"Doesn't the Bible say there will be trumpet blasts before the end of time? Let's chronicle every unexplained or weird event occurring. If *Sojourner* contacts me, I can ask if the Dominion or man caused the events. I think we are at a point in believing that God, aliens, or government conspiracy is causing this. When I go to work, I will make a copy of Reliance for my protection. I created it and am the only person without a copy, it seems."

"Can you do that?"

"Yes. I will figure a way. And I want it for protection."

"Okay, get going, and I'll work on my assignment at home."

Simon leaves for JPL.

⁂

Meanwhile, across the continent, Dr. Beckett is also watching the news report on the death of Salem. He shuts off the show and explodes from the chair and runs around the room in exhilaration. "It worked!" he shouts. He clasps his hands in prayer and reaches them skyward. "Thank you, God! Thank you, Simon Northstrum! And thank you, sis! I'll get the bastards, as I promised you!" He thinks of the quote from General Patton: *"May God have mercy upon my enemies, because I won't."* Beckett calls Caritta. "Did you get the news?" he asks

"Yes, it's remarkable. It was Reliance?"

"Yes, unless he died naturally, which I doubt. Either way, he is gone." He pauses a second and then says, "Are we ready to expand?"

"I'll go up the chain of command," Caritta responds. "If we get approval, how soon can you begin, Tristin?"

Beckett replies, "I've got my phones cocked and loaded, waiting to call."

"How many?"

"I programmed an even hundred. I've not set up a speed dial for death yet." Tristin smirks at his joke.

"Let me get back to you," Caritta tells him. Tristin returns to his work and builds a second target list of villains.

⚖

President Matherson has convened an emergency session of the United Nation's Security Council. It is unprecedented for a president to sit in on one of these sessions along with the US–UN ambassador. Yet these are extraordinary times. The body is meeting in an attempt to avoid a world war. Tensions are high, as no country is sure who the villain in the email hacking is, and now the worldwide doomsday clock is ticking down. The entity known as the Dominion has somehow invaded the electrical systems of the earth and can move through them with impunity. In the room today are the world's geniuses. Each is proposing a solution to end this nightmare, but countries are posturing for power. They have not heeded the message of the first email and selflessness.

Cooke Carver, renowned in many fields, has proposed a test to remove this hack from systems throughout the world. He proposes to make Times Square in New York go dark for a short period. This will allow the circuits to lie dormant before a small power surge scrubs them, purging the problem. He likens this procedure to clearing the cache of a computer. Countries argue for and against the idea.

President Matherson says, "Mr. Carver, you are proposing to make Times Square go black? It is one of the busiest intersections in the world."

"Yes, it is prominent," replies Carver. "We must do this in a visible traffic site to show the Dominion we can stop them."

"I recommend we use the internet kill switch and shut it off," says Matherson. The Chinese delegation erupts at the mention of an internet shutdown. Many delegations react negatively to the suggestion. The president sits back in his chair as the yelling continues. He ponders that these countries are incensed by a shutdown. *Maybe they are the ones creating this mess and I struck a nerve.* The Chinese would lose three million dollars a minute during the internet outage. Many countries would suffer immense losses, including the United States.

"Mr. Carver, explain why your option of shutting down Times Square only is better than an internet kill," Matherson says.

"As far as I can tell, Mr. President, the internet is working fine. Maybe you know something I don't, but I can't find where anything has been broken, stolen or transferred. No countries have reported espionage, with a crucial defense plan divulged. I would assume in traitorous terms that would be the coup de grâce. We've only been told to live a benevolent lifestyle. I don't know what will take place when the clock strikes zero. Our best option is to stop the clock. If it works, we will give the technology to everyone to run the fix. You can turn off the internet, but you will only scare people even more. The clock's electronics doesn't care about the internet, but somehow, they have found a way to control it. If it doesn't work using Times Square, we are no worse off than before, and the countries here will get off the warpath."

⚓

Alexis has been called back to work at the funeral home. When she was called in, she wondered why, because she understands that no one is dying, and her clients have said they have no business for her. But nevertheless, she is in the office, alone, waiting for an explanation. That's when Adam steps through her doorway.

"Hello, Alexis," he says. His face is upbeat—not common for him. "Did you see the census?"

"No, are we still empty?" Alexis responds.

"Absolutely not," Adam chirps. "We have a full schedule." This confuses Alexis. Her clients have had no business for them, and her research shows no one is dying.

She asks, "Where did they come from, Adam?"

"They have been coming in from the county morgue and hospital ERs. They are strange, in a way."

"How so?" she asks.

"Research is showing the deaths are among what we would call 'bad guys.'"

"Okay. So we've got shootings, knifings, overdoses, and stuff like that? Bad guys killing bad guys? Drug dealers and such?"

"No," Adam tells her. "The interesting thing is they've all died from natural causes, with the medical examiners finding no cause of death. It is as if these people just quit living. Gang members and thugs usually come in with obvious wounds, pretty straightforward."

"You're right, Adam. This is weird," Alexis says, very perplexed.

"We have a full week's worth of funerals. Most need no dramatic measure for viewing."

"We are burying a bunch of creeps?" Alexis asks.

"A good percentage, but there is at least one priest, one rabbi, and one protestant minister in the mix. It sounds like a bad joke." Adam gives a little laugh, which is highly unusual for the sourpuss.

"So you called me in. Do you need my help inside?"

"Yeah, you can work inside in the mornings, then hit the road in the afternoons to see who else is dying and where they are."

"Okay," the still-perplexed Alexis says.

Adam leaves the office, and Alexis logs into the computer to see the list of the people in the back. It is unusually high. The screen floods with the list of the deceased. She picks up the phone and dials a counterpart at competing funeral home. "Is Laurie in, please?" she asks when connected. Shortly, she says, "Hi Laurie, this is Alexis from Sable."

Oh, hi, Alexis."

"I have a strange question to ask you, Laurie."

"Okay," Laurie says.

"We have an overload of clients, and they are stacking up like cordwood."

"It's funny you called," Laurie says before Alexis can ask her question.

"I was told to call to ask for help from you for the same reason. I've not seen anything for days, and now they arrive in busloads. The other homes reported the same."

Alexis is silent and then asks, "Are you getting many criminal types?"

"Yes, predominately, but not all. But they are all natural causes, regardless of age. Weird, huh? If we get any more, I might have to put them in the freezer at home."

Alexis laughs. "That will go over big with the family," she says.

"Yeah, dead guys in the fridge."

"Thanks, Laurie. Let's keep in touch and we can help each other."

"Good deal," Laurie replies, and they hang up.

Alexis sits back in her chair, brushing the hair behind her ear. She thinks back to what Simon told her about his discussion with *Sojourner*, with the robot saying the Dominion would be reclaiming souls off the path and that it will surprise us which people are sent packing. *I understand the criminals, but what would priests, rabbis, and protestant ministers do wrong?*

Alexis dials the phone, and Simon answers, "Hello, honey. What's going on? Did you find out why you were called in?"

"Well, we've got business. That's good but strange."

Simon knows this is an opportunity for a dead-people joke, but something in Alexis's voice causes him restraint. "What is strange? Is the census back up?"

"Yeah, and that's the problem. Not only is the census back up, but we're backed up. People are dying again, and it's weird. No one dies for days, and now they are dropping all around us."

"Really? I've not seen or heard anything on the news."

"Well," Alexis says, "I've got to start calling around to find freezer storage space. We are overflowing with the dead."

"Okay, but you are a funeral home; dead people get sent there, and apparently the moratorium on death is over.

"But Simon, we're talking about an overload of dead people, and the huge majority are criminals dying from natural causes."

"Good. They are off the streets."

"Yes, Simon. But when we get criminals in, most have noticeable damage done to them. They don't usually die from natural causes, and certainly not at this rate. Do you remember what *Sojourner* told you about reclaiming people?"

"Of course."

"Simon, I spoke to another home, and they report the same. Mostly obvious criminals, but not all, and they are overflowing. Simon, is this the Dominion doing what *Sojourner* predicted?"

"Crap!" Simon reacts.

"Simon, can you research this or talk to *Sojourner*?"

"I can research it, but *Sojourner* contacts me. I can't initiate contact."

"Can't you try on your Reliance program at JPL?"

"I don't know, Alexis, because talking to *Sojourner* from here anymore is dangerous. Everyone suspects me of everything. I was beginning to think that everything was settling down."

"But Simon, you told me that *Sojourner* said the Dominion would turn up the heat."

"Yeah, it did. I'll try to find out something. We'll talk about it tonight. Apparently you'd better get busy at work."

"Right. Talk to you later."

The call ends, and Alexis starts trying to contact some families of the dead to discuss interment plans. Meanwhile, Simon has been electronically connecting with the rovers, and they are all working perfectly. After his conversation with Alexis, he realizes that he never actually tried to contact *Sojourner* to start a verbal conversation. As he told Alexis, it's always been the other way around. He goes back to the initial screen, where it was set when *Sojourner* first talked to him.

Simon thinks about the surveillance on him by the FBI and the NSA, ponders it, hesitates, and then goes ahead and clicks the button. He sits back in his chair, now thinking himself crazy for doing this—or downright stupid. The computer runs through its programming and ends with a screen saying, "Communication is not available."

Simon rubs his face in exasperation, thinking, "This is like praying to God. You do the talking and get silence."

He checks another screen and sees that the rovers are still connected. He then calls funeral homes in a few states to substantiate Alexis's claims, quickly finding that everything is accurate. He then opens his desk and grabs a slip of paper with Tristin Beckett's number scribbled on it. Simon dials the number, and a woman answers. "This is Dr. Simon Northstrum. May I speak to Doctor Tristin Beckett?"

"Sir, he is traveling, but I can put you through to his voice mail."

"No, it won't be necessary." Simon hangs up. He has Beckett's cell number at home, and it will be better not to leave a voice mail at his office. He works the rest of the day, with no word from *Sojourner*. The day ends with no surprises, and he makes his way to his car. Entering the car, he breathes a sigh of relief that neither the FBI nor NSA has been on his back. He looks forward to a peaceful evening with Alexis, hoping she won't want to talk much about dead people.

A quarter of Simon's drive is uneventful, though he encounters several people in a hurry, and no matter his speed, it isn't fast enough. Simon lets them pass. The solitude is broken by a voice from the radio.

"Hello, Simon. I saw you called."

"*Sojourner?*"

"Yes."

"So I did get through to you. It did work."

"No, not really. The Dominion knew of your questions, even if there was no reply to your contact."

"Oh, them again."

"Not again, Simon. The word is 'always.' Still don't believe, do you?"

"I don't know."

"Doesn't it say, 'Eyes that have not seen'?"

"Yes, I suppose."

"Well, Simon, you have seen much. You question the deaths? Is the Dominion the cause? I told you of the coming rapture. You did not understand."

"No. If people are off the path, I can't change them, and you will take them."

"They can get back on track. They must listen to their souls. Your Reliance has linked the world and is bringing people to their rapture. You and Alexis have witnessed it and are the only humans that see the truth. The rest of the world will postulate that aliens are here or new government programs have been implemented to rid the world of scum. If you don't start your mission soon, many will be removed without the opportunity to change. Noah was a slow learner, but he was not as learned as you. Don't let your scientist's nature impede your faith."

"Why don't they just flood the world again?"

"They could remove water or make it scarce, but that would bring out the selfishness of man, Simon."

"Do they delight in mankind at its worst?"

"Natural death is a celebration of a journey's end. Unnatural death caused by someone's selfish ripple is an experience of learning. No one may end a soul's journey, be it for water or survival."

"*Sojourner*, you said the Dominion walk the earth."

"Yes, occasionally."

"Do I know their names?"

"Yes. They are teachers and spend much of their time in the Dominion and need not come to Earth as often to learn. Your biblical prophets come to mind. Are you familiar with Fatima, Lourdes, and Medjugorje? It was the Dominion directly teaching a soul."

"Is that why the people were in a trancelike state?"

"Exactly. Their souls were in the Dominion while their bodies, or vessels, were earthbound. They were in direct touch with their stories, remembering the twists and turns they created. They see firsthand the lessons they need to learn in this lifetime. I recall many died young and did not have joyful lives. Most people consider a happy life one that is successful and that provides material possessions. The Dominion considers a happy life as one that allows a person to live his or her soul's story and to learn or receive payback from a past-life mistake. This is learning, as the ancients have done throughout eternity.

"Where do the Dominion travel on Earth?"

"They travel everywhere."

"Have I seen or met them?"

"Yes."

"Who?"

"You would not know them. They would seem like every other human.

"What do they want from me?"

"I told you. They are intertwined in you and Reliance and are helping with your project. Remember, Simon: Your prayer was answered. You are back at JPL. Now they want something from you. Do as they ask."

"Are many people being reclaimed?"

"I don't know, Simon. I'm just a robot."

"Was it the Dominion in Mosul?"

"Yes, but humans believe it was an angel or a new government weapon or some such. Simon, tell Alexis the answer to her prayer has begun, even though she is already aware because of the backup in the funeral home. Have a good evening, Simon."

The car is silent as Simon's drive continues. He enters his home. Alexis sits in the kitchen in silence. "Hi," he says, and he moves to hug her.

"Simon, I'm scared." She looks at him for reassurance. "Are aliens killing people?" He slides into a chair, grabbing her hand. "After you called, I researched more in-depth and found that every parlor is experiencing overloads."

"Everywhere?"

"Yes. Everywhere."

"Well, I found the screen I was on when *Sojourner* first spoke to me. I thought that if I tried to initiate a conversation with *Sojourner* at the same place it might work.

"Did it?"

"No. But when I was in the car, *Sojourner* spoke to me."

"Are they, the Dominion, doing this to the world?"

"It appears that way."

"So aliens are killing people?"

"Not exactly. *Sojourner* says humans are the aliens because they live outside the peace of the Dominion."

"Does it … or he … or she … or whatever … mean heaven?"

"I guess so. Yes. *Sojourner* reminded me of my responsibility in saving people. He also said I had met the Dominion, and they are helping me.

"Have you recognized them?"

"He said I wouldn't. He also said prayers are being answered, including yours. Did you pray for anything in particular?"

"Well, I recall a lot of prayers. But when you just asked, I especially remember being sad about a client of mine, and I lamented that the good ones die and the creeps keep going. I asked God if He could get rid of the creeps. Oh, Simon, is this happening because of what I prayed?"

"No, I reckon it is because of what we both prayed."

"What do we do?"

"I guess I should try to reach people about their journey. *Sojourner* suggested blogs, saying they can reach many people."

"What would you tell them without sounding crazy?"

"*Sojourner* suggested I use my connection to government to calm the nerves of the countries anxious to go to war over an email. *Sojourner* said the email was the key."

"Figure out every word, Simon. Isn't it text from the Bible?"

"Yes, most of it. But it's the last part of the messages dealing with names and dates that's the most important, *Sojourner* tells me. The most brilliant people throughout the world are researching the whole thing. I have to look at it from a different perspective."

"What would that be, Simon?"

"Maybe pure faith. Faith in life after death. Heaven again. Alexis, I have concluded and taken on faith that this is real and the Dominion is real, so I'd best get started."

"What can I do to help, Simon?"

"Not a clue, other than having faith in me when everyone wants to accuse me."

"Oh, Simon, you know I do, and I will. She stands and embraces her husband as he sits.

"So is it fun embracing a crazy man?"

At that moment, the commander's lens reads: "Simon has embraced his mission. Give him support when needed."

CHAPTER 19

"Good morning, everyone. Welcome to *America's Newsroom*. I'm Bill Hemmer. Hello, Martha."

"Hi Bill. Good morning, everyone. I'm Martha MacCallum. Earlier there was a Fox News alert saying that for a time there were no people dying. Newspapers across the nation had no obituary sections printed for a while. But now the latest reports say that people are dying again—but seemingly only those we would call the bad people."

"So what you're saying, Martha, is that hoodlums, thugs, and downright criminals are dying, but the good folks are staying alive?"

"That's right, Bill."

"Well, it's great to see that we're still here."

Simon is at work before dawn, when the lab has limited staff. He has decided to protect himself from the government as best he can. Doing this will require him to disconnect the rovers. The data line will read only a short disconnection of no significance. The managers will consider it a hiccup. They will chalk it up to electrical charges. With Reliance shut off, Simon copies the program and renames it Common001. Common is a program on millions of computers worldwide. He hides the file in a folder not related to any operating systems or programming software. The name will not be a flashing red light to the geeks looking for security flaws. This is his creation, and he needs to make a copy. His big problem now is getting the program off the JPL computer. Security is fierce, and no disks, drives, or storage devices can enter or leave the building. The light of morning is filtering into the lab's windows. He can see increased motion on the mission floor, with the staff circled, talking, with coffee in hand. Simon issues commands for the rovers, moving them into other activities on Mars. These are new procedures not tried since the communication breakdown.

Once the commands are complete, Simon realizes it's now late morning. A government assassin has not visited him; nor has Kelly been back. Simon looks down the hall toward the offices of Norm and Earlman. The two are in the hall, talking with Kelly. Next to them are two other people. They are somewhat hard to see, the way they are standing, but both look unfamiliar to Simon. The one he can see best is a large man, and Simon thinks he has a military look about him.

The two men and Kelly began moving up the hall toward Simon's office. He quickly moves back to his seat, but not before getting a glimpse of the second man, who he thinks he has seen before. Norm and Earlman have returned to their offices as the trio stop at Simon's door. He does not look up, because he wishes he could slither behind the console. There's a knock, and he says, "Come in."

"Hello, Simon," Kelly announces as they enter. Simon hesitates before turning to face them, pretending he is highly focused on the computer. "Hope we are not disturbing you."

"No," says Simon, "just finishing up something. Good Morning, Kelly. Good to see you back." Simon stands.

"I'd like you to meet our team," Kelly tells him. "This is Brock Chesterfield, my partner."

Chesterfield extends his big hand to Simon and squeezes tightly as they shake. He then looks to the other man and says, "This is Michael Cott, a private security consultant brought on to help with this email issue."

"Hello, Michael," Simon says, now recognizing him. "You were in my Bible study not long ago, weren't you?"

"Yes. It's a small world." He steps over to shake Simon's hand.

"Pleasure to see you again," says Simon.

Brock turns to Kelly. "Cott goes to Bible study?"

"Apparently," Kelly answers, smiling.

Michael says to Simon, "So this is your window to the universe. We didn't get to talk about your robots at Bible study."

"This is it," Simon replies, and he then looks at Kelly as if to ask, "More investigation?"

She says, "Michael will find any security holes in the JPL system and plug them."

"Relax, Simon," Michael says. "I've already worked with Reliance, and it has nothing malicious in it." He nods toward the terminal Kelly has been using and says, "Kelly and I will work from here for a few days. Go about your day like we're not here."

Later that evening, Dr. Tristin Beckett pulls up in front of the Northstrum home, parks, and exits his car under the watchful eye of Brock Chesterfield. Chesterfield is curious about this visitor that's arriving so late. Beckett approaches the front door and knocks. Simon and Alexis are lying on the sofa in the family room, exhausted, all talked out, both dozing. The knocking startles Alexis, leaving her fully awake. She nudges Simon and says, "Simon, someone's at the door."

Simon rubs his eyes, gets up, and goes to the door. He looks through the peephole, opens up, and says, "May I help you?"

Beckett asks, "Dr. Simon Northstrum?"

"Yes," Simon says.

"I'm Beckett," he tells Simon.

"Beckett? Dr. Tristin Beckett?" Simon opens the door wider, sticking his head out to scan the street. "Come in," he says, quickly closing the door after Beckett enters. "It's good to see you, but what are you doing here at this hour?"

"I caught a night flight. Sorry for not phoning ahead, but I didn't want to alert anyone of my arrival. I know you contacted my office, and I'm aware of your surveillance. I want to discuss Reliance with you, and we should talk here, not at JPL."

"Sure," Simon says. "I was going to call your cell, but with everything going on, I misplaced your number. This was probably good, though, because like you said, they're tailing me."

The two stand there momentarily, and then Simon says, "My wife is here, but she's aware of everything. We talked ourselves to sleep about it tonight."

Alexis calls from the kitchen, where she is straightening up some things, "Simon? Who was at the door?"

The two men walk back to the area. "Alexis," Simon says, "this is Dr. Beckett, Dr. Tristin Beckett, the doctor from Washington I spoke about to you. I believe he is one of the good guys, on our side."

"Is that correct?" Alexis asks in a protective manner.

"Yes, Simon is correct. We both work for General Bosman, but in different capacities." Simon gives Beckett a quizzing glance, not quite understanding that response.

"Hi, Tristin," Alexis says, reaching out to shake hands.

"A pleasure to meet you, Alexis. I apologize for coming here so late, but I need to talk to your husband in person."

Simon says, "And I want to learn more about our General Bosman connection."

"Should I leave?" Alexis asks.

"No," Tristin says, "You can stay."

Simon gestures. "Let's take a seat." They gather about the kitchen table.

Tristin begins. "Alexis, I'm NSA, working with CART, the catch-and-release program that detains terrorists, then eventually lets them go."

"And that's not a good thing," she replies.

"It hasn't been," Tristin replies, "but it's changing, and that's what I'm here to talk about." He looks at Simon and says, "Simon, we spoke of your Reliance program and how it worked with my nanos."

"Yes. Explain that."

"Did you hear on the news of the death of Sadek Salem?"

Alexis jumps in, "The bomb maker terrorist? Was that you with your nanos and Reliance?

"Yes. In simple terms, we dialed his number and used the nanos to kill him with Reliance."

"I didn't write my program to kill people. How did you change it to kill?"

"Simon, I touched no line of code in Reliance. I'm here because Reliance is doing something else it did not do in our trials."

"Trials?

"Yes, we tested the program on ill animals to be euthanized."

"And?" Simon asks.

"The phone displayed an image with the text 'Your rapture, created by Reliance, delivered by the Dominion.'" Simon glances at Alexis and then looks back at Tristin, who continues. "I see from your faces that you are familiar with this phrase."

"No," Simon says, "not the entire phrase, but the words 'rapture' and 'Dominion' are very familiar." Simon again looks at Alexis.

Alexis cuts to the chase with "Tristin, can you be trusted?"

"You have nothing to fear from me," he replies. "My sister died on 9/11, and I am in this to get the bastards responsible. I'm not interested in any government stuff—emails sent or hacking. You can trust me, and you need a government guy in your camp."

Simon and Alexis both nod in agreement. Simon then says, "Tristin, what I will say now must not leave this table. I am telling you in advance you will call me crazy. Do I seem crazy?"

"No. You seem brilliant."

Alexis smiles, and Simon says, "Good. Thank you. I'll start at the beginning. I was out of work." He pauses. "Are you religious, Tristin?"

A little taken aback, Tristin replies, "Well … I could do better."

"So you have faith?"

"Yes. Yes, I believe in a higher power."

"Okay then. This is what Alexis and I have put together, and we don't know what to conclude. Do you believe in prayer?"

"Yes. I pray, but I do the work."

"Okay again. Well, I couldn't find a job in the space program, and I got mad at God. I gave him an ultimatum of sorts—He helps me or we're done. A few hours later, I get a job offer to come back to JPL. Coincidence? At the time, I thought maybe. So I get back to JPL and get the rovers working again. Everything is good, right?"

"Yeah. Bosman says You're JPL's golden boy."

"He isn't aware of everything. After the rovers were working, something strange happened … Very strange." Simon pauses and looks at Alexis.

"Go on," Tristin says. "Strange in what way?"

"Well, the rovers were designed to communicate with JPL in code."

"I understand that," Tristin responds. "Rather the standard."

Simon again looks to Alexis. "Tell him, Simon," she says.

"Tristin, this is where the crazy comes into play."

"Okay. I'm ready."

"Tristin, *Sojourner* spoke to me. It—he, she, or whatever—talked to me. Called me Simon. Just like we are talking now."

Tristin doesn't speak; he just listens intently.

"The thing is," Simon continues, "we started carrying on a conversation. I responded to *Sojourner*, and he responded to my questions." Simon pauses again. "Conversing, like we are now."

Tristin, with elbows on table, raises his forearms, opens upward the palms of hands, and says in amazement, "This is new territory … hard to take in."

Simon says, "I thought someone was playing a practical joke on me. You know, 'Simon is back, and we need to break him in right …' or some sort of something like that."

"I would think the say way … if a computer started talking to me," Tristin agrees.

"But *Sojourner* told me things only I would know. He also told me he was better now since his injured foot had been taken care of. His foot, which is really a wheel, had been jammed by a rock, and *Sojourner* couldn't move." Simon pauses. "Now the weirdness increases. *Sojourner* told me 'friends' had visited and fixed the problem."

"Friends?" Tristin asks.

"Yes, called the Dominion."

"Dominion … like in the email messages?"

"Yes."

"Who are they? Aliens?"

"I don't believe we can call them aliens—not in the sense of the word as we've always used it. But the Dominion holds the power of the life and death of humanity. They are on Earth to reclaim souls that are not following the correct path designated for them."

In awe, Tristin says, "Simon, this is so weird."

"It gets better."

"Okay. I've been listening to this, unsure of what to say … or do."

"Tristin," Simon says calmly, "Alexis and I believe prayers are being answered."

"Answered?"

Alexis tells Tristin, "We both prayed for help. I prayed for God to get rid of the creeps in the world. Now the bad guys are dying."

"So," Beckett says, "the ones I'm taking care of … I'm not really doing it, but it's being done through your Reliance program and my nanos by the Dominion?"

"That's the way I figure it," Simon answers. I don't really know for sure. It's hard to get my head wrapped around it."

"I can believe that! My head is spinning now!" Tristin says.

"But I seem to be catching on more, because *Sojourner* talks with me often."

"Okay …?" Tristin responds, seemingly waiting for the next revelation.

"At first the dialogue between *Sojourner* and me was relegated to my office—always when nobody else was around to hear it. Now he talks to me in my car."

"How?"

"It was through the radio at first. But now, when the radio is off, *Sojourner* still talks to me and responds to what I say. He told me the

Dominion doesn't need any appliance in order to contact me. He emphasizes that he is not doing the talking but that it's the Dominion contacting me through him."

"What do they want?" Tristin asks.

"Tristin, let me take weird up to another level."

"If that's possible," says Tristin.

"Oh, yeah. It's possible. *Sojourner*—the Dominion, really—told me they were responsible for Noah and the flood."

"Okay. Yes. It can get weirder, Simon."

"They are here to do it again if people do not listen to their souls and the souls' stories."

"Stories?"

The Dominion say we have a perfect life story created within the Dominion. Our job is to follow the true story. The communications of today are drowning out the stories, infecting people with self. We get many lives to learn our lessons."

"Is this reincarnation?"

"Tristin, all I know is that they are on Earth and have started their mission."

"Simon, tell me about the snipers killed and the Christians saved. What took place over there? Did the government do it?"

"It's not my area, but I believe all this was done by the Dominion, even though the government probably has weapons that everyone is unaware of."

"Aliens killed the terrorists?" Tristin asks.

"Remember: not aliens as we commonly understand the word. But *Sojourner* told me to watch the news for events."

"The robot predicted the events?"

"The Dominion speaking through the robot … yes."

"Ooohhh, boy!"

Simon continues. "People have seen flashes of light going across the sky. The electromagnetic field has flashed."

"Most scientists have explained those occurrences," says Tristin.

"Yeah, but have you asked yourself, 'What if they're wrong?' The

Dominion wants to see what people do. You and others ask, as I did, 'Is it aliens, God, or government?' Well, *Sojourner* said the world will blame me for everything."

"Blame you for everything? Including what?"

"The emails, Reliance, deaths, rapture—you name it."

"What do they want you to do?"

"Get people to listen to their souls."

"How do you do it?"

"Good question. *Sojourner* recommended a blog."

"If you don't, what happens?"

"*Sojourner* said we will be reclaimed into the Dominion."

"Killed?"

"You've got it."

"But you're only one guy, Simon."

"I said the same thing, and *Sojourner* said, 'So was Noah.' They want me to get people to communicate in person, soul to soul."

Tristin reacts to all of this with "Wow!"

Alexis says, "Tristin, I have more. "I work at a funeral home. Our intake census was down at the home. I mean it got down to zero."

"Okay …" Tristin says. Alexis's remark causes him to raise his eyebrows because of what he has heard and seen in the news, and what he has already heard so far this evening.

Alexis continues. "The funeral home sent me out to see if it was a relationship problem. I called on our best clients, and everything was fine. They just had no deaths to report."

"Go on," Tristin says. "I'm following you."

"Well, after a couple of days there were still no clients, and we found out no people were listed in the obituary section of the paper."

Simon inserts, "The papers even dropped the obits section during this time."

Tristin states, "I had no idea it had gotten to that degree. I mean, I had heard and seen things on the news, but, well, I was pretty tied up with my project."

"I thought it strange and called the paper to see if we missed a section," Simon says. "The lady at the paper said they had no obituary section in the paper that day. Alexis called newspapers and funeral homes on both coasts, and they had no deaths or clients. Tristin, there are deaths again, but only bad people are dying … as I understand it, worldwide."

"The creeps," Alexis interjects, "like I prayed for."

"Well," Tristin says, "regarding Reliance and the nanos, we have scheduled other villains to be eliminated, but now it appears the Dominion are running the show."

"What will you do with what I told you?" asks Simon.

"I will let it stew. The question is, what are you going to do?"

"First of all, only four people now know about me talking with *Sojourner*. They are Alexis, you, Norm, and me.

"Who is Norm?" Tristin asks.

"Norm is what I call Ed Proctor, my boss and longtime friend at JPL. Long story."

"I know of Ed Proctor," Tristin replies.

"Well, anyway," Simon continues, "only you, Alexis, Norm, and I know about the conversations. I prefer to keep it that way. I believe you can agree to that; otherwise, I wouldn't have opened up to you."

I do agree, and I believe you will not share with anyone else what I have told you tonight about the relationship between your Reliance and my nanos."

"We indeed have a pact," Simon tells Tristin. Alexis nods as the three of them look at one another. Simon goes on to say, "The Dominion will use our technology to bring a reverse rapture to Earth."

"Simon," Tristin responds, "Let's keep in close touch. My department will continue attacking terrorists. Let me know of developments with *Sojourner*."

"I will."

Tristin shakes his head slightly, amazed at what they have discussed and what has been happening. He says, "It's amazing that I found your Reliance program, which magically works perfectly with my project without any tweaking. I have been pulling my hair out for years to get it working. Then Reliance, and bang—everything falls into place. You realize that if it continues to work, you and I will be disowned, Simon?"

"What do you mean?"

"The bigger wheels will take the credit for ridding the world of evil, even though the Dominion are doing it."

"Oh. I don't care, if I can keep my space missions."

"Okay, I just wanted you to realize how government works."

"Believe you me, Tristin, I know *exactly* how government works."

Tristin pushes away from the table and rises, saying, "I'd best be going." Simon and Alexis stand with him. Handing Simon a card, Tristin says, "Here is my private contact information. I recommend using it instead of my office."

"Got it," Simon says.

"Alexis, it was good to meet you," Tristin tells her.

"My pleasure," Alexis replies.

Simon and Tristin head to the door. Before he leaves, Tristin scans the street and says, "Simon, you are being watched."

"Yeah, I figured as much."

They exchange good-nights, and Tristin heads to his car.

⚓

After leaving Simon's home, Tristin drives toward his hotel. On the way, he tries to absorb the discussion with Simon and Alexis. The discussion was interesting and bizarre. He had come to get an education on Reliance but ended up talking of aliens, speaking robots, and biblical rapture. *Have my nanos brought on a rapture of sorts? Simon is a normal guy, and if his wife has faith in him, then he is not a fool. Simon has too much credibility in the scientific world and is not a quack.*

Tristin arrives at his lodging and enters the room. He throws his case on the opposite bed and crashes on the other. His phone rings and pulses. He sees it is Major Caritta.

"Hello, Major."

"How was your meeting with Doctor Northstrum?"

308

"Excellent. As I mentioned, he is brilliant but humble."

"Did he explain Reliance to you?"

"No. He does not know why the program is working for us. He said it should not work, but he is glad it does if it helps the war effort."

"Will he try to sabotage the program? Remember: we are working with a guy considered a hero and a villain by the government."

"You mean the email problem? Big deal—people got spammed. Simon could not care less about the hacking and would not waste his time."

"Okay, Tristin."

There's a knock on Tristin's door.

"Major, someone is at the door. May I get back to you?"

"Sure."

Tristin hangs up, moves to the door, and peers through the peephole. A large man is holding up a federal ID badge. "Brock Chesterfield here," he says. Tristin removes the security chain and opens the door. Chesterfield stands there and shows his full credentials to Tristin. "We need to talk," he says.

"Come in." I'm Dr. Tristin Beckett," Tristin tells him. Chesterfield enters, and Tristin closes the door. "You were watching Dr. Northstrum's house, weren't you?"

Rather taken aback, Chesterfield says, "You are observant."

"We work for the same people."

"Bosman?" Chesterfield asks.

"Yes. We are both NSA."

"What do you want with Simon Northstrum?" Chesterfield asks.

"Chesterfield … Brock, you said, right?"

"Yes, that's right."

"Well, Brock, you don't have clearance for my program, and I am consulting with Dr. Northstrum on his Reliance communication software."

"I am too," Brock replies.

"No. Your investigation is on hacking and espionage—another area entirely. I'm trying to see if his program can help us find easier ways to find terrorists."

"Why go to his home and not JPL?"

"You have people looking over his shoulder at JPL, and I don't care about hacking."

"The FBI and my department believe he is dirty."

"Do you have concrete proof?"

"No."

"Did he tell you anything important? Enough to cause additional suspicions?"

"Well, no. Not yet."

"There you go. On the other hand, Simon and I spoke of computer code and communication programming. Reliance is brilliant software and might help in the effort on the war on terrorism. I can't tell you any more without you getting special clearance, which you can't get on this."

"Beckett, you see what is going on around the world. Everything is on heightened alert. Countries want to blame someone or a country."

"So you need a scapegoat to pin it on so we have no war?"

"Why not, if it stops a war? He looks guilty."

"So sacrifice one for the many, even if he's done nothing? It sounds a bit like Pilate with Jesus and the Pharisees."

"What?"

"Brock, you'd better look at other avenues than Northstrum. If you don't, you risk the real culprit getting away."

"Getting away where?"

"You realize that with everyone connected electronically, the culprit could be on a beach somewhere with a computer, watching the world burn?"

"We are on top of it," Chesterfield huffs.

"My impression is that you know nothing. Brock, it was a long day—and night—so if we are done, I'm retiring."

Tristin shows Chesterfield out. He enters his car and bangs the steering wheel in frustration, knowing the scientist schooled him. He must find evidence of Northstrum's involvement. Chesterfield glances toward the window of Tristin's room, and the lights go out. He drives away from the hotel.

⚓

"Good evening, folks, and welcome to this special report. This is a Fox News alert. I assume the major networks have broken into your regular scheduled programs for this important message from the president. You will see a picture of the oval office. We are told he will address the nation on the countdown clock. Our sources tell us they have come up with a plan to stop this clock and will test it on the one displayed in Times Square. If it is successful, it will be shared with the world. Here we go, folks."

"Hello, my fellow Americans. You are all aware of the email messages and the doomsday clock, as it's now being referred to. I want to assure you the government had no hand in this clock or any hacking. Our top scientists have devised a plan to remove the clock and restore our computer security. In a few moments, the power to Times Square will be shut off. Our scientists will send a power surge through the line to scrub the circuits of any malicious software or viruses. I am told it is much like rebooting a computer or phone, taking it back to the factory settings. I want to assure everyone not to fear."

The president signals for the reboot countdown to begin. The screen returns to the news program. "Well, folks, I guess we must sit and watch the jumbotron and see. The screen shows the clock ticking down." Moments later, one by one, the lights go dark around the square. People on the street who are unaware of the president's warning gasp. Fifteen minutes go by in darkness as the wires are scrubbed. Once the procedure is completed, the power returns, with preclock advertising filling the screens on the square. The largest jumbotron illuminates with an advertisement for a new Broadway show. Cheers go up on the street. In the oval office, there is back slapping.

"It looks like the flushing has worked," the newscaster says. It will go a long way toward reelection when you can say you destroyed this menace. Saving the world looks great on a political résumé. Now we have an electronics expert with us—Dr. Tarin Mayer." Turning toward Dr. Mayer, the newscaster says, "Thanks for coming on such short notice. "What took place?"

"Well," Dr. Mayer says, "the president explained it accurately. It seems to have solved the problem, as the screens in Times Square are back to normal."

"Yes," the newscaster replies, "you can see the lights in the square are back, but what of the rest of the world?"

"It will take time. The quickest way to fix the problem is for the world to go dark."

"Can we do it without people dying? There are folks on life support, pumps that keep oceans out, and other such electronic devices."

"True. I'm sure they are discussing this as we speak. An alternative is to do it in segments, but all the power must eventually be cut."

"Dr. Mayer, we have disabled this clock tonight, but what of the messages? Is something terrible going to befall us at the end of the month? Although we can't see this countdown clock, are we still on a countdown? We are getting tweets that people are terrified. They fear a surprise attack like Pearl Harbor or 9/11."

"I don't know. I'm in electronics, but hopefully this stops the hacking and get things back to normal. Stopping it this way can lead to discovering ways to stop future attacks."

"I hate to break in," another reporter says, "but we are getting an alert from Times Square, and our cameras are there." The largest jumbotron flickers, and large letters scroll across the screens. The message reads, "Nice Try. The Dominion." The screen returns to the countdown clock and the message of self.

The word "crap" escapes Mayer's lips.

"I guess it failed," says the host newscaster. "I don't know who these Dominion are, but they have the world by the ————. If they control the electrical grid of the world, they can send us back to the stone age. We are seeing posts in which people are telling their loved ones to not contact them through electronics. They are afraid to use them and are now shutting them down. Is that what this is about—getting people to turn off their electronics?"

As the sun breaks over the horizon, soldiers remove a tarpaulin covering a large drone. A technician opens a bay on the underbelly of the aircraft, revealing a circuit board. He opens a laptop and attaches cables to the board. He enters a code into the computer. The screen reads, "link complete and control passed to central command." Pilots can now control it in air-conditioned comfort from far away. They can target the bomb placement to limit collateral damage. Straight computer control cannot add the human touch. The engines whine to life. The pilots sit before a screen in a control room, looking like grown-ups playing a video game. But this isn't a game in which one reaches different levels. One doesn't kill ghouls, demons, or half-life gnomes. This is life and death on the screen. Humans play this game, wreaking real death and destruction. The pilot must decide in a heartbeat who are the good people. Most times, the villains intertwine themselves with the innocent. Sadly, it's a common trait of those who believe they are the supreme people. The Germans, Japanese, Communist Chinese and Khmer Rouge did it. Isis, Muslim terrorists, and other terrorists are the new rendition. Man must dominate others.

Today's mission will send the reaper to Mosul, a city of one million people and the largest dam in Iraq. ISIL has established a stronghold here. They arc ruthless, killing anyone not bowing before them and swearing devotion to their form of faith. The mission will target an area near the dam where the militants have created a human shield. Destruction of the dam will flood lower Iraq and bring devastation to those living near the Tigris River. This is a surgical strike to kill four thousand ISIL fighters without killing the people held as human shields around the dam. The Iraqi army has made little progress in pushing back the insurgents. The drone will be their support. Central command is wary of the Iraqi army. They tend to cut and run.

The drone lifts off on its mission, with the pilot reviewing the landscape of the Persian Gulf and vast deserts of nothingness. Someone might mistake the landscape for that of the images of Mars sent by the rovers. Who'd want to die for this dirt, dust, and rubble? The four winds have blown the dust from every human body ever existing and settled it here. A Biblical verse seems pertinent: 'And to dust you shall return.' The drone flies along at three hundred miles per hour. It should be over the target in two hours. This is the mindless part of the mission—watching the expanse of desert for two hours before a human takes control.

The drone arrives over the target, and the computer puts it into an elevation where it is not in harm's way from enemy fire. Now it is in a reconnaissance mode, sending pictures to loyal forces at command centers below. Iraqi forces shell the insurgents, making small progress. The pilot sees a window of opportunity to free the people, as the enemy has left itself defenseless for the moment. The pilot arms the onboard missiles, and after receiving the command to fire, a missile accelerates from the drone to its preprogrammed target. There is no sending it back.

The drone circles silently as the missile approaches its target. Cell phone ringtones erupt simultaneously near the target. There is a flash of white light, and the missile veers off its target, falling harmlessly into an empty field. The light vanishes, and one by one, people emerge from their hiding places. Some are crying, while others look into the sky to see if other missiles are coming. More fall to their knees in prayer to Allah. The sky is clear, and the street has a peaceful silence. As more people emerge, they realize the insurgents are dead. Thousands lie lifeless in an untouched state. Some shout, "The Americans have brought a new weapon to bear!" A message blasts from the town's minarets: "Your rapture is brought to humanity by the Dominion … Where are you in your soul's contract with us?"

The commander's lens reads, "I send you the selfish. There will be more."

⚅

Magdala of Swaddling Clothes stands at the front door of the Northstrums' home. Inside, Emma is in her room, laboring on her homework. Simon and Alexis have assumed their positions in front of the television. Alexis mentions to Simon she hears someone at the front door. He stands, but Alexis stops him. "I'll get it. I need a sip of water. Anyway, your usual nighttime visitors are people from the NSA or CIA, and this knock seems softer than that. Simon looks at Alexis sheepishly.

Alexis sees Magdala through the peephole and pauses for a moment, not knowing who it is and not sure if she should open it, but she does. "May I help you?" Alexis says.

"Mrs. Northstrum?"

"Yes."

"I am sorry for arriving at this late hour. I am Magdala from Swaddling Clothes. Is Emma in, please? I missed her at school."

"Oh, yes," Alexis replies. "Emma has spoken highly of you. Please come in. I'm Alexis."

Magdala enters and pauses in the foyer. Alexis calls for Simon to get Emma. Simon yells back, "Who is at the door?"

"It is the lady from Swaddling Clothes, the company Emma works with at school."

Simon goes to the bottom of the stairs and calls for Emma. She appears at the top of the stairs. "Gee, Dad, what's wrong?" she says, sensing that recently, when her father has called up, she has been in trouble.

"Nothing, hon. You have a visitor."

"Really?" She descends the stairs and walks past her dad. As she arrives in the foyer, surprised, she says, "Maggie?"

"Emma," Magdala replies.

"Is something wrong?" Emma asks, a worried look crossing her face.

Magdala smiles. "Does there have to be something wrong to visit a friend?" Emma is relieved, and Simon appears in the foyer to see what's going on.

"I'm Simon, Emma's father," he tells Magdala.

She steps forward and shakes his hand, "I'm Magdala. As you may have heard, friends call me Maggie."

"Okay, Maggie," Simon responds. "Good to meet you. Emma can't stop talking about Swaddling Clothes. And my wife is happy, because they are the same size. It is good on the wallet." Alexis and Simon look at each other and smile.

Maggie says, "Don't you love it when a plan comes together?" She then turns toward Emma and says, "Emma, sorry I missed you at school today."

Simon interrupts. "Girls, invite the lady to sit. Would you like an iced tea, Maggie?"

"Tea sounds good," Maggie tells him. They move into the kitchen. Emma gets the tea from the refrigerator, Alexis gets the glasses, and then they all are seated at the table.

Emma, still in her something-must-be-wrong mode, asks, "Is there is a problem with the internship program?"

"No, Emma," Maggie replies, "everything's fine, and you're doing wonderfully."

Emma blushes and says, "Thank you."

Maggie pulls a shirt from the bag she brought in and says, "I wanted to give this to Lennon today, but he has an after-school job, and I missed him. I thought you would give it to him." Maggie grabs the shirt by the shoulders, and it unfurls to the table. The shirt is white and bears an image of John Lennon holding his trusty Rickenbacker guitar. Magdala says, "Lennon has his uniform, I know, but I thought he might want an alternative choice at times."

With sort of a frown and a nod of her head, Alexis says, "Yes, his *Abbey Road* shirt. I think Lennon sleeps in it."

"Mom, you don't understand", says Emma. "It was the last gift his mom bought him before she was killed."

"Oh, honey, I didn't know."

Emma says, "He hand washes it to protect it."

Alexis's and Maggie's faces show a sadness mixed with sympathy.

Maggie says, "I know he is a big Beatles fan and thought he would like this one. Maybe he can put it into his clothing rotation."

"He will love it," Emma tells her, "because he dreams of owning a guitar like the one on the shirt."

"Good. Will you see that he gets it?"

"Oh, yes. I'll see him at the bus stop in the morning. He might even want to wear it for the big talent show that's coming up. Mom, Dad, I forgot to tell you that a new recording company in town is sort of turning this into an audition type of thing, and they will be awarding a recording contract to the winner. Lennon is so pumped!"

"That's great," Alexis says.

"Knowing Lennon, I'm sure he is excited," Simon adds.

"Yes, and many people have signed up for the event. The church really needs a larger place now."

Maggie tells them, "I've heard about the show, and I'm planning to attend."

"Cool," Emma tells her.

Addressing Simon and Alexis, Maggie says, "I want you to know Emma is doing a great job for our company. We are proud of her."

Emma glows.

Alexis says, "We are more than happy to lend our support." She then places here hand on Maggie's and tells her, "You have helped Emma blossom in just a little while."

Maggie replies, "Sometimes it takes an outsider to help people look at how great they are. Like Emma—she knows you love her and support her, but she doesn't know if the world will." She looks at Emma. "Right, Emma?"

"Yes, Maggie. That's about it. You seem to be able to look inside people, and that's cool—really cool."

Maggie turns toward Alexis and says, "Emma tells me that you really like and enjoy our clothes."

"Oh, yes. With Simon out of work for a while, new clothes were not in the budget. It is funny how just putting on a new outfit can lift your spirits, even if you're just trying it on when you can't actually buy it."

"You sound like a selfless woman," Maggie tells Alexis.

Simon interjects, "Yes, her picture is in the dictionary next to the word. She's always putting others first."

Alexis blushes and swats Simon. "It is not."

Maggie smiles and can see the love Alexis and Simon have for each other, and how lasting couples play well together. She has seen couples who have been married for sixty years still playing with their best friends. She turns to Simon and says, "When I interviewed Emma, she said you were the inventive Q of James Bond fame when it comes to the space program."

Simon, not realizing she held him in such high regard, says to Emma, "I appreciate that, honey, but many people working together put the probes on Mars. But I appreciate the comparison."

"Lennon thought of the Q comparison," says Emma.

"I knew I liked that boy," Simon replies.

Maggie addresses Simon with "I guess there is much going on in the computer and space world today. What do you make of these hacking issues and emails, Simon?"

"Everyone keeps asking me that question, but it is not my area or focus. But, to tell you the truth, I liked the messages."

"Has any harm come from the hacking?"

"I'm not privy to that information, but people seem ready and willing to kill each other."

Maggie shakes her head slightly and says, "Yes. It's sad that people always seek to gain advantage for money, power, and control. Many will perish if cool heads can't prevail. We must have faith that goodness and selflessness will win."

"'Selflessness,'" replies Simon. "I keep hearing that word."

"Yes," Maggie says. It is a strange trait in humans. When there is a disaster, people become selfless. They crawl into holes in a collapsed building, claw with their hands in the muck, and swim in turbulent waters. I might be a dreamer, but just imagine if everyone behaved that way each day. Think of the positive ripples it would create in the world."

The Northstrums are focused on her words, impressed with the manner in which she is presenting them. Maggie then presses her palms on the table and says, "Well, I apologize again for coming at this hour, and I do need to get going to a special meeting that's been called. My boss is gentle but demanding and punctual."

They all rise and exchange parting words, and then Simon and Alexis walk her to the door as Emma returns to her homework that must be finished tonight.

At the door, Simon asks Maggie, "Do you think everyone can be selfless every day?"

Maggie looks into Simon's eyes and says, "No, Simon, that would be heaven, but here on Earth free will is a problem for people."

Simon recoils at the term and exchanges glances with Alexis before asking Maggie, "Did I touch a nerve?"

"No, Simon, and I apologize."

"No. No need," Simon replies. "I understand. With all that is going on, others have mentioned free will, and I have responded just like you did."

Again they exchange good-byes, and Maggie says, "I will see you again at the talent show." The door closes, and Maggie disappears.

CHAPTER 20

"Good morning, everyone. Welcome to *America's Newsroom*. I'm Bill Hemmer. Hello, Martha,"

"Hello, Bill. Hi folks, I'm Martha MacCallum. There was a major offensive yesterday in Mosul, Iraq. I have with me today retired general Peter Weslon, a Fox News contributor. Good to have you here, sir."

"Thank you for having me, Martha."

"General, we have startling news out of Mosul that this offensive resulted in the deaths of thousands of people. We are getting pictures of dead people lying around everywhere. Sir, in truth it looks like the pictures I've seen of the D-Day invasion and the carnage on the beaches."

"Yes, Martha. My sources tell me over four thousand died."

"These pictures are odd, General, because I see no blood or torn flesh. There is no trauma associated with blinding from the explosives. The skinny on the street is that the military has unwrapped a new technology. General, we are getting word it may be biological or nuclear in nature."

"No, Martha. If that were the case, then everyone would have perished, like Hiroshima."

"Good point. General, unconfirmed reports coming out do say only terrorists died—no innocents. Some reports say the terrorists had been using their cell phones even more than usual, and some have talked about lights flashing from the phones at one time or another.

We are getting images of people praying in the streets, thanking Allah or the new American weapon."

"I have no knowledge of that report, Martha."

"General, do you believe we have a new weapon that can kill people using their phones? What do you make of the radio message broadcasting after the strike?

"Well, Martha, on that first question, let me remind you I am retired and not in on things—especially current top secrets that need to be kept under wraps. But it's interesting the message is biblical, about the rapture and the Dominion. You ask if maybe the US or a rebel group or some other country has a new weapon. I don't think a country would go on the radio after an attack. It is the terrorists who are now dead that would do that. The Dominion, I believe, is a diversion to get us to look in the wrong direction. We had better be careful and keep our eyes open and watching 360 degrees. Honesty has been my policy, Martha, and I simply tell you, on this I am in the dark."

"Thank you, General."

"You're welcome, Martha."

"Can you come back as more information filters in on this military operation?"

"I am ready to come back and offer my assessment as more is learned."

Martha turns toward her cohost. "Bill, many weird, unexplained events are going on in the world today: strange lights, the northern lights going crazy, new weapons, and curious emails."

"Martha, this just came across the wire. Let's hold the general over for this Fox News alert. We have a report from Lawrence, Massachusetts, of the deaths of over one hundred members of a wild "Latino gang." It is strange, but our producers are reporting that the deaths were not related to violence. No turf war, reprisal, or mayhem is associated with the deaths of so many in this gang. They are dead from natural causes. They were all over the age of thirteen. The CDC is on the scene to investigate possible infectious diseases. And we have just had it come across the wire that similar deaths have happened in various places around the world. The World Health Organization is in panic mode as to whether this is a start to a new pandemic."

Martha comments, "Of course, we are at the start of the flu season."

"Yes, Martha, but it seems that a flu outbreak does not kill in one spot."

"I don't know, Bill, but I guess if people are congregated together, then they could infect one another. It would make sense." She turns toward Weslon again and says, "General, do you think what occurred in Mosul may be happening in other places?"

"I don't know, Martha. But it's hard for me to wrap my mind around the fact that a government could have a weapon that only kills bad people."

"Yes, General," Martha replies, "you're right. And the question then is, Who becomes the prosecutor, judge, jury, and executioner?" She pauses. "We will hold the general over and will be right back after the break."

The Northstrum family is at home doing normal weekend chores. Emma is dusting in the family room, Alexis is tackling the kitchen, and Simon is out in his garage workshop, honing his carpentry skills on a broken cabinet door handle. But the quiet peace of the morning is suddenly broken as dark SUVs with flashing lights screech to a halt, blocking the driveway and parking in front of the Northstrum home. Many men with blue FBI jackets pile out of the cars. Steele is in the lead and rushes to the front door but breaks away as he sees movement in the garage. He yells, "Stop!" and Simon turns. He isn't running but is only working on a door handle. Emma and Alexis rush out to the garage before Steele reaches Simon.

Alexis confronts Steele. "What's going on here?"

"Your husband took part in worldwide espionage. I know it.

We will sort this out, but your husband's fingers are all over this problem!"

Angry, Alexis says, "How can a man back with his company only a short while be a part of such a worldwide event?"

"It is my understanding that a number of people believe Simon Northstrum—and maybe you—is the idiot who infected the government computers."

Alexis is now in Steele's face, and Steele realizes he has kicked a hornet's nest. He suggests she back down if she doesn't want her daughter to see both parents in handcuffs.

"Calm down, honey," says Simon, now out in the driveway. "I'll go with them. I've nothing to hide, and I'll answer their questions. But Inspector Steele, I have nothing more to tell you." Simon glances at all the people in blue with their guns pulled. "Really?" he says sarcastically to Steele. "A whole army?" Steele bristles. "Am I being arrested?" Simon asks.

Steele adamantly replies, "Yes!"

In tears, Emma yells, "Daddy!"

Alexis backs off and comforts her crying daughter. Steele quotes Simon's Miranda rights to him while applying handcuffs to his wrists. Simon nods his understanding of the monotone words and says a quiet "Yeah, yeah, I understand." He then says, "Are these cuffs necessary? It's scaring my family, not to mention that you've got the whole neighborhood in an uproar."

"Yes. Who knows what kind of nut you are? I've seen them, and I take no chances. But this can be avoided if you come clean."

"I've nothing to come clean about. I hope you like hearing a repeat of what I already told you and every other government employee. Do I need an attorney?"

Steele laughs. "With espionage, most attorneys won't be able to find you."

Simon says to Alexis, "Call Arnold Farina and tell him the situation."

Alexis, still fit to be tied, asks Steele, "Where are you taking him?"

"This is a serious government issue, and we will tell you when ready."

"What you're doing can't be legal!" she replies.

"I don't give a crap about legal! The world is on fire because of your genius husband!"

"No, Mr. Steele. You are taking the easy route to lay the blame on Simon, too lazy to look any further!"

Steele leads Simon toward the van. Alexis and Emma follow, with Emma sobbing and Alexis still ready to bite somebody's head off—specifically, Steele's. Alexis is already searching on the phone for the number of their attorney, Arnold Farina. She finds it and leaves a message. Neighbors have gathered, concerned with the flashing lights. Some are taking photos and videos. None are allowed on the property, which has been designated a crime scene.

Simon is pushed into the van and seated next to an emotionless agent.

Simon says, "Hello," and he is met with a grunt. He notices the agent's gun in the holster. His head slumps in dismay, realizing that he is in deep trouble. He remembers what *Sojourner* said about being brought to his knees. He silently prays, "I'm on my knees now. Will you help me?" The door to the van is closed, and the government vehicles speed away.

Neighbors rush to Alexis and Emma. The true friends comfort them and offer help, assuring them that everything will work out because Simon is a straight-up guy. Others mumble behind their backs, deriding them and accusing them of being traitors. These are probably the ones that fed their views to Steele. Alexis sees what they're doing and is shocked by it, because she thought everyone in the neighborhood had their backs and believed them to be upright Christians and citizens after living beside them for many years. She remembers what *Sojourner* told Simon about knowing someone soul-to-soul and what people do out of fear. Alexis pulls away with Emma beside her, stating that she needs to talk with their attorney. They make their way inside and lock the door.

Her phone chirps. It is Farina. "Hello," she says, "this is Alexis."

Farina says, "What's going on, Alexis? My secretary said you sounded very anxious."

"Arnold, thank you for getting back to me so quickly." Her voice is now quavering as she conveys the events of the last hour and Simon's predicament. Farina consoles her and asks her to take a few breaths. Emma listens in. Farina asks her the who, what, when, and where of the incident involving Simon. He tells her he is not a criminal attorney but will look into it and see if one of his colleagues can help. Arnold assures her that no matter the reason for arrest, he is entitled to legal representation. He calms her, saying, "We will let these power-hungry government officials have their testosterone feast; then we will bring them back to the real world. Remain calm, and someone will get back to you."

Alexis thanks him, hangs up, and moves to Emma, who is highly shaken. She brushes Emma's hair back and pats her wet cheeks with the tip of her blouse. "He said it will be okay. We should clean up and wash our faces. We might have to go and get your dad out of jail."

"Mom, Dad didn't do this, did he?"

"No, honey. He is the most honest, selfless man I know, and if you are selfless, it is impossible to do such an act." She kisses her daughter's cheek. "But you know that, don't you?" Emma weakly smiles and nods in agreement. "Let's get ready," Alexis says.

Hours later, Simon sits in a barren room with a chair and table, reminiscent of those in cop shows where alleged perpetrators are taken. But today it is him. Steele bursts through the door, holding paperwork and a box. He throws the papers at Simon, yelling at him, "Is that your work?"

Simon squints to focus and reviews the pages. "Yes," he replies. "It is the code for Reliance. But you know that already, don't you? Why are you showing it to me now? You know I reviewed it with your guy Aldis Montgomery, and he ran it through your Bertha computer and found nothing wrong with it. Where am I? I need to call my wife and talk to my lawyer. Where are my rights you should have Mirandized me about?"

"Yeah, yeah, rights! Not here, buddy boy! No get-out-of-jail-free card for you! I think you are a corrupt genius who believes he is smarter than everyone. There is indetectable code placed in there by you. Show me where it is, and maybe you walk away."

"Steele, I can spend the whole day going through the code with you, Kelly, Michael, Aldis, or any other government computer techies. I can't find code that does not exist. And nobody else can. However, if you still think it's in there, you might consider the military guys at JPL who were brought on while I was sacked. Everyone had access to it. Am I the only programmer you are harassing? I am sure you have gone through my immense financial holdings and found all the offshore accounts with piles of money flowing from a foreign government. Listen, Steele; I write communication code to talk to space vehicles, period. End of story."

"We have looked at everything and everyone," Steele tells him. "How do we know you are not talking to extraterrestrials?"

"You are delusional, Steele, along with your Star Trek generation— all of you who believe a super geek will raise an eyebrow while contemplating the laws of physics in relation to the universe. Then, with one minute left, he will rewrite said laws and save the *Enterprise* and the world. We might have too many TV fantasies of superheroes who destroy most of a city to save the world from the evil villain but don't show up to rebuild the city. It doesn't work that way, and I could not have had time to pull off such a scheme—and certainly not the slightest interest. Face it; you found nothing. You are looking for a scapegoat to save your pride and butt, so you persist with me."

"You might be on the dark web trading in stolen goods or Bitcoin," says Steele.

Simon laughs. "Now you are really grasping at straws, old man. Do you think I'm a Lex Luthor super villain who is in a subterranean lair, preparing to rule the world? That is rich, Steele! Why would anyone want to rule the world? There are seven billion people on

Earth bickering, bickering, bickering with one another. You can have all that if you want it."

Steele stands and retrieves the box he brought in and pulls an ankle monitor from it. Simon sees it and asks, "Why a tracking bracelet in here?"

"We may move you, and we want to keep tabs."

"The NSA isn't getting the job done or isn't sharing with you. How sad."

"You don't want to piss me off, Northstrum. You're the one in shackles in the middle of nowhere."

Simon's face goes slack, almost as if in resignation. Steele pulls Simon's leg from under the table and places the band on his leg. He presses a button, and the band blinks.

"There we go, working perfectly," says Steele. He removes Simon's handcuffs as a guard opens the door, telling Parker the cell is ready for Simon. Simon is ushered to the barren four-by-eight-foot cell. He notices the other cells in the area are empty. It is just him. Once in the cell, he asks again to make a call, and the guard smirks. He gets a feeling of what it was like to be in Nazi Germany. The door closes and bolts, which triggers a claustrophobic response in him.

⚅

Meanwhile, the yellow being walks unnoticed through the gates, barbed wire, and fences surrounding the facility holding Simon. Before entering the building, it transforms into a large man close to seven feet tall. The man has a ruddy complexion, with hands like hams. He could play either a post position for the NBA or left tackle in the NFL. A guard confronts the man and asks how he got in here.

"I was dropped off by my driver, and I have all clearances. I am Earl Connery Hardin, the attorney representing Dr. Simon Northstrum. Get your superior this instant. The guard tries to stonewall the man. "Listen, sonny," the man says to the guard, "take your fancy phone, type in my name, and then you can see if you want to give me a bunch of crap." The guard does as directed and discovers

327

that this man has been the adviser to many presidents, along with many in cabinet positions. Earl says, "Isn't it wonderful when you make choices based on knowledge and wisdom." The guard presses the intercom, requesting Inspector Steele's presence. Moments later, a weary Steele arrives.

"What is it?" Steele asks. "I'm busy."

"Sir, this is Earl Connery Hardin, the attorney for Dr. Northstrum.

Hardin towers over Steele, whose face grows pale. "Mr. Hardin, why are you here? You have no authority in this place."

"No, Inspector Steele, you are mistaken. As of this moment, *you* have no authority. We have laws, and you are not the Gestapo. Let me show you my phone. See those numbers? Those are the personal cell numbers to people like the president and even your boss at the FBI. If I press any of these, you will ride a Segway as a mall security guard. Your rogue operation will not please them. Now, I want to see my client and hear the charges against him. Do I need to make the call?"

Steele presses the intercom, requesting Simon be moved back to the interrogation room. He asks Hardin to follow him. The duo arrive at the room. Hardin tells Steele to give him time with his client and to get the paperwork listing the charges. Steele leaves, and Hardin enters the room.

Simon is uncuffed as Hardin crosses the threshold of the room. Simon's eyes go wide in fear as this immense man closes the door and approaches him with a stern face. As he faces Simon, Simon wonders whether this is when the torture will begin. This man's hands could palm his head. Hardin draws closer, and the huge man's face breaks into a compassionate smile.

"Hello, Simon. I'm your attorney, Earl Connery Hardin, but you can call me Earl. I understand you are in a fix. Let's get right to the matter. Did you do it? Did you break into every computer system on the planet, and maybe even beyond? I like my clients to be honest with me, but I'll represent you either way. I've taken many showers in disgust and have had clients who were outright thieves, thugs, and murderers, but they had the right to representation."

"No sir, I had no part in the email or any hacking. You have my word." Simon pauses. "How did you arrive at being my attorney?"

"The grapevine. I have knowledge of your attorney, Arnold Farina. He is not an attorney for cases such as this, but I do know he is a man of integrity. He believes in you, and I learned of you plight."

"I don't think I can afford you, Mr. Hardin," Simon tells him.

"Call me Earl, Simon, and let's not worry about money. Think about the publicity to be gained by defending the man that started World War III."

"Earl, I did nothing," says Simon.

"So you said, but governments don't need you to be guilty. They will make you out that way for their best interests."

Steele enters the room with the paperwork listing the charges. Earl reviews the documents. He looks at Steele and then to Simon.

"It seems like every government agency is doing a proctoscopy on you, Simon." Earl lets loose a barrel laugh. "Steele," he says, "these charges are a bunch of crap. In the morning, I will have all of it thrown out, and your thin ice will crack. Now, here is the deal. My client will only talk in my presence. You will release him now and remove the tracking."

Shaken but trying not to show it, Steele says, "I can release him, but the device stays, just as the FBI director suggested. Call him if you like."

"Is it all right with you, Simon? No need to poke people for a silly band."

Simon nods in agreement.

Earl, who has been sitting, now stands, again towering over the FBI inspector. "Steele, you will get him back to his family ASAP so they are no longer inconvenienced."

※

Hours later, the FBI van drops Simon in front of his home in the dark of night and speeds away. Simon makes a beeline to the locked front door and bangs. Alexis is startled by banging and makes her way to the door, afraid they have come back for her. She stretches to peer through the peephole. Realizing it is her husband, she frantically opens the locks. He steps inside, and Alexis wraps around him, holding on for dear life. She is now crying.

Emma appears at the top of the steps, concerned by the commotion. She sees her dad in the doorway and bolts to her parents. "Daddy, you're home!" she screams. She jumps to them, embracing both and pushing them against the wall. Simon's long arms envelop his girls, not wanting to let go.

Alexis breaks the moment by asking, "Did Arnold help you?" The trio unbundle and separate. "I tried to locate you but couldn't."

"Yes and no," Simon replies. "I'll tell you about it later. Right now, is there anything in the house to eat? I'm starving."

"They didn't feed you?"

"All they fed me were words of garbage."

Alexis pats his arm and heads to the kitchen. Emma grabs her father's hand and leads him behind Alexis. She and Simon sit at the table as Alexis rushes to provide food. While scrambling around, she knows Simon is safe for the moment and teases him to break the tension with levity.

"So honey, did our jailbird con man not run his tin cup across the bars, screaming for the screw to bring food?" Simon looks up with a weak expression, and Alexis realizes it was in poor taste. She rushes to Simon, apologizes, and hugs him, saying, "I'm glad you're safe."

"Hilarious," Simon manages to respond, reaching down for his normal sense of humor. "I wasn't a con, though, just the alleged perpetrator. Somehow, through Arnold, an attorney named Earl Connery Hardin came to see me, and they backed down once he got involved. Apparently he is well connected, and his connection got me out of jail."

"Dad," Emma says, "We talked about Earl Connery Hardin at school in our current events studies. He's terrible, defending guilty celebrities, politicians, and crooks."

"I don't know about that, honey … but I do know that he's the one who got me sprung … and I'm no crook."

Alexis turns with food plates in hand saying, "Honey, you were in jail for less than a day, and you're talking of getting sprung. The place hasn't rubbed off on you, has it?".

He swats her. "I never want to see it again. Let's pray."

Michael lands in Columbia near the home of Cortez Mora, the most wanted cartel leader and drug lord. Approximately 60 percent of cocaine delivery flows through his organization. His henchmen have been responsible for thousands of deaths resulting from drug overdoses and gang warfare. Michael sits near his heavily guarded compound. Mora is by his pool with more security than a country's president. His wife, half his age, reclines nearby in a bikini. He is a vicious middle-aged man with a belly and salt-and-pepper hair. Many have crossed him or his organization and found themselves impaled on stakes in the center of town. Most police and politicians are in his pocket and do his bidding, turning a blind eye.

Michael muses, "Your power will not help you now, because your dominion will soon belong to the Dominion." Michael places his hand on the phone, and it glows. Cortez grabs his phone and looks at the number. It is his daughter away at college. He presses to connect and says, "Hola miel." His eyes go wide, and he falls face down on the table.

His security team scrambles in all directions, looking for an assault or a sniper, but there is no blood. Mora was not eating, so there was no poison. His food taster is still alive. One guard removes the phone from his hand, and the screen reads, "Your rapture is brought to humanity by the Dominion … Where are you in your soul's contract with us?"

Michael stands, glows yellow, and fades. The commander's lens reads, "I give you Cortez Mora."

Lennon's house is still, with light coming from the family room. Inside, Mark Thomas stumbles from Lennon's room, having clipped the strings of the guitar again. He falls into the recliner and swallows a beer. The bottle then joins the many empty bottles on the side table. A video of his wife, Samantha, plays on the television. Mark stares at it until the beer and sleep overtake him. A green being lands on the sidewalk at the back door. It steps forward, dissolving through the walls. Entering the family room, it sees Mark's body and the television playing. The being's lens reads, "Commander, May I connect them?"

The commander replies, "I trust your judgment." The being turns its palms outward, facing the television. A white light flows from both palms and joins as one, hitting the television screen with the image of Mark's wife singing. The light withdraws, and the form of his wife stands next to the being. Samantha looks into the being's kind eyes, as if in a trance.

The being says, "I grace you the unique opportunity to come back, but you have little time to help your husband. Release him from his heartache so he can discover his important journey." Samantha's face glows with delight. She approaches her husband and kneels beside his chair. Her face grows sad at his disheveled state. He is not the man who captured her soul so long ago. She brushes his hair back, and her lips press his in a kiss.

A white light connects them, and they talk soul-to-soul. The being's lens reads, "Mark, you are off your soul's journey. I know of your sorrow for me and how you miss me, but you must let me go. I'm at peace and with friends in the Dominion, watching over you and Lennon. Lennon needs you to help him on his journey. Mark, I know you blame music for my death, but it was a person off his soul's journey. It was his choice to get behind a wheel drunk. No one may end a soul's journey and its wonderful possibility. You are traveling the same path in your current state. Lennon has music within him, and he needs your approval. You are the love of my life, and with this final kiss I release you from your mourning. I will wait for you when your time arrives to enter the Dominion. Good-bye, my love."

Samantha breaks the kiss, returning to the being. The being has a warm, loving smile for her and assures her that her family is now on a good path. It steps forward, telling her, "You will be reunited again." Samantha has a sad face as she listens. The being continues. "You are recalling the starkness of returning to a mortal existence and not being in the light. The joys and the lows of learning on Earth are coming back to you. Humans see only one side of the mirror of life, but now you are in the full Dominion." Magdala wraps Samantha in her glowing arms, and they vanish. The television goes dark, and the VCR spits out a torn strip of tape before ejecting the cassette. Mark snores in his chair.

CHAPTER 21

Michael enters the largest megachurch in the nation. The fiery lead pastor is Gordon Thatcher. The arena can seat over twenty-five thousand people, and on most church days it is overflowing. Many are sick, seeking healing from Thatcher. Today is one of those days, with the believers flowing to their seats. Many are on crutches and in wheelchairs. It is said that Reverend Thatcher has made the lame walk and has cured cancer. Thatcher is in his forties. He has built a massive church that stretches far outside Houston. Social media, the internet, and other forms of communication have allowed Thatcher to reach the world with his message. This is evidenced by the satellite dishes surrounding the building.

Michael goes to a seat near the pulpit area. Today he will be one of the infirm, as a lesion appears on his temple. Michael knows the healing is a ruse and false. The reverend's church is for his selfish 'divine profit.' Michael sits and listens to Thatcher go on and on about how we are sinners in need of his saving. He wants to stand and turn him to salt like Lot's wife, but he shows restraint. He is on the commander's mission. *Giving false hope to the innocent is not his only crime against the faithful, and today we will have dominion over him. He had better get his soul in order.*

Michael approaches the stage and the reverend for healing. The reverend takes Michael's hand and looks into Michael's eyes. Thatcher takes on an odd look, as if he has been caught with his hand in a cookie jar. He recovers and has words of comfort for Michael, assuring him that his healing will begin shortly. The Reverend wipes his brow and takes a sip of water, making a joke that sometimes the word of God can make one sweat, but Michael knows better. Thatcher feels as if someone climbed into his soul, where the human crap hides, and exposed him.

Michael retreats to his seat and watches as the unsuspecting seek help from Thatcher. The reverend finishes preaching, and donation buckets move through the assembled. If everyone gave a dollar, that would be $25,000 on this day. Michael ponders how religion became such a business. He scans the dispersing crowd and wonders whether they listened to the half-truths coming from Thatcher. The Dominion will set it straight.

The reverend leaves the arena and retreats to his office, which is rich in decoration like Caesars Palace. He sits at his desk and writes a letter. The heading reads, "The Sins of Gordon Thatcher." He spares nothing from his soul, just as Michael instructed him when they touched. Michael's message, soul-to-soul, was "You'd better be sorry when judged, because you are far off the journey you planned before your birth." The message went on to tell about bringing false hope, deceiving, having sex with people he counseled and with minors, out-and-out infidelity, blackmail, theft of church money for personal gain, and destruction of prayer cards.

The list Thatcher writes is extensive. He finishes the letter, admitting his fraud and everything the authorities need to shut him down and lock him up. His church assistant, whom he has blackmailed into a nonconsensual relationship, sits at her desk. She is a notary, and he asks her to stamp the letter. She does so without question because of fear. He addresses the envelope to the attorney general for the state of Texas and places it with the other outgoing mail. Thatcher leaves the office and makes his way to his car, but he never reaches it. On the way, he answers his ringtone of "How Great Thou Art," falling dead as the light scans his face. The dropped phone reveals the words "Your rapture is brought to humanity by the

Dominion … Where are you in your soul's contract with us?" An autopsy will find he died of natural causes.

𝕁𝕉

The commander's lens reads, "I send you Gordon Thatcher."

𝕁𝕉

Another day ends at JPL, and Simon makes his way to his car. His pant leg obscures the ankle bracelet provided him by the FBI and the NSA. Norm doesn't know about the hardware. Almost unbelievably, little has spread about his arrest and short stint in some jail or prison somewhere. Friendly neighbors have disregarded the whole thing as a huge mistake, and the busybody neighbors are now keeping their mouths shut.

Once in the car, Simon breathes a sigh of relief that nothing earth-shattering has descended on him today. Glancing at the dashboard, he sees a sticky note from Alexis with a list of groceries needed written on it. He smiles, as this is a task he can complete without causing the world to explode. The list is long, so he heads to their usual store for the heavy shopping. He directs the car to the store and turns at the next intersection. In a short distance, his ankle hardware beeps.

He pulls over and realizes that he can no longer shop at this store because it is not within the travel parameters set by the government. Simon grabs his phone and searches for grocery stores he can go to without setting it off. He is not keen on discovering what happens if he breaks the rules. He thinks, *Will it blow my leg off, start a drone attack, or surround me with an armored SWAT team?*

He decides on a store not on the normal path but within the bracelet's parameters. In a short distance, he is at this store he has never visited before. It is now a discovery mission to see how this store entices him to stay to drain his pockets. Simon doesn't do big shopping trips often, usually just picking up a few things on the

336

way home. Shopping is Alexis's domain, and he has accompanied her a few times. Alexis and he are different shoppers entirely, which amuses him, as this trait hearkens back to the caveman days of the hunter-gatherers.

As in his work at JPL, he is laser focused, driven at full speed to the intended target to kill it and drag it home. Alexis is the "let's circle it ten times and then move to another tangent in hope for something better, only to return to the original target to circle it again until it dies from exhaustion by my many passes" shopper. He supposes each method works in the end. He grabs items on the list and drops them into the cart, weaving in and out of slower shoppers nearby while leaning on the cart for support. Simon believes one should behave when shopping as if one is in a car, staying on the right side. He also thinks that each side aisle connected to a main one should have a stop sign.

As he quickly shops, he thinks that people should not cut across traffic into the other lane and should never talk on the phone while driving or when deciding on a product. As he sees someone doing this very thing, he thinks, *For goodness' sake, decide and quit blocking the aisle. It's pasta, woman, at $1.50. Just get it and move on.*

He then notices a woman following him in the store. Now he thinks, *The government can't have people in the cereal aisle at the grocery stores trailing me.* He maneuvers his cart as he did his car to discern whether or not she is in pursuit. Stopping his cart, he grabs a box of Cap'n Crunch and reads the box. The woman heads toward him and passes without looking at him. Once past his cart, she turns and calls him a traitor.

"Excuse me," he replies. "What did you say?"

"You heard me, traitor. You broke into the computers, and now we have this mess and possible war."

"How would you know anything about me? I've never met you."

"I know people at JPL, and they say the government is investigating you. My husband lost his job there, but they hire a traitor like you." Her voice rises, drawing attention. "How do you sleep, traitor? God should make a special place in Hades for you."

"I've done nothing, lady, and you get your panties in a knot because you get an email suggesting people should love each other."

"Well, the word is that the government's going to nail you, and deservedly so. I hear you're wearing an ankle monitor. Why that if you are not a criminal?"

A crowd forms around the two as the conversation escalates. The woman educates the crowd on Simon, and they call for blood, so management intervenes. "Ask him to lift his pant leg and show you the ankle monitor," the woman tells management. "He shouldn't be in here." Sensing he might be dangerous, management calls for a security guard, and he is escorted into a locked loss-prevention office to wait while they call police.

Simon is bumfuzzled. He is not sure what to tell the police when they come. He is unsure whether he can explain the device to them without having another agency on his butt. The wait seems to go no for hours before the door finally bursts open and Kelly's face is smiling at him. "Are you trying to wreck the commodity prices now?" she asks.

"Freaking Kelly. I was buying cereal!" he replies.

"I know you did nothing, Simon, and I cleared it with the locals. We saw it come over the police network."

"Does this mean I can go nowhere?"

"Simon, we can't protect you from people. We looked at many at JPL, and word got around among the lower-level personnel that you were questioned more than anyone else, and … well, you know how people talk and point fingers. In this day and age, you get accused and convicted at the same time with no evidence. The unknowing who have been cleared spread gossip like lightning. Humans must find someone or something to blame, as you found out. We shared no information on our discussion with you or others at JPL without proper clearances. You would be sitting in a cell so deep that God's light could not find you if we had found any criminality. They are still digging." Kelly pauses, looks at Simon, and says, "What's wrong? You look funny."

"You mention God's light, Kelly, but it isn't pointing my way right now."

"Simon, if you must shop, I suggest doing it as little as possible, maybe stopping it altogether and letting your wife take care of things. And maybe she should shop in another town, away from JPL people and other people caught up in the gossip mill, just to be on the safe side. Keeping this from the media's prying eyes will not last forever. They will go down every avenue and follow every lead, which at some point will lead to you if we don't get it cleared up."

"Do I need to call Hardin, my attorney, for help?"

"That's up to you, Simon. But for now, we'll get you out of here. Give me your keys, and I will bring your car around to the back. Management can let you out through the back door where the trucks unload, keeping you away from the crowd out front." Kelly leaves and Simon is ushered to the rear—with no groceries, of course. Not even the Cap'n Crunch cereal.

He soon hears a pounding on the door. Opening it, Kelly stands there with his keys in hand. "I will follow you home for safety," she says. Simon drops into his seat and rubs his face. He is now a man on the run. He thinks, *Do I need to get some type of disguise? Maybe then I can go out in public.* The last time he was in the car, he boasted to himself that nothing earth shattering had happened today, but he spoke too soon. As he pulls out from behind the store and onto a main road, he sees in the review mirror that Kelly is following him, her mouth moving. He knows her conversation must be with the NSA, FBI, or both.

Traffic backs up, which is a relief to Simon. The solitude and tinted windows are welcome. He will have to clean the junk from his garage after dark so he can slip into his cave unnoticed. He turns on the radio, and the tune playing stops in midsong. It is suddenly replaced by the phrase from "The Ballad of John and Yoko" about being crucified. Simon thinks it odd, but he realizes how everything has become odd, which is now normal for him.

And then the familiar voice of *Sojourner* says, "Good evening,

Simon. Is it evening there? It is hard to see from here. I thought you would enjoy your theme song."

"Hilarious," Simon says. "So now the Dominion are jerks."

"No, they care about you and selected you. They wanted you to see what man can do to each other. You saw firsthand what people believe when they choose not to know someone. The lady was full of hate for you out of jealousy and poor information from the electronic grapevine. If she had taken the time to know you personally, she would think differently. And that, my friend, is the mission."

"They were testing me?"

"They are not throwing obstacles in your way to see how you react. Humans will do that without the Dominion's help. But they are allowing it to happen so you can better understand exactly what your mission is."

"I guess I failed."

"No, Simon, you performed well. You nicely asked the woman why she was so mad about getting an email telling her to love others. The Dominion says, 'Well done.'"

"The people in that store wanted to lynch me."

"Simon, can you imagine the vileness thrown at Noah by the people calling him a fool? These same people became his best friends when the rain kept falling. They wanted to go aboard, but it was too late."

"Oh, yes, *Sojourner*, I am sure they wanted on his boat."

"Simon, the woman that attacked you and caused the ruckus goes to church each Sunday but is full of self."

"Am I done now?" Simon asks.

"We've only just begun," *Sojourner* replies. "'Peace be with you,' Simon."

The voice is gone, and the radio returns to normal. The drive is over, and Kelly beeps and powers past his house. Simon is at his castle, but the word "castle" now brings vivid memories of the old Frankenstein movies. It reminds him of a mob of people with pitchforks and torches assaulting the castle and the purported beast within its walls. He twists and turns in his seat, looking to see whether any of his neighbors have joined the mob. Seeing the coast is clear, he darts to open the front door and bolts it behind him. He yells for Alexis. "Come here! Come here!"

She rumbles down the stairs, asking, "What is it, Simon?"

"I couldn't get the groceries."

"That's all right, hon. I can do it later."

"You don't understand. I was assaulted at the grocery store."

"Someone attacked you?"

"Not physically, but verbally. A woman knew of my questioning on the email hacking and called me a traitor."

"What? Did you know her?"

"Never saw her before in my life. But her husband knew of me from the JPL grapevine. He lost his job a while back like me. Alexis, the stupid woman shouted to everyone around about what a traitor I am, and a crowd gathered. Alexis, the management saw my bracelet and called the police."

"You were arrested? Why didn't you call me?"

"I was buying cereal, and I did nothing. This woman started it. They took me to an office to wait. But then Kelly from the NSA showed and cleared everything. During the ride home, *Sojourner* spoke, telling me of my experience at the store."

"They are watching you?"

"They knew everything. *Sojourner* said the Dominion were pleased with my actions."

"What? Getting arrested?"

"No. When the woman was shouting at me and calling me all this vile stuff, I kept my cool and asked why she was so worked up about getting a message asking her to love other people. I guess the Dominion liked the response. *Sojourner* said she was a good Christian in word only and, like the rest of the world, absorbed in self. Kelly suggested I quit shopping for the time being and let you take care of it. And she suggested you might shop in another town."

"What? Where? New York … or someplace like that?"

"No, no. Some little town nearby. You know how it is; people in the outlying areas don't know what's going on in this JPL town."

"Okay, Simon." She pauses and then asks, "Are we in danger from our own friends?"

"No. *Sojourner* said those that know us soul-to-soul will understand and have our backs. Those that don't—those that rely on media and hearsay—might be a problem. The bottom line is, I will keep my head down."

"Other than shopping out of town, I'm staying at home as much as possible and at the funeral home. Those in the back can't assault me."

"Funny. I need a laugh. Is Emma all right?"

"Yeah. Emma's a real trooper, Simon. Other kids might let this whole thing bring them down, but not Emma."

"Great. I'm really proud of that young lady … more than ever."

"Yeah, me too. Did *Sojourner* say or want anything else?"

"No, just for me to get started saving the world. I said I didn't know how to begin, and it said that what I did at the store was a good step. And *Sojourner* mentioned that blog thing earlier."

"Well, you spoke to one person today. It is said that revolutions begin with the first step. So what now?"

"I can reach more people on that suggested blog, so I need to get started on that. But, changing the subject, what's for dinner?"

"We will have leftovers, since this bad boy didn't bring home the bacon." She scurries to the kitchen with Simon in pursuit.

The journey to the studio today couldn't go too fast. Lennon wished he had wings. As he pushes open the door, the smiles of Macy and Oz greet him. The sound machine is flashing to the beat of music coming from the recording room. "I see you brought your guitar," Macy states.

"Yeah, I'm embarrassed by it after touching the new ones."

"Hey, I like the tape design," Macy says. Lennon smiles and rubs his fingers along the tape-covered case. "Don't worry, Lennon; everyone here has had instruments held together with string, tape, and glue. Such is the life of musicians."

"Good news, Lennon," Oz interrupts. "You ready to play music today?"

"Yes!"

"Our musician friends are in the back and will help us get everything working. Macy and I thought you could sit in on guitar."

"Me? I've never played with professionals."

"Relax! You've played together with friends?"

"Yes."

"These will be your new friends, except they have played on major albums."

"I'm nervous," Lennon says.

"Don't be," Macy tells him. "They started where you are and understand the game. We played them your rendition of 'The End' you played for us."

Lennon gets a huge grin. "I'm still scared."

"You'll be fine," Oz encourages him. "Follow me, and I'll make the introductions."

The trio leave, heading to the studio. The studio has a new life, filled with musicians talking and laughing as if they know each other well. Oz enters the studio, followed by Macy and a shaking Lennon. The group razz Oz as friends do, one mentioning to another he has gotten no better looking since they last met. Lennon sighs in relief that the people are not stuffy. Darrel Higgins sits behind the drums, with a headband holding back his long hair. "Macy," he says, "you still hang with Oz?"

She responds by sticking her tongue out at him. He laughs, and she says, "Hi Darrel. Thanks for joining us."

"I wouldn't miss it for you guys," he replies.

"Yeah, Darrel," Oz joins in, "appreciate you taking this on." They nod in agreement. "We have a newbie with us today," Oz announces to everyone. The musicians glance at Lennon, and he gives a shy wave. Darrell claps, and the others join in. Lennon doesn't understand.

The applause dies, and Darrell says, "You are Lennon, and your guitar lick is impressive." Lennon hopes his smile will unhook from his ears so he can speak. Real musicians—not parents, friends, or relatives—complimented him.

"I'll go around the room and make the introductions," Oz tells him. "The ugly guy on the drums is Darrel Higgins." He does a quick drum roll and hits a cymbal.

"Next up, on bass guitar is Kristi Jenkins."

She says, "Hi, Lennon. Welcome to the team."

"Next to her is Zane Weiss, on a harmonica."

He gives Lennon a wave.

"Near to him is Matt Hawkins, sitting behind the piano."

Lennon feels a brief sadness as Oz then introduces Jeni Cate, who is holding the red guitar he tuned. "Next to her, holding another new guitar, is Pat Brady."

Brady says, "Hi Lennon," and pats the empty chair between him and Jeni Cate. "Come on and plug into the system," he tells Lennon.

Lennon looks to Oz and Macy. "Go ahead," Oz tells him. "We will make music and have fun. If you're unsure, ask Jeni or Pat." He makes his way to the chair, trying to hide his wreck of a guitar case. Once seated, he opens his case, hoping this will not be the time it crumbles.

Jeni smiles and pats his case. "Nice tape job," she says. "I still have mine, and you will keep yours when you move up to better." She then says, "We liked your Beatles song. Do you mind if we play it with you?"

"I would love it," Lennon tells her.

Jeni says, "You did each of the parts before, but today we will split the parts among us. Do you have a favorite section?"

"I like the last part," Lennon tells her.

Okay," she replies. "John did that part, and it goes with your shirt." Lennon grins and looks down at his new shirt from Maggie. "I'll do the first, followed by Pat. Don't worry if you mess up; we do it too." Lennon plugs in and sits with his broken, dull instrument, sliding his palm along the neck. Oz's voice breaks his nervousness as he barks out instructions from the control room. The musicians get ready.

Oz says, "Everyone prepared? Lennon, you have your part?" Lennon nods to indicate he is ready. Matt begins with piano. Lennon waits for his part, wondering whether if he pinches himself he will wake from this dream. His part arrives, and he slides into it like an old friend connecting. Years of solitary practice are coming home. Eyes in the room fall upon him as his fingers move across the frets. He glances to Pat and Jeni, who smile back. He returns the grin and keeps playing, with a feeling of belonging running through to his soul.

The song ends, and Macy's voice over the intercom says, "It was wonderful, and Lennon, you were perfect." Lennon blushes.

Pat fist-bumps him and says, "You've got chops, man. Do you play at other studios?"

"No," Lennon replies, "just high school dances for free, and in my room.

"Where did you learn?"

"My mom taught me before she died."

"Sorry, man, my sympathies to you. But I thought you might have gone to a performing arts school."

"No, no formal teaching."

"If what we heard continues, we have nothing on you, because some here are classically trained. You make your mom proud." Macy enters the room and distributes a playlist to the artists.

Oz says, "If you can do that number you just did, Lennon, these will be no problem." Lennon studies the list, realizing he has played the songs many times. He hopes they aren't taking it easy on the new kid. After a few hours and many songs played, night has fallen outside, but this goes unnoticed by him. Everyone breaks as Oz ends the session from the control room. They put their instruments to rest, and Lennon cases his guitar.

Matt comes over to Lennon and says, "You did great." He points to the case and says, "It still has life."

"Yeah, I guess."

"Like your shirt, too, Lennon."

"Thanks, Matt. I'd love to have a Rickenbacker 325."

Matt asks, "Just like the one on your shirt?"

"Yeah," Lennon replies as he pats the image.

"Matt taps his shoulder and says, "Dreams come true. If you keep playing the way you just did, and you treat the music right, you will have it one day.""

Lennon leaves the studio and steps into the darkness. He walks slowly, not wanting to go home, because his father will be long into the beer. He is tired of being the grown-up. After the bus deposits him on his street, he stands at the end of his walkway and takes a breath to prepare for what awaits him. The house is dark, which is unusual for his father. His dad is not in his recliner, the TV is dark, and no bottles cover the end table. He thinks it strange.

Lennon walks to his father's bedroom and sees him sleeping. He sighs in relief that his dad is not driving. Lennon's room is undisturbed, and his mom's guitar rests on its stand, with the strings intact. This is really strange to him, because coming home late is usually disastrous. He turns on the light and sees a package resting on his pillow. On the package are the words "Zachery Music." That is the shop where he buys his strings, and he is their best string customer. After setting his case against the wall, he opens the package. It is full of many sets of guitar strings.

A letter inside reads, "Dear Lennon, I am so sorry I've been a terrible absent father. I hope you can forgive me. Friends helped me realize I have become the person who took your mom, and I blamed music for her passing. In a dream of your mom, she gave me an attitude readjustment. I mourned her loss, but she told me to stop mourning her and start helping you with your journey. Let's return to how we were before the accident. I know I will be with your mom one day, but she is with us every day, and I want to be with you in everything. Love, Dad."

Lennon places the letter on the table and sits on the bed. He grabs the bedsheet to wipe the tears from his cheeks. He prays, "God, thank you if you had a hand in this; my prayers are being answered since Swaddling came into my life. Emma hugged me, I have a dream job, and maybe, just maybe, my dad has returned." Lennon, worn out physically and mentally, doesn't undress but pulls the covers over him, hoping the dream of today doesn't end.

Simon climbs the home stairs up to his bedroom on legs weary from the pressure of the government surveillance. He now understands how people in communist countries felt and still feel, never knowing whom to trust. Alexis has proceeded him to bed, and he sees her form on the bed covered by the blanket tucked under her chin. It gives him solace that the family is safe and together at home. He drops his clothes on a chair in the room. Alexis calls it his pile. A night-light illuminates the bathroom, and he moves there to brush his teeth.

Before sliding into bed, Simon drops to his knees and says his nightly prayer. Even though he is in a perilous state of faith, he still prays. Tonight he will pray for his family and his sanity. How does he save the world, or is he slipping into insanity? The pillow caresses his head as his body surrenders to the softness. A prayer escapes his lips as sleep overcomes him. "Let tomorrow be better," he mumbles. Simon's eyes twitch as he gets into a deep sleep with his head partially tented by the blanket. It is funny how the way we sleep as a child follows us to adulthood.

His dream or nightmare starts with a grotesque nonhuman creature grunting and dragging itself down the water aisle of a supermarket. The skin of the brute is burning, as if molten lava flows beneath the dermis. It howls and grunts, with steam pumping from every orifice. Patrons flee in its path as it moves through the aisle. It scans the shelves from side to side, with unopened water bottles littering the floor as it discards them after sniffing their contents. We pay a dollar for the most plentiful substance on the planet, but it may not always be that way. The creature reaches to a shelf with leprous, gnarled hands and grabs a bottle, tearing off the cap and guzzling the contents.

It repeats this six times. Its face turns skyward and unleashes an ear-shattering ungodly howl and belch. It marches forward with its skin no longer having a lavalike appearance, and it molts like a snake. The outer skin peels away to the floor, and a white light being bolts through the store's ceiling. A store employee picks up one empty bottle. A holy man in a white robe sits by an idyllic waterfall with the words "Holy Water" emblazoned on the label.

Simon rolls over and issues a restless mumble, returning to a quiet snoring. The peaceful sleep is interrupted by another dream filling his mind. Today he will appear as a presenter on the *ABC* television show *Shark Tank*, six wealthy business personalities (the sharks)in attendance who may want to invest in his product. He paces behind the big wooden doors ready to swing open. He will show a new water drink. The pitch to the sharks is in memory, and his worry is not tripping during the walk down the aquarium-lined hallways. It is ironic he will walk between water to talk to sharks about water. The doors fly open, and Simon marches to his pitch. When the door opens, a video of his product plays to educate the sharks during the walk. It precisely ends when he takes his position on the carpet.

The shark Damon responds, "Nice timing."

"Hello, sharks, my name is Dr. Simon Northstrum. I am the man who talks with space probes around the universe and the rovers on Mars."

Eyebrows rise on the sharks' faces.

The shark named Mark says, "I love that stuff. You're the guy?"

"Yes, he replies."

"Cool. Guys, this is the real Mr. Spock."

"Did you enjoy the video?" Simon asks.

"Yes," replies Barbara, "a very professional display. You are a space genius; why water?"

"Before I continue, I have samples for you." He takes a tray and distributes a bottle to each shark. They sample the water, downing the contents.

"Mr. Wonderful remarks, "It's water. I can buy it anywhere and get it at home. Why is yours any different?"

Lori asks, "Why the name Terrormist? It sounds frightening."

Simon chuckles. "Will you please take out your cell phones?" Each shark pulls out a phone; they all have weird looks upon their faces. Simon reaches into his pocket and retrieves a remote.

"The product is Terrormist because this water can kill terrorists in any form."

Barbara pipes up. "Is this a joke, and how did you get on the show? I'm out."

"Please be patient. It will impress you. I have a product that can rid the world of terrorists."

"How do you do that?" asks Lori.

"I will show you now. You all had a sip of water." Simon presses a button on his remote and the sharks' phones glow to life. They all stare at the screens. They wince and grab their temples in a short-lived bout of pain. Simon says, "Did you feel a pain in your temple?" The sharks stand, wanting to run. Simon quiets them and tells them, "Stay calm; you are in no danger."

Robert asks, "Did you do that to us?"

"Yes." He holds up a vial of clear water in his left hand, and with his right, he points to the video screen. The image of the vial appears, with millions of nanos swimming erratically in it. "The water you drank contained these nanos, and I control them. Here is a test I ran to show you how much control I have over the robots."

Simon moves to another video that shows the nanos' erratic behavior changing. In a few seconds, the nanos have lined up in a message. The sharks squint to read the message. Robert stands to move closer to the screen, since he is the nearest shark. He puts his face near the screen and turns to the other sharks, telling them, "It says, 'Be Not Afraid.'"

"You did this, Dr. Northstrum?" he asks.

"No, my software, Reliance, controls them. I could have them form a blood clot in your brain, killing you."

Barbara replies, "You put this in us without our approval?"

"Yes. Would you have done it if I had asked?"

"No."

Simon explains, "We cannot go to terrorists and say, 'Here, drink this for me.' When we detain them, they must hydrate more than they must eat. This is when they receive the robots. We can track them anywhere and give the nanos commands, and they'll die from natural causes days or weeks later. Let me reassure you that the nanos in you are dead and the body eliminates them unnoticed. You are in no danger."

Robert asks, "How far can you communicate with these nanos?"

"Here and around the world," Simon replies.

"This is creepy," says Barbara.

"So are terrorists who put explosives in pressure cookers and strap children with bombs," Simon replies.

"How did you get our numbers?" asks Mark.

"The government has your numbers. You give them away willingly with each new app and advanced cell phone." The sharks nod in understanding.

Damon asks, "Is this the same program running the Martian rovers?"

"Yes."

"Who else has this software?"

"No one. Not even the government. It is up here," Simon says, tapping his head.

"This might be creepier than the guy who wanted to put a cell phone in your brain," Mark says. The sharks nod. "For that reason, I'm out." He leaves, and one by one others follow, until only Mr. Wonderful remains.

"Well, good doctor, one shark remains—and the best one. I like the concept, and we get rid of the terrorists. I can think of a thousand uses for this beyond terrorists. What a negotiating tool in business! I could say, 'Give me my terms or else.'"

He stands with his arms outstretched and points toward the other sharks. "You're fools and cockroaches to me. We can obliterate the competition and rule the world. You are dead to me now." He turns to Simon and says, "Dr. Northstrum, you've got a deal at this ridiculous valuation, and I won't need a royalty." He walks to Simon with his arms out and screams a loud evil cackle. Simon wakes from the dream with sweat on his forehead and sits upright in the bed.

CHAPTER 22

Simon backs the car from the garage en route to the office. He looks for oncoming cars and is startled by the bright letters spray painted across the facade of his home. "Traitor," the message reads.

He pulls the car back up the driveway and places his head against the steering wheel. "*Sojourner* was right; this will kill me." He prays, "I'm trying, can't you see."

He is thankful Emma needed to get to Sable early and took Emma in for a before-school meeting with Swaddling Clothes. Leaving before sunrise, they apparently could not see the graffiti. *It would frighten them, so it must be repaired before they return.* He messages Norm that he will be late to work, along with a sad emoji. He goes into the garage and locates the extra paint to start the repair. Painting was not on his planner for today. Fortunately, the people who sprayed the message were short, so he doesn't need a ladder to fix it.

Across the street, Ezra Crockett stirs in his kitchen. Ezra is ninety-five and has lived on this street since when it was not much more than a cow pasture. His wife died a few years back. Now Crockett hears shouting from across the road and peers out the window to see Simon verbally abusing the wall of his home. Adjusting his glasses to focus, Crockett sees the bright red paint and the word written. He mutters, "Oh, my." He has known the Northstrums since they moved in before they had Emma. He and his late wife watched them become a family and shared in the joyful events, as good neighbors do. Crockett's wife was like a nana to their Emma.

He puts his coffee on the counter and moves into the bedroom, returning moments later dressed in overalls and a paint-covered ball cap. He makes his way to Simon's, shuffling across the street with a paint roller in hand. Simon faces his home, still muttering. Ezra stands behind him and says, "I'm old, but can I help."

The voice startles Simon, who turns to see his elderly friend. "Ezra, my gosh!"

"I heard the shouting and saw the vandalism."

"I can handle it, Ezra. I don't want you to get hurt."

Ezra holds up his arms. "They may be spindly, but they painted many things over the years and survived D-Day. Anyway, a friend helps a friend in time of trouble." He pauses. "Do you know, Simon, you were the only people on this street who sat with me, cried with me, broke bread, and checked on me when Millie passed? I'm helping if it kills me."

Simon smiles and gives the man a hug. Ezra returns the hug like a father to his son. They both hold on, needing the closeness of a selfless friend. They break away, and Simon says, "Okay, Ezra, I have another pole to put on your roller so you don't have to bend or stretch." They begin their work, and Ezra asks Simon about everything going on in the world.

"Are you responsible for the problem?"

"No," says Simon.

"I knew the answer. We know one another on a soulful level, and I know you are incapable of the crime. You think you know your neighbors, but until you relate honestly with them, you know nothing. One of your neighbors did this, I'm sure."

Simon replies, "I've had strangers assault me. Our cars have had eggs thrown at them. My daughter gets abused at school. I'm the only one accused, and I've done nothing. The sad fact is, I have no way to prove I've done nothing. It is a dilemma, Ezra."

"Yes," Ezra replies, "like having faith in something you cannot see." Ezra then notices a change of expression on Simon's face and says, "You've got a funny look on your face, Simon."

"Everyone is telling me to have faith. I've done nothing, but I can't send up a flag showing the absolute truth of my innocence. They only want me to show them how I did it."

"Simon, it's like when we met our wives and we knew they were the ones. If a person asked you to show proof, you couldn't do it; you just felt it and had faith in it."

They continue talking until they cover the graffiti; then Simon puts the supplies away.

"Thank you, Ezra. It was great having the company. And you will never fully know how much I appreciate you and your help. Alexis made some sweet rolls—delicious. Will you join me for coffee and a roll?"

"It would be nice, since I usually eat alone." They move into the house, wash up, and then go to the kitchen and sit around the table.

Simon says, "What do you make of everything going on around the world?"

"I'm old, but I worry our country is rudderless and has lost its way. Politicians run the world, and their only concern is staying in power at any cost. They remind me of the royalty during the French Revolution who fled the scene with their riches while the country sank. We have no statesmen today, only politicians controlled by their money handlers. There is a quote from the legislator who cast the final vote to impeach Andrew Johnson. He said that when he voted against impeachment, he dug his own political grave and jumped into it. He chose the health of the country in twenty years over his future career. The founding fathers put their necks in a noose for the good of the country. Our leaders refuse to make difficult decisions needed because they want to please everyone for votes."

Ezra takes a bite of his roll and sips some coffee before continuing. "I remember being on the landing craft on D-Day, waiting on the ramp to open. We knew when it did that most of those first off would be cut down, and most were. I don't remember seeing anyone with an emotional support animal on the boat. When the war was over, many of us probably needed one, but there was nothing. They called it war fatigue. They didn't know of brain damage or PTSD. You sucked it up. Those boys with emotional problems from the horrors of the war and the pounding of the artillery that rattled our brains took to drink or held it inside or committed suicide. We had weapons used to kill lots of people; it was our job to get them before they put us in a grave."

Another bite, another sip. "I don't recall the men with issues going into a school and killing innocent children. It might be because the children of the war ran to us for food and protection from the Germans. We were killers, but they knew we would lay down our lives for them. I know, because I saw many of our guys fighting to keep strangers' children safe. Many of these same guys never came home. In the last thirty years, something has changed. Back then you could go to a high school and see pickup trucks with rifles in the rear window, but it never entered someone's mind to use them against the students at the school.

"Simon, it boils down to respect. They taught us that your rights end at the start of my nose. I think the youth of today believe in little and their 'god' is their electronics. When you're mad at the world, someone must pay, and the innocent pay the price. I believe the electronics of today have given the youth instant gratification, thinking if they can't get it in seconds, then someone must pay. They are unprepared for adversity. We on the boats learned adversity in seconds. You grew up fast back then; if not, you were dead. Grown men pissed on themselves before the doors came down." He pauses. "Sorry, Simon, I guess I am venting on you. It is nice to have someone to talk to, but I haven't given you a chance to speak."

"Ezra, it is fine. It must have been horrible. I've never been to war and can only imagine."

"I don't talk about it anymore, except for today. "One minute you're talking to a friend, the next minute his head explodes across your face. It becomes a nightmare when I talk about it—again, except for just now, with you. Back then, six months before the war, most of us were trying to impress a pretty girl back on the farm or at the soda fountain. And then we had our innocence ripped away in a minute. My worry with today's media and power-hungry politicians is … Well, let's just say that if we had it back then, we could never have mounted a secret invasion. Some idiots would think it cool to divulge the plan."

Ezra shakes his head at the thought and then continues. "These social media companies can't control their own bits and bytes or soulless programmers. We no longer strive for excellence; we try to reach the lowest common denominator. Television is packed with people behaving poorly, and the youth now believe that is normal. If it feels good, do it. They want theirs, no matter the cost. Lying, cheating, stealing—all the sins are okay if it gets me what I want. I was watching a show on artificial intelligence. It is a scary concept. There is the word 'artificial,' for one thing, and then to combine it with intelligence seems stupid. They miss the fatal flaw in the plan."

"What is that fatal flaw, Ezra?"

"Man does unthinkable actions for power. Look at D-Day and sitting on those boats with the bullets pinging off the bow. The Germans firing, in most cases, had never met an American and had no reason to want revenge on us. Yet they willingly cut us down to keep power. Man creates this AI and believes it can give it a moral compass when the man creating it cannot control his own. The man building the AI cannot code it with selflessness, love, knowledge, and wisdom. Man has not learned it yet. It will start out with good intentions and be corrupted for money, power, and control. Simon, I'm nearing one hundred, with one foot in the grave, but I have doubts about faith."

He sips his coffee and then says, "I've never shared this with anyone, outside of Millie. When we were on the boats, ready to charge, I was with my best bud, a guy named Albert Wilone. He was an older guy at twenty-five. He had a wife and two kids. He was a farm boy and a terrible poker player, but we became friends. Simon, do you ever wonder if people are in your path for a reason?

"In a way," Simon responds.

"I ask because when the door came down, the hail of bullets rushed in on us, and suddenly I was wearing my friend's face. The bullets plowed into him. His body became a shield I wore all the way to the beach, taking the repeated machine gun blows. I was the same weight as I was then, but somehow I could hold on to him for one hundred yards. I thought at the time a medic could help him, but he was dead. It's been many years, and I still wrangle with why I wasn't the one killed. The bullets hit him, leaving me with scratches. As I've gotten older, I've wondered if his life's journey brought us together for that moment, where his was to end and mine continue." Ezra eats his last bit of the roll, takes his last sip of coffee, and then says, "Simon, you have that strange look again."

"Ezra, I was meeting with a priest, and he was telling how people we meet intersect our lives for a reason, some positive and others not so much. It's the decisions we make from those interactions that are important. He described it as ripples in a life, and he said our free will is our hell."

"Did he mention anything about the inaccuracy in the email messages sent to everyone?"

"Yes, as a matter of fact he did. He said the dates might not have been wrong and that a selfish action by someone may have caused them to be delayed."

"It would make sense. While we are on the subject of selflessness, thank Alexis for me. Do you realize she has been slipping a goody bag into my mailbox each week since Millie died? It's full of the little goodies she would bring home from grocery trips. We've both been blessed with angels as partners. It would be wonderful if the helpers like them could run the world. They do a thing because they don't have to." Ezra takes a deep breath and then says, "I suppose you must get to work and don't have all day to sit and talk to a geezer."

"Ezra, I've enjoyed our talk, and we should do this again without having to paint a house. We must cross the street more often. Please don't mention the graffiti to Alexis. It would scare her." Ezra zips his lips. Simon walks him to the door, they exchange parting words, and Simon returns to the kitchen for another cup of coffee. He sits and thinks about how the people of Ezra's generation were different and were connected personally.

The yellow being touches down on the Black Sea shoreline of a wooded area. This is a massive estate on the outskirts of Sochi, Russia. The being assumes the image of Michael while walking through the forest. He breathes in the peacefulness of the unspoiled nature around him. He comes to a large rock and sits, pulling a phone from his pocket. Michael views the screen for his assignment. On the screen, he reviews the life of Serge Shogun.

He views the file, and a tear falls to his cheek. He breathes a sorrowful exhalation, knowing what must be done. This is not the life path Shogun chose before birth; he is now so far off the path. His free will has led him to sell drugs and weapons, and to enslave people for power, money, and control. It is said, "Whatever you do to the least of my children, you do unto me." *Today, Shogun, you will begin a new journey with many debts to pay. It didn't have to be this way, but that is the dark side of free will.*

Michael stands and walks toward a large fortified mansion sitting on a rise in the forest. The fortifications do not concern him, since they hold no control on the Dominion. Michael can now see the mansion and is a good distance from the building. He leans against a tree and dials his phone. Inside the home, Shogun sits with his wife on a long sofa, with a large television playing. They are snuggled together. This is odd for a ruthless man who sells death and destruction to the world while being hailed as a great business leader. Shogun's phone rings a familiar ringtone. He does not lift his head from the sofa back but brings the phone to his face, barely moving. He looks at the screen, his eyes go wide, and his hand slides down his body, resting on the sofa cushion. The image on the phone is peaceful, and the text reads, "Your rapture is brought to humanity by the Dominion ... Where are you in your soul's contract with us?" Shogun is gone. His young wife notices nothing, assuming her husband has fallen asleep as usual.

※

The commander's lens reads, "I give you Serge Shogun." Michael's lens reads, "Simon needs your help. You are free to use the power of the Dominion."

※

Kelly Sellers is on her way to JPL to meet with Michael Cott at Bosman's direction. The investigation at JPL is at a standstill, with no evidence of a hacker's presence. Simon remains the main person of interest. The FBI's blunder with Reliance put the NSA in full control. Steele continues to act as a lone wolf, conducting his own investigation and believing Northstrum guilty. He must save face.

Kelly meets with Michael at his car before they walk through security and Alvarez at JPL. "Have you found any holes at JPL?" she asks.

"No, it is a tight ship. They will be fine unless an insider creates a problem. I see no reason to keep the heat on Simon."

"He is still the top choice."

"I have found nothing leading to him."

"The FBI has failed big time, so the NSA wants the heat turned up on Simon."

"Michael says, "Continuing to look for a scapegoat." He shakes his head. "How are we supposed to apply this heat?"

Kelly grabs a laptop from her bag. "I believe Simon is innocent, but we've got jobs to do—if we want to keep our jobs. Michael, I want you to give this to Simon. General Bosman, for whatever reason, had the NSA build it, if you know what I mean."

Michael erupts in laughter. "So you are giving the guy a state-of-the-art NSA computer. He's not a dolt and will see right through it. Rich, very rich, Kelly."

"That is why you will give it to him. He trusts you."

"You want me to screw him?"

"I know how you feel about this. I feel the same way. But we've got jobs to do."

With resignation, Michael takes the laptop. "So, it's 'Et tu, Brute?'"

"I'm sorry," Kelly says, looking remorseful. "Jobs."

Later, Simon is in his office, and Michael enters, saying, "You got a minute?"

"Sure, Michael; come in.

"I have a new laptop given to me by Kelly."

"A new computer?"

"Yes."

"Why?"

"The government wants you to have it."

Simon erupts in laughter. "This beats all," he says, still laughing. "You give me a computer from an NSA agent." He wipes his eyes. "I bet that baby is full of special sauce aimed right at me. Thank her for me, but I don't need it; I'll stick with my clunker."

"I believe it is not a choice, Simon. But you're right, they tinkered with it and set you up—big time. But I fixed it for you. It will be okay to use. I give you my word. It will be all right now."

"Your word, Michael? Are you sure?"

"Yes, you can trust me. I have your back because I've been in your shoes. It's still in my car for now. I wouldn't dare try to take it through security. But when you go to lunch or home, I can give it to you."

CHAPTER 23

"Good morning, everyone. Welcome to *America's Newsroom*. I'm Bill Hemmer. Hello, Martha."

"Hello, Bill. Hi, folks, I'm Martha MacCallum. You might recall a while back, after we reported there were no deaths in the world, people—bad people, not good ones—started biting the dust. Our producers tell us now that such deaths are continuing. And it seems now that it looks to be a contagion spreading. People are now perishing in pockets here and there. We are following reports that the fallen include not only terrorists and other criminals, but also politicians, clergy, CEOs of big companies, university professors, and others from all walks of life and careers, even including children over thirteen years of age."

"Yes, Martha," Bill joins in. "The CDC is struggling to discover a common cause. The dead had no known interaction. They died from natural causes. You will remember the Reverend Gordon Thatcher's recent death revealed he was not the good shepherd we took him to be. At the same time, one of our viewers posted that a neighbor of his died for no reason, but they saw him as a vicious, selfish man and stayed away from him. We learned his own family detested him. He died in his yard, with his cell phone next to him.

"At the same time, Bill, we are getting reports of many natural deaths that have come as huge surprises, affecting various people of various ages. Folks, if you know of such sudden, unexpected deaths, text us.

"Good idea, Martha," Bill replies. "And if you know of any so-called 'cell phone deaths,' we would also like to hear from you."

🎼

Macy and Oz sit in the control room, reviewing the upcoming sessions booked for the studio. They turn as Lennon enters the building. Oz forgot to tell Lennon not to come in today, but he hides his mistake and welcomes him. "Hi, buddy," he says. "There is no session today; only Macy and I am doing the yucky stuff of business."

"Oh. What should I do?"

"Make sure the guitars are in tune."

"Sure." He goes to the back as Macy and Oz continue their discussion. While tuning, Oz's voice comes over the speaker. "Lennon, Macy and I will step out for a bite; can we bring you back a burger?"

"Yeah, that'd be great. Thanks."

"I've left the board on to record if you want to play with it while we are gone."

The duo leave. Lennon, alone in the studio, explores the instruments surrounding him. He picks up the red guitar, connecting it to play. His fingers play a few riffs from his favorite songs. The last riff is one of the many he wrote for Emma. His book of words and music grows thicker; he is afraid to leap for fear she doesn't feel the same. Lennon sets the guitar in the stand and walks into the control room. Once there, he presses a button and its light glows. He bolts back to the studio and grabs the red guitar. His fingers slide over the strings, playing Emma's song, careful to be perfect as this recording is the first for him.

After the song is complete, he gives a smile of satisfaction. He feels his song has left his room at home and made it into the universe. Lennon rushes back to the control room and presses stop. The recording rewinds as Lennon adjusts himself in the chair. He looks around to be sure he is alone. The play button illuminates, and Lennon's guitar comes over the large speakers. Lennon leans backward in the chair with his head back and eyes closed. The song continues with Lennon in his trance.

Unknown to him, Oz and Macy watch through the window. They sneak inside the entryway. Macy stops, Oz and motions for them to be quiet, with a finger to her lips. She puts a foot out to hold open the door a crack to better hear the music. Macy whispers to Oz, "It's beautiful." Oz nods in agreement. They wait for the song's ending before making their presence known. Lennon notices them shortly after the song ends, and they enter.

"Hi," Lennon says.

"Sorry it took so long," Oz replies. As he hands a burger to Lennon, he asks, "Were you busy while we were out?"

"After tuning everything, I was playing with the machine and my red guitar."

"You like that one?" Macy asks.

"Oh yeah!"

Oz says, "There is not much to do until we get through with the boring business paperwork, so you can take leave." Lennon nods in agreement while gulping his food. Macy and Oz head back to the paperwork. Lennon finishes his meal and leaves the studio. Oz and Macy lock the door and sit at the sound board. Oz maneuvers the machine to replay what Lennon was listening to when they arrived. The music plays, with Oz and Macy smiling at one another. The entire guitar instrumental is perfect in every way, and the words and phrasing are great—soul touching.

Oz says, "Macy, I'm calling the guys in early before Lennon arrives tomorrow so they can hear it. They will want to add other instruments."

Macy replies, "Hold off on that thought. I have a better idea. I'll tell you if it works out. If not, then we will do it your way." A puzzled Oz agrees. They both continue with their work.

Simon leaves the bus and moves toward the entry into the Pasadena Pueblo's library with its Spanish facade. He enters the building, going through a hall with rich wood paneling surrounding the stacks of books. The hall has two rows of large tables where people are quietly working. Simon looks for Michael. His eyes home in on a young man in a yellow T-shirt waving both arms over his head, signaling for Simon to come his way. He goes toward him. When he reaches Michael, he stretches out his arm in a greeting. Instead, Michael wraps his arms around Simon in a hug and then steps back.

"Hi, Simon, good to see you again."

"I hope you can help me," says Simon.

"Let's go around the corner to this alcove, where we can talk without disturbing others." Simon follows Michael to the alcove. Once there, Michael removes the backpack he carries and retrieves a laptop computer.

"Michael," Simon says, "I researched you and your criminal past."

"No problem," Michael replies.

"So you're on a straight path now, working for the NSA? Tell me your story."

"Well, the government sometimes hires a thief to catch a thief. I was in trouble with the law for hacking, and I got caught and turned over to the NSA. Now I am hacking for a living for the government, and I do side jobs for companies. They pay me to break million-dollar security software. Go figure." He then looks down at Simon's pants and asks, "You still wearing your fancy ankle bracelet? If so, are you close to out of range?"

"Yeah, about as far as I can go—probably another block. But I'm sure someone is following me."

"A regular Tom Clancy novel character, but I know the feeling."

"Right," Simon responds.

"So I got your message, Simon. Here we are. What can I do for you?"

"Well, you said you had my back and helped with the computer."

"Yeah, NSA has found nothing yet in order to move forward with any stickable charges. I know you are a good soul, and I've got to tell you, if you were guilty, you'd be the computer god.

"Michael, I'm too busy trying to get robots that are millions of miles away connected. I don't have time to even think about such a weird idea as hacking the world. And if I don't get a steady stream of information from the rovers, our funding will stop."

"And you're doing a great job, Simon."

"Yes, but *Sojourner* behaved strangely when I came back to JPL and reconnected with it. I hope I can trust you with what I'm going to tell you."

"You can, Simon, whatever it is."

"My intuition, my soul, for some reason tells me I can. But if this gets out, I promise you, I'm toast—burned, dried-up toast."

Michael zips his lips, just like Simon's ninety-five-year-old friend Ezra did when they talked over coffee and sweet rolls.

"*Sojourner* spoke to me, Michael," Simon says softly.

"That's the whole idea, isn't it? To communicate and get the data? I mean, isn't that why they brought you back—to reestablish communication?"

"Yes, but in computer language. When I say *Sojourner* spoke, I mean like we are speaking to each other now."

"Go on," Michael says. So Simon lays it all out, just as he has done with only three other people: Alexis, Norm, and Dr. Tristin Beckett. Then he tells Michael that he needs a world-class hacker.

"Why do you need a hacker?" Michael asks.

"Well, I've tried a few things, but they haven't worked out like I wanted. What I need now is to get a pure copy of my Reliance program, straight from the JPL server. As you know and have seen, I created the program, and I want a pure copy for my defense."

"You naughty boy." Michael smiles. "Let me guess. You saved it in an obscure location on the JPL server and renamed it to a file name common to computers."

"Yes."

"Simon, you might be a better hacker than you let on, because that is smart hiding it in plain sight."

Simon frowns, saying, "But I can't get it out. Can you do it? We're talking about life and death here."

Michael says, "Yes."

"Where and when can you get me a copy?"

"Right here, right now." Michael scans the room and says, "I see no people with that 'government look' about them. However, before I start obtaining Reliance for you, I want you to begin searching for Bible verses on a library computer. While you do that, I will do the same on my computer while I get Reliance. If stopped, and if the FBI, NSA, or any other entity wants to browse our search history, it will show we were both on a Bible study."

Simon initiates his assigned task.

Michael opens his laptop, and his fingers tap the keys. He smirks. "The folks at JPL don't listen. I told them of a security problem, but they have not addressed the issue."

"You're in that easy?" Simon asks.

"What did you name the file, and where did you put it?"

"I called it common001. It is in the rover image directory."

Michael finds the directory and the file. "Is this the one?"

Simon leans into the screen and scans the files until he sees his file. "Yes, that's it."

"What do you want to do with it?"

"Can you make a copy and then delete the copy on the server?"

"Yes, I'll do that and remove any electronic footprints of my presence."

Michael's task is quickly completed. He asks Simon, "Where will you work on your Reliance copy?"

"I have an old computer hidden at home but no internet access. So it can't be bugged."

"Great. To keep it away from government goons, I've put it on an SD card for you. The disk is small enough to hide in your home. I recommend the spine of a well-read book or your Bible. It will have space to hold the disk."

Simon realizes that Michael is very observant. Michael reaches into his backpack and pulls out a tattered Bible. Standing the Bible on end, he shows Simon how to slide the card into the binding. Michael looks at Simon and says, "An old trick learned early in my hacking days." Michael then glances past Simon and removes the SD card from the Bible. He takes a piece of gum he has been chewing and sticks it under the library table.

He tells Simon, "Your government handlers have just arrived," as he nods toward two men in suits approaching. "Remember: we are in a Bible study at your church." He takes the SD card and presses it to the gum. "We can get it later." The two men arrive.

The FBI's inspector Parker Steele says, "Northstrum, it concerns us that you are meeting with Michael Cott. Even though I know he now works for the government only because he has to, my belief is that a leopard cannot change his spots."

"Inspector Steele, you may be unaware, but Michael and I are Bible study members at my church."

"Mr. Cott, my friend here will search your computer." He grabs the laptop and sits next to Michael.

"I guess a warrant isn't something you need," Michael says.

Aldis Montgomery puts a flash drive into the machine, and the screen scrolls a search. "We will see what you two are doing," Steele says.

"Be my guest … as if I had a choice," Michael responds.

"Well, what is it saying?" Steele impatiently asks Montgomery.

Montgomery says, "They have looked at Bible sites and verses."

Steele says, "check the library computer."

Montgomery moves to Simon's library computer and repeats the same scan with identical results.

"You both are Bible-thumpers?" Steele roars.

"Guilty as charged," Michael smiles.

Steele is frustrated and furious at Michael besting him. "I know you two are up to something."

"Oh, ye of little faith," says Michael.

"Search them both for any drives or disks," Steele instructs Montgomery.

"So much for a constitution," Michael mumbles as he stands,

arms raised. He then tells Steele, smiling like the cat that ate the canary, "I sure hope the FBI and NSA don't get word of this. He glances at Simon, saying, "Just go with it. They get a thrill out of intimidation." Simon is amazed at Michael's lack of fear from the government.

"They are clean, sir," Montgomery says.

"Dr. Northstrum, your association with Mr. Cott does not look good. You know you are under surveillance."

"How could I not know?" Simon retorts. "I've got an ankle bracelet to remind me."

"Inspector Steele," Michael says, "stop threatening the guy without solid proof. He has done nothing wrong."

"Cott, because of Northstrum, every computer worldwide has been breached," Steele huffs.

Michael replies, "How do you know that, Inspector Steele? I think it's interesting that worldwide government hacks came from your FBI's supercomputer, Bertha."

"Yeah, when we put Reliance on the FBI computer for analysis," Montgomery complains.

"So you admit it," Michael retaliates. Montgomery's demeanor changes, becoming much different from his former defiant attack mode. Michael continues. "Both of you should be wearing a dandy bracelet like Simon's. You, me, and the NSA examined Reliance and found nothing malicious. Do you have any other prospects but Dr. Northstrum?"

"We are investigating everyone and everything connected," Steele lies.

Michael doesn't let up. "The big governments had their feelings hurt because they are not the cyber kings anymore. In the hacking messages, the writer is laughing at the governments, which are pointing fingers at one another. The worst that has happened is that a super geek told the world 'Peace be with you.' You are told that, and now you have attack planes, carriers, and missiles on high alert."

"Enough," Steele says, with a lot of his vigor gone but anger remaining.

Michael continues. "It's amazing how people will use something created for a peaceful purpose and weaponize it. And look at the current forms of communication. Folks are addicted to its immediacy. Humans are naive, thinking the software they build is the ultimate. They fail to realize someone might be smarter or have figured out something someone didn't see. Yeah, with all this, people are ready to cuss, fight, and blow up the world for 'Peace be with you.'"

Inspector Steele moves away in a huff, saying to Montgomery, "Let's go."

Michael shouts, "Hey, inspector! Remember: It's Cott to be Good."

"What was that?" Simon asks.

"Just a dig. We have crossed hacking paths in the past, and Steele is livid that the government didn't lock me up instead of giving me freedom to keep on hacking. 'Cott to be Good' is my slogan for my security website." Michael clicks the screen on his computer, and his website displays with his image and slogan. I borrowed the slogan from a drink company. Now back to business." Michael moves to the library computer and strokes the keys.

"Simon, I created a back door on the library server. Use your first name and 'Doctor' backward to gain access. They won't be able to find it, so you can work here without worry if you ever need to do so." Michael inserts the SD card and copies the files to the library system. He removes the disk and hands it to Simon. "You can leave after me, but check out a novel and secure the disk."

Michael packs up his belongings and extends his hand to Simon. "I hope I was of help to you."

"Big time." Simon nods. "I hope you don't get into trouble."

"They can't touch me. If you own nothing, what can they take away? I helped a friend who it just so happens might have started World War III." Michael grabs Simon by the shoulder. Smiling, he says, "Just kidding. This, too, will pass." Michael exits the building as Simon picks a T. S. Eliot favorite from the stacks and secures the disk.

CHAPTER 24

In the morning mist outside the Northstrums' home, Brock Chesterfield sits with his seat reclined and a blanket covering him. He is on a side street with a direct view of the home. The health craze has made this surveillance troubling. Morning joggers make it difficult to stay unnoticed. Fortunately, it is not January, with the sidewalks jammed with resolution-makers who last through the second week in February. He can see why, since no one jogging or exercise-walking is smiling. The solitude of the morning breaks with the chirping of his phone. He glances at the number and sits to attention.

"Yes sir, General Bosman," he says. "Chesterfield, your report shows nothing on Northstrum. I don't have you both out there on vacation. I want results. Dig deeper. If there is dust, then look under it."

"Sir, do we have warrants?"

"Warrants? This guy may have lit the match to World War III and may get us blown to cinders, and you're worried about laws. We will put the constitution aside to protect the folks, because we won't have laws in the coming misery. I want every piece of electronics for him and his family under our control. Do it today without a trace. You know the drill."

"Yes sir. I get the message. I'll turn up the heat on the doctor and associates." Chesterfield throws the phone on the seat. In moments the garage door opens, with Emma walking to the bus stop. Brock records the time, as he does each day, to develop a family pattern.

Shortly thereafter, Alexis's car backs out of the garage as she goes on her way to work. He notes the time, relaxing, knowing that in twenty minutes Simon will exit the house on the way to JPL. Like clockwork, Simon's car leaves the house.

Brock sits still and scans the neighborhood. He leaves the car and retrieves a pack from the backseat containing the tools of his espionage trade. After a scan around the neighborhood, he walks to the home and around the back unnoticed.

After a quick manipulation of the back door lock, he enters the house. Once in the kitchen, he stands still and breathes in the smell of bacon and thinks of how eating cold food out of a bag in a car sucks. He begins his search and moves to the drop point found in every kitchen—the place where folks drop their mail, keys, purses, papers, and magazines. Things are uncluttered, signaling that the Northstrums have a pretty organized life. He shuffles through the magazines and mail for evidence, but it is all normal bills and the daily barrage of offers from cable companies.

Walking around, Chesterfield thinks of how mad he gets when the new guy gets a great cable rate and the old, good customers get the shaft. Drawer by drawer, he digs but finds nothing of suspicion. The kitchen is void of any interesting electronics, save for a flat-panel TV. Brock moves to the dining room and continues his mission, with no results. The family room or den is always of interest, as it is a gathering room and has heavy electronics use.

He realizes the Northstrums use an antenna for television viewing, and he knows their internet provider. One last cabinet opened has a laptop within it, and a smile of satisfaction crosses his face. The laptop fires up and displays the login screen. Brock laughs. The screen reads, "Windows XP." He expected a scientist of Doctor Northstrum's caliber would have the F-35 of computers, but he knows of the super-duper computer given to Simon by Kelly.

He inserts a special flash drive into the computer. Once inserted, the computer password is bypassed, and a scroll bar moves across the screen. A dialog states, 'software installed.' With the same flash drive, he downloads everything on the computer. Brock clicks to close the screen and returns the computer to the cabinet. The intrusive search continues for hours, with the dust searched, as asked by his handlers. The final room is the bedroom. He scours the room, with nothing of importance found until he pulls up the mattress and discovers a tablet tucked underneath. *So, good doctor, this is an odd place for a computer.* Once activated, he soon realizes the machine belongs to Northstrum's wife.

He hacks the device in the same fashion as the old computer. He supposes he could plant something auspicious in both computers found, but he could get in deep trouble if discovered doing so. While searching the room, he picks up a book from Simon's night table titled *T.S. Eliot: The Complete Poems and Plays—1909-1950.* He thumbs through the voluminous tome, notices the library stamp, and places it back on the table. It is too cerebral for him, and he thinks, "Three hundred ninety-two pages of this stuff!" Michael was right to hide Reliance in the book's spine, as Brock never noticed it.

He finishes searching the room, disappointed to find nothing to report, pointing blame on Northstrum. He finds nothing of value to him at all in Emma's room, but he is not surprised, realizing most kids keep electronics like phones and computers attached to them twenty-four hours a day.

After going through all the other rooms, his last stop is to carefully search Simon's home office. The only thing electronic there is the printer, and he realizes Northstrum has no homebound computer but only the laptops he keeps with him. Chesterfield reviews the scientific journals Simon is reading and the ones in which he is mentioned in articles, thinking he can link colleagues and search them as coconspirators. Brock leaves the home with nothing out of place. Once back in the car, he texts General Bosman that his mission is complete. A nap at the hotel is in Chesterfield's future before he begins looking at the information from the flash drive.

The morning is uneventful at JPL. Simon works at his desk while gazing at the people on the mission floor. He is still recovering from his ordeal at the grocery store and wonders again whether he needs to go to a disguise store and go incognito for safety when outside. The rovers are operational with the Reliance program's support. He has not spoken to *Sojourner* in a few days, but he thinks that maybe that is not a bad thing. It sometimes seems *Sojourner* takes too lightly the terror brought to the world, what with people around the world dying from unknown causes.

Simon's thoughts are broken by the intercom. Earlman asks, "Simon, can you join us in the conference room for a discussion?"

He responds, "Sure." He exits his office. When entering the office, he sees that along with Norm and Earlman, Parker Steele, Brock Chesterfield, and Kelly Sellers are sitting around the table. A lump lodges in his throat as he thinks this can't be good. Is he being fired, arrested, or executed? Norm usually gives him a heads-up, but he can't always shield him. Earlman greets him when he crosses the door's threshold.

"Be seated, Simon," Earlman says. "You know everyone, so I won't make introductions. They are here to ask you more questions on Reliance."

"Okay, but I don't know what more I can share."

"We spoke with Ed about Reliance and its workings." Simon is unsure what Norm may have said about Reliance, *Sojourner*, the Dominion, or anything else. "Have a seat," says Earlman.

Steele starts the conversation with a direct question. "Did you sabotage our computer systems and create this clock to scare the crap out of people?"

"No. As I have told you, maybe a hundred times by now, no."

"You got me in a heap of crap with your little trick," Steele continues.

"I tricked you into nothing. I have been honest with each of you. You have been through every bit of my code and found nothing." He addresses Earlman, "Tom, is my program working well for the rovers?"

Earlman nods. "Yes, excellently."

Chesterfield says, "If you did nothing, then who are the Dominion?" Simon refuses to look Norm's way in fear of triggering a guilty response on something he may have divulged.

"I don't have a clue. I do know, however, I've not the skill to do what they have done in so short a time."

Steele interrupts. "I want this guy put back into prison and the key thrown away. I don't care about rights or a constitution. If we keep Northstrum locked up, away from any electronics, all these continuing messages and other mysterious happenings will probably disappear."

Meanwhile, a large man approaches Alvarez in the lobby of JPL while the meeting continues with Earlman, Norm, and the government operatives.

"I need to see the director of JPL now," the giant of a man says.

"Sir, are you on the list?" asks Alvarez.

"I don't know; nor do I care about your list. Get the director on the phone this instant."

"I don't report to you," Alvarez says, pushing back. Two giants stand face-to-face, neither backing down.

"My client, Simon Northstrum, is being interrogated without his attorney present. If this goes to court, I will drag your ass there under obstruction of justice charges. Your military pension will never cover your legal fees, and you would be foolish to think the government will back you."

Alvarez steps back and reconsiders his position. "Let me see if I can reach the director." He presses a button on the phone. "Colonel, there is a lawyer here in the lobby who represents Dr. Northstrum and is demanding access to your meeting." There's a pause. Alvarez asks, "What is your name?"

"I'm Earl Connery Hardin."

Earlman interrupts the meeting. "Do any of you know an Earl Connery Hardin?"

"Yes, he is my attorney," replies Simon.

Steele's face glazes over at the mention of the man who dismissed him. Kelly and Brock know the name from political investigations during election times.

Earlman asks, "Are we at a point in this where we need attorneys?"

Steele says, "This guy is dirty, and I want him in prison. If we lock him away, he can do no harm, and the world will settle down."

"Parker," Earlman says, "we at JPL have found no reason to crucify Simon for this problem, but if he needs an attorney, I'll not deny him his rights." Earlman unmutes the phone and tells Alvarez to send Hardin up.

Alvarez turns to Earl and says, "You may go to the conference room on the second floor. Here is your security badge." Earl grabs the badge, enters the elevator, and soon arrives in the conference room.

"Colonel Earlman, I am Earl Connery Hardin, and I represent Dr. Northstrum. My client will not answer any more questions. Steele, I warned you about your rogue investigations."

"Calm down, Mr. Hardin," says Earlman. We are not investigating Simon. We at JPL have found nothing to make him culpable in the hacking. No damage has been done, and nothing has been taken or distributed from JPL. Have a seat."

Hardin asks, "Why are these NSA and FBI people here? They spy on everyone, and I know that from experience. They become political operatives run by politicians seeking to keep power by destroying people in their path. They are insane if they believe one man could complete the communication wizardry in so short a time and leave no trace. Heck, it takes America twenty years to build nuclear power plants, and there are still mistakes. Big deep-pocket governments or companies have the know-how to pull this off. They run secret programs. Do the NSA and FBI have teams storming those offices? I think not. You stomp on a penniless little guy because it is easy."

Silence reigns for a few moments, and then Kelly says, "Mr. Hardin, I'm Kelly Sellers with NSA. I reviewed Simon's software after the government hack and found nothing wrong with it. I've done nothing to be ashamed of. We started our search at JPL because the original email problem started here. Brock and I want to get this resolved and find the guilty party. At the present time, Inspector Steele is speaking for himself and the FBI."

"I appreciate it, missy, but I hear politicians say it all the time. Look at the legislative investigations. Useless, lacking any power to prosecute. Then you have a world of seedy attorneys who are the new ambulance chasers. Find the dirt or make it up, then let the media run with it. Job done; lives ruined. Their only reason for existence is to retain power or stay close to it. These same people would be putting innocent children on train cars if it kept them in power."

There is silence again before Hardin continues. "So government officials will not railroad my client. I agreed to the tracking and nothing else." Addressing Steele and Chesterfield, he says, "I am sure you two have turned his home and life upside down to get the goods, which don't exist."

Steele stews in silence. Chesterfield remains stoic but soon retorts, "I thought you were in a country club prison."

"Oh, Sonny, they won't touch the man with the world's secrets at his fingertips. Putting me to death would be a better choice, but they don't know where I store the secrets and what may be published if I die. So here I am."

Steele squirms, and Chesterfield remains quiet. Kelly has a little half-smile, and Simon is eating all of this up, learning things about Earl about which he had no idea. Meanwhile, Norm seems to be enjoying it all, and Earlman is rather at a loss for words. It is an interesting situation.

Earl Connery Hardin continues. "Don't believe what politicians tell you. They'll cut your throats for power. Remember Julius Caesar? This hacking might be the best thing to happen to mankind. It upsets the world not because the email had a nice message but because someone has figured a way into the secrets of humans. The world has too many secrets, and this joker can expose them. Your electronic convenience and interconnectivity have allowed it. No one is immune, with no place to hide. You are afraid of the secrets and lies told to hold power. I know because they tried to hang them on me."

Earl pauses and then asks, "Do you have other suspects you are pursuing? There are many at JPL with computer expertise."

Steele responds, "We are looking at everyone."

Earl says, "Give me a list of the others with tracking bands on their legs."

Steele looks despondent at being played once again by Hardin.

"It is what I thought," Hardin goes on. "You are trying to convict my client and ignoring everyone else because he wrote great software, which solved JPL's problem. You are the one, Steele—you and your FBI, who infected the government computers. So why aren't you and your accomplices wearing the bands? The NSA should shred your lives."

Silence reigns before Hardin continues. "You have subjected Simon and his family to injustice because people only believe what they read on the first line of the internet or in a tweet or text message. Celebrities get involved in things like this because it keeps them in the public eye when they don't know their butts from a hole in the ground, and they put people like my client and his family in jeopardy. It has leaked too much from the investigation. The government can't be trusted with information."

Colonial Earlman finally speaks up again. "Mr. Hardin, General Bosman is running the investigation. I have no power over it, but Simon is in good standing with JPL. I've no intention of letting him go. However, that being said, if word comes from higher up, I might have to put him on leave until we clear things up with the hacking."

"Fair enough," says Hardin. "Bosman is an honorable man. I've had dealings with him and his wife, so I'll think about contacting him. Meanwhile, I will escort Simon back to his office."

Later, after another challenging day, Simon is at peace at home in his castle. He knows the government is tracking his every move, but he is safe at home unless they drop a missile on him. He feels led to open the machine given to him by Michael. Emma has installed software that will enable him to act on the blogging he has been encouraged to do by *Sojourner*—or, more precisely, he assumes, by the Dominion. He recalls Emma telling him that social media is about followers, and right now he has none. Laughing to himself, he thinks, like the kids, that he must do something absurd to get everyone's attention. The government wants to crucify him, so he'd better find the truth.

He says to himself, "Didn't *Sojourner* say the trouble with the internet is there is no truth button, with people posting accusations, whether they are true or false, and then expecting people to defend themselves?" Simon thinks that people who do stuff like that should have it turned on them. Maybe we should go to a system where the loser pays. He taps the keys, wondering what to say or post. Michael has maintained the computer is safe, and he now trusts him.

Simon copies the email from the Dominion, and he keys in some questions, asking ordinary people what they make of the message and whether any harm has come to them from it. He is impressed by the professional-looking WordPress site Emma has set up for him. She told him a clear majority of blog sites use it. She has given him an avatar, and he has named the blog Selfless-Reliance. After thinking about it, he realizes he has seen no conflict with the Reliance program he created for JPL.

Blogging is as foreign to him as is social media. He considers much of it an addictive waste of brain power and a harbinger of drama. People are being tracked and sold for a dollar. Sitting back in his chair, he chuckles that his thinking reminds him of his sessions with *Sojourner*. The robot stated the Dominion would help him, but no one new has come forth except for Michael, and he certainly isn't an angel. Simon's heard his foulmouthed discussions with his superiors and his in-your-face attitude.

He thinks of Alexis, saying that when you find a white feather or a lucky penny, smell a floral scent, or revisit an old friend from the past, all can signal an angel's presence. Michael doesn't seem the sort to wear white or care much for flowers. He was, as a matter of fact, in the church Bible study and, in dealing with Steele, extremely fearless and in an attack mode—not angelic. He dismisses the angel notion, not believing Michael to be a part of the heavenly choir, as he continues with his blog in a clueless manner.

His only social media link is a Facebook page with his family and friends that was set up by Emma, which he seldom uses. He has it for good photos of Emma and Alexis. He clicks on the Facebook website and sees a list of friend requests. There are some he knows. Others are women from the other side of the world, half-naked. He deletes those people and clicks through to the ones he knows. He is clueless as to whether they are real or have been sent by a hacker. When he is done, he is proud he now has seventy friends, or, as he describes it, acquaintances.

He considers friends those who have his back and are hard to find. Again on the main page at Facebook, he is tickled by a picture of a dinner plate of someone's meal. He points his finger in a pistol fashion to his temple and pulls the trigger. He feels that many brain cells have died.

He returns to his attempt at a blog. He reads the Domain message he copied onto the page, along with the questions asking people what they think about the message. He wonders whether the Dominion made a mistake in selecting him to save the world. He has seventy Facebook friends and is now brain-dead. He decides, "What the heck?" and hits Post.

☞

The commander's lens reads, "Simon has contacted the world."

☞

While on the special computer, Simon decides to poke around the internet at the social media sites, many well-known, others obscure. As a communication specialist, his big question for most of them is "Why?" The kids say it is how they talk today, but Simon knows he likes speaking to a warm body. When he talks in person, he can read body language. Many of the sites are here today, gone tomorrow, as the fickle public move along like herd cattle. He also finds some blogs and studies them.

He goes to his blog to see if he has received a few comments like those on the other blogs he just viewed. Emma told him he would get spam from internet bots, and she set up protection for such. But she also told him that he must manage the blog because some spam always slips through. He moves cautiously around the page.

Here is the man who got the space rovers talking, now afraid of clicking the wrong link on a simple blog. He shakes the nonsense from his head and clicks to see whether anybody responded. The first response is from a person who is vicious, calling him an asshole and asking why we should love each other. He tells Simon it's kill or be killed—dog eat dog. A gross emoticon follows.

He leans back. Since he had only asked a nice, simple question, he is offended at the response. It seems the Dominion's email has set an angry fire in some people. He hits the button to remove this subscriber, and he will do so with others who are full of hate and self-purpose. Looking down the list of about ten responses, he finds one with a smiley face. This response is heartwarming. It says, "If we learn to love, then there would be no evil, but I guess I'm a dreamer."

Simon replies, "Thank you for your wonderful message. Keep on dreaming, because dreams do come true. I can attest to that." But he is still unsure of what to say on this blog; he does not want to be labeled a lunatic from the start. But he gets a warm feeling knowing there are others with good souls. *If there are more people like this replying, then maybe it won't be impossible to get the world to the safety of the ark, as* Sojourner *suggested.*

Meanwhile, Raph says, "Commander, Simon has spoken."

The commander replies, "Yes I have heard. Reliance will help him bring the sheep to safety. He is only responding to people of faith and not the faithless. The helpers of the earth will be his best bet. They are abundant yet have gone unnoticed each day. These are the selfless. They will help him. However, he must also eventually touch the nonbelievers, as did the apostles. He has a great weight to bear. I have faith in him."

Energized by the positive comment and smiley face, Simon thinks maybe he should go deeper into the Domain's email message and post more about it. He rereads the email message from the Domain for a clue. He focuses on the two names below the Bible verses. He is familiar with Fleming and penicillin. Pixii is a different story, so he does a web search, discovering him to be the man who invented the dynamo.

It is ironic to Simon that the Dominion would reference a man so vital to electricity. It runs the world and our communications. *Why, in both messages, are the dates so wrong?* He remembers *Sojourner* said every action people take while alive has a ripple throughout time, and the Dominion records everything.

Simon removes his hands from the keys, clasps and stretches his fingers, and then types out a message about the dates in the email and how maybe the dates are not wrong. He suggests maybe someone else could have made the discoveries of penicillin and electricity earlier, but some people, through selfishness, caused the first discoverers to change direction and fail. He writes about how things we say and do affects others.

"Let me know your thoughts," he writes. "Are our own human actions holding us back? Could they be holding others back?" Simon now realizes that his mission is to tell the people of the world to look inside themselves and the selfless stories their souls provide." He hits Post.

The red being responds, "The Reliance program on his computer will help spread the word as I helped Noah reach the beasts of the planet. His followers will bring more heat from the governments around the world. Those without selfless faith will revile and scorn him. It is good to know he has accepted his mission."

The commander replies, "His faith is strong, though he doesn't know it. He will need it, as many humans will try to burn down the society, putting blame on others for their condition. I will bring many home in rapture as they work in complete selfishness. The world will realize many are dying, but they will assume it is for criminal activity or natural causes, not realizing the self-caused demise."

The red being touches Earth, unnoticed in a back alley of town. "I am here, commander," his cornea reads. He transforms into a disheveled old man dressed in rags. Once the transformation is complete, he leans against the wall of the building he will soon enter. Across the alley, the green being appears and transforms into an old woman. She walks to her cohort, saying, "Sorry I'm late. The commander had me meet a needy soul."

Raph smiles because the interaction between souls is the ultimate communication. Helping with their lessons is fruitful and selfless. Magdala scans Raph, frowns, and says, "Isn't it sad we must transform into the downtrodden and lost to find the true character in people."

Raph replies, "You find the truth when they perceive no one is listening or watching, but they don't realize you can't deceive the light."

Magdala responds, "Humans fail to see everything has an effect or ripple on life, like a stranger you bump into on the street who may cause you to pause for a second, thus keeping a bus from hitting you."

Raph nods his head. Magdala continues. "I remember getting on an airplane and asking a man to move to his assigned seat so I could sit in mine. He sneered at me. Little did he know that due to the seat change, he would sit beside and meet the woman he would spend the next sixty years with, answering her prayer—and his."

Raph says, "Gabe told me when he was having lunch one day, a man and his three teenage daughters were dining at the lunch courter. In an hour, they never looked up from their cell phone coma, never shared a word, and never thought about or glanced at one another. Gabe began to boil. Did they not realize their life journey is short and these toys suck up precious time to connect? He thought of sending them packing, but Michael handles such things. As Gabe left the restaurant, he turned their devices off for a few hours. They were tapping on them like the world had ended. Very unhappy campers."

"Funny but sad," Magdala says.

"What do you make of Lennon and Greg?" asks Raph.

"I can see Lennon but not Greg. However, Joseph selected them, so he must see something we don't."

"Michael wants to wipe the slate clean of human existence," says Raph.

Magdala frowns. "They repeat the same mistakes often, but such are children."

As Raph and Maggie talk, Lennon and Greg arrive at the door to the Demon Den. Greg is dressed in his signature goth black, with it highlighting his eyes. Lennon arrives in clothes provided by Swaddling, except for his trademark beret.

Greg says to Lennon, "You'd better be in black if you want to continue in SureDeath."

Lennon stiffens his back and replies, "I'll wear what I want, and if it isn't good enough, then I guess you will be minus a guitar player tonight."

"Jeez, Lennon, we are trying to project an image our fans will follow."

"You have no fans, and you'd do better to practice your instrument than worry about what you're wearing. If you don't get better, the only one seeing you will be you in the mirror doing air guitar alone."

"Our interns are here, and Lennon gave Greg an earful," says Maggie.

"He has character, but I guess we are here, unsuspected, to discover their truth," Raph replies.

"Yes," Maggie agrees. "Greg is changing the rules. Let's begin."

The two move toward the nightclub and the line forming in front of the bouncer.

Maggie says while walking, "The place is a dive, yet they reject people. How sad."

The two move behind Lennon and Greg unnoticed. A large man is jockeying his way to the front of the line and pushes Maggie to the ground. He sneers at her unmercifully, saying, "They will never let a bag woman into this club. Get out of the way; crawl into your box and go to sleep."

Raph looks on, knowing he must not intervene. His cornea reads, "Commander, may I bring him into the light since we are beginning the rapture?"

"No, this is a learning moment for the interns."

The bouncer scans Lennon and Greg as Greg shows him the band credentials. The bouncer then moves toward the commotions, with Maggie still on the ground. "You two should leave, you're not wanted here," says the bouncer.

"We only wanted to hear the music," says Maggie, "and this brute trampled me." Greg signals for Lennon to follow and enters the club. Lennon stays behind to watch the turmoil in line. Lennon sees kindness in the woman's face, as if he knew her. Lennon reaches down to help her up.

"What's wrong with you?" he says to the bouncer. "She is a person, for heaven's sake. Help me to lift her up." The bouncer doesn't move. Lennon gets in the face of the large bouncer and says, "These two are my friends, and I am part of the band. If they don't get in, then you will have many angry people with no band. What is it going to be, buddy?"

The bouncer says, "Okay, okay. Fine." He helps lift the woman and ushers both Raph and Maggie into the club with Lennon.

"Thank you, young man," Maggie says, "You are kind."

"You are welcome, ma'am," Lennon gently tells her. "I hope you weren't hurt."

"No, I'm all right," Maggie tells him.

Looking at the two old people, Lennon asks, "Do you want to hear the music? Pardon me for saying it, but you don't seem to be the type to listen to a band called SureDeath."

"Yes and no," Raph replies. "We listen to all music, but mostly it gives us a chance to get inside for a while."

Lennon reaches into his pocket and retrieves some money Jozy gave him. "Here," he says. "I don't know if you have money for food and refreshments, but someone helped me, and he asked me to pay it forward. Now is as good a time as any." Magdala smiles as Raph accepts the cash. She and Raph both thank him.

"You are certainly welcome," Lennon tells them. "I have to go now and join the group. I apologize in advance, but the band stinks, and you might run out of here screaming. I told them I would play with them, so I'm keeping my word tonight."

Raph says, "We don't hear as well as we used to hear."

Lennon smiles. "Tonight that could be a blessing."

He leaves as the duo find a seat. They look at each other and in unison say, "Joseph chooses well."

Lennon makes his way backstage where the other band members are waiting to do their four-song set.

"Where have you been!" yells Greg.

"They knocked an old woman to the pavement, with no one helping her."

"Big deal," Greg says sarcastically. "Are you ready, Lennon?"

"Yes, are you?"

Greg ignores his question and tells him, "We get to do four songs tonight, and if they approve us, then we may get more time on a busier night. Is your guitar going to make it?"

Lennon clutches his case tighter. "It will get the job done," he says. The other band members snicker at Lennon's beat-up case.

The stage manager grabs Greg's shoulder, saying, "You are next. This band on now is getting the ax, so get ready."

The music from the stage ends with boos from the crowd. Lennon opens his case and gets out his guitar. He places his ear to the strings, and in seconds the guitar is in tune. The other band members do nothing to their instruments. The manager leads them to the stage, and the crowd is a mixture of cheers, claps, and, "I'm on the planet without a clue. I'm here for the party."

Each member takes a position, with Greg as the front man. He fancies himself a rock god, the want of every woman. Lennon stands out as being the only one on stage not in black. He laughs inside as he looks at the patrons without natural black hair. He thinks, *They must have a sale on black at the dollar store. A dollar and a bad dye job.* He hopes it doesn't rain once they get outside. Greg's screaming into the microphone, introducing the band, stops his thoughts. Most of Greg's dialogs start with expletives rhyming with "witch" this and "witch" that. Lennon interrupts him by beginning the song with "And a one, and a two, and a three." Greg sneers at Lennon but starts into the music.

Raph and Magdala have their hands up to their ears to cut out Greg. They remove their hands at Lennon's musical prompt.

"Thank you, Mr. Lennon. That was painful," says Raph.

Greg is now screaming out the words to his own composition—a song filled with hopelessness, darkness, and death. As the front man, he is the only one who gets to sing.

Maggie watches Lennon's face as his eyes wince.

"What is wrong with Lennon?" asks Raph.

"Nothing," she says. "The band is the problem. Lennon's ears hear every note his bandmates play. They are out of tune and off beat, and he is trying to hold it together. They are racing each other, and the singer is out of pitch, tune, and tone, but the crowd doesn't care. Greg will blame Lennon and his old guitar for the issue after they finish."

The band finishes their set without being pulled off the stage, but they don't get the standing ovation that was expected by Greg, the rock star.

Once backstage, Greg goes off on Lennon as the others sit and watch. "Your guitar is a piece of junk. It was off key the whole set and caused us to suck tonight." He turns toward the others and says, "Right guys?" They nod their heads, afraid of Greg. "We may not get any cash tonight because of you, Lennon."

Lennon cuts loose. "There was nothing wrong with my guitar or playing. The truth is, you can't play guitar or sing, and you need to buy a thesaurus for other words." Lennon turns and addresses the drummer. "Hey, drummer boy, it's your job to keep the beat, not mine. Do you know what that is?" He turns to the other member and says, "You did okay on bass, considering garbage surrounded you."

The bass player smiles. Really pumped, Lennon faces Greg and says, "I quit the band. I want nothing to do with it." Lennon packs his case.

Greg gets in his face and asks, "Are you out of the talent show?"

"You bet. If you are in it, you can call it the talentless show."

"I'll get you back for this, Lennon. You're to blame."

"You can blame me all you want, and keep my money if you get anything, because *we* should have paid *them*, as we were so terrible."

Raph and Maggie watch Lennon leave. The hour is late, and he is walking home, since Greg was his ride.

Maggie tells Raph, "You should get him home."

"Sure thing, Mom," Raph says, kidding her. Maggie remains seated as Raph leaves the building. Once outside and unobserved, he transforms into the person Lennon is familiar with from school.

Lennon walks rapidly, since it is a long distance to home and he was expecting a ride. The buses don't run this late. Cars stream by as he pushes toward home. A car slows and parks up ahead of him, which gives Lennon pause. One doesn't know what creeps may be lurking at night. The car reverses and moves back toward Lennon and stops. A head emerges from the driver's side window and calls, "Is that you, Lennon? It's me, Raph." Lennon smiles at his good fortune and scampers for the car. "Why are you walking so late, Lennon?"

"I was playing at a club, lost my ride, and my dad isn't feeling well."

"Get in. I'll take you home," Raph offers.

"I like your clothes," says Raph. "The beret adds flair." Lennon touches his head and smiles at the compliment from a fashion expert.

"Were you playing at that Demon Den tonight?"

"Yes, trying to get more money for a new guitar."

Raph looks at the guitar case jutting between Lennon's legs and comments, "The duct tape is artistic."

Lennon caresses the case and says, "Duct tape is my friend."

"Did you play alone at the bar?"

"No, I was part of Greg's band, but I quit."

"Why, may I ask?"

"Mr. Raph, I don't want to put anyone down, but they are terrible. The vocals are a bunch of screaming with nothing much to say. No one can play worth a crap. They look ridiculous in black, like they are dead. I realized that even though I lost out on the money, it is not me. Emma told me Greg wanted me for my guitar skill and would do me wrong. I guess she was right."

"I pointed to your heart once before, saying that you will find your answer there," Raph tells him. "Tonight may have been disastrous, but it might have been the kick in the butt you needed to play your music."

"Right, like anyone wants to hear music from a nobody."

"Lennon, all famous artists were unknowns at one time." Raph then asks, "What song have you selected for this talent show I've been hearing about?"

"I've not decided. Maybe my favorite song by the Beatles, 'Here, There and Everywhere,' because it has melodies played within the melodies. I've played it a million times and can play it blindfolded. It might make me stand out in the show."

"You should play something for that girl you adore," says Raph.

Lennon looks at Raph. "For Emma?" he asks.

"Yes. Why not? You like her, and she likes you."

"Did she say something?"

"No, but everyone can see it—except for yourself?"

"Here we are," Lennon says, changing the subject.

Raph parks at the curb, stretches his arm across the seat top and looks at Lennon. He says, "In every man's life, there comes a time when he must take a leap of faith. You must take a leap for love, for faith of belief, and for career. If you don't, you are hiding from the abundance life offers—a scary prospect for sure. There is no safety net, and you might crash and burn, but you will not die. Whatever you do, do it from your heart and soul and not because others want you to go on a different path."

"Heavy stuff," Lennon says. I'll think about it. But it would be terrible if it didn't go well."

"Yes, it can be, but you will never know unless you jump." Lennon thanks Raph for the ride, leaves, and walks to his home.

The being's lens reads, "He is ready to jump."

CHAPTER 25

"**G**ood, morning. Welcome to *America's Newsroom*. I'm Bill Hemmer. Hello, Martha."

"Good Morning, Bill. Folks, this is a Fox News alert. They have reported the giant cyber company ConnecTooU is moving its headquarters from Silicon Valley. Switzerland is now the base of operation for this behemoth. I have Bryer Wilson with me today, who is a Fox News tech contributor and computer expert. Mr. Wilson, what is going on with this company? They got their first start in the United States, and much of their funding came from American citizen investors."

"Thank you for having me on today, Martha. Everything you stated is true. This company is mammoth and connects everyone. When you get up in the morning and experience your smartphone alarm, alerts in your car, traffic light controls, and many other things, you have met ConnecTooU. It is mammoth and invasive. They are a quiet giant with a huge amount of control over us."

"So," Bill says, jumping in, "Why do you think they are moving their headquarters from America? Is it a corporate tax issue?"

"No, Bill. They have excellent tax benefits. It comes down to sheer numbers and war. The United States does not have enough people."

"We have over three hundred million people and a large economy, Bryer," Bill says.

"True, Bill. But in numbers and growth, we are small. I saw a study showing that India has more people studying computer science than we have people. This company is preparing for war."

Martha interjects, "You mean they are choosing sides?"

"Yes. From a money standpoint, they have more customers outside the United States. It is important to realize that these social media companies make millions collecting and selling data from everyone. They must protect their data reach. If we go to war, the US government has a large reach and can shut them down for national security. They are taking a money position; they can afford to lose the US market to save the rest."

"Wow!" Bill says. "That thinking sort of blows me away."

"And well it should, Bill. When the two last world wars began, our major manufacturers transitioned and produced for the war effort. I saw a story about A. C. Gilbert, the creator of the Erector set. He transformed his toy factories to produce for the war effort."

Martha asks, "Are you saying these companies will fight against America?"

"Martha, many of these companies are just algorithms running other algorithms. They always catch the nefarious aspects of the internet after the fact. The CEO is apologetic for not catching it beforehand. Yet the people still bleed. You cannot catch what you do not know."

The elevator lifts Simon to his floor while he contemplates what awaits him on the other side. The door slides open, and no SWAT guns attack him. He moves to his office. A young woman passes him and says, "Way to go, Simon." He responds by thanking her, without a clue to why he received the praise. After arriving in his office, he scans the mission floor and flips through yesterday's task notes while the computer loads. A 100 percent success rate using Reliance on new rover projects will help him. A loud roar from the mission floor breaks his studying, and he jumps to view the racket.

The floor crew is fixated on the big video screen and a Martian image. Simon smiles, pleased *Curiosity* sent back new images per his commands, but the crews are pointing at the screen and doing high fives. Simon is too far away to identify what is causing the excitement. He is rather afraid to find out exactly what the news is, so he dials up Norm.

"Hey, Norm," he says, "I just arrived and noticed the commotion on the floor and—"

"You've not seen it, Simon?"

"What?" Simon says. "Have not seen what?"

"I'm in my office with Earlman, Simon. You'd best get to my office right now."

Simon walks a few circles around his office, collecting his thoughts. He clasps his hands together and prays. "God, what will I be blamed for now? Bless me, Lord. Bless me." Simon heads to possible doom as the phrase about being crucified from "The Ballad of John and Yoko" plays in his mind.

Simon arrives at Norm's office and appraises the situation by analyzing the faces of both men. He relaxes. The faces are upbeat. "Hi," he says.

"Come in, Simon," Norm says to him.

Earlman begins, "Well, you sure are the golden boy."

"What did I do?"

"You don't know?" Earlman asks.

"Curiosity sent us new photos," Norm tells him.

"Good," Simon replies. "I asked it to send them from a different vantage point."

"Come around here, Simon, and I'll show you what everyone has been cheering about," says Earlman. Simon makes his way to the men, and they point at a *Curiosity* photo.

"Okay," Simon responds, sounding not very excited at all. "It sent a new image from a different spot and angle. Reliance is working as expected. It is a photo of *Curiosity*'s wheel. I know what it looks like. You can trash it."

"Yes, Simon, but look closer," says Norm. Simon moves closer to the screen.

"All right," Simon says. "I see red dirt."

"Yes, but don't you see what is exciting everyone?" Norm asks.

"No …" Simon replies.

Norm points on the screen. "Keep looking Simon. I didn't notice it at first."

Simon studies closer. He turns to the men.

"Is that a footprint?" He turns back to the screen and increases the magnification.

"Sure looks to be a footprint," says Earlman.

"This can't be. We get messages about faces on the planet, and rats and pyramids. People detect something weird in every image."

"Our guys discovered the image, and it isn't public. Look closer," says Norm with a grin. "Are those toe prints?"

Simon presses the keyboard and increases the magnification. "It is a foot pattern, but we know it is not a foot. If it were, where is the second foot, a trail, or a heel? If it were a creature here on Earth, there would be a trail or path," Simon says.

"Right," Earlman states. "Point made. No creature of Earth made this footprint."

"Are there more pictures of the spot from a differed angle?" asks Norm.

"No. *Curiosity* is on another project in a different direction."

"Can we send it back?" Norm asks.

"Yes, but is it worth it for a weird impression?"

Earlman says, "No. We don't need to. For now let's just release this image to the public website. As you saw, our JPL people are excited about it, so putting it on the public website will give us better exposure and get people talking about it—and talking about the success of JPL. I know General Bosman will like that."

"Okay," Simon says. "And when I get back to my office, I'll examine the images for anomalies. Is this all you have for me?"

"Yes," Norm says. "Good work, Simon."

Simon returns to his office and retrieves the images from *Curiosity*. The photos are excellent, but none shows weird forms from millions of miles away. He gets to the image he saw in Norm's office and increases the magnification. Simon can't deny the footprint on the screen, and *Sojourner* told him the Dominion had visited Mars. Simon has all types of questions running through his mind.

Did they visit each rover? Will I catch flak from this image? Sojourner *said they will blame everything on me, but I didn't walk on Mars. Why one footprint?* The speculation and pointing continue from the mission floor. It might be good to have a distraction from the email problem. He realizes some people still believe we have never gone to space or landed on the moon, convinced that it was all done in Hollywood or in a desert somewhere. *The image will feed the delusion. The networks will have a field day with this, and the people believing The US government housed aliens in Area 51 will come out of the woodwork.*

Simon smiles at the positive twist produced by the photo. A person walking on Mars will trump earthly hacking problems. He enters the code into the screen to navigate *Curiosity* back to its earlier position. *Curiosity* will photo the image from another perspective. Shadows and light can play tricks on the human eye. Tomorrow, new images will be available. It is time now to do his job as he issues commands to each rover.

Later Simon enters his home and yells for his girls to come see the footprint picture. They appear in the kitchen with questioning faces. "We were trying on new Swaddling clothes," Emma says. "What did you want to show us?" He reaches to a stack of papers and pulls out the photo, laying it on the table. He tells them to examine the photo and tell him what is strange. The girls scan the image.

Emma asks, "Is this from *Curiosity*?" Simon tells her it is and that he knows because of the wheels. The women continue their investigation until Emma's head pops up. "Is this a footprint?" Her finger rests on the image by the wheel. Alexis asks her where the footprint is, and Emma says, "Right here."

Alexis moves closer to the photo and then says, "Simon, it is! That's a footprint! What does JPL say?"

Simon says, "They're excited. Some very excited. It'll be on the public website. People find many images in the Mars photos, and this will stir up things and, of course, bring out the nuts. I've sent Curiosity back to the spot to take another look at the area."

"This is so cool, Dad. Can I tell my friends things are walking on Mars? It would be so cool."

"No, I wouldn't go that far. But it's okay to tell them to look on the site because the newest image on Mars looks like a footprint. Between us, for now I'm calling it an optical illusion. If I find out differently, I'll tell you first."

۞

Michael makes his way to Umm al-Quran, a great Baghdad mosque with four towering gun-barrel-shaped minarets. Today he will attend the teachings of the grand Imam Abu Karim Sadek, the leader of this Sunni region. Michael is dressed in the usual garb of the local men, entering the mosque with men, women, and children. The women and girls wear required hijabs. The men worship separate from the others and divide themselves from the females once they enter the building. Mankind always makes faith into a religion, causing the countless problems throughout time. *If they only knew their souls were sexless in the Dominion. They become a gender at conception, based on the soul's story. Each learns as a man or woman through many lifetimes. The phrase "Walk a mile in my shoes" comes to mind.* Michael follows the crowd and moves into a smaller room. Cameras, lights, and electronics obscure the holiness of this place. It resembles the set of a newsroom on network television with an ornate stage setup. Ushers guide him up a side aisle. He passes one camera and lays his hand on it. A yellow spark enters the camera. He moves on with the flow of worshipers and into an unoccupied row, where he kneels on a prayer carpet.

In moments, the Imam enters the room to thunderous applause, and the footlights bathe the stage. He quiets the faithful with his arms raised and begins a prayer. Abu is an older man with a gray, almost white, beard. A white kufi sits on his head. Today he wears a light gray-blue robe of exquisite cotton with short open seams on

395

both sides of the waist, and a white shirt with gray stripes to match the robe. Sadek fancies himself a Gandhi leader, but he is a man interested in only power and money. The men kneel forward, placing their faces to the floor in prayer. Michael does the same, but his prayer is different, going straight to the commander. The commander's lens reads, "Today will be Sadek's day to prove his faith."

Michael says, "He set the plan, and the world will see his deceptive life."

Michael's lens reads, "I trust in your judgment; it will fit the plan. You may pull back the curtain of his faith."

The devoted sit back and view as a list of martyrs' images are displayed on the large video screens. Sadek praises them as true believers in Allah. He says, "They are now with God." He tells of how these faithful have taken many nonbelievers and infidels with their sacrifice. The crowd applauds the photos of men, women, and children. Michael droops his head in anger. He knows too well the trappings of religion throughout history. They all get that way. If you are not like us or believe like us, then you must repent or die. If he had his druthers, he would send all humanity back into the Dominion.

The cleric continues teaching that the quickest way to God is by removing an infidel. Michael hopes the verbal diarrhea coming from the cleric's mouth is not the promise of seventy-two virgins. In the Dominion, everyone is pure, full of the endless love, knowledge, and the wisdom it holds. How a mother and father could strap a bomb to their children is beyond him. The cleric is a powerful persuader, but he preys on the fringe people—the outcasts and disenfranchised of society. *Does he not realize that every soul put into a body is another drop of hope given to the world? If it is the quickest way to God, then why haven't all clerics blown up themselves?* He is growing weary of the cleric and his explanation of what it will be like to come to God as a martyr. *How could he know?* The cleric pauses for a moment to sip water.

Michael takes the opportunity of the quiet time to begin his plan. Rising to one knee, in a strong voice, speaking perfect Baghdadi Arabic, he bellows, "Abu Sadek! What part of 'Thou shalt not kill'"

(Exodus 20:13 KJV) escapes you? Moses gave you the rule chiseled in stone so man could not abrogate it." Michael is standing erect, looking toward the stage. Sadek takes his last swallow and places down the water. A stillness fills the room, with all eyes on this unknown guest. The scene is like a gunfight in the old west, but the cleric is wearing the white hat.

"I do not know you, young man, and it is rude to interrupt the teaching, since everyone wishes to learn. Michael isn't deterred by being disciplined.

"I will ask you again," Michael repeats. "What part of 'Thou shalt not kill" do you fail to understand?

Abu addresses Michael. "You misunderstand, for the book tells us we can kill for justice."

Michael replies, "God gave the law to mankind long before Muhammad walked the earth, and Gabriel would not adulterate the laws."

Abu is momentarily silent and then says, "You know your religious history."

Michael responds, "I know no religion. Religion is a man-made faith used to subjugate people for power, money, and control."

"May I continue my teachings, young man?"

No, Abu, your days of teaching hate are over. These are good people, and if you look into their souls, you'll see they have plans for them worked out between them and God. You don't get to God by being a bomb. You recently got emails. Your recent sermon showed how outraged you were at the emails you thought driven by a nonbeliever."

Michael asks the crowd, "Did everyone read the messages?" He turns back to Abu, asking, "Abu, did you take it to heart? I don't care where it came from or who sent it, but what a wonderful message. Love and one another. How simple, Abu. Today your faith will be on display for the world to see. The cameras in this room are streaming worldwide. You see, Abu, I need not die for my God. I let him into my soul. We will find out who you are and the darkness of your soul."

Michael tells the crowd, "If you look at the screens, you will see the misdeeds of your revered cleric. While most of you toil in service to faith, he has spirited your tithe away for his personal gain." There is a gasp from the crowd. Abu's assistants usher him from the stage, with armed security coming for Michael.

"Wait," Michael calls out to Abu. "I wouldn't leave yet, because you and I will have a faith gunfight. Michael holds up his arms, displaying a remote control. He reaches for the buttons of his shirt. tearing open his shirt, he reveals an explosive vest. The crowd moves back from him, and the security team stops their approach. "Be not afraid; no harm will come to you. I am here for Abu," he tells the crowd.

Abu and his assistants halt in their tracks, carefully watching Michael and his explosive vest. Michael tells Abu, "You have a similar device near you that will tear you and your family apart, so you must be still. Walk to the podium and stand and listen." Abu does as told, very gingerly. Michael continues. "You have spoken of hate and death for too long. You have persuaded innocent people with a different plan designed by them and their Creator. They had not found their heart songs. Since you believe your bomb way is the swiftest way to get to God, today is your day to show your followers and the world your faith."

Quietness fills the large mosque, and then Michael breaks the silence. "In your terms, Abu, I am an infidel, and under your teaching, if you die while taking a nonbeliever with you, you move straight to heaven. Today is your lucky day. Behind the Koran is a remote like the one you see here."

Abu stares toward the Koran. There is silence. Then Michael again speaks. "I stand here ready to die for my beliefs, but are you ready? Press the button and you will kill both of us." Michael then tells the crowd, "Relax, everyone. I am a trained expert with bombs. The charges will destroy only the hearts of Abu and me. They will harm no one else." He then speaks directly to Abu. "If you move from the platform now, Abu, your charge will expand, killing not only you but also your family. But to you that should not matter, because you and your entire family will be martyrs and I will be dead." The faithful have distanced themselves from the cleric. He looks at his crying family and at the screens showing a history of his deceit.

"Do you want to see if your cleric leads by example?" Michael asks the crowd. "Abu, have you ever played an American game called Monopoly?" He nods to show that he has, while dabbing the sweat running down his forehead. Michael continues. "In the game, you can get a card that allows you to get out of jail free, should you land on that space. I have given you a green release button. Press it, and you can walk away with your family intact. If you select it, you will show your followers you believe nothing of what you teach. God has always given you a get-out-of-jail-free card called forgiveness. Jesus told the woman caught in adultery, 'Sin no more.' If you select green, I tell you to love one another and for you to sin no more. What will it be, Abu? Red or green?"

Michael increases the intensity of his voice with his last instructions to Abu. "Jesus carried his cross all the way to Golgotha. Now is your chance to do the same. You audience here and on worldwide TV will witness your 'Do as I do, not as I say' statement. You have ten seconds to decide."

Michael's arms relax to his side, and he breathes out, closing his eyes. His lips move in prayer. Abu wipes more sweat from his brow and views his terrified family. He reaches for the remote, and a few female family members collapse. He looks at Michael, who is standing there so calmly while he, the renowned Abu, is a sweaty mess. Large screens and TVs worldwide show Abu pressing the green button. Michael's eyes open, viewing the family huddled around the disgraced cleric.

Holding up the remote in plain view on the screens and on television, Michael presses the red button. The crowd screams and falls on the floor. The device explodes with a bang, and a white powder is lofted into the air, filling the room. The dust settles onto the crowd. A young man near to Michael swipes his hand on his face to clear the powder away. It filters onto his lips, and his tongue tastes it. He looks up at Michael and smiles. In Arabic he yells, "Sugar!" He turns to show the crowd and repeats, "It is sugar!"

Michael's words, spoken with authority, have made an especially strong impact on one young woman who has been searching for real faith. Believing that Abu's device would be set similar to Michael's, she runs to grab the device, and before anyone can stop him, she pushes the red button. The screens and televisions display an identical, extremely loud sugar bomb.

The studio lights dim, and the cameras go dark. The large monitors display a message: "I forgive you. Sin no more." It is followed by an email message that is again delivered to the world. Beautiful music comes from the video screens, and the crowd turns, seeing the images of what being with the Dominion will be like if one follows one's path. This diversion creates a hypnotic trance, allowing Michael to exit. He backs out of the church unseen. Abu and his family exit from the building, surrounded by his handlers, and get into his expensive bulletproof car. He reaches for his phone and pulls open a banking app. Abu has an escape plan. He will transfer his wealth and leave town before anyone finds him. His family will follow later. Good thieves always have an exit strategy.

He quickly directs his phone to transfer his funds to an untraceable account. He presses Transfer, and the progress bar glides across the screen. The screen reads, "Thank you for your donation of 100 million dollars to the American Red Cross." He screams. A new screen appears, bearing the writing, "Abu, you asked for forgiveness, but you paid with deceit. God also has the supreme exit strategy." The screen glows white, and Abu slumps sideways. The dropped phone shows an image that reads, "Your rapture is brought to humanity by the Dominion … Where are you in your soul's contract with us?"

JR

The commander's lens reads, "I give you Abu, unrepentant."

JR

Outside the Forestville campus, a combination rehabilitation hospital, senior residence community, and nursing home, Emma sits with Jennifer in one of the expensive cars owned by Jennifer's family. Emma scans the car and the luxury, thinking about how she drives her mother's car that still has a cassette tape deck in it. The queen bee laments to Emma, "First we've got to pick up poop for useless dogs, and now we must hang out with people waiting to die."

Emma turns to Jennifer and says, "Turn your brain on before the words leave your lips."

Jennifer frowns and defends her comment, "What? We're talking about a bunch of old people we don't even know. I mean, like, I didn't put 'em here."

"No, you didn't put 'em here, because you don't care about anybody that much. But Lennon's mom was here because of a stupid drunk. They took good care of her before she died."

"Like, I didn't know."

"Then just shut up, Jennifer. And as I've told you before, and Lennon has too, you need to lose your 'likes' every time you open your mouth. And another thing, in this age of texting and Twittering, people get involved in discussions because they can, but most are ignorant of the facts. And when you don't know what you're talking about, don't add your two cents' worth."

Silence reigns.

Unbeknownst to the girls, Maggie has arrived in her car, parked behind the girls, and is walking toward them. Overwhelmed by Jennifer's costly perfume, Emma has powered down her window, which has allowed Maggie to overhear the scolding Emma has unleashed on Jennifer. Maggie thinks again, as she has before, that Emma is the only peer to challenge Jennifer, unafraid of any consequences. Also as she has done before, she tells herself, "I made a good choice in choosing Emma. Simon and Alexis raised and nurtured a strong woman with character; Emma will help Jennifer grow."

Maggie then knocks on the driver's side window, which startles the girls. Greg and Lennon, with the dog Rudy in tow, have come with Maggie and are now trailing close behind. Jennifer rolls down the window; Rudy's head and paws meet her face. Jennifer swats and says, "Down! Down!"

Emma yells joyfully, "Rudy!" She swings open her door, leaps from the car, and yells again, "Rudy! Come here, boy! Come on, Rudy!" The dog is around and on her in a flash, with tail wagging.

Jennifer, now deeming she is safe from Rudy, steps out as Maggie opens her door and says, "Hello, girls. You look nice in your new Swaddling Clothes."

Jennifer sort of smiles; Emma, with Rudy shadowing her, thanks her. Maggie tells the crew, "We are here today to introduce Swaddling Clothes to the nursing home residents, and you will be modeling for them."

Taken by surprise, Jennifer says, "We are selling Swaddling Clothes, the same kind we have on, to old people?"

"No," Maggie replies. "We are not selling anything. Clothes have been delivered here as gifts for the residents to keep. Many of them wear the same clothes every day. Swaddling is ageless and should make them feel much better."

"I know I feel good in mine," Emma inserts.

"And you look good," Maggie replies. "Other outfits are inside for the four of you to model, similar to what the residents will be wearing."

Jennifer rolls her eyes, while Emma says, "This will be fun." She pats her shadow-dog and asks, "What about Rudy?" She then sees that Greg is holding on a leash the dog that Jennifer picked when she was instructed to choose one at the shelter. "And what about Jennifer's dog?"

Jennifer, now noticing her chosen dog for the first time, says, "What's that one doing here?"

"They are both going inside with us," Maggie tells the girls. "Animals can be very nurturing for nursing home residents." She then asks Jennifer, "What is your dog's name?"

"I don't have a name, and that dog's not mine. I just had to choose one for that day, remember?"

Maggie tells her, "Pick a name for your dog before we go inside so the folks can call her by name."

Looking down at the dog and then rolling her eyes, she says, "Okay, Blackie, I guess."

With a laugh, Lennon comments, "Very creative, Jennifer."

Maggie says, "Blackie will work."

The five of them enter the building, with the girls controlling the dogs on leashes. Residents are in the day room, awaiting the unique event that is to take place. Around the room are displays of the various clothes the group will model. The director of the facility greets Maggie and the foursome. "I'm Marsha," she tells them, "and we are excited to see your show. I don't know how I can thank you for all the clothes in these boxes."

"The looks on the residents' faces will be thanks enough," Maggie tells her. She then introduces the foursome to Marsha and says, "These are their four-legged friends, Rudy and Blackie."

"You can let them roam. The residents are accustomed to animal visitations, and most of them love such visits." says Marsha.

Emma kneels next to Rudy and rubs his ears. "You are a good boy," she says, and Rudy's tail polishes the floor in excitement. Once freed, he darts to the crowd in the dayroom, not knowing whom to visit first. He makes short stops at everybody. The tenants liven up at the swift-moving dog and signal to him for attention.

Maggie says, "He brightens the room." Emma beams. Jennifer releases Blackie; she follows Rudy but takes a differed approach to the crowd. She is fearful, approaching the residents with caution. Each reach down, however, to scratch her head, she seems to enjoy. Blackie wanders to a silver-haired old woman in an easy chair. Her dress should have been in the rag bin long ago. Blackie eases up to her, and she is unresponsive. Blackie sniffs the woman for a moment, but instead of going on, she leaps into her lap, turns around, and sits.

The old woman's eyes widen, and her face brightens. She strokes Blackie, and the dog's head moves with the caresses. Maggie gathers the interns around and tells them of the outfits on display. "I want you to go into these two rooms and change into these, and then come back here."

Emma asks, "What are we expected to do?"

"Just stroll in front of the residents in a fashion walk. You have watched them on television and in the movies. Just be yourselves, not put-on or anything like that. Enjoy it and have fun. If the residents have questions, answer them as best you can. You're showing the clothes, so let them know how they feel."

Jennifer responds, "I must talk to these old people?"

"Yes, Jennifer. They were young once and wore the fashions of their times."

"These old geezers will be staring at me," she retorts.

"No," Maggie tells her, "they will be observing you, admiring the clothes and the beautiful children created by God."

"Yuck! Creepy!" Jennifer responds.

"They are not creepy," Emma tells her. "They're just old or in bad health. They have great-grandchildren your age."

The four interns file into the assigned dressing rooms as the director gets the audience's attention. She says, "Hello, everyone. As you can see, we have two four-legged visitors. One wants to meet everyone, and the other has found a home with Bessie." She pauses. "I'd like to introduce Magdala, a representative with Swaddling Clothes."

Maggie steps up and says, "Hi, folks, I'm Magdala, but I go by Maggie. I am with Swaddling Clothes. We have started a new clothing line and will show it to you today. Each of you will pick a free outfit to keep for yourself or, if you choose, present as a gift to someone else."

The residents buzz with excitement. Nothing beats free. Maggie continues. "Our interns from the high school will model the clothes displayed around the room. You can ask the interns questions as they model." She pauses and then says, "Now, boys, no whistling at the pretty girls."

The crowd laughs—some of them for the first time in a while.

Maggie goes on to say, "You have slips of paper and pens. When you decide on an outfit, write your name and the outfit number on the displays on your order form. Please include your sizes for a complete outfit. If you need some help, there are workers present who will assist you."

Maggie gets the cue that the interns are ready. She places an instrumental CD in the player and picks up the attached microphone. She says, "First up is a young man named Lennon. He's sporting a golf shirt with our logo and a pair of khaki pants. His footwear is the tried-and-true penny loafers."

Lennon makes his way down the center aisle of the room. Not knowing exactly what to do, he twists and turns so everyone will get the best angle of the clothes. He smiles as one woman mentions to her friend how cute he is. He departs to change outfits, and Maggie introduces Jennifer, who strides in front of the group with purpose. She makes no connection with the people and never stops to let them see the floral dress she is wearing. She returns to Maggie, who tells her, "You can talk to the people. They don't bite. Now go change."

Jennifer heads to the changing room. Emma is up next, in a colorful suit for exercising, which the home tries to get the elderly to do. She has a pickleball paddle in her hand and saunters along the runway. She twists and swings the paddle, and then bends as if reaching for a low serve. Her eyes meet an old man's, and she winks. Whistles erupt as Emma continues to walk through the crowd, pausing to answer a few questions and respond to remarks.

Lennon, already changed and standing in the wings, whispers to Maggie, "I thought they weren't supposed to whistle."

Maggie smiles. "Boys will be boys at any age. Emma is having harmless fun with them, giving them attention."

"I guess," Lennon says.

On the way to change, Emma tells Maggie, "I don't know what got into me. I didn't mean to cause a scene."

"You were great," Maggie tells her, "and you entertained everyone. This outfit might be the big seller."

Greg is up next and picks up on the enthusiasm started by Emma. He wears well-pressed jeans with a blue dress shirt covered by a black vest. He follows Emma's lead and slowly travels through the crowd. Most of the women are rather old, but they are no better than the men viewing the eye candy. Greg returns to Maggie and asks, "Did I do well?"

"Yes, they liked your choice. And you did get to wear the black vest, which should please you." Greg sort of lowers his head, knowing she and others are aware of his fondness for black. Maggie grabs his chin and lifts his head, telling him, "It's okay, Greg. Black works." Greg smiles. He is warming to Maggie since she has taken an interest in him more so than his parents, who are indifferent about what he wears and does.

Greg goes to the changing room, and Lennon steps up to Maggie. He is in a pair of shorts and a compression shirt that accents his slim figure, accompanied by sandals and a ball cap. "Is the shirt too much?" he asks Maggie. "Maybe too small and tight?"

"No," Maggie says. "Many men dream of washboard abs, and the ladies have grandchildren."

"Okay," Lennon affirms. "Got it." He begins his march through the residents. One woman touches his shorts to feel the material— or, as Lennon thinks, maybe his butt. Rather shocked, he smiles at her. Friends sitting next to her giggle like teens at her forwardness. Lennon moves on and back to Maggie.

Maggie tells him, "You made a girlfriend, and her soul's alive and well."

"It's nice to make them smile," Lennon replies.

"Even better to connect with them," Maggie responds.

Jennifer is back, dressed in a black pencil skirt with a sleeveless white dress shirt. It is prim, proper, and stylish. She has watched the others and launches in front of the audience, not to be outdone. She walks slowly, allowing both the men and women to ask questions. It amazes Maggie that Jennifer answers their questions without being condescending. Some women mark their tickets, with one woman asking Jennifer her size, telling her she has a great-granddaughter about the same size. A few men give some low whistles.

Jennifer glows at being the center of attention. She returns to Maggie. "Did I do well this time?" she queries.

"Yes, much better." Maggie tells her. "I noticed some ladies filling out forms as you spoke with them. See what happens, Jennifer, when you listen and respond?"

"Yes. It made me feel good, and they were interested in what I had to say."

Emma reappears wearing a fifties-style bright yellow dress with a fitted dark belt around her waist. She is in matching flats. As she starts her walk, the men stare at her, and the women applaud as she exudes an Audrey Hepburn elegance. The color is an excellent contrast to her skin and hair. She stops, as residents want to know whether Swaddling has their sizes. Emma answers and returns to Maggie wearing a wide grin. She is beautiful in the outfit.

"You look marvelous," Maggie tells her.

Lennon and Greg gaze at Emma, and then at each other with raised eyebrows. Then they smile. "Where did she come from?" Greg seems to be asking, but Lennon has always seen her beauty.

Maggie steps in front of the group and says, "Ladies and gentlemen, that concludes the fashion show. If you will complete the order slips and pass them up here, the interns will fill them for you. You can get the Swaddling Clothes today." When the forms are completed, Maggie asks the interns to pass the orders to her for review. She then tells them, "You guys can change into your other clothes while I review the slips."

Maggie sits at a table while the residents chat. Her lens scans the order forms. In another prearranged room, clothes appear on previously empty tables based on Maggie's scan. These clothes come straight from the Dominion. Maggie processes each order, and the interns return from changing. "Great," she tells them. "Open the door to the next room over. There we have the correct sizes and clothes for everyone. I want you to deliver them to the right person."

The interns follow her directions. They open a door to another room, and on tables are the clothes just modeled, in stacks, with order slips pinned to them. They stare at each other, wondering how this happened. Lennon jumps in first, lifts a pile of clothes, and returns to where the residents are seated. He shouts the first name on top, and a man raises his hand. Lennon gives the clothes to the man and continues until the pile is gone.

The other interns follow. The residents are boisterous as they show off their new clothes. Maggie smiles at the interns as they show a look of satisfaction. They are receiving so much more than they gave, realizing to various degrees how they have connected with and touched the lives of people at the point of need. Maggie addresses the crowd, thanking them for allowing the Swaddling Clothes group to come. She tells them, "If you have problems with the clothes in any way, let the director know, and we will fix it." She knows everything is perfect because it is perfect in the Dominion. The folks give her and the interns a round of applause. Maggie and the group depart the room.

Emma asks Maggie, "What about the clothes we wore today?"

"Those are yours to keep." The foursome all show pleasure in the revelation, with Emma being the most excited. Maggie then shifts the mood toward one of a more serious nature. "Emma, Lennon, I understand your church is hosting a talent show?"

"Yes, Lennon replies.

"I have good news for you both. Swaddling Clothes is now partnering with the church in this event. The civic center can accommodate a larger crowd, and there is a larger cash prize. Also, as I realize you may have already heard, a local recording studio is pitching in a recording contact for the top-rated musical performer." Lennon and Emma exchange glowing-faces looks. Greg appears surprised by the news but shows a look of interest. Maggie continues. "And for the young ladies, Swaddling Clothes will have a fashion show in conjunction with the talent event." Addressing Emma and Jennifer, she asks, "Are you girls up for another fashion show?" Neither hesitates to answer positively. Maggie says, "Good. For now, however, you'd better be getting home, girls, and I've got to get the boys home."

They exit the Forestville campus. Maggie's lens reads, "The interns grew today."

CHAPTER 26

"**G**ood morning, folks. I'm Bill Hemmer, and welcome to America's Newsroom. I assume you have seen what happened last night all over the world." Turning to his cohost, he says, "Good morning, Martha."

"Good morning Bill. I'm Martha MacCallum. We are witnessing some strange occurrences with communication worldwide. This cleric video preempted all programming on every network and platform around the globe."

"Martha," Bill says, "the federal government cannot do that with private networks. Whoever pulled this off has control of the world's communications. Nations are on the warpath, concerned the United States or a proxy called the Dominion has new communication software and has compromised foreign governments. This video is like a prayer, with the deaths of snipers, arms and drug dealers, creepy ministers, and now this cleric. Someone is killing the lowlifes of the world."

Martha says, "Bill, I know we have hoped and prayed someone would stop these types of people. Our producers are trying to track down this brave young man who called out this supposed holy man in the Middle East."

"Yes, Martha. We are drawn to such courage, strong faith, and resolve. We are getting reports, Martha, and saw on the video he had no explosives, but only sugar in the pack. What a brave or crazy man to call this guy's bluff."

Martha adds, "I am sure we wish our faith was that strong. After escaping and being rushed from the huge mosque, Imam Abu Karim Sadek died of natural causes in his vehicle. We understand he used his cell phone to transfer one hundred million dollars from a personal account. The Red Cross reports it is the largest private donation in the history of the organization. Our technical people are trying to find out who videotaped this entire event and broadcast it worldwide. If you watch the video, you never see videographer, but you can hear his voice."

There is peace and quiet for Simon, as the battle between the Imam and the courageous young man diverted the world's attention from him. The kid confronted the cleric with his hypocrisy. *Maybe humanity will look inside ourselves to find our own selfish nature.* Simon has not heard from *Sojourner* in days and wonders whether this was the work of the Dominion or government nanos. Nanos scare him, leaving him wondering who determines those people who are to receive the robots. Simon feels governments can't be trusted; anything can be used against the innocent.

The good news for Simon is that the space projects are on course, and his ankle bracelet beats its rhythm, confirming he is still alive and well. His silent thinking is broken by the intercom requesting his presence in Earlman's office. After the many interrogations, he has no idea what more information anyone could want. He wonders how he is supposed to explain something he had no hand in creating. It is like trying to prove love or faith in something one can't see or touch. And then, on a brighter note, Simon thinks maybe Earlman might want to talk about space stuff.

When he walks down to the office, he sees Earlman standing, with Alvarez and Norm on either side. Their faces are glum. "Come in, Simon," Earlman says. The four of them sit. The faces of Earlman, Alvarez, and Norm are rather expressionless. Norm looks ashen. Earlman initiates the conversation. "Simon, I have bad news. I wish

I didn't have to do this, but I have orders from the top to put you on administrative leave."

Simon is shocked. "They have not charged me with anything," he states. "I've just been accused, but no evidence for the accusation has be found."

Earlman responds, "I know, and I believe you, but we have funding to consider, and the crowds outside keep calling for your head. They are turning on the other staff. I can't allow it to happen."

"Am I being fired? If so, who will run Reliance?"

Norm sheepishly raises his hand.

"Norm?" Simon asks.

Earlman says quickly, "Simon, Ed has had your back the entire time, but he and I have families and pensions."

"I guess it always comes to having the money rather than having someone's back."

Norm says, "Simon, you know better than that. You know I tried as hard as I could to fight for you. The final straw that broke the camel's back and caused this current upheaval was your blog."

"My blog? There is nothing nefarious on my blog. The NSA gave me the computer. I am sure they review every keystroke before I hit Post. It must be chock full of the latest tracking known to man. They might even know stuff before I think of it. All I'm doing is trying to calm people—you know, the 'love one another' part of the email. I'm being fired for because of my faith?"

"Not fired, Simon, Earlman says. You are being placed on administrative leave; you will still get paid fully—same benefits. After we get though here, I want you to give Ed a run-through on the rover projects. Alvarez will meet up with you later to get your badge and update your clearances."

Norm says, "Simon, the top brass wanted you gone, but it's better for all of us to have you still on staff, getting paid, but away from JPL for a while. When everything gets resolved and returns to normal, I can reinstate you."

Simon stands and says, "Well, I guess I should be grateful. But I might just go make apps to steal stuff, seeing as I'm the guy who is supposedly responsible for everything electronic going on in the world. I'm sure my résumé will demand an eight-figure salary from an unknown government or dark web entity." He understands the situation but is still livid. "Are we through here?"

Earlman nods, and everyone else stands. Simon leaves the office without looking back. His travel to his office seems to take place in slow motion. He straightens his back and walks with fake confidence. Inside he is a pile of goo, wishing he could find a place to hide and cry until he melts away. Once back in his office, he retrieves a box and empties his desk, glad that he didn't have time to accumulate much clutter in about a month. He reexamines the stuff in the box because he doesn't want to be arrested for stealing a JPL paper clip.

Norm appears at the doorway. "Simon," he says, "I didn't ask for this, and I tried everything to keep it from happening. Please don't let this ruin our friendship."

Simon stares at him. "Norm, let's don't talk about it. Not now. I need to process this. Deep down in my mind and soul, I need to process everything." Norm nods. "You know Reliance," Simon continues. "I've got everything running correctly. Everything is okay with the rovers right now. There is the command center and a list of the command codes to reach the rovers. You have the knowledge to take it from there."

"Simon, you need to know I told no one of *Sojourner* speaking, of the Dominion, northern lights, Noah, and the stuff happening with Reliance … and I don't plan on telling anyone. But what do I do if *Sojourner* speaks, believing I am you?"

"That won't happen. *Sojourner* knows my voice. He knows my presence—where I am. He won't speak to you." There's a pause, and then Simon continues as his anger gets the best of him. "He certainly won't speak to a traitor."

Simon steps away from the console. Norm, shocked by Simon's words, walks toward it. Alvarez knocks and enters the doorway. "Dr. Northstrum, may I have your car keys?"

"Why?" Simon replies.

"There is a mass of demonstrators out front. It is safer if you go out through the loading docks. I will bring around your car."

Simon shakes his head. "Out the back again?"

Norm turns from the console and asks, "What do you mean, 'again'?"

"At the grocery store, I … never mind," Simon replies. He walks toward Alvarez, hands him the keys, and says, "I guess you need these," giving the guard his clearance badge and credentials.

"Yes sir. I didn't want to ask for them, but I have orders. Dr. Northstrum, I'm a pretty good judge of people. It's my job. I like you and believe you. I will see you again once you get over this speed bump."

Simon turns toward Norm and sarcastically says, "Good-bye, buddy, have fun." He and Alvarez exit the office.

Norm sits. With tears in his eyes, he fears a longtime friendship has ended. After rubbing his eyes and looking at the console, he finally picks up the phone and makes a call. When connected, he asks, "May I speak to Alexis Northstrum, please?" Shortly, he says, "Hi, Alexis, this is Norm."

"Oh, hi, Norm," she replies. "Is Simon okay?"

"No, Alexis, he is not. He was put on administrative leave just a while ago by Colonel Earlman, who had no choice. Orders from the top brass. Long story. They ushered him out of the back of JPL. I wanted to tell you, and I think he hates me. I did everything I could to protect him, but he called me a traitor."

"Oh, Norm. He doesn't believe that of you. He must be hurting with nowhere to turn. I will speak with him. Where is he?"

"On his way to his car, probably there by now."

"Okay, Norm. Thank you for letting me know. I'll call now."

"Alexis, tell me the truth. Do you think the pressures he's been under are causing him to hallucinate?"

"No, Norm. If I thought it, I would demand he see a professional for help."

"Do you believe the stuff about Noah, *Sojourner*, and Dominion?"

"I know my husband and believe him. You should too."

"I'm trying."

"I know, Norm. I know. You two will be all right when we understand these events and Simon is eventually cleared."

"I hope so, Alexis." The two exchange good-byes.

Simon sits in his car in the loading area where the rovers left JPL to be sent on their missions. He feels that when he puts the car in drive it will be a mission of no return for him. He wonders why God would answer his prayer for only a little while. He wonders where his supposed angels are in his moment of need. His face is wet from the trip to the docking area, along with the emotional strain and the feeling that his soul is melting away. He swipes his forearm across his face to dry it. His grasps the gearshift just as his phone chirps. He sees it is Alexis and hopes she won't be emotionally injured by this more than she already has. He brings the phone to his ear and tries to sound normal so as not to upset her.

"Hi, honey," he says. "How is your day?"

"I'm fine, but how are you?"

"Well …" Simon begins.

Alexis interrupts him with "I heard, Simon."

"How?"

"Norm called me."

"Oh, him. I won't be contacting him anytime soon."

"Don't be that way, Simon. The man was in tears."

"Well, I …"

Alexis interrupts him again. "Norm is your friend. He has your back, and don't throw it away because it hurts right now."

"Well, I'm still processing everything."

"Don't kill your relationship with Norm. That's an order. Remember: *Sojourner* said you can never undo everything you say. Are you on your way home?"

"Yes. But I might stop in a bar and down a few shots."

"The only thing that would do is make you feel worse in the morning, and maybe make you spend the night in jail or the hospital—or worse."

"Yeah. But it looks good in the movies."

"In the movies the guy gets into a bar fight. You are not a bar fight type of guy, so just come home. I'm leaving work and will see you at home. I love you, Simon. And I fully believe in you."

As Simon exits JPL, he feels the doors and an era close behind him. Rounding the corner, he sees the demonstrators and the hatred being spewed toward JPL. He hopes they hurt no one. It calls to mind what *Sojourner* said people do when they are afraid or fail to see the truth. He speeds off toward home.

The silence of his drive is broken by *Sojourner*, who says in a light manner, slightly laughing and giggling again, "Hi, Simon."

"What's so funny?"

"It amuses me how humanity is going bonkers over an email, and now a blog."

"You think it's funny my life and family are being destroyed?"

Sojourner continues. "Your life isn't destroyed. You keep going back to the material stuff of life. No one on the planet has lost anything. Yet they will destroy it instead of following the message. They can't win. Either humans send the souls through selfishness by annihilating the human race through a holocaust, or we take the selfish. Actually, we are much better at it. It is clean, peaceful. I see they gave you the sack. I saw it coming."

"You could have warned me."

"I can't do that. Remember the first time you rode a new roller coaster. We spoke of this before."

"Yes."

"Then you know why."

"Where is the Dominion on Earth here to help me?"

"They are there; you have seen them, but you would not know. Do you realize you do not have to die to be an angel? Those who live a selfless life are angels in the eyes of the Dominion."

"Be a doormat and become an angel?"

"Remember: it is about the ripples you cause. It is your choice. Free will causes positive and negative ripples. What you are experiencing is due to your prayer, so you must accept the consequences. Everything has consequences, or ripples. I sense you dislike these consequences.

415

Noah had a similar experience, but he dealt with it for over one hundred years. The Dominion has sped it up in your time. Simon, the world is at a boiling point. The Dominion is happy with your blog. Many are taking heed of your message of selflessness, togetherness, and fellowship. Yet there are still those who would prefer to be buried with their electronics. Keep reaching for them, and direct them to the helpers. They can see them wherever they live if they open their eyes."

"I'm worried I will be gunned down in the street."

"This will not kill you. The Dominion are not your enemy. Your faith will sustain you, so lose not hope. Bye, Simon." With that giggling laugh, *Sojourner* closes with "Keep your head down."

Simon pulls into his garage, and the door closes behind him. A large gasp escapes his lungs as he plops his head onto the headrest. His slow breathing calms his heart rate, and he makes his way to the kitchen table and a cup of stale coffee.

Moments pass as he feels sorry for himself, but his lamenting is ended when Alexis bursts through the door and envelops him with her arms. "I'm so sorry, honey."

Simon stands and hugs her. While in the embrace, he recalls *Sojourner* saying how important a deserved hug from a selfless human can be. Alexis looks into her husband's eyes and tells him, "You're going to be all right, Simon."

"Yeah, I know. It's just the feeling that my best friend stabbed me in the back and everyone at JPL hates me. But I'm still breathing."

"Well, with what is going on around the world and people dying, others aren't so lucky."

"So I'm lucky now?"

"You call Norm and apologize. You would be jobless with no pay, benefits, or retirement plan without his help."

"Well, he did say that he did all he could."

"You would have been flat-out fired if it weren't for Norm. You wouldn't listen to him explain because you were too upset and angry or hurt to listen."

"Maybe. But all I hear about is listening. The more I try to listen, the deeper my hole gets. I'll call tomorrow. I need to calm myself first." He pauses and then tells her, "*Sojourner* spoke in the car after I left JPL. He … it, or whatever … keeps laughing at humanity."

"*Sojourner* laughs at people dying?" she asks.

"The Dominion don't think in the same way we do. We are hung up on survival and accumulation of stuff. They concern themselves with our learning."

"Oh, right, learning selflessness before they exterminate us. How many years have humans been on Earth, and we've not learned our lesson? Our time has run out is my thought."

"*Sojourner* said I can succeed, and the Dominion do like my blog, which is showing promise, they say. Many more would have been recalled, but they changed because of me."

"Simon, what if they are aliens or governments using you to get us to exterminate one another? Do you know Betty from the end of the block?"

"Yes, marathon woman."

"Her family called about funeral arrangements. She died yesterday. Do you think she was a bad person? I thought she was nice."

"I don't know. We only knew her outwardly. But she must have been in pretty good shape with all that exercise."

"Everyone is dying. When will they come for our family? Is the Dominion the new Nazis? Didn't Pastor Martin Niemöller write about the purging of their chosen targets?"

"You mean the communists, trade unionists, and then the Jews?"

"Yes, Simon. Remember: 'and then they came for me and there was no one left to speak for me.' If a person did not buy into Hitler's view of Germany, they were trashed. The Dominion have our numbers. I'm sure we've all impeded or hurt someone in some way. And what about an evil thought or action from twenty years ago? Is it still a death sentence to the Dominion? No one is perfect, so we must die when the clock strikes midnight. I'm scared we kill ourselves or they do it for us—a flawless plan with the same ending."

"They have given us time to change, Alexis. Modeling Jesus, who died for our sins, they want us to move to selflessness and realize the effects our interactions with others cause."

"But Simon, how can we change a misdeed from ages ago? Did I cause this because of my prayers, and now our neighbors are dying? I didn't mean it that way. It is only the bad people."

"You can't change the past. But we can repent and move forward. At the same time, *Sojourner* said we are to be careful of what we pray. Our learning requires us to recognize the positive and negative things we say and do, learn from them, ask for forgiveness, forgive ourselves, and move on. Jesus said, 'Go and sin no more.' I guess we can't determine who the bad people are. We don't know the negative ripples people have caused."

"Do you really believe in the Dominion, and it is something good?" she asks. "I'm having my doubts."

"I understand. At times, I've had doubts—different doubts at different times. But I know *Sojourner* is conversing with me. Through *Sojourner*, the Dominion said Noah had doubts until the animals arrived."

"Yeah, his wife must have been ready to leave him. What was her name anyway?"

"I think it was Naamah."

"It's a wonder Naamah didn't hit him with one of the boards from the boat. I can hear her now: 'Boat, boat, boat!'"

"You're not saying, 'Reliance, reliance, reliance; *Sojourner*, *Sojourner*, *Sojourner*; or Dominion, Dominion, Dominion,' are you?"

"I don't know, Simon. I'm confused and terrified. They've accosted, interrogated, arrested, and shackled you. And now this administrative leave … Is Reliance doing this without your knowledge? You created it, but apparently it's out of your control."

"Alexis, I just—"

"What if they come for Emma?" Alexis interrupts. What if something is in her water or on her phone? We can't keep her in a cocoon. Maybe they did kill our neighbor Betty. How do we protect our child? You can ask your robot friend who laughs at death, but we must protect Emma."

"Listen, Alexis. I would offer to plead guilty to anything if it would protect you and Emma. But deep down, I know the government is not behind all this. We're not at the point of Star Trek yet, and the government can't talk to me in my car without the radio playing. *Sojourner* knows things before they happen.

"Well, I think you should call this Dr. Beckett and see if the NSA is behind this and is killing the selected."

"I'll call Tristin, but I think he's doing just what he said he's doing. He's come around to understand how Reliance, and maybe the Dominion, is helping him and his nanos take down some really bad guys. But I don't think the NSA is even involved with this wide-scale stuff or the emails." There are a few moments of silence, and then Simon says, "Alexis, if I lose your faith in me, life is not worth continuing, and the Dominion can come and take me."

Alexis embraces Simon and then steps back. Clasping and holding tightly both of his hands, she says, "Hon, I've had my ups and downs in all this, but I have faith in God and in you."

Simon gives Alexis a kiss and then tells her, "I'm going upstairs and checking on my blog that seems to be causing problems and got me placed on administrative leave. I haven't checked it since I posted."

She understands and gives him his space while she straightens up in the kitchen and fixes herself a cup of hot tea so that she might relax some.

Simon opens up to the blog and again reads what he has written. "Simple words and pure, simple thoughts," he says to himself. He looks for a way to see how many subscribers have joined. After a few clicks on the screen, he finds the number displayed. Simon blinks a few times to clear his eyes, not believing the total. He presses Refresh, thinking what he saw must have been a mistake.

After refreshing, the number still reads over one million subscribers. Simon now sits erect in his chair, in full focus. He expected around ten more people than last time. A feeling of celebrity churns inside him, and he realizes this is the feeling influencers get from being on social media.

However, his recalled *Sojourner* discussions quickly smash that feeling, because it is about ego. The reason the Dominion have come to Earth is to rid the planet of egos seeking power and control over money and people. They have come to replace selfishness with selflessness. No matter the number of subscribers, it is not about Simon Northstrum. It is about humanity finding and living their stories.

He logs out of the blog, waits a few minutes, and logs back in. He wants to check the number of subscribers again, just to make sure he got his blog numbers and not someone else's the first time. He finds the icon again and punches it. It now reads over ten million subscribers.

Simon goes to the bathroom and splashes cold water on his face, dries it, and then lies down on the bed to think and to let things soak in as best he can.

🙰

During this time, Emma, who has been driving her mother's car, parks the car at the end of Jennifer's driveway and gets out. The house is huge, with professional landscaping. She is sure Jennifer's hands never have touched the dirt. It is near dusk as she approaches the ornate glass-paneled door. The lights inside illuminate the wealth of the family's possessions. She reaches for the doorbell button but pulls back after she hears crying coming from within the house.

Emma backpedals enough to peer through a nearby window. Pressed against the wall is Jennifer, with tears causing her makeup to run. But what she sees on the other wall shocks her. Jennifer's father has her mom by the throat. His arm swings around and lands a slap to her neck, and then he punches her stomach. She doubles over, and he throws her to the floor. She lies there a few seconds before crawling to get away. Jennifer moves to help her mother, but her father intervenes by grabbing and twisting her arm, and then pushing her down and stepping on her legs. He shouts at Jennifer, "Don't you dare help the tramp! You both are tramps! I'm the mayor, and I demand respect from my own family!" Jennifer crawls away in pain toward the door. Emma freezes in the window, not knowing what to think or do.

While dragging herself, Jennifer sees movement outside and then recognizes Emma's face. Jennifer shakes her head and silently mouths, "No," warning Emma not to interfere. She then places her face to floor, preparing for more blows that may follow. Emma steps away and runs sobbing to her car. Jennifer has verbally tortured her for years, but she had no idea Jennifer was being physically tortured at home.

Once in the car, she grabs a tissue to wipe her eyes and then quietly backs out of the driveway. She parks along the curb about a block away. Needless to say, she is shaken, and she calls home. Alexis answers and Emma says, "Mom …"

Alexis picks up on her tone. "What's wrong, Emma? Are you okay?"

"I'm fine, Mom," she replies in a broken voice.

"Okay. But why are you crying?"

"I saw something horrible when I went to drop off some clothes at Jennifer's house as Maggie asked me to do."

"What did you see, hon?"

"The mayor was beating, kicking, and punching Jennifer and her mom."

Fear enters Alexis's voice as she asks, "You were there when it happened?"

"No. Not inside. I was about to ring the doorbell, and I heard crying. I looked in the window."

"Did they see you?"

"Just Jennifer. When she saw me, she shook her head. I took it to mean that I shouldn't come in, or maybe that I shouldn't call the police or get involved in any way. Mom, she hasn't been my friend, but she doesn't deserve to be beaten."

"Emma, where are you now?"

"I'm parked at a curb about a block from Jennifer's house. Mom, what should I do?"

"Are you up to driving home?"

"Yes. Sure, I can do that, but—"

Alexis breaks in, saying, "Well, that's what you should do for now. Just be careful, come on home, and we can discuss this." There's a pause before Alexis asks, "Are you positive you are okay to drive?"

"Yes ma'am."

"Well, take your time. We'll talk about it when you get home."

"Okay, Mom. I'll be careful."

Simon is still upstairs, so Alexis meets Emma at the door when she arrives. "Oh, Mom," Emma says as Alexis wraps her arms around her. Alexis kisses her on the cheek and brushes her hair, and then they go to the kitchen, the favorite place for Northstrum family discussions. They sit side by side. "What should we do?" Emma asks. "Call the police?"

"No, I don't think that would be wise, Emma."

"Why not? If only you could have seen what he did."

"I know, Emma. I understand what you're saying. But apparently this is not the first time for something like this in the Bittle household, and apparently neither Mrs. Bittle nor Jennifer has ever reported it."

"So?" Emma asks.

"They would have to file a complaint. We could tell the police about it, but if they don't file a complaint, it will be dropped. And, well, I don't want to think about what might happen then."

"We do nothing?" Emma asks.

"For now, Emma, just keep in mind that Jennifer knows what you know. She needs a real friend at this time—not just the girls you call the Bittlets. Talk to her. Tell her you are sorry about what happened, and then maybe listen more than talk. She needs to share this with someone she can trust, and I know she can trust you, now that you know the situation. I'm sure she is pent up with hurt and anger. That could be a big factor in why she treats others as she does."

"Yeah, maybe so," Emma replies, relieved to be discussing the situation with her mom.

"Unless the right person says and does the right thing at the right time, Mayor Bittle will have the police sweep it under the rug," Alexis tells her daughter.

Simon comes downstairs and hears talking in the kitchen. Going into the room, he senses something is wrong. "Are you both all right?" he asks.

Emma sees her father and bolts to him, wrapping her arms around him. "I love you, Daddy, and you too, Mom!" She begins to cry.

Comforting Emma, Simon says to Alexis, "What is going on with her does it involve JPL and me?"

Alexis rises from her chair and says, "No, Simon. Emma got a glimpse of another side of life tonight."

"Daddy," Emma tells him, "it was terrible. I went to Jennifer's house, and her father was beating up Jennifer and her mom."

"Oh, my! Did he touch you?"

"No, I was outside the door, and he didn't know that I was there—that I saw what was happening."

Simon turns to Alexis and says, "Do I need to go over there? Maybe call the police?"

She responds, "No. You know how that would go, what with Bittle being the mayor."

"Swept under the rug?"

"Exactly what I told Emma. I suggested to Emma she could talk to Jennifer alone. Simon, that girl needs a real friend, someone she can trust."

Emma looks at her father. "Jennifer is the only one who saw me outside the door. I heard the commotion and looked in the window, and Jennifer saw me. Shaking her head and mouthing 'No,' she signaled that she did not want me to get involved."

Simon asks, "Is she okay? What about Mrs. Bittle?"

"I don't know. I got out of there."

"It is good you did. Bittle must be an animal, and he may have hurt you. I have never cared for the guy and the way he tries to be a dictator, but this? I never imagined."

"Dad, Jennifer has always had this air of being better than everyone, but she lives in a nightmare."

"Honey, a friend told me we never know the pain behind another's eyes until we really get to know the person. I'm learning more and more each day that the best way to do that is with person-to-person talking. And what you're telling me now is another part of my learning."

With the three of them now standing together, Emma wraps her arms around her mother and father and says, "I've been taking for granted how great you two are as parents. I mean, there's Lennon's situation, and now, much, much worse, Jennifer's."

"We try, hon," Simon tells her. Alexis gives her a kiss on the cheek and wipes away the wetness under Emma's eyes as her own tear up.

"Now," Simon says, "How 'bout you gals freshen up a bit and then we go out for a bite to eat? I hear there's a great new Mexican place in the little town just south of here."

"Yes!" says Emma.

"Sounds good to me," Alexis joins in.

As Alexis and Emma get ready, Simon thinks of how he recited to Emma what *Sojourner* had told him about listening. When everyone gathers in the kitchen to depart, he marvels at how lucky he is to be surrounded by two amazing women. He tells himself, "There's much more to life than being upset over the administrative leave from JPL."

They enter the car and speed away to the new Mexican restaurant, loving the fact that it's out of town but still in ankle bracelet range. Simon plans to tell them about the amazing numbers on the blog. Of course, lurking behind is Brock Chesterfield, still looking for some real arrestable evidence.

A misty rain falls as Lennon moves toward his job at the studio. It has been a few days since he played with the other musicians, and he has been doing manual work. Such work certainly doesn't bother him; he gets to play on the instruments and electronics when finished. He folds his coat together as a gust of wind slices at him. Approaching the studio, he notices the window of the studio has a constant river of droplets making their way down to the sidewalk and into the street. He peers through the rain-distorted glass, hoping today the band might be inside and needing him to sit in on a session. But he discovers the control room is empty, so musicians would not be in the soundproof room adjoining it.

The lights are on in the building, but no life or movement is visible. Finding the door locked, he uses his own key, which he is thrilled to have. He pulls open the door and removes his jacket, hanging it on the wall coat hangers. The control room is bare, so he calls for Oz and Macy, thinking somehow they might be there even though the door was locked. No answer comes, but he sees a note on the control board that reads, "Lennon, we stepped out; will be back soon. The boxes in the office need attending to. Also, we have a guest in the studio wanting some alone time. If he needs help, you can handle it. See you later. Oz."

Lennon wipes the wetness from his face and adjusts his John Lennon shirt, which is now his studio uniform. He glances into the studio and to a figure with his back to the control room. He is an older, slight man dressed in a blue jean shirt and dark slacks. His guitar is backward to Lennon, and headphones clamp his ears. The sound from the studio is off, and the control room is silent. Lennon turns to work on the boxes. He unloads some supplies and puts them in their proper places. Then he sees some things he is supposed to sort, box up, and tape. On his knees, taping a box, he is startled by a voice.

"Hello," the man says. On his knees and with his back to the voice, Lennon swings around. From his vantage point, the view is feet first, and it then moves upward as he rises. When he gets to the man's face, his jaw drops open. His mouth becomes like cotton; his tongue feels swollen and useless. The man who has stepped from the studio is Paul McCartney.

"Surreal," Lennon thinks. "I am standing alone with Paul McCartney, my idol." Frozen in place, he wonders why his mouth won't work. He asks himself, "Why can't I say something inspirational?" Finally he is able to get out, "Hi, I'm Lennon"

Paul responds, "No joke?"

"No, sir. No joke. It's Lennon. Lennon Thomas."

Paul moves toward Lennon with his hand extended. Lennon brushes his hand against his pants and then clasps hands with Paul. Paul says, "Someone must have been a fan?"

"Yes sir. My mom."

"Nice. There are a few Lennons running around the world. You have a neat shirt. I don't recall ever seeing one like it in my travels. I can't remember if John ever posed with that guitar, but in the day, every time we turned around there was a camera."

"It was a gift from a friend," Lennon replies as he brushes the shirt and asks, "He liked the Rickenbacker 325?"

"Oh, yes. At one time we each had one."

"It's my dream to own one. I'm saving up right now."

Paul smiles. "So this is your job?"

"Yes, an after-school job, and I love it."

"I take it that you play guitar?"

"Yes sir."

"You can call me Paul. I remember how scared I was to meet the Everly Brothers. You can relax." Suddenly a calmness enters Lennon at the words of Paul, who seems to be a normal guy.

"You know Oz and Macy?" Lennon asks.

Oh, yes, very well. Oz and Macy worked at Abbey Road until they moved to the States."

"Cool," Lennon responds. "They are skillful and talented."

"What do you do for them?" Paul asks.

"Well," Lennon says, "I do whatever they need. Today it is unpacking and packing boxes."

"Your expression, Lennon, tells me it is a paying-your-dues job."

"I guess. It pays well though."

"Hey, we all pay our dues; no way around it."

Lennon adds, "They let me play with the instruments and electronics."

"You have a plus while paying your dues, huh Lennon?"

"Yes. And they asked me to sit in on a studio session the other day."

Paul's brow rises. "So you must have a skill they see in you."

"I practice a lot in my room."

"Paul smiles. "John and I practiced in the bathroom in our flat. Good acoustics."

Lennon nods in understanding. "Like singing in the shower."

Paul gives a slight laugh and says, "I'm impressed, Lennon, that Oz and Macy asked you to sit in. They have a good eye for talent."

"Can I ask you a question?" Lennon queries.

"Sure."

"Do you know a man named Joseph Deuss?"

Paul's face perks up. "Yes," he says. "A name from the early days. Why do you ask?"

His company is doing an internship with our school for his clothing line, Swaddling Clothes, and I'm one of the four interns. Mr. Deuss helped me get the job cleaning up this building before it was a studio, and there was an old picture of the Beatles with Mr. Deuss."

"Wow!" Paul responds. "I've not seen him since those days. He was the guru of fashion."

"At first I thought he was giving me a bunch of bull when he talked about those days, but I began to learn better."

"You'll never meet a better man. If you see him, give him my love." Paul smiles. "You and I will be friends, Lennon. We know the same people and we play guitar, and any friend of Joseph's is a friend of mine."

Lennon is in heaven at Paul's words. *A friend of Paul McCartney!* He asks, "What brings you here?"

Paul tells him, "I have business here in town, and the grapevine at Abbey Road told me of Oz and Macy's new venture. I rang them to catch up, and I knew I could slip in here unnoticed without the paparazzi swarming the place." Paul puts his fingers to his lips. "You can keep this between us until I leave?"

"Your secret is safe with me," responds Lennon.

Oz and Macy enter the studio. Hugs and embraces go around between Paul and the duo. "I take it you have become acquainted with Mr. Lennon," Macy says.

"Yes. It seems I've met another musician named Lennon." Lennon blushes at the comparison to John.

"Were you able to get any work done?" Oz asks.

"Guys, this studio is great. I wish you the best in your endeavors. To answer your question, yes. Thanks for letting me work alone. I got stuff done."

"Would you like to work on it now?" Oz asks.

"You bet, if that's okay with you."

"Let's do it," Oz replies.

Macy and Oz move around the control board, and Paul exits to the studio. Lennon is standing awkwardly, wondering what to do, until Oz pats a chair, indicating for Lennon to sit next to them. Macy says, "Today you get to work with a legend. You up for it?" Light speed couldn't get him in the chair any quicker. Paul is in the studio, but this time he is facing the control room with headphones in place. Paul plays, and Macy and Oz adjust the sound machine as ideas are passed back and forth among the trio. Lennon sits in awe, realizing Paul's songs are put together piece by piece.

Lennon's awe coma breaks when Macy asks Lennon what he thought about things. Caught up in the action, Lennon blurts out, "This stanza should be in a different key. It will sound better." He suggests the key. Lennon then gets an embarrassed look on his face; he has just told a master musician that something he is doing could be better.

Paul, Oz, and Macy have questioning looks on their faces until Paul says, "Let's give it a go." They finish the new rendition, and Paul listens to the playback. His voice comes over the speaker. "Thank you, Lennon. This does work better. You remind me of the days working with John in our bedroom, running different stuff by each other."

Macy and Oz slap Lennon on the back as he is hoping not to explode with excitement. "I never want to wake from this dream," he remarks.

The workday ends, and Lennon makes his way home with a new sense that dreams can come true. A huge smile is still plastered to his face. He helped his musical idol craft a song. He turns up his collar up and twirls in exhilaration, screaming, "Thank you, God!"

CHAPTER 27

"Good morning. Here we go again! Welcome to *America's Newsroom*. I'm Bill Hemmer. Hello, Martha."

"Good morning, Bill. Folks, this is a Fox News alert. On the screen are shots of the riots taking place in almost every major city around the world. The word from our reporters is that people are afraid of the drumbeats of war and annihilation. They are looting for food and provisions. Experts are with us to make sense of what is happening. We have Dr. Alice Ritelli, a psychologist, clerics Rabbi Joseph Hertzog, Father James Milan, Imam Wafa Sani and Pastor Robert Jefferson, along with medical examiner Dennis Clary."

Bill says, "We are glad to have you here to understand what people have coined 'The Days of Desperation.' Dr. Ritelli, let's lead with you. What is going on with people? Have they gone mad?"

"The simple answer to your question is fear. It scares them that the powers around the world are turning on each other and are looking out for power and control, not looking out for the people. In the backs of their minds, they consider this an insidious scheme by one unknown government. When the war starts, you had better have supplies of foodstuffs, water, medicine, and guns. We might fight our friends. People will leave the cities, searching for food and where it grows."

"Dr. Ritelli, this is Martha. You paint a bleak picture of mankind. It is a portrait of human nature and survival of the fittest."

Father Milan asks, "May I break in?"

"Yes, Father Milan."

"Martha, these riots are curious. The individuals initially leading the protests did not show up on the succeeding nights. On later nights, the crowds diminished. Dr. Clary, bad people have taken a whipping. We're talking about various criminals: thieves, thugs, and many you would not expect to die. Even the powerful preacher Gordon Thatcher died and left behind a note detailing his dishonesty and immoral behavior."

Having been addressed, Dr. Clary says, "I am swamped with dead bodies from all walks of life. And it is taking place not only in the States but also in pockets around the world. I learned from another coroner that a large group of Central American gang members were eliminated. I know the government keeps an eye on these types, but according to what I hear, they just died of natural causes. Here in America, coroners have appropriated former supermarket locations that have gone out of business, turning on the electricity and using the large freezers to help hold the overflow of dead bodies."

Bill shakes his head, saying, "Unbelievable … here in America."

"Yes," Dr. Clary says. "These people just quit living. I don't know how else to explain it. Other coroners have dissected the corpses, just as I have, and all of us have found nothing but natural death. We have performed every scan and toxicology test known, but, well, they just quit living."

"Absolutely no biologicals have been found?" asks Martha.

"No, unless it is something new and we don't know what to look for."

Bill says, "A while back, we had a scientist on the show who speculated that the government might have a nano program where they implant little robots in captured terrorists. Could something like that be the cause?"

Dr. Clary replies, "Rumors exist of such a program, but the people I've examined were not terrorists. Some had police records, but others did not—just ordinary people. I've no clue why they passed."

Martha asks, "What about nanos? Did you find any?"

Dr. Clary shrugs, gives a little laugh, and responds, "Well, I wouldn't know what one of these so-called nanos look like. But no, I haven't found anything foreign to the body."

Bill jumps in. "I'd like to address this question to the clergy. We have seen in recent days the churches filling, and people gathering and talking. The major cell and internet firms have announced a dramatic drop in usage. Old-timers are reconnecting their land lines and going back to simple phones with no apps or tracking. What are your takes on this?"

"May I tackle the question?" asks Rabbi Hertzog. He gets an affirmative reply and says, "People are afraid, as Dr. Ritelli suggested. In response, I believe people are turning away from electronics and toward each other."

"You mean like the Dominion's email suggested?" asks Bill.

"Well," the rabbi explains, "the email triggered a response like the kind you might get during a natural disaster. It was once said people are at their best when things are at their worst. I read on a blog that maybe this disaster has been triggered to get us to be at our best and selfless."

"I believe annihilation would fall within that 'worst' category," says Bill.

Martha joins in with "Pastor Jefferson, it is reported that the phones of the deceased had the message, and I quote, 'Your rapture is brought to humanity by the Dominion … Where are you in your soul's contract with us?' What is it, Pastor? Are we seeing the rapture according to the Bible? The original email was biblical. There is an urban legend spreading that a program on cell phones is scanning your soul, and if you are not a good person, you die. Could the Dominion be God? Or maybe extraterrestrial things, what with the weird flashes going on around the world? Are our electronics killing people, and is this a government plot to get rid of people opposed to it?"

Pastor Johnson replies, "Huge questions you have there, Martha. I don't have an answer to what's happening, but I can tell you this. When the rapture comes, it will not be the bad people that are taken. With the rapture, it is the good souls that are taken to be united with God. As far as the known-bad and maybe-bad people dying, I am clueless, and I feel this must be a man-made thing." He pauses. "Maybe it is the nanos that you've described."

Dr. Cleary says, "With all due respect to the clergy present, we can't deny that religious texts are full of deities killing or assisting in killing humans. The flood is an example of this."

Martha asks, "Doesn't the Bible say God will never kill man by flood ever again? Has God maybe selected a new twenty-first-century method?"

Rabbi Hertzog says, "It appears this entity called the Dominion—be it God, a government, a programmer, aliens, or whatever—is causing these deaths to teach us selflessness and togetherness. I think every human in existence has prayed to rid the world of liars, thieves, murderers, and other vultures."

Martha asks Imam Wafa Sani for his input, and he says, "I have been listening, and all viewpoints are very interesting. My response is what is found in the Koran: 'For in its own works lies the fate of every soul.'"

Martha says, "Stay with us, folks. We will be right back after this short break."

⚜

Simon has all types of thoughts running through his mind as he drives around performing family errands. He remains careful regarding where he goes and when he goes, choosing to travel to the little town to the south as much as possible when needing to visit stores. It's a quiet drive, with only Simon and his thoughts. Simon feels weird having not been in touch with his Mars rovers for a while. He thinks especially of *Sojourner*, who has not spoken to him in several days, and he strangely misses the one that has brought the wrath of the world on his head.

It is at this moment of pondering that the radio glows to life and the familiar voice of *Sojourner* fills the car, beginning with a laughing little giggle, which confuses Simon more and more as to whether *Sojourner* is an "it," "he," "she," or "whatever."

"Hi, Simon. I miss you too. You find it difficult being the new Noah?"

"What do you think?" he says sarcastically. "Where have you been?"

"I've been busy reclaiming souls and meeting the returning children. So very many have gotten far off their stories. Many assumed they were on the right path, but they were on a path of selfishness." *Sojourner* pauses. "I saw your blog. Thank you for getting the original message out, and for your follow-up. Nice. You messaged the world in your own words."

"Did you get all those subscribers for me?"

"No, Simon. Reliance did it, and Reliance is doing the reclamation."

"Reliance can't kill people."

"You still don't get it, Simon. Dying and killing is a human construct. In the human school, you're born, you live, and you die. It holds no water in the Dominion. There you live, you learn, you reflect, and you live again. Snap, snap, snap. Your souls are eternal. Remember that as you see many reclaimed on the news. It will get ugly, Simon. Your problem now is determining how you become Noah. Let's play a game. I will be God, and you will be Noah."

"*Are* you God?" asks Simon.

"No, but humans look to a deity. It will surprise them when they pass from Earth that the deity in whose name they kill and judge might be the same for all, no matter whether they call it Jesus, Allah, Yahweh, or Mother Nature, along with the other names throughout history. As I said before, they brought the flood into the world because of self, as it is today."

"You expect me to save the world?"

"No, that is impossible. But you must lead people to the safety of a selfless life. They must reach into their souls and find their stories to live. We spoke earlier about ripples. No matter how tiny a ripple begins, it can grow to a tsunami. I give you Hitler as an example. He was not born evil but grew that way because of small, selfish ripples that scarred him, causing him to become despicable."

"Where is Hitler now?"

"He has crossed, as all do, and he has many debts to pay. As Lucy said in her old TV show *I Love Lucy*, Hitler had a sad face when he arrived. And as Lucy's husband Ricky said, he's got a lot of explaining to do. I assure you, every ripple that affected his time and other people's time on earth was discussed in detail. Free will cuts both ways but is the best teacher. Humans only think of it for this lifetime."

"So how do I get more people's attention?"

You have already begun that with your blog, and it will continue to grow. Just go back in now and then to respond to some of the comments, both the positive and the negative. And write some more words from your heart. You'll have time during your administrative leave. It took Noah a hundred twenty years to build the ark, and yet only his family got on board. Many were pounding on the hull once the boat floated. You have advanced communications today—and much less time than Noah.

"Exactly how much time are we talking about?"

"I don't know, Simon. I'm only a robot. Just preach the word of coming to the safety of a selfless life."

"I'm trying. I've told people about the rapture and your plan to save them, but they laugh. Many think I'm a lunatic who's lost his mind."

"But Simon, many are also paying attention to your words. Just keep preaching the selfless life. You are not responsible for the results. Your responsibility is to share the word. Warn humans. Invite them to enter a selfless life and avoid the rapture playing out. Remember: it is the ones who mock and hate you that are in the most peril. Find the helpers of your world—those that help regardless of religion or challenge. They are your salvation."

Evening falls on the Bittle household, with the lights in the palatial home giving off a false glow of love and warmth. Michael stands nearby, knowing a crafty decorator helped hide the truth of this house of torment. Inside, Jennifer and her mother sit at the kitchen table. They peck at their food in silence, afraid to speak. Conversation terrifies them. Should any misplaced or misused word come from their mouths, even a small spark of something, the spark can intensify into a physical beating should the mayor overhear or enter the room. Simple conversation is a battle point, so they don't do it. Jennifer wonders how great it would be to have parents like Emma's. She is jealous that Emma's parents' faces are bright when Emma is around. She has witnessed them with one another.

Jennifer's parents' faces are usually pallid when the three of them are together—especially her father's, which is stone-cold. She wonders what it would be like to live in a home without fear. The mayor is in his home office. He never dines with his wife and daughter at home; he does so only sparingly in public places in order to fabricate the image of a happy family, which is always a tough act for them all.

Jennifer hears her father on the phone now. His voice is loud and enraged. She knows someone is in for a butt-kicking tomorrow. Employee talks often lead to problems in the family and are not good. Jennifer slips out of her chair and then washes and puts away everything she used at dinner. She knows not following through on a chore can become a flash point to her father. She asks to go to her room to get out of harm's way. Hiding from her father is her normal. Her mother signals her approval as she prepares a plate for her husband.

Jennifer hears her father yell to himself, "Who is calling now!" He switches the phone to the new caller, and a white light flashes. An expletive escapes his lips as he switches back and continues to eviscerate the person on the other end.

The commander's lens reads a message from Michael: "I give you Landon Bittle."

Michael reads a message from the commander: "Landon Bittle will find himself in the Dominion tomorrow."

Florence is in front of General Bosman. She scolds him for not getting back to his daughter and grandson; she is the only person who dares to do this. He accepts her tirade, knowing in his heart she is right. Florence adds, "Robert, you can fire me. It is your right. But even though the world seems to be deteriorating, the two people who need you the most are calling, and you avoid them."

"Florence, everybody is my responsibility, not just my family."

"Don't get on that tangent," she says. "The beautiful souls of your own family are your pressing need. Look at the picture Billy made for you. It will take less than a minute. He was trying to cheer you up, but it seems you don't care. Cassie calls every day asking if you've taken time to just look at it, for heaven's sake. I will lie for you no further. You look at the picture this instant. I have placed the phones on hold, so your procrastination is over. Robert, I'm facing a soulless man and not the man of faith I knew when your wife, Anna, was living."

"I had faith and prayed," he retorts. "But it did no good. She still died."

"Yes, she did. But the Bible says the rain falls on the just and the unjust. God never promised to keep us from all hurt and harm. But He did promise to give us strength and courage to deal with troubles and tragedy if we will turn to Him and trust Him. Would Anna be proud of your behavior?"

"No, the little dynamo would kick my butt. Cassie is a whirlwind like her mother."

"There you have it. Make Anna proud of you. Forgive yourself. No one could save her when the cancer metastasized. No matter your position or influence, you were helpless, so she put herself in God's love. I am certain she is one of his angels and is behind you right now, slapping the powerful general on the back of the head to get him to look at Billy's picture and reconnect with his family."

There is silence, and the general doesn't move.

"Well, Robert, I've said enough. Do I need to clean out my desk?"

"No," he replies. "Thank you. Good friends tell you what you need to hear, not what you want to hear. You have my word. I will look at it before I quit today and will leave a note confirming it." He then tells Florence, "You're a tough, relentless hombre. Maybe you should have five stars."

"Silly man. I already have those. Earned them years ago. I call them my children, who have finally grown up and flown the coop. You're a puppy dog compared to them."

Florence exits the office, and he hears the door lock. He muses about how a slight woman can imprison a commander of the most powerful military on Earth. Rather than subject himself to her further wrath, he clears his desk of national security issues in favor of Billy's artwork. He recalls the refrigerator art stuck in every imaginable place by his wife so Billy could see it in a place of honor. Many of the compositions were simple crayon lines. But to her, they were treasures she wouldn't trade for the *Mona Lisa*. Bosman recalls how she would listen as Billy explained the art to her.

He opens his desk drawer and retrieves the tube and unfurls the scrolled picture over his desk. The picture tries to roll up, so he weights the ends. A smile crosses his face as he recognizes the home he and his wife once shared. He grasps the fact that when she passed, the soul that kept the home fires burning stripped the family of its binding glue. He dials Cassie's number. Her voicemail comes on.

"Cassie," he says, "this is Dad. I looked at Billy's picture, and it is beautiful. Mom would have it framed and placed over the mantle. I have ordered pizza for the three of us, to be delivered right there at Grammy's house at six thirty tonight. It'll be nice to eat in the old home place again, and Billy can explain his painting, and we can get in touch. Perhaps I can put back some of Mom's family glue. I'll see you then. Love ya, Dad. Bye." Bosman sits back in his chair, feeling a burden lifted from his shoulders. He mumbles, "I listened, honey. I needed a head slap."

After a few hours' work, he leaves his office and stops at Florence's desk to place the promised note. It energizes and excites him to get back to family. It took a simple step. He misses his daughter and grandson.

Bosman makes it to the outside and is greeted by his driver, Lieutenant Konner Fry, who is at attention. The general nods a salute and then tells the young man to relax, adding that it is just a night with two guys on a drive. Bosman climbs into the backseat. Fry asks, "Straight to your apartment, sir?"

"No," Bosman replies. "Tonight I'm going back to my old home place."

After a pause, Fry says, "Sir, I don't think I've ever been there. Could you give me the address? Bosman tells him the address; Fry keys it into his Android GPS and pulls out toward the main road and then onto the highway.

Bosman asks, "Konner, what are six- or seven-year-old boys buying at the toy store nowadays?"

"I am not sure, sir. As you know, I'm still pretty fresh from graduating West Point. Not married yet, no children. But my nephews go crazy for these remote control cars. They want to go to empty parking lots where they can let them scream."

"Good. Take me to where those cars are sold." The lieutenant pulls to the roadside, googles the directions, and then reenters the road.

After some silence, Fry says, "Sir?"

"Yes, Konner?"

"Sir, my mom called me, and she is worried. She wanted to know if we will have a world war. It scares her." Fry gazes through the rearview mirror for a response he can relay to his family.

General Bosman tells him, "Things are bleak. I grant you that. But we have good people working, trying to figure it out. Everyone is going crazy over an email. It is not the email but the breaking into all the computers that's the problem. As far as I know, there is not a computer anywhere on the planet that's secure. That's why everyone is rattling sabers."

"Mom says many people are not using computers and electronics as much. She goes to a church social group, and its meetings have tripled. She and her friends have been reading a blog by a Doctor Northstrum. He says maybe the email is a way of being told to look inside ourselves and become selfless. Northstrum said the email has a wonderful message but the second part is the most important. He believes the dates in the email were not wrong and that selfish acts in humans have a ripple effect in time, no matter how minor."

"What do you mean?"

"Well, according to Mom, let's say that with penicillin there may have been a person who was meant to discover the drug earlier, as the date suggests. But because another human's act caused that person to veer off his or her true life journey, or even die, the discovery had to wait for Fleming."

"Your mother got this through the email messages and Dr. Northstrum's blog?"

"Yes sir."

"And the idea is that everything everybody does affects everyone else?"

"Yes sir."

Bosman makes a note to question Northstrum about this.

After the trip to the toy store and the purchase of a super-duper race car, Bosman arrives at his home. Happenstance has it that the pizza delivery guy pulls up just after Lieutenant Fry drives away. The general takes the pizzas and tips the guy, who is quickly in the wind. After juggling the pizzas and setting the race car and Billy's picture in the mailing tube on the porch swing, he unlocks the door, steps inside the dark home, and places the pizzas on a nearby entrance hall table.

He retrieves the packages from the front porch and places them on the table next to the pizzas. He then turns on a light and closes the door. With things brighter and warmer-looking now, and with the smell of pizza refreshingly in the air, things feel much homier already.

He has a cleaning service that takes care of things, dusting and such, on a regular basis, and he has a landscaping service that takes care of outside needs. All utilities are set on autopay, and he has someone pick up and bring home-delivered mail to his office. So as far as all that is concerned, he is set. But now he needs a family back in the house to make it a home.

He goes to the kitchen and flops down the pizzas and packages. He searches the kitchen drawers and finds some tape he wants to use in order for Billy to attach his picture to the current artwork hanging above the mantel over the fireplace in the family room. He hides the race car he got the store to gift wrap for him. That way he can pull it out later as a surprise after they have reunited, eaten, and visited for a while. His wife was the entertainment specialist, and she would give him directions on the correct way to do things.

Bosman then hurries upstairs to get out of his military attire and rummage through his closet and chest of drawers to locate and change into some Dad and Grampa clothes. Having not been in the house for a while, his rummaging around takes longer than he hoped it would. Finally he gets re-dressed and makes his way downstairs as the front door flies open.

Rushing through the doorway is Billy, and Bosman braces himself for the tackle hug he sees coming. While grabbing him around the legs and waist, Billy shouts, "Grampa!"

Bosman shouts back, "What's happening, Billy Boy?" A wide smile caresses his face as he picks up Billy and swings him around.

"I missed you, Grampa," Billy tells Bosman as he lowers the boy to the floor.

"I missed you, too, Billy," he replies. He then asks, "Where is your mom, young man?"

"She's coming up the walk."

About that time, Cassie emerges in the doorway through the wide-open door; her arms are loaded with packages.

"Billy," the general says while rubbing the boy's hair, "you could have carried something." Bosman rushes to Cassie and takes a couple of the bundles. He then leans over, kisses her on the cheek, and says, "Hello, hon."

Cassie pecks him back and says, "So great to see you, Dad. As you might have known, I cried when I got your message."

"What's with all this?" he asks, referring to the bags.

"I stopped at the store because I know your fridge must be empty. When was the last time you were here?"

"I don't know," Bosman replies. "A while. But I'm here now."

They move to the kitchen and place the bags on the counter, and Cassie opens the refrigerator, revealing only a few nonperishable items. "Really, Dad? Really?"

"Like I say," he responds, "it's been a while. The cleaning service takes care of things and gets rid of stuff that could ruin." He quickly changes the subject. "Hey, the pizzas are getting cold!"

"Yeah," Billy says, jumping in. He flips open one of the boxes and says excitedly, "It's my favorite! You remembered, Grampa!"

"Yes, Billy. Of course I did!"

"Okay," Cassie replies. I brought some things to make a quick salad and some drinks. Let me take care of that, and we can microwave the pizzas, just like when they come out of the oven."

"Sounds good," Bosman responds.

"And," Cassie adds, "It just so happens that to top things off, I got some of those little moist cupcakes from the bakery, along with some vanilla bean ice cream."

"Wow!" Billy yells

"I say, 'Wow!'" Bosman responds, overtly loosening his belt.

Cassie, taking after her mother, tells the guys to get the plates, eating utensils, and glasses, along with the paper napkins she brought. She tells them to set up things while she prepares the salad. As they get closer to being ready, Cassie instructs Billy to go to the bathroom, because he probably needs to, and to be sure to wash up for dinner.

Alone with her father, Cassie says, "Dad, are you okay?" She's halfway kidding him, but the other half of her question is digging to see if he's physically all right. "I mean pizza, your home, we are together. What's up? Did Florence hit you in the head?"

"Well," he replies, "she did give me a talking-to today."

"I like her," Cassie tells him. "She has fire, like Mom."

"Yes," Bosman agrees. "I sometimes wonder who really runs that office—Florence or me."

"She talks to you like that because she really likes you."

"I like her too."

"No, Dad. I mean she *really* likes you."

Taken aback, Bosman says, "Oh, Cassie, I'm not ready for anything like that."

"Yes you are, Dad. She is already your work wife; her husband passed away several years ago, and all her children are grown, with children of their own."

"We … we work well together."

"Consider it, Dad. You need companionship."

"I'll think about it."

"Good."

Billy is back, and they sit down at the kitchen table to enjoy pizza and all the fixings, already conversing. It seems just about like old times. Things ingrained deeply are hard to destroy.

When everyone is full and the table is cleared, Bosman gets the mailing tube, removes Billy's picture, and says, "Now, let's take a look at this and discuss its artistic ramifications."

"Ram-if-i-ca-tions?" Billy asks.

Cassie tells Billy, "Dad, being a great lover of art, and a bit of a clown, simply means he wants you to explain the picture to him."

"Great!" Billy exclaims.

"Help me here, guys," Bosman says, spreading the picture on the table and telling them to place near the corners some of the paperweights he has rounded up. "This is a wonderful picture," he tells Billy, who glows with the compliment. Bosman folds four bits of tape and attaches them on the back side of the picture at the corners, and he then says, "Let's carefully take it over to the family room area. I have the perfect place to display it. And then, Billy, we can discuss it."

They go into the family room. "Here, Cassie; you hold the two top corners," Bosman tells his daughter. "I will lift Billy onto my shoulders, and then you can hand us the picture and we will press it onto the glass covering this old picture. I believe Billy's is just about the right size to cover it exactly."

He lifts the boy, the task is completed, and Billy is lowered down. Cassie says, "Amazing, it does fit perfectly, just like that frame was specially made for it."

Bosman rubs the boy's head and tells him it is a job well done. Billy grins and, as some people down south say, "looks like he is as happy as a pig in a peach orchard."

The three of them sit on the sofa facing the fireplace and the picture, with Billy seated between Mom and Grampa. "Now," Bosman tells Billy, "tell me about your picture."

"Well, first of all, Grampa, I guess you know whose house this is in the picture?"

"I sure do," Bosman replies. "You did a great job drawing it, I might add, and the yard looks nice."

"You always take good care of your yard, Grampa." Bosman smiles and nods. Billy then points to the stick figure representing himself. Next he points to Cassie, saying, "Mom is right here, close to me." Bosman and Cassie exchange knowing looks, acknowledging the closeness of mother and son. Billy then moves on to show Grampa where he is, and he specifically describes his medals. Bosman smiles inside and out. Billy then points and says, "This is Grammy. She is holding your hand like the two of you used to do. The general's face warms, remembering especially the walks the two shared while holding hands. "I drew it that way to make you happy, Grampa. My teacher said this project was to make someone happy. I chose you."

Moisture forms in Bosman's eyes. "Who are those other people?"

"They are our guardian angels, and God is up above them." Billy pauses before saying, "Grammy's an angel too."

"You've got that right, Billy," Bosman immediately responds. Looking at Billy, the grandfather asks, "How did you get to be such a budding young artist?"

"I wanted to make you smile again, and to be with us, and to be happy together like we used to be."

"Well, Billy, this was certainly the ticket I needed in order to get back in the groove again. I'm sorry I haven't been available, spending too much time with my work and not enough time with my family."

"But you're back now, huh, Grampa?"

"Yes, Billy, I'm back, and ready to pick up where we left off." Bosman stands, steps out in front of his daughter and grandson, and says, "Come here, kids!" They spring from the sofa, and he pulls them toward him. Quoting from the Bible's Ecclesiastes, Bosman says, "A cord of three strands is not easily broken!"

"Oh, Dad," Cassie says, "I've missed you so much."

"Me, too, Grampa," Billy looks up at him and says.

"And I've missed you two," Bosman responds. "I didn't know how much I missed you until I saw Billy's drawing ... and I knew it was from his heart."

Backing away slightly, Bosman looks down at Billy and says, "Wait! I almost forgot something." He winks to Cassie and points to a nearby cabinet. "Go over there and open those bottom doors. I believe there's a package under there that might interest you."

Cassie gives a questioning look toward her father as Billy bolts to the cabinet. A yell soon erupts from the room, as he quickly tears into the package and sees the race car photo on the box. "Oh! Oh! Wow! Thank you, Grampa!" Running back to his grandfather and mom, he says loudly, "This is amazing, Mom! It's a remote-control car like I was telling you about! Jimmy Newland has one, Mom. Remember I was telling you about it?"

"Dad, this is great. And, yes, Billy has been talking about this very thing. How would you know?"

"Grandfather's intuition, I guess," he replies.

The car is out of the box, batteries are in, and Billy goes around the corner chasing the fast-moving car on the hardwood floor. "Dad, this is so sweet of you," Cassie tells her father. "But it is a pretty big present, and Christmas is coming, you know."

"So Santa came a little early this year. And isn't that what grandfathers do—spoil their grandchildren?"

Billy pops in and asks, "Can I take it out to the driveway?"

Cassie replies, "Well, I don't know, Billy …"

"Please … Grampa has a long driveway."

"Well … if you promise to keep it close to the garage, Billy. No letting it get out into the street."

"I won't."

"All right then, for a little while."

Billy picks up the car and shoots out of the house.

Cassie and Bosman get some coffee and sit at the kitchen table. "It's wonderful to see you, Dad. Billy is so excited."

"That's certainly easy to see; I noticed even before he opened the car."

"Of course. The car is just icing on the cake, Dad." Cassie sips her coffee and then says, "And this has got to be really good for you, Dad, taking your mind off all that's going on in the world—especially in your position."

"Cassie, the world is a powder keg. The president is breathing down my neck to find the guilty party behind what's going on."

"It's really bad, isn't it?"

"Definitely. The hawks want to attack everyone, which is impossible and would bring the world to extinction."

"Dad, I can't believe a brilliant hacker would envision annihilation, especially since the hacker would perish along with everyone else. I would not want to crawl out from any bunker to witness the devastation."

"Like you say, Cassie, I'm away from that right now. So let's get away from the subject for the time being." She nods, again sipping coffee. Bosman asks, "How did Billy come to make such a wonderful picture? Tell me about the project he mentioned."

"Helping people to be happier has been a recent theme at school. They had an after-school program with a visiting priest. It was unusual."

"Oh, how so?"

"He didn't reference the fire-and-brimstone types of things. He walked into the room dressed in a brown monk's robe, like in Star Wars."

"Okay …"

"Then he underlined words written on the blackboard and turned toward the children with a big smile and laugh. He said, "I bet you thought I was Gandalf or Obi-Wan." He goes on to say that the words on the board are in different languages from countries where he has preached, including Klingon, among others. He laughed again, saying that actually the Holy Father had not sent him to the Klingons' home planet yet. He said the words underlined meant 'Peace be with you,' and that the words disarm people."

"Sounds like an interesting man," Bosman says.

"Very," Cassie replies. "While he was speaking, Kelly Sellers was face first in her phone." Bosman's jaw tightens in reaction to the name. Cassie continues. "He walked to her and covered her phone with his palm, and the phone went dead. It was odd. Then he told the parents and children that we would not want the last face we see on Earth to be our phones."

Bosman's elbows are on the table, coffee cup to his lips, as he listens intently to what Cassie says about the priest. She says, "He spoke of how these electronic devices have interfered with connecting with our souls, which he described as an unbreakable, unlimited power source. He said we are on God's time and one's life is a blink of an eye to God."

"Interesting," Bosman says. "Sounds similar to the email messages that have people in an uproar and something I've been told a Dr. Simon Northstrum has written on a blog."

"He loved Billy's picture, Dad. Billy told him that God was on top in the picture because He is God. But the father—Father Gabriel, to be exact—suggested God was all around and part of us all. He said you and Mom were parallel souls traveling together. He said she is still with you every day."

"He is correct about that," Bosman interjects. "No doubt."

"And he said Rich and I were perpendicular souls, and that we only intersected for a moment in our souls' stories."

"Sounds deep," Bosman says, pursing his lips. "Soul's story? What is that?"

"He said we are born with a story inside us and are judged by how we adhere to it. He said Rich was unwilling to move to a parallel position because of free will."

"This guy got pretty heavy with the kids."

"No, not the kids or the rest of the audience. He was talking with me while he viewed Billy's drawing. He spoke of faith, of our souls, and of Star Wars."

"Star Wars?"

"Yes. He said Luke had to believe in a force he could not see but had to learn to feel, much like we need to feel God and our own souls. Dad, he was so interesting … different. I came out feeling stronger somehow. He was the one who suggested we mail you the picture."

"He was right in doing that. He got it into Florence's hands, and she did the rest."

Cassie smiles, arises, and goes over to give her dad a hug. She tells him, "You need to treat Florence to a nice dinner for doing that, Dad. I know she would enjoy it." He shrugs and nods. It has gotten dark outside. Billy's car comes careening on two wheels into the room. Cassie looks at her father and says, "I guess he's got a pretty good handle on how to control it."

"I think so," Bosman replies.

♫

Days have passed since Lennon met Paul McCartney, and the work at the studio for Lennon has been more manual labor than musical. But he has had time to play his red guitar and work on Emma's song. Today he must go over the Beatles song he will play in the talent show. When Paul was here, he should have asked which would be best. On the other hand, confusion freezes his mind, with him wanting to play his song for Emma but fearing that if she

447

doesn't feel the same, he will look like a fool and upset her. If he takes the leap of faith, there is no going back. He has seen in other relationships that if both sides are not on the same page, then one or the other gets creeped out and the friendship ends. Lennon thinks that the worst thing that could happen would be for Emma to say, "I want to be friends." It is the kiss of death for a guy.

The Trojan computer is open in front of Simon, and he is on his blog. He responds as best he can to some comments, both the positive and negative, as advised by *Sojourner*. As he writes simple, new blogs about faith and selflessness, he wonders what Noah said to his neighbors. Was it something like, "Hey, everybody, I'm building a big boat that is this many cubits by this many cubits." Most would probably wonder what in the world a cubit was. There must have been major thigh-slapping and laughing. They probably asked him what he was drinking. Simon knows the Dominion will not wait for him as long as God waited for Noah to build that ark, and he also knows he won't live as long as Noah did.

Simon then thinks about how everything moves so much faster today. Truth and lies spread in an instant, and the internet and social media companies have little care for either. If we had a war, he wonders whose side these ruling electronic companies would be on, since they have more customers outside the United States than inside and would probably generate much more income outside. "Is there someone watching these companies?" he asks himself.

Simon rereads the Dominion's original emails that got the world so upset in the first place. He then rereads his messages, which put the biblical statements in his own words. He then looks at his messages about how everybody affects others. He writes more about the ripple effect—the ones of old plus those currently going on in contemporary society. He writes of individuals finding his or her own true journey.

Continuing to talk to himself, though inaudibly, he says, "Maybe the robot was correct. Free will is our self-inflicted hell, and we don't know it. We think it's our life, but it belongs to the Dominion." Simon now sits with the cursor blinking, unsure or fearful of what more to say. He does not want to bring more wrath on himself and his family. He asks, "Then again, do I want to make people mad, or do I make the Dominion mad?" He follows his gut and revisits the second part of the original email, since it had to be written by man and not carved in ancient tablets. He wonders how many other discoveries were delayed or halted throughout history.

He sees some sense in his thinking this way, asking himself, "In human history, has anyone ever been truly unselfish?" A discussion with *Sojourner* comes to mind. He mentioned that only one had completed his soul's story perfectly. Jesus stands above the other spiritual leaders. Was He one of the Dominion—or above them? He was, as it is written, born of a virgin mother. That is unusual, to say the least, and he ascended to heaven in a "beam me up Scottie" fashion. Simon suddenly looks upward, hoping no lightning bolt will fry him. He gets back to pondering Jesus and how the perfect selfless person lived, died for everyone who has the faith to believe in Him, was resurrected, and lives today in hearts and minds as a model to emulate.

Studying the model, Simon says to himself, "I suppose that to be selfless, a person must have the "fruit of the Spirit" mentioned in the Bible, which includes unconditional love, forgiveness, patience, and willingness to go the long haul with people, among other things. He touched and dined with outcasts that many religious leaders would not touch or dine with because they were absorbed with self-importance, position, and power." Simon now has a firm grasp of what he will continue to say in his blog.

His next post will be named "Maybe." He thinks as he writes again about the important word "selflessness." *Maybe the entire point of the original email mail is that we need to be selfless. Maybe we must understand we connect with one another for a reason. The interaction, however small, produces a ripple in us and in those we touch. In human history, have we ever knelt in unison in a unified prayer? I mean on our knees, hands clasped, at the same moment around the world.* Simon thinks of the many Facebook posts he has seen in which people are praying for this and that. *Is that action a prayer or just a feel-good reaction with no force behind it?*

Simon's thoughts and writing continue. *People may call me mad, but the email is telling us to connect with each other selflessly, soul-to-soul. Many of these tragedies might be averted if we were selfless, because at some point, someone noticed something that wasn't right and turned a selfish blind eye. This recalls the happening at Fatima in 1917. The image observed by three children asked us to pray for Russia. Did the world ever do it? Maybe not, because it took seventy years for the regime to decline. Imagine if the force of unified prayer had been all that was required to make it happen quicker.*

These three children who had such conviction were never promised happiness in this life by the image or being. Maybe the being was the Dominion teaching the children's souls. Maybe they've always been with us. It makes sense, what with the current deaths of selfish characters and the sightings of flashes of light. I don't know. Maybe people assumed seventy thousand people at Fatima who saw the sun dance in the sky were crazy. Are we all so crazy that people perish for no reason?

It cannot be chemical or germ warfare. The powerful, wealthy, poor, and criminal are gone. We look for culprits in this devastation and want to destroy the world to get to them. Maybe this is the miracle, ridding the world of the selfish ones. Maybe we should look at the helpers, the selfless, to discover if they are passing in high numbers. Get off your phones and computers and meet people. I was told you will be amazed at what you find if you let someone know you—a scary thought for sure. Look for the helpers and make a friend. They surround us and are the first ones there when calamity strikes. We will find security in each other, soul-to-soul. What do you think? Let me know. Am I crazy?

Do you think the second part of the email contains the real message of connecting—that everything happens for a reason? Our lives are a mirror, but we see just one side of that mirror. When we pass, we see each side and the meaning in our choices of human interaction. I guess we will find out that our free will is both our heaven and our hell. Maybe living is a school to teach us a selfless life. Won't we be surprised if, when we cross over, we find there is one great power or force for all? You may call it God, Jesus, Yahweh, Allah, or many other names. It will sit with you to judge how you did in your soul's story. Did you stick to the script in the story you developed with it before conception to learn and discover a selfless existence? I want to hear from you. Am I crazy?

As all these thoughts of Simon are committed to the blog and passed on to readers, Raph says, "Commander, Simon is on his blog."

The commander replies, "Yes I saw. He is leading, unafraid of the consequences. It took Noah longer, but we will move swiftly this time. The reclamation has begun, and the humans are turning on each other. They are afraid of the secrets they hide and the vulnerability of their electronic world. We will cull the people looking to gain from others' suffering. The electronics of this world will bring them home unless they annihilate themselves through fear. They will get the message, but many will fall before they understand. Simon will help them."

CHAPTER 28

"Good morning, folks. Welcome to another edition of *America's Newsroom*. I'm Bill Hemmer. Good Morning, Martha."

"Hello to you, Bill. I'm Martha MacCallum. What can we say, folks? The clock is ticking down. The world is on the brink of war against an unknown. We can't say we have good news for you this morning, but the latest update of deaths around the world stands at five million. The CDC is comparing this to the Spanish flu pandemic of 1918, which infected five hundred million people around the world and resulted in the deaths of fifty to one hundred million, equal to 3 to 5 percent of the world's population. That pandemic is one of the deadliest natural disasters in human history. The CDC has isolated no pathogens, biological agents, gas, or weapons to cause the deaths. There is no rhyme or reason the deaths of these healthy people. We have been hard at work to get an interview with the man at the center of the computer hacking. Dr. Simon Northstrum and his attorney, Earl Connery Hardin, join us today. Take it from here, Bill."

Bills asks, "Dr. Northstrum, the world wants to know, and I must ask. Did you do it? Did you break into the world's electronics?" Simon looks to Hardin, who responds to the question.

"My client cannot speak about ongoing investigations or litigation."

But Simon does speak up. "Bill, Martha, thank you for having us. I in no way had anything to do with the hacking and the electronic misfeasance taking place. I talk with robots on Mars, period, and I do not have the time or the sophistication to compromise the world's electronics."

Martha joins in. "Mr. Hardin, you are an accomplished attorney, so I ask you, what charges are facing your client?"

"Martha, you can fill a few legal pads with charges the government and foreign powers want to hang on Simon. I recommend he not travel outside the United States, since other countries are not so gracious as America and would execute him on the spot. He has been put on leave from JPL, investigated, and temporarily imprisoned by the FBI, accompanied by the NSA, who both have found nothing to implicate him. They have examined none of the powerful corporations who have much more brain power to apply to this. Simon is one guy."

"You mean companies like Apple, Microsoft, Google, and Facebook?"

"Exactly. Neither the FBI nor NSA has raided them to search for bad operators. Who is watching them? They employ thousands of programmers yearly, and we're to assume they are all good apples. Excuse the pun. A tactic they might employ is to create a problem, then sell the solution to billions of people for twenty bucks a month. And then you have the first tech trillionaire. Who is to say a silicon chip with a microscopic switch on it is not letting the world into your electronics? Somebody or some entity is hanging all of this on Simon."

Bill says, "You mean my cell phone could have a switch in it to record everything?"

Simon jumps back in. "Why not? Programmers are people who will do anything for money, and we go smiling to the executioner. They already write software to keep you coming back. They've created intentional addiction."

Martha looks at her phone and shuts it off. She then says, "Our sources tell us this started when you activated a new program called Reliance. What is this program?"

"I wrote the program before they let me go from JPL the first time, when funding for the Mars rovers was cut. It is an ultrasophisticated software designed especially to communicate with the Mars rovers. It could have been run by many people at JPL after I left."

"We hear it now has reconnected with the rovers, which have regained power that was lost when you left … the first time."

"Yes. And, Martha, I want to assure people my software communicates with rovers on Mars, not with people worldwide."

Hardin breaks in. "The FBI are the individuals responsible for infecting government computers, not Simon. They put Reliance on their supercomputer Bertha. The world is on the brink because, thanks to the FBI, a genius has discovered a way into our electronics. People and countries are afraid an entity can pull back the curtain and break the anonymity of computer connections. This Dominion, be it an individual, a group or a country, has access to our secrets, truths, and lies. I know this, because as an attorney I harbor many secrets about the powerful, and this is the reason they leave me alone and I can talk as I'm talking now."

"Mr. Hardin, would a government have the capability to be the Dominion?" Bill asks.

"Well, both governments and cyber companies have the resources. Mankind has always employed the latest technology as a weapon. Cyber is it today. It was predicted years ago that the next big war would be a cyber war."

Martha asks Simon, "Dr. Northstrum, what do you make of the pandemic and the people dying? Is your software being used by a government to kill people? Do you think a government is now the judge, jury, and executioner?"

Simon responds, "Repeating what I said previously, I hear the urban legends that cell phones scan your soul, but my software can only speak to the Martian robots. It is not related to people passing away. I have looked at my phone every day since this began, and I'm still here, and so are my friends and family. I see that you, Martha, and Bill and Attorney Hardin, along with your camera crew, are here, still alive. Bottom line, the government took my program to analyze it. I do not know the different parties who now have access to it. I've not been asked to reprogram it to work on other projects, but I'm sure a good programmer could do it."

Bill asks Simon, "Are you concerned about the emails and messages?"

"Bill, people are enraged by an email telling us to get along, to do unto others as we would have done unto us, for people to share unconditional love and quit being so selfish. It dumbfounds me why anyone or any government would be resolved on creating a weapon to turn off the power creating such a message."

Martha now says to Simon, "We understand you write what has become a well-read blog. What do you believe will happen when the clock strikes zero?"

"My blog simply emphasizes that I am hoping people take the email messages to heart and try to get along and live altruistically. If we show good faith and honesty, it might stop the clock. Some call me crazy when responding to the blog, and some government people also believe me to be either a nut job or a crook. Yet, as I keep saying, it was through the FBI's intervention that the real problem started."

Still probing, Martha tells Simon, "We have had many who say aliens are here and hate us, causing these many deaths. Others are saying we are in the final days and that the rapture is near because of sinfulness."

Simon gets an odd look on his face, growing rather pale under the hot lights of the studio.

Bill breaks in, "Did we strike a nerve, doctor?"

Simon says, "You can't beat the message. But getting on the offensive against others seems more important to many, rather than listening to the message. A young man who came into my church's Bible study told me that the world is infected with self and that our electronic communication exacerbates it. I've no idea what will happen when the countdown ends. It makes no rational sense for one country to start a war throwing around atomic weapons. Everyone would die. It is crazy, so our leaders, who are full of love, knowledge, and wisdom had better prevail, but those are in short supply."

"Back to your blog," Martha says to Simon. "As we have been

talking, our research team has informed us that your blog, which speaks to living a selfless life, is making you one of the most followed bloggers online."

Simon replies, "Well, the blog simply says what I have been saying to you today. It speaks of doing unto others what you would have done unto you. It's repeating in my own words what the email messages have said before. Pertaining to the blog followers, there are those who love the message and are looking for reassurance. I try to be a helper for them. And then there's the group who wants to curse me out or crucify me. Others are somewhere in middle of those two, just watching and waiting."

Bill asks Simon, "A common theme on the blog is listening. To whom or what are we listening?"

"In my view, the Dominion are telling us to have faith in our souls' stories created before birth. When you pass, you sit with your teachers and review your life story and how close you came to completing it."

"If you are rotten, then you are sent to Hades?" asks Martha.

"Well, a priest told me our free will choices can be our undoing if we get derailed from the paths of our stories. Derailing occurs when we are selfish in various ways. As he stated, free will is a double-edged blade. No matter the deity or faith, you will sit and review the lessons you failed in your lifetimes."

Bill asks, "Are you talking about reincarnation?"

"Reincarnation? I don't know. They tell me time is a human construct. The past, present, and future are one. One person's soul journey can take place as a king in some realm, and maybe that of a pauper in another. Since the email messages, I've had to do much soul-searching myself. If this is aliens, God, governments, or a super smart dude, I am clueless. But I have seen on your program and others that more people are talking face-to-face and are congregating without riot or protest."

"Yes," Bill responds. "Everything is unusual. Our producers tell us many more are showing up in churches, restaurants, and other gathering places."

"So," Simon tells him, "more and more are taking the message to heart."

Martha presses her finger to her earpiece and then says, "Our producer wants me to ask you what you make of the last parts of the messages—the names and the dates?"

"Well," Simon answers, "the dates that appear to be incorrect may be correct. For example, maybe a person with whom you interact may be on the path to cure cancer. But you may selfishly say or do something that knocks him or her off that path. So the cure for cancer, rather than coming in two years, may be delayed for another twenty years or more. That could have happened with the discovery of penicillin, electric lights, or anything else."

"Heavy," Bill utters, "very heavy."

"Yes," Simon replies. "The Dominion says that the universe records every word and action, no matter how insignificant. Everything makes a ripple that affects others. Our free will enables us to choose the ripple to be positive or negative. A friend used Hitler as an example. He was not born evil but became that way through human interaction and selfishness." Simon pauses and then says to Martha, "I understand you meditate."

"Yes," she replies, "it helps clear my mind."

"Sort of being still and listening to your soul?" Simon asks.

"I never thought of it that way. I think of it more as just getting organized and mindful each morning."

Simon nods. "After talking with my friend, my understanding is that the messages want us to connect with our souls, and connect person-to-person with others who have connected with their souls."

"Doctor," Bill asks, "what do you make of the bad guys killed in recent weeks? The grapevine has it that your Reliance software has been involved in these deaths and in the attacks on the terrorists."

With a little chuckle, Simon says, "Remember what I told you? All of this began after the FBI put my Reliance program on their supercomputer."

Changing the subject, Martha says, "We hear from viewers that God is now answering prayers the way true, honest, sincere people ask for them. We had a tweet from a viewer stating that this is the reverse of 'Only the good die young.'"

"That's in the Creator's ballpark, not mine," Simon responds.

"Okay, Bill says. "Before we let you get out of here, Dr. Northstrum, we've got to ask you about the footprint on Mars. Everyone here has viewed it with interest."

"Yes," Martha interjects, "and we hear some people have accused JPL of hiding the discovery of a race on Mars called the Dominion, the very organization we've been receiving messages from and talking about today."

"Ah, yes, Martha," Simon replies. "The footprint. I have been swamped with questions about this. First of all, anything is possible. And let me just say for the conspiracy theorists, the image has not been edited in Photoshop or doctored in any way. This has already been proven by outside specialists. And, of course, real robots sent by JPL exist on Mars, and from these we get real pictures."

Simon lets this soak in and then says, "JPL continues to examine the image, and some experts believe the footprint is a rock formation. There are images of formations looking like people standing, a woman, and heads peeking out of caves. We used to think there were canals on Mars, but we got smarter and gained the ability to look closer. We have found no life called the Dominion, no bacteria, no microbes, and no Marvin the Martian. JPL wishes we had, since it would help funding tremendously."

Getting back on message, Simon says, "But the bottom line of why I am here today is to say our society's tech companies have developed an interconnectivity through electronics, which has greatly eliminated person-to-person, face-to-face contact. Electronics will someday come crashing down, because if man made it, man can break it. Someone is always smarter or more nefarious, as you can see with hacking daily. I am at times ashamed to be a programmer, since many of us have gone to the dark side for money."

Bill takes it from there with "Folks, we will be right back after the break."

⚿

The commander's lens reads the message sent: "Simon has taken another jump in faith."

"I see," he responds.

⚿

The halls of the school are bare, except for Jennifer clearing out the contents of her locker into a box and a backpack. She is going away after losing her father, the mayor. Emma steps out of the principal's office and sees Jennifer for the first time since the tragedy.

"Jennifer," Emma says, "I am so sorry."

Jennifer looks at her and says, "Thank you, Emma. Thank you for many things."

"Are you okay?" Emma asks. "Is there anything I can do to help?"

"I'm doing all right," she replies, halting her packing and rising from a kneeling position. "Under the circumstances, I think I'm doing about as well as can be expected."

"How is your mom, Jennifer?"

"She's doing fine. Mom and I are going away for a while to be with family. I told Magdala I could not be an intern anymore. She understood and said a spot is open when I return." Jennifer smiles for the first time and says, "And here I thought she wanted to get rid of me."

Emma says, "She is kind and understanding. And very intelligent."

Jennifer closes her empty locker. "Bye, Emma," she says. I hope the fashion show goes well; you will do great. I wish I could be there, but my mom needs me."

"Oh, yes," Emma affirms. "It is much more important than any show." Jennifer initiates a hug, which surprises but pleases Emma,

"I'll see you when you get back," Emma tells her. She helps Jennifer with her backpack and box.

Jennifer turns, and Emma watches her walk away. A short distance from the door, however, she stops and turns back to Emma. "Emma, can I talk with you?"

Emma closes the distance between them. "Sure, what is it?"

Jennifer looks into Emma's eyes. Tearfully, she says, "You don't owe me anything, and I have been really mean to you. You know my family's secret. My father is gone, and I am struggling. He was my father, and I should be sad, but right now I'm relieved. What is wrong with me? He gave me everything, and I am emotionless."

"He failed to give you unconditional love, Jennifer, like in the email messages we all read. Not only that; he abused you and your mom physically and mentally."

"Mom has not shed a tear, but she took much of the abuse for me. She is also relieved he's gone."

"I'm so sorry, Jennifer. But neither you nor your mom is to blame at all. Really, I'm amazed you could live and survive under such conditions that he put you through."

"Emma, I understand that many in school despise me, and I deserve it. Most of my so-called friends have just been hangers-on because of my father being mayor. When I get back, I will be friendless. I was wondering, and it's okay to say no, but would you keep my family secret between us? Also, and this is big, would you be my friend when I get back?"

Emma hands Jennifer a tissue; both girls are now tearful. "Jennifer, I will not repeat anything about what I saw. I promise you that. As for being your friend, you are right; you have treated everybody as second class. But now only I understand where you've been coming from. And I've learned from Maggie that in order to grow as a person, I must learn forgiveness. That's the unconditional love I mentioned earlier." Emma pauses. "But, you know, Jennifer, it will certainly make things smoother if you say you're sorry and ask for forgiveness. Real, all-around forgiveness involves a two-way street.

The offender shows true repentance from the soul, and the forgiver shows true forgiveness, not just saying the words."

Without hesitation, Jennifer says, "I am sorry. Truly I am. Will you forgive me?" She dabs her eyes and says, "I've never had a true friend, Emma."

"On one condition will I forgive you, Jennifer."

"What is it?"

"I wish to be friends with this Jennifer—the one with her defenses crumbled. No put-ons, no secrets."

"I'd like that, Emma." She stretches and hugs Emma again. Emma embraces her and then advises her to go heal, telling her the two of them will start afresh upon her return. Jennifer walks on toward the exit, turning back once more to wave and say, "Bye, Emma." She walks away with a new confidence, because the exchange of true forgiveness is a dynamic thing.

Emma turns and makes her way back to the next class as the bell rings at the class change. A herd of students bursts from the rooms, and the once vacant hall fills with bodies moving in different directions. A scream of "Emma! Emma!" rings out over the commotion. Emma looks around to see Sophia charging to her.

"You won't believe it! You won't believe it!" She catches up, out of breath from running. She takes a deep breath.

"What won't I believe, Sophia?"

"Bobby Fuller asked me out."

"Oh, Sophia! I'm so happy for you." Both girls jump straight up and down as Lennon appears. Jestingly, he joins the jumping ritual.

"It's a girl thing," Emma tells Lennon as she swats him. "Bobby Fuller asked Sophia out on a date."

"You go, girl," Lennon says. "Good for you—and for Bobby."

And then Emma, noticing something about Sophia, says, "You really look nice today, Sophia."

"That's my other news, Emma. Magdala called my home and invited me to be a Swaddling intern with you." The girls jump again. Lennon refrains from this round of jumping. Sophia says, "I got my first clothes today," as she spins around.

"Wow!" Emma says.

"Yeah," Sophia tells her, "and I learned Swaddling is inviting other students to take part in the fashion show. It's wonderful; the never-chosen students got picked, like Sally, who has a leg brace."

"Really?" Emma says. "She is nice. I've always liked her."

"How many are going to be in the show?" Lennon asks Sophia.

"I don't know, but with the boys being in the talent show, they needed others for the fashion show."

Simon again sits in a sterile room in a top-secret federal military prison. This time it's the NSA, under direct instructions from General Bosman, that has whisked him away. Surveillance cameras record his every move, but Simon is motionless, his arms shackled to the stainless steel table. He is here because the government has no one else to blame for the hacking that has brought the world to the brink of Armageddon as *Sojourner* predicted. So they came for him again. He has pleaded to speak with General Bosman to change his mind. Bosman wants to strike first to avoid complete destruction, believing that if America strikes first, the country can be better prepared and inflict more damage on the enemy, even though Bosman does not understand who needs to be destroyed first. Simon now sits upright, tapping his fingernails against the cold steel.

The door to the room opens, and General Bosman himself enters, wearing a shirt and tie, no jacket. He orders the guard to remove Simon's restraints and demands water. The door clinks shut. Bosman places a computer on the table.

"Are you familiar with this machine?" Bosman asks.

"Yes. It's the one I use for my blog and Bible study."

"You did not disclose it to the FBI during its investigation."

"I can't disclose an item I didn't own when asked."

"You were under investigation for cybercrime, and you bought a new computer."

"I didn't buy it. One of your investigators gave it to me. I assumed you knew, since he works for you. Michael Cott is his name. I also assumed it was a Trojan horse of a machine."

"How so?"

"I get a spiffy new computer from a computer hacker working for the government. I am sure it is jam-packed with tracking stuff I can't even imagine."

"We didn't approve his giving it to you."

"Maybe someone has gone off the reservation or works without your knowledge." There's a pause. Simon's look grows stern as he says, "Let's cut to the chase here, General Bosman, You accuse me of espionage and hacking. They drag me from my home again, traumatizing my family. My daughter is subject to derogatory remarks about me daily. They compare me to the antichrist in the news. All because of a simple email I had no part in. And you have no proof. I am held in an unknown prison without due process. "Is that about right, General Bosman?"

"Northstrum, at this point I don't care about your rights or your family. You and I have no rights at this moment. I must care for all families. You're correct we have no concrete proof you did anything. It serves no purpose to convict you, because in a few minutes I must advise the president to destroy most of the world. I was hoping to appeal to your humanity and confess to something to defuse the situation."

"Do you believe the world will accept a scapegoat you put up coming from the United States? What about the other countries that hate each other? Do they also have scapegoats? It seems everyone would need one, because anyone is capable." Bosman frowns. Simon continues. "I am speaking to you as a husband and father. I had nothing to do with this problem. Have you been reading my blogs?"

"No, but others check them."

"I'm sure they do. What did those who read my blogs for you tell you?"

"That it is a bunch of mumbo jumbo on faith and loving each other. They found Reliance on the machine."

"Yes, I wrote the program and kept a copy for my protection.

They found nothing out of the ordinary in Reliance, and no message left the computer."

"Correct," says Bosman.

"Do you have faith, General?"

"I used to, but I am losing it."

"Well, General, you had better grab hold of it and not let it get away from you. I am trying to get the world to listen. In the world today, everyone is talking, and the volume keeps getting louder as we talk over each other. Then it becomes a shouting match, and the message is lost. The email is a good example."

"How so?" Bosman asks.

"Everyone screams about his or her violated security, so everyone misses the important part of the message," says Simon.

"What part?"

"The part about loving each other," Simon tells him. "We hear it in church, yet we continue to hate."

"They tell me you now have two billion subscribers to your blog. Is this true?"

"Yes. It took off, and I don't know how. I suppose people feel powerless and are looking for words of hope."

"You mean like 'Be Not Afraid'?" says Bosman. "They told me about that."

"I can't take the credit, General. I believe an angel coined it. But I think he'd be okay with the rip-off if it's helping people."

"Our guys review it every day. Nothing but mumbo jumbo to them."

"Have they said anything about the last part of the messages from the Domain I post on the blogs?"

"Yes. They say some names and dates are wrong."

"Maybe they are not wrong, General. Maybe they are telling us that our actions are wrong. What if the date pertaining to penicillin was correct? Someone else might have discovered it years before, but the person died or never pursued medicine because of another's selfish act. The act may have caused a ripple, changing the course of things. Maybe the email is telling us to look within ourselves and our journeys and to realize every word, thought, and act have outcomes beyond ourselves. The ripple continues through time."

"My people are right, Northstrum. You're crazy. I'm supposed to tell the president your crazy speech. I'll be sitting right next to you here if I do."

"Bosman, has anything been lost, stolen, or broken?"

"No."

"So go destroy the world for nothing? It would be a huge ripple. That's your choice, General. Go destroy the world or save it. The ripple is your free will. A wise man told me free will is our perdition."

"If I open the computer, what will I find?" asks Bosman.

"I don't know what's been added since they confiscated it from my home. It has been in your hands. Who else has opened it?"

"No one. I received it with the security tape in place."

"Fire it up. I don't even have a password on the machine. Seemed useless with the hacking issue," says Simon.

Bosman opens a pocketknife and cuts the tape. A faint violet spark jumps unnoticed from the knife into the machine. The computer loads up, and the Windows icon appears, soon replaced by a rotating theme of beautiful images supplied by Microsoft.

"What should I look for, Northstrum?"

"I don't know. It's a blank machine except for blog texts and Bible study notes. As I told you, I blog and do Bible study with it. Your people might have added stuff. Who can you trust in the cyberworld?"

Bosman taps the computer, unsure of how to go ahead. He then glares at Simon and barks, "What the heck is this?" His tone startles Simon. Bosman then spins the computer screen toward Simon.

"I don't understand," Simon says. "It's a child's drawing, and I don't have children that age."

"Where did you get this image?" Bosman asks in a hyper-sounding voice.

"This drawing?"

"Yes, Northstrum. This drawing!"

"I suppose it came with the machine and the themes. I don't mess with that stuff. Why such a huff? Is it important?"

"It's a paper drawing my grandson drew for me, and the only copy of it hangs over the mantel at my home."

"General … I've never met your grandson, didn't know you had one, and have never been in your home. You have had this computer locked up. I am clueless."

Neither one says anything for a few moments, and then Simon breaks the silence with "General, don't you think now that maybe something wonderful is happening and it's not a catastrophe? Maybe something higher and bigger than us? Look around you, General. It might be our last days alive, yet people are together like never before, reaching out to each other and discovering the humanity of one another. Maybe the ordinary, everyday people of the world, especially those without much or with nothing, have already discovered the true meaning in the email message. General, maybe you need to catch up."

Bosman jumps from his seat and opens the door in full stride. He orders the guard to release and drop the charges against Simon and get him home. "And," he tells the guard, "get that ankle bracelet off him!" As he runs, he presses his phone to his ear, eventually saying, "This is General Bosman. Get me the president, now!"

The commander's cornea reads, "Simon has succeeded."

CHAPTER 29

"Good morning, folks. This is Bill Hemmer, and this is a Fox News alert. Martha, what do you have for us today?"

"Good morning, Bill, and to everyone, I'm Martha MacCallum, and you are now seeing on the split screen the Oval Office, where we are told the president will address the world. The president will speak of the world being nearly at war and the measures he has taken to keep us safe. We have a Fox contributor with us, General Jerrell Pope."

She turns and says, "General Pope, what will we hear today?"

"Martha, we are expecting the president will declare war."

"General, some people seem to have peace, while other people are afraid, with things seeming to be spiraling out of control. Some are ransacking grocery stores, sucking gas stations dry. Up north, heating oil is hard to find."

"Yes, Martha. We have a mixed barrel. While some do seem rather tranquil, many are stripping gun stores bare, and seed stores are targets."

"Seed stores?"

"Yes. If things get worse, then you must grow food at some point."

"What would an act of war mean, General Pope?"

"It means we can get our military moving quickly. It means we can attack. Military enrollment centers are jammed to a point not seen since Pearl Harbor."

"General, with everything going on around the world and the threats being hurled at each other, I don't understand. Who do we attack? In other wars, there was a defined enemy, the Germans, Japanese. Today, everyonc is a suspect."

"True, Martha. I suspect the military will go after the entity that has most often crossed the line."

"Go after in what way? Are we talking about nuclear war? World War III?"

The general responds, "What other options do we have? I suspect diplomacy doesn't work, and each country has no faith in the others."

"It is interesting, General. This started with an email asking people to get along, and we now stand at the brink of a horrific war—an end to the world as we know it. What will it look like, General, after everyone hits each other?"

"I imagine the world will resemble scenes from apocalypse movies. Not a pretty sight."

"Can this be avoided, General?"

"We are at the highest DEFCON level. Cooler heads can prevail if the right people listen to one another."

"Interesting, General," Martha tells him. "We keep going back to the emails about listening."

"Yeah, I guess," the general responds.

Bill cuts in with "We are being told President Matherson is ready to speak. We will take you now to the Oval Office."

"My fellow Americans, and the good people of the world, we all will acknowledge the world is in turmoil. This started with an email sent from something or someone called the Dominion. I want to assure the world, its people, and their leaders the United States of America had nothing to do with the transmission. We've used every means at our disposal to find the perpetrators and have been unsuccessful so far. America and all other countries received the same email."

The president pauses to let those words sink in. He then continues: "The messages have circumvented the most sophisticated security in each country. Country leaders have come to not believe one another. Therefore, we are all pointing our weapons at each other. Our country is at the highest alert level since the Cold War. The Dominion have set governments' doomsday clocks at one minute to midnight. This is the closest it has ever been to midnight. I will today ask Congress to declare war on every nuclear power."

The president pauses and bows his head as if in prayer. He raises both his palms and rubs his face. He refocuses on the camera. "People of America and every country in the world, what I have said so far and communicated to you, my advisers and speech specialists wrote for me, and it is scrolling from a teleprompter. I want to speak to you now as a human, a man, a husband and father. This is unscripted. It is true that in one command I can destroy the world. And other countries can do the same. A trusted adviser told me we own nothing and we leave this earth naked. I have declared war on the world, but I command our military to stand down."

He pauses before continuing. "I will clarify myself. We are at war and will defend ourselves, but I command our military to stand down. I will not be the man who destroyed the world because of unfounded mistrust. I ask other world leaders to do the same. There will be no winners if we attack. I am a man of faith and will take the advice of the email messages we all received. Let us get along as humans. No harm has come from the breaches. Only the harm people have done to each other is evident. When I finish this speech, I will gather my family and bring them close. Then I will talk to my staff and listen, discovering what is going on in their lives."

It is evident the president's eyes are moist, but his voice is strong as he goes on. "A wise man told me recently the emails were a warning for us to connect honestly with one another. I suggest we take the advice. Put your electronics away and walk outside, sit on your porches or in your yards, and discover your new neighbors and friends. It connects us in a human bond. There are forces out there who may want to use this opportunity to seek power and control. But if we go to war, you will have control only over a wasteland. I realize many of you will consider my actions as weak or traitorous. I believe with all my soul we will wake in the morning to a world not smoldering. If this is my last act as president, I commission every human throughout the world to understand his or her neighbor, as the email asked. Maybe then we will learn to listen without speaking. God bless America, and God bless the peaceful people around the world who want to live in harmony."

The president's transmission ends, and the network discussion returns.

Bill Hemmer begins, "Well, what can I say? This is unprecedented. General Pope, as a military man, what do you make of what the President did?"

"I am dumbfounded. In my mind, he surrendered our country."

Bills responds, "He declared war but asked the military to stand down. What now? What will the military leaders do? Are they beating their war drums?"

"The military does not want to go to war, but they want to protect our country."

"We still have no defined enemy," Martha says, "and the president didn't cite one. Is it true that striking first or second is irrelevant?"

"Probably, but if you strike first, you have the element of surprise."

Bill tells the general, "It does not seem there will be any surprises when the rockets launch."

General Pope replies, "Bill, Martha, this man is the biggest fool or the greatest of poker players."

"So is he bluffing?" asks Bill.

"If he is, he is doing it with our lives," Pope replies.

"General," Martha asks, "with due respect, do we want to start a horrible war over an email?"

Bill jumps in with "I don't want to go there. Folks, hopefully we will be right back."

✴

Joseph, Gabe, and Raph make their way to the civic center for the Halloween trunk or treat talent and fashion event tonight. They smile at the abundant ghosts, goblins, superheroes, and princesses surrounding them on their walk. The youngsters can't wait to get inside to the sugar overload. They hear the children telling their parents to hurry, which is usually the other way around. What they don't realize is that inside the doors is not only candy but also amusements and rides provided by Swaddling to put a smile on everyone's face. Inside the arena are the local vendors from various businesses, their booths stocked with goodies.

Booth owners dress as goblins and ghouls to entertain the kids. The trio walk through the civic center. Raph alerts Joseph to a young lad who is crying and is wearing an unusual costume. A smile captures Joseph's face as he looks at the boy, who is dressed in a tunic like those worn in Jesus's time. Over his shoulder is a cross made of brown pool noodles. Joseph makes his way to the boy. The mother sees Joseph approaching and apologizes to him. "I'm so sorry" she says. "I tried to convince Tommy to be Iron Man, but he insisted. We have gotten the ugliest looks and comments."

Joseph looks up at the woman and gently grabs the boy's shoulder. "Nonsense, young lady," Joseph softly tells the mother. "One should never be ashamed to imitate or walk in the shoes of the most selfless man. Most people carry their crosses only when it's in their best interest." He tells Tommy, "Your outfit is wonderful—the best one here. I am sure Jesus in heaven has a smile right now that could light the universe."

Tommy smiles and says, "See, Mom. This man understands."

Joseph says to the mother, "Tommy has a strong soul. I have it on the highest authority."

The mother tells Joseph, "Tommy is afraid to go up to the booths for candy because of the remarks."

Looking at the boy, Joseph says, "Mr. Raph has something to help you."

Raph kneels next to Tommy and says, "Hi, I'm Raph. Everything is okay. You will be fine." Tears roll down Tommy's face.

His mother tells Raph, "It was all I could do to get him this close to a booth again. He was scared away the first time and won't go any farther now."

"I see," says Raph. He then tells Tommy, "I admire your costume. Imitation is the highest form of flattery." Tommy wipes his cheeks as he listens to Raph, who asks, "Do you realize Jesus was the original Iron Man, and Hc had something special you need?"

"No sir," says Tommy. "What did he have?"

Raph tells him, "He had courage when he was verbally attacked and intimidated by others." He then asks, "Have you seen *The Wizard of Oz*?" Tommy nods. "Remember the lion who was nervous and had no courage?"

Tommy again nods, and then he says, "But he got courage later on."

"Right!" Raph replies. He then reaches into his jacket pocket and pulls out a small brown bag. He holds it out toward Tommy and says, "I have something here that will help you. Look into the bag and you will see."

Tommy glances up at his mom; she nods that it's all right. He spreads the bag's opening, looks into it, and says, "Red jellybeans?"

With a chuckle, Raph says, "They do look like jellybeans, don't they? But these are courage beans. When you are afraid, take one of these to ease your fear. It will work. And by the time all of them are gone, you will have enough courage in you to last a lifetime."

Raph exchanges glances and smiles with Tommy's mother. He then says, "Let me make sure they are fresh." He takes a red bean from the bag, sticks out his tongue, pulls it back in, and chews. "Oh, yeah!" he says, "Very fresh!" He then takes another from the bag and says to Tommy, "Here, let me help you with the first one."

Tommy looks at his mother again. She says, "Go ahead Tommy, stick out your tongue. I believe you can trust Raph."

Tommy opens his mouth, Raph places a red bean on his tongue, and a red spark flashes for an instant, unnoticed. The boy chews and then says, "Delicious, Raph!"

Raph stands up, hands Tommy's mom the bag of beans, reaches out his hand to Tommy, and says, "Come on; let's try out the beans together," as he steers the boy to the closest booth. Once there, Raph asks him, "What do you say?"

The boy initially splutters, and he then blurts out, "Trick or treat!" with a powerful, excited voice. A glow radiates from Tommy's face as he gestures to his mom. "Come on; I need more candy!"

While being pulled by her son, the young mother says quietly to Raph, "Courage." Holding tightly to the bag of beans, she then says, "Thank you. It's a miracle."

The Commander's lens reads, "Yes a miracle. If she only knew."

Gabe and Raph mingle among the various booths as Joseph makes his way into the staging area where the talent and fashion show will happen. Magdala stands on the catwalk jutting into the audience. Joseph touches her on the shoulder. He asks, "Is everything coming together with the new interns?"

"Yes, Joseph. They are so energetic."

"How is Emma doing?"

"She is a little mother helping the younger ones, and so selfless. She is showing the new ones the ropes."

"What is up with the musicians?"

"Lennon is on the fence on what to play. He might go safe and play a Beatles song."

"Maggie, he will surprise us tonight."

"Greg is disgruntled because Lennon will not play in their band. Joseph, they are terrible. I wish I could suggest a career change."

"Mr. Greg will decide it on his own tonight." Magdala looks at Joseph questioningly, wondering exactly what he means.

The auditorium fills with families of the participants, sellers from the booths, and interested community members. It is a packed house. Sophia, who follows Emma like a puppy dog, says, "Emma, "I'm so nervous."

"You'll do fine," Emma assures her. "You look beautiful."

"Bobby said he was coming to the show."

"Super," Emma responds.

Sophia tells her, "My mom, who works in the checkout at the supermarket has invited people to come."

"Now don't go getting a big head on me, Sophia."

"As scared as I am? No way! It's just that being Hispanic, we invite everyone to the fiesta." Sophia pauses and then says, "Emma, do you think Lennon will ever ask you out on a date? You know, a romantic date?"

Emma slightly shakes her head and sighs. "I don't know, Sophia. I keep hoping, but I might have to hit him with a stick to wake him. He's shy."

Magdala slips in behind them and says they both are stunning in their outfits. Sophia asks, "Where did Jennifer go?"

Magdala responds, "She went with her mom to be with her family and get some healing time." She is about to say something to the girls when a movement distracts her. "This is unexpected," she says to them.

The girls turn and see that Jennifer is crossing the stage. She says hi, and Emma asks, "I thought you left to be with your mom?"

"Yes," she responds, "She is with her brothers and sisters. I was moping, and she suggested I come and help with the show. I didn't want to let the team down." Maggie's face brightens. Jennifer asks, "I know I have missed some things, but may I still take part?"

"It is up to the other interns," Maggie says. She calls them together. Jennifer stands alone, surrounded by those she tormented. She realizes her chances are slim. This is their time to seek revenge. A voice comes from behind the group. They turn and see a slight dark-haired girl sitting in a wheelchair. "Jennifer, I have been the brunt of your hurtful barbs, as others have. The cuts you inflicted on us will heal as we mature and grow. The scars will remain, but maybe they will stay as a lesson for us to learn. Maybe everything happening in the world with emails and such is about being benevolent. And just maybe this intern gig is not about clothes at all but about giving selflessly to others. I'm sorry you lost your father, but you can only have our forgiveness and inclusion if you are sorry for the past. There is nothing in the past we can change, so we can't go back and start over. We can have a new beginning. Do you want to be an unselfish friend?"

With tears streaming from her face, she nods. "Yes, oh please."

The interns surround her in a group hug.

Magdala's lens reads, "Isn't it wonderful when they claw their way to the truth and reach their souls."

The Commander's lens reads, "If only the humans could see the intersection of true contrition and forgiveness and how the soul develops and grows. It is one of the hardest lessons in a lifetime."

Maggie breaks in. "You'd better get in position. Jennifer, your clothes are in the dressing room. You can follow Sophia on the runway." Jennifer beams and scurries to get ready. "You will do great tonight, Sophia. Just be yourself."

"Yeah, that is what Emma said."

Maggie asks Emma, "Is everyone excited and ready?"

"Oh, yes. Of course they are nervous, but yeah, everyone's ready."

Simon and Alexis have enjoyed looking at all the costumed kids and visiting some of the booths. Alexis is feeling quite a bit younger herself now that things have been cleared up and Simon is back at JPL, even receiving a large bonus, compliments of General Bosman, which has allowed her to depart the Sable Funeral Parlor.

They have now moved on into the civic center auditorium and found good center seats on row eight. Lennon's father, Mark Thomas, finds a seat on the end of the same row. He nods a hello to the Northstrums. It surprises them he is at the show, since he's been absent in Lennon's life for a while. They also notice he looks very nice—and very sober.

Macy and Oz have planted themselves a couple of rows in front of the Northstrums, wanting to hear and see everything up close and personal. With them are the studio musicians with whom Lennon played.

The lights in the room dim, and the stage spotlights come on as Father Irwin comes on stage. The audience quiets as he begins speaking. "Hello, folks, thank you for coming out tonight. Wow! A few weeks ago, we had a small show prepared to present within our church. Here we are now, with the civic center jammed with representatives from the whole community. I want to thank the Swaddling Clothes people for their partnership, inclusion, and guidance." There is hustle and bustle behind the curtains, and the participants are excited.

Father Irwin continues. "We need a reason to breathe with the events in the world. Many believed our world would end, but we of all faiths are here. It amazes me that a few days ago governments wished to destroy one another because an email said to love each other. The true message of the email was about selflessness—how everything in our lives affects other people in ways unknown to us but known to the Creator. I can't tell you what to believe and whether or not this Dominion group are government hackers, aliens, angels, or God. All I know is that they have given us the wonderful gift of insight, to look at ourselves."

Father Irwin is impressed with the rapt attention of the audience. He says, "This hard glimpse brought us near annihilation. We have a hero among us who doesn't consider himself one. His wonderful blogs on faith helped change the mind of our president, world leaders, and people throughout the world. Instead of people destroying communities, burning our neighborhoods, and going to anarchy, they've connected with each other. Churches have filled, gathering places have been packed, and people have been talking without fear of judgment. Of course, all of this might have been out of fear itself."

Joseph, Gabe and Raph, seated at the end of a last row, look at one another and smile as Father Irwin continues. "I sensed people realized that if this was the final war, there would be no winners, since we had no villains. We were all in the same boat. Our status—famous or unknown; wealthy, middle class, or struggling—was of no importance to the Dominion. If my time were to end today, I'd wish to be with a loved one, a neighbor, or a friend. I've never seen on a tombstone the words, 'I wish I'd sent one more text.' You hear stories of an afterlife and loved ones there to greet you. I have never heard of a laptop, cell phone, or computer in the white light of passing. The Dominion asserted you must be benevolent, and this man here tonight, the blogger, discovered the message through the shouting and blame going on in the world. I consider him another Noah, leading us to the safety of an ark."

The Swaddling Clothes trio in the audience give each other looks, understanding the priest has received the intended message. Father Irwin goes on to say, "The ark this time is each other and the discovery of humans we pass each day. One man was the first to receive and distribute this message through his blogging. I'd like to meet the billions he has reached and discover their wonderfulness. Folks, Dr. Simon Northstrum has put us on the right path, using blogging technology. Maybe now we will all use limited technology in a selfless way to discover one another, instead of using it as a brag sheet or for drama or deceitfulness."

Father Irwin points into the audience, and a spotlight shines upon Simon. "Dr. Simon Northstrum," the priest says, "please stand and be recognized. Here is the man who I believe silenced the drumbeats of war and stood tall when the world wanted to crucify him." Simon reluctantly rises to a standing ovation. He waves a quick acknowledgment and sits, not wanting the spotlight.

Father Irwin continues as the people sit. "Now, I would like to introduce the person who put this event together in such a short time and under challenging circumstances. Please welcome from Swaddling Clothes a young lady with a sweet and beautiful spirit, Magdala." As the audience applauds, Maggie comes to the stage and thanks Father Irwin. He leaves the stage.

"Good evening everyone," Maggie greets the audience. "Thank you for supporting us tonight. I listened to Father's message, and I agree with his words—a message that is a wonderful introduction to what is in store for you this evening. It appears parents have rounded up their children who have been visiting booths and enjoying the amusements. We at Swaddling Clothes have added many interns from the local high school, and they are so excited to show off our new lines of clothes. Not only are they attractive, but when you wear them you will feel very comfortable; it's like being wrapped in your blanket as a baby."

Maggie looks offstage right and says, "First up is Emma. She is wearing a yellow pencil skirt and a navy-blue sweater." Emma strolls the runway, copying the moves she has seen on television fashion shows. The whistles from the crowd start. Offstage, Sophia looks at Lennon and says, "She looks beautiful."

Lennon replies, "She always looks beautiful to me, but yeah, tonight she looks especially great."

"Other guys think so too. You'd better jump, or they will."

"I know, Sophia. It's a secret, but I plan to tell her with my song tonight."

"Oh, so instead of crashing and burning in front of one person, you want to do it in front of the whole town." Lennon looks at her quizzingly. She pats him on the back and then says, "It's my turn; wish me luck."

"You will do great, Sophia," Lennon tells her.

"I hope Bobby thinks the same." Then, before stepping out from the wing, Sophia tells Lennon, "By the way, to take the pressure off you, Emma feels the same way about you as you feel about her—but don't tell her I told you so. Just go get her."

Lennon displays a huge smile. The potential money and recording opportunity he could receive from the talent show is no longer the most important thing. His thoughts now are focused on hoping his song is perfect and hits Emma's heart.

※

The commander's lens reads, "Prepare for our meeting tomorrow." Michael, who is not at the event, responds, "I am on it."

※

The interns each have had at least one turn on the runway. Jennifer walks with a new confidence given by her new friendships. She even wishes good luck to Lennon, the man who took none of her abuse. The parents and everyone else fully enjoy the show. Even the children take time every now and then to look up from their bags of candy. Simon says to Alexis, "These Swaddling people are nice. They have selected people that never get chosen. We have seen kids with braces, crutches, wheelchairs, and special needs."

"It's wonderful," Alexis replies. "Everyone has looked so happy."

"I know," Simon agrees. "Everyone on stage has been glowing."

"Yes," Alexis tells him, "but I'm really talking about the looks on the parents' faces. The joy in their eyes makes me want to cry."

"Don't start the waterworks, honey."

Greg's band SureDeath gets ready to play as the fashion show ends.

Magdala tells the audience it's time for the talent show and gives them a preview of what's in store for them. She then introduces Greg and his group. They come on stage decked out in black, going against Swaddling's instructions. Free will can be a bummer. The band has a new guitarist who is a clone of Greg. Lennon listens from the side stage to gauge the competition. He knows SureDeath will implode without him. Greg starts with his rant and verbal diarrhea. He forgets he is playing to a different audience, and they respond with boos, rants, and thumbs down, as in Roman gladiator times.

Magdala's face expresses her sadness. As the boos and rants reach a crescendo, things get thrown at them, including pieces of candy. Greg unleashes obscenities at the crowd. Magdala has the stage crew signal Greg to stop, but he continues until they cut off his microphone. The band storms off, with Greg enraged. Passing Lennon with fire in his eyes, he says, "This is your fault, jerk. I'll get you for it." Lennon steps away from the maniac.

Some members of the crowd rise, almost ready to leave, but they return to their seats as a young lady calms them with beautiful music from Mozart. Magdala looks at Lennon and says, "Good timing for classical." With his John Lennon shirt on, Lennon smiles and nods.

The show rolls on with various audience-pleasing performances. Emma, who has been assisting Maggie in getting groups on and off the stage, eyes Lennon and says, "You are almost up, aren't you?"

"Yes, I'm the last act," he replies.

"Have you decided on a song?" she asks."

"Yes, but I want it to be a surprise."

"Goody," Emma says, beaming, "I like surprises."

"Emma, you did great in all the clothes you modeled, and the new people you helped followed you really well."

"Thank you, Lennon." She turns away, and then faces back toward Lennon. "One more thing." She leans in and kisses him on the cheek. "You will be great no matter the song, because it comes from your heart." She then leaves.

Lennon is euphoric, wondering if what just happened really happened. He tingles to his toes.

Emma muses as she walks away, hoping the kiss was the push he needed in order to get the courage to ask her out on a real date. Magdala's lens reads: "Isn't true love delightful?"

♫

The commander's lens reads, "Splendid."

♫

Meanwhile, Greg is backstage fuming. The rest of the band has left, figuring that if people threw stuff at them, there will be no prize money. Greg paces and comes upon Lennon's guitar case. An idea strikes him, so he scans the area and sees no one to interfere. He pulls a black knife from his pocket and opens the case. The knife slides over each fret until it rests on the string saddle. He saws the strings enough that they will break when Lennon starts. Greg knows the rules of the show. If Lennon can't continue, it will disqualify him. An evil smirk crosses his face, and he moves out of the stage area.

Magdala's lens reads, "What should I do with Greg?"

The commander's lens reads, "You gave him hope and were paid with treachery. I have him in hand."

Emma and Sophia sit with their parents, with Sophia next to Bobby, who has heartily congratulated her on her looks and performance. Emma glances at her and gives a happy clap.

"Dad," Emma says, "Lennon is coming on now to wrap up the show. I'm nervous."

Simon replies, "He is good and will do fine." Alexis pats her hand.

Lennon takes the stage with his guitar. A loud voice of approval explodes from the group of studio musicians, saying, "Go for it, Lennon!" He puts his hand to his eyes to block the footlights and look into the audience. He waves to the group and smiles. They respond, "Whoop! Whoop!" Lennon feels like a rock star.

He sits on the provided stool and adjusts the microphone on stage. He plugs his guitar into the preplaced amplifier. He then says, "This is a song I wrote for a beautiful girl here tonight. It is full of what I carry inside, so this is my leap of faith for you. I hope in my heart you will catch me."

With surprise in her eyes and on her face, Emma just knows he is talking about her. She looks at Alexis, who gently grabs and holds her daughter's hand. "I'm sure it will be marvelous," she tells her daughter.

Lennon strums his guitar twice to check the tuning. On the second stroke, the strings break one by one. Lennon is perplexed and devastated. He has never had every string break at once. He has extra strings but not enough time to replace them all and stay within the time limit allowed. His shoulders droop, and he hangs his head.

In horror, Emma looks to her mom. "Something is wrong, Mom. I need to help him." Alexis shakes her head slightly and softly says, "Not now, hon."

Embarrassed and almost in tears, Lennon says to himself, "God, why did this happen now on my big night?" Then, even though he knows he probably won't have time enough, he reaches into his case to start applying new strings.

Maggie approaches Mark Thomas in the audience, who is sitting on an end seat. She says, "Mr. Thomas, your son needs you now. You can comfort him."

"What should I say?"

"Telling him you believe in him is a good start."

"Okay. I'll … I'll try."

Lennon's father hustles to go to the stage while the judges decide whether Lennon will continue. He does not have much time left. On the way to the stage, Oz intercepts the father. "Mr. Thomas," Oz says, "I work with Lennon at the recording studio. Here is a guitar someone asked me to bring tonight to give to Lennon after the show. Give it to him now so he can continue and not be disqualified." Thomas accepts the cased guitar and rushes to his son.

He sees his son's eyes tearing, but they brighten with surprise as he walks onstage with the guitar case. "I believe in you, son," Thomas says. He hugs Lennon and gives him the guitar case, saying, "A man named Oz gave me this." Lennon wipes his eyes. Mr. Thomas watches Lennon as he kneels and opens the case. A handwritten note to him sits atop a cloth covering the guitar. "Dear Lennon," it reads, "I thought of you on my way back to England. You are at a crossroads in your life. 'Do I play other people's songs, or do I play what my heart writes?' is your decision to make. John and I were at a similar crossing and chose our songs. I guess you can say it worked out pretty well. If I can give you fatherly advice, it would be this: quit playing Beatles songs and play yours. Someone special inspired every love song ever written. Oz played me your song for your special lady. Don't change a word or note. You remind me of another Lennon, and it would be an honor to work with you anytime, and someday we can walk the Abbey Road strip together. In the guitar case is my gift to you for helping with my project. John would not want it sitting in a case or behind glass in a museum or a themed restaurant. Let's honor him by playing it well. Give the world your gift of music. Go get them, Lennon. All the best—your friend Paul."

Lennon peels back the cloth covering the guitar, exposing a Rickenbacker 325—the actual one on his shirt and poster. He turns to his father, this time with tears of joy welling up in his eyes. "What's wrong now, son?" he asks.

"It's my dream guitar, Dad, once owned by John Lennon."

"The one on your shirt and on the poster in your room?"

Lennon nods and says, "Paul McCartney gave it to me, with a note to me."

"You know Paul McCartney?"

"Yes, from the studio."

"Wow!"

The stage manager interrupts, asking whether Lennon will continue.

"Yes," Mr. Thomas answers. "Lennon is ready."

Lennon lifts the guitar and hugs it tightly. Looking up toward the ceiling, he whispers, "Thank you."

His father hands his son a handkerchief. "You'd better clean up to sound good for Emma."

"You know?" Lennon asks.

"I may have been a drunk, but I've always had good eyes." Mr. Thomas then walks toward the wing to watch as Lennon prepares to resume.

Lennon apologizes and states, "A dear friend stepped in with a replacement guitar. It seems miracles have surrounded me lately. I need one more, so here we go."

He launches into his song, full of his deepest feelings for Emma. With every word, Emma's face glows brighter and Alexis clutches her hand tighter. Simon beams at his happy daughter. The final line of the song is the repeated refrain "God, I didn't know heaven was here on Earth." The entire audience gets on their feet, singing the refrain along with Lennon. Emma knows the refrain means she is his heaven, and she is lifted higher than she's ever been before.

The song ends, and Lennon himself is lifted high as he sees the crowd and listens to the thunderous applause. As he humbly bows, he realizes that even though he wrote the song for Emma, maybe everyone had it wrap around their hearts. Sharing it with the world is what John and Paul would do, but he will ask Emma's permission.

"Mom, I am going to the stage," says Emma.

"Yes," Alexis replies, "now is a good time."

Emma looks toward Sophia, who is standing with everyone else and who has her arm around Bobby. She removes her arm and jumps up and down, doing her happy clap. Emma responds in kind and then dashes for the stage.

Lennon is still waving to the crowd, with his father, Magdala, and Father Irwin near him. All the talent show participants then come onstage and spread out to be acknowledged, and the audience claps loudly again. There are no sad faces anywhere around, except for one. Greg walks to his car alone, guitar in hand. He pops the trunk and violently throws the guitar inside. As he plops into his seat, he mumbles, "This internship is worthless." At that moment, his phone rings. He gazes at the screen and punches it to answer. Dropping the phone, he hangs his head. The dropped phone reveals the image. "Your rapture is brought to humanity by the Dominion … Where are you in your soul's contract with us?" An autopsy will say he died of natural causes.

The commander's lens reads: "I send you Greg Mindoro."

Back on stage, Lennon continues in his revelry, the session group egging him on with chants of "Hail, Lennon!" Emma gets on the stage and runs toward him. His entire focus is now on her.

Throwing her arms around his neck and looking into his eyes, she says, "I will always catch you, and I loved every word and note. It was magnificent." He holds her, discovering his arms fit her perfectly. Lennon loosens his embrace but is stopped by Emma. "Aren't you forgetting something, mister?" Lennon looks at her, questioningly. "Your love letter needs a spectacular ending," she hints.

"Ending?" Lennon asks.

"Kiss me, silly! Kiss me!" They close around each other in a long, loving kiss. Alexis and Simon snuggle in the audience as they watch the love between Emma and Lennon unfold on stage.

"Our little girl has grown into a wonderful young lady," says

Simon. "You did good work, Mom." She clutches her husband's hand tightly.

After the onstage kiss ends, Emma asks, "What happened when you first started?"

"Emma, a miracle happened here tonight."

"A miracle? How?"

"When I began, all the strings on my guitar broke in the same place at once."

"I noticed. Were they new?"

"Yes, put on yesterday and tuned. I thought I was done, but then, as you saw, Dad showed up with another guitar from Oz."

"Yeah. Go on."

"There is much more you don't understand." Lennon shows her the letter.

She reads it and looks at Lennon. "He gave you John Lennon's guitar? It's worth thousands—maybe millions!"

"Oh, I would never sell it. See it, Emma? It's exquisite."

"This is the one from your dream poster?"

"Yes, the actual one. I said a miracle happened. Look more closely at my shirt. See?" He holds up the guitar; they are the same.

Emma gasps. "Exactly!"

Father Irwin steps to the microphone and thanks everyone who helped with the event, especially the Swaddling folks. No one is surprised when the talent show prize and recording opportunity are awarded to Lennon. In fact, if he had not, people would have been disappointed—even the other participants.

The civic center eventually empties after a lot of talking and congratulations among all the families and participants. The Swaddling trio exit to the street and slip unnoticed into the atmosphere. Magdala addresses the interns and thanks them for their service. She advises them that in the back is a room filled with clothes for them to take. She says, "If you need nothing, give it to someone in friendship or with need."

Simon and Alexis go onstage to congratulate Lennon, who is stuck like glue to Emma; both of their faces are glowing. Simon and

Alexis converse with Mark Thomas, who says, "You have a beautiful daughter."

"You have a very talented son," Simon tells him.

"That's his mom's doing," Mark Thomas replies. "I can't take any credit."

Alexis, touching Lennon's arm, says, "I know your mom was here tonight and saw and heard everything. She is the proudest angel in heaven right now."

"Thanks," Lennon replies. His eyes moisten as he smiles.

Simon interrupts. "After a wonderful night like this, pizza is in order for everyone, my treat. Mark, will you and Lennon join us?"

Lennon looks to his father and nods. "Thanks," Mark says, "that would be nice."

Simon sees Magdala and steps up to her. "You did a wonderful job with everything."

"Thank you," she says. "I see you have two new lovebirds."

"Yeah, Lennon finally got his nerve up." With a slight laugh, he adds, "And he broke the barrier in front of a lot of people."

"Yes. Yes he did," Magdala replies, with a slight laugh of her own.

"We are going for pizza, and we'd all like to have you join us," Simon tells her.

"Oh, thank you. It sounds lovely. But we have a corporate retreat tomorrow, which I'm overdue in preparing for. I'll probably be burning some midnight oil as it is."

"I understand," Simon replies. "I've experienced my share of those nights." He pauses. "We'll see you again, I hope."

"Oh, yes. Our paths will cross again, I'm sure. I have it on good authority. Tell everyone good-bye for me. Your family has a wonderful faith binding you. Never lose it. Take care." She heads for the exit and disappears into the night.

The Northstrum and Thomas families head out for pizza. As they exit the center, Simon puts his arm around Lennon and says, "So I guess I need to keep an eye on you now that you are a famous musician. We won't have any drugs, sex, and rock 'n' roll stuff with my daughter, will we?"

Lennon's jaw drops in surprise. A fearful look covers his face. Simon breaks into a smile and hugs Lennon tightly. "I'm pulling your chain. Welcome to the family." A relieved Lennon thaws quickly, realizing he's been had by a man with a sense of humor.

Alexis and Simon are alone in their car, with Emma riding with Lennon and his dad. As their conversation swings from one thing to another, Alexis asks, "Has *Sojourner* spoken to you lately?"

"No. I've heard nothing since the president's address to the nation and world."

"Well, with everything working great, it appears you are off the hook, Noah."

"I'm no Noah."

"Father Irwin thinks otherwise."

Simon gives a silent laugh.

"Honey, how do you feel, honestly?" Alexis asks.

"Good. Why?"

"No, I mean with everything that's happened, how do you feel deep inside?"

"Are you going into funeral home psychiatry?"

"No," she says, giving him a punch in the arm. "Be honest. Are you still a little scared? The whole thing terrified me, yet I watched you. The world wanted your head, and you kept going. Sure you got angry, got down a little bit. That's understandable. But all in all, you never really lost your cool. How did you do it?"

"It's strange, Alexis, to be honest with you. I've learned to have more peace now. It's taken a while, some knocks on the head and the feeling of being overwhelmed, but I've gained more and more peace lately. Sort of like in the Bible—'a peace that passes all understanding.'"

"I saw and felt that in you, Simon. And seeing and feeling that in you helped me when I was most terrified—terrified for you and for Emma and me."

Simon replies, "Like I said, it's strange to have a feeling of peace when the world was on the brink of imploding."

"How do you account for it, Simon?"

"Well, even though *Sojourner* has really gotten on my nerves at times, even telling me early on that they would crucify me, the more I talked with *Sojourner*, the more I learned to gain peace within. I could get upset outwardly, but I had that strange peace within. It just grew in me slowly.

Alexis responds, "Strange but wonderful."

"And you know, Alexis, I felt the same way after they selected Emma for the internship program and Magdala came to our home. She was warm and calming, and I felt Emma was in caring hands."

"Me too," Alexis replies.

"Magdala is a name not taken by many people," Simon tells her. "Do you know anyone with that name?"

"No. But I think it is Middle Eastern, going by her complexion. Actually, I was rather jealous her skin was so perfect."

"She couldn't hold a candle to you."

"Liar! Liar! Pants on fire!"

Alexis grabs her phone and types "Magdala" into Google. "Wow!" she exclaims.

"Jeez, Alexis, what's wrong?"

"Do you have any idea of what 'Magdala' means, Simon?"

"No, but you'd better tell me, based on your reaction."

"It is another name for Mary, the mother of God, or Mary Magdalene." She pauses and then continues. "Who are those Swaddling people, Simon? Didn't *Sojourner* say the Dominion were on Earth and would help you?"

"Yes."

"Also, *Sojourner* said they answered your prayer, and mine was answered." Alexis quickly calls Emma and says, "Emma, listen, and only give me short answers."

"Okay," Emma replies in a rather questioning manner.

"Did you pray for anything in recent weeks, like Lennon getting help with his father and winning the talent show?"

"Yes, every night."

"Anything else?"

"Yes, for Jennifer to stop bugging me."

Alexis hears Lennon whispering in the background. "Is everything all right?" Emma smiles, nods her head, and shushes him.

"Remind me of the names of the other Swaddling people," Alexis says.

"Along with Magdala, whom we call Maggie, there is Raphael, whom we call Raph; Gabriel, whom we call Gabe; and Mr. Deuss, the leader of the group. There was another one named Michael, but he was back at corporate. We never met him."

"Thanks, honey," Alexis tells Emma. "See you at the restaurant." She writes down the names and then asks Simon, "Can you think of any new people you have met with since your prayer?"

"Yeah, a bunch, and their names are followed by every abbreviation like FBI, CIA, NSA, and ATF. Why?"

"Outside of these, did you meet anyone unexpectedly with whom you discussed the *Sojourner* talks in passing?"

"I've told you, Alexis, apart from the two of us, only Dr. Tristin Beckett and Norm know of my talking with *Sojourner*." Simon pauses and then says, "However, as I think about it, I did mention *Sojourner* later to Michael Cott from the NSA—the one who helped me in many ways."

Alexis reads off the names she wrote down and then asks Simon, "Do these names mean anything to you?"

He thinks, slowly shakes his head, and then says, "No … I … Wait. Two of the names do come to mind, along with Michael."

"Which two?"

"Raph and Gabe—or, as Emma told you, Raphael and Gabriel."

"If you can remember, tell me about them."

"The day I went for my processing in returning to JPL, I had to wait for my background check, so I went to Jimmy's. A dog was out front, chasing a ball. It spilled my coffee. The man with the dog rushed up and apologized and refilled my coffee. His name was Raph."

"And …?" Alexis says.

"Well, a few days later I was back at Jimmy's, and Raph and the dog were back. He bought me lunch. I thought it strange at the time, eating with a stranger. He was in electric power systems. I was in the middle of processing *Sojourner*. We ended up speaking of faith and listening."

"What about this Gabriel?"

"I was back at Jimmy's again, this time with the NSA woman Kelly, and she ran into a missionary priest she knew. His name is Father Gabriel, or Gabe for short. He dined with us, and he and I had a marvelous discussion on God's Dominion when Kelly left to talk with someone on the phone." Simon hesitates and then says, "Wait just a minute here … Surely … How could I be so stupid as to not realize?"

Alexis catches his thought and asks, with tears in her eyes, "Were you … were we in the presence of angels?"

"That's what I … but I don't know. Maybe. Maybe."

"Simon," Alexis replies, "Raphael, Gabriel, and Michael are the names of archangels. And we've discussed Magdala."

"True, they are the names of archangels, but I've not heard of an angel named Deuss."

Alexis starts to say something. "Well—"

Simon interrupts with "Wait a minute. Wait just a minute. It's coming back to me from grad school. When I was working on my doctorate, we translated a lot of things from Latin. It stuck in my mind that the Latin word '*Deus*' means 'divine' or 'deity' or 'god.' Remove that last *s* from 'Deuss,' and you see what we've got?"

"Wow!" Alexis responds. "He's been walking around in plain sight with his name veiled, just adding an extra letter."

"You know, Alexis, *Sojourner* told me of an incident that happened here in the States, in Cokeville, Wyoming. I didn't research it because I got busy with the investigations. We're almost to the pizza place, but quickly google that town and see what you find."

Alexis searches on her phone, which leads her to a YouTube video. She puts the phone near the dash so both can see. The video ends as they arrive at the pizza joint. The others are already inside. Alexis and Simon look at one another before Simon says, "Angels saved the Cokeville children because everyone was selfless, focused on one need."

Silence follows momentarily before it is broken by Alexis asking, "Simon, have you been talking to God all this time?"

"Alexis, I believe God is always talking to me, to us, to the peoples of the world. But, as *Sojourner* said, we all made the world about us and worldly things, and we quit listening to God. Maybe we told Him what we wanted, but we didn't listen to hear what He had to say about our requests. We damaged our relationships with God and with our very own souls." Simon pauses, and then says, "Alexis, before we go in, I need to give thanks." She and Simon sit with hands clasped as Simon softly, almost inaudibly, prays. It may be rather quiet in the car, but the prayer screams into the Dominion.

In the darkest part of the night, four colored beings pulse through the magnetic field and move into the white light crowning the earth.

The light spreads, blanketing the whole planet in a faint veil of the Dominion's grace. The haze flashes like a person taking a picture. It is accompanied by a thunderclap; suddenly the light disappears and the blue oceans of the earth are crystal clear. Mankind will discover a wondrous sight left by the visitors when daylight breaks. The earth becomes a bright star to the beings.

CHAPTER 30

"Good morning. Here we go again, folks! Welcome to America's Newsroom. I'm Bill Hemmer. Hello, Martha."

"Good morning, Bill. What do you have for everyone?"

"Well, Martha, I say to the world today that unless you have been in a submarine on the ocean floor, you have seen the celestial light show in the sky. People have tweeted us saying they feel as if they were back when the shepherds and wise men saw the star of Bethlehem. Some of our contributors say this is a rare planetary alignment. The sun, Jupiter, Saturn, and the moon are all in Aries. Venus was close, in Pisces, with Mercury and Mars on the other side, in Taurus. They say Aries is the location of the vernal equinox. Folks, I am clueless on what I read to you. Let's call it an amazing miracle. After the events of the last few weeks, it seems that the president was correct in his decision. We are all still here, and this morning is spectacular."

Upon hearing this, Simon breaks from his breakfast station and bolts through the front door. There in the sky is a beautiful star.

Alexis calls to him, "What are you doing outside in your PJs?"

"Come here, Alexis! Hurry!"

Alexis descends the stairs and goes out the door Simon has left open. Looking up, she holds her hand to her mouth, saying, "Oh, my! A star in the daytime! A bright star at that!"

They look at each other and say, "Angels!"

Simon tells her, "Well, no one can accuse me of moving the planets that I just heard about on TV. I'll call Norm to get the details on this event." He then pauses, struck by the strange look on Alexis's face. "Is everything okay?" he asks her.

"Yes, but I just had a thought. Remember when you told me Magdala couldn't go for pizza with us because they had a corporate retreat she had to prepare for?"

"Yeah," Simon responds. Alexis points to the bright star. Befuddled, Simon asks, "So what are you saying?"

"Simon, there are all the angels looking over humanity, gathered at their corporate event. Don't you get it? They are showing us All Souls' Day and the grace they left us. In answer to your question, everything is as it should be." She kisses him on the cheek and says, "Go call Norm and see what he has to say." She watches him go back into the house, looks up toward the star, and whispers, "Thank You." A smile crosses her face as though the star winked back at her in response.

⚓

In another place, there is a room presenting the gift of unlimited sight. It has a window into the universe that provides panoramic Hubble-like telescopic images as far as the eye can see. A pulsing white light encompasses the room waist high, as if one were skiing in a powdery white snow. A brighter light, even more brilliant than the other, forms the upper edge of a channel. The trough curves around the room and goes on forever, like reflections between two mirrors.

Beneath the thin membrane of light is the rainbow river of life. It flows in from the universe and to the top of the canal. The river washes over everything in the moat and then exits back into space. A white light being is slightly bent to peer into the furrow. The dives into the rainbow and uses its thin hands to widen it, as though parting a curtain or whisking away fog. As the gap widens, a small, spinning, marble-like blue planet appears. The river washes the earth with life.

The white light being moves along the line, repeating the action and exposing the other planets. There are countless worlds in the bath. A large red ball spinning within the rainbow of light resembles Mars. The next orb is Jupiter. The being examines each like a gardener tending a nursery. When the being's hands leave the rainbow, the light membrane returns to covering the river.

Four childish light creatures surround the white being. They are playful children, wiggling and full of innocence. These tiny beings pulse with various colors, as if they are part of the rainbow. The white light being is surgeon-focused, with hands moving in and out of the river. The brightly colored beings scurry to line up to the right, and the white being addresses them as a teacher would instruct a class. The white being's lens reads, "I am so excited with your stories you have developed for this lifetime. I will miss you in your absence and look forward to your return and the discussion we must have about your learning journey."

Three of the colored lights, one by one, jump into the river flowing through the earth and disappear. But as the fourth one jumps, the violet one, the white being reaches out and jerks the violet being back by the scruff of the neck.

The white being's lens reads, "*Sojourner*, I know of your mentoring of Simon and the disruption of the river of souls." The violet being's innocent face grows sad. "I forgive you," the message continues, "because it worked well for my plan; but you will pay for your actions in this life story." The childish being's face glows brightly as it jumps to embrace the fatherlike being. After a quick hug and childish laugh, the violet being does a swan dive into the rainbow after its friends. The white light closes over the river and flows back into the room's light.

CHAPTER 31

Simon lies motionless in bed with his eyelids trembling in REM sleep. They flicker and pulse, trying to open reluctantly, as if waking up is too painful. A large white bandage covers his head. He is in a hospital bed surrounded by his family and friends. Alexis sits near him, holding on to his hand, with Emma on the other side, watching the eyes move. Lennon is at Emma's side. At the foot of the bed is Norm, standing watch over his friend.

Each person in the room has a little smile of relief, as if they have received some wonderful news. Suddenly a text message notification on Emma's phone breaks the silence. "Sorry," Emma says to her mom. "I forgot to mute it." She mutes it now, looks at the message, and shows it to Lennon. He just sort of rolls his eyes and shakes his head.

"Important?" Alexis asks.

"Not really. Sophia saying she was outside the principal's office and overhead him talking about a clothing company planning to come to school for a program of some kind. You know how Sophia gets excited about things." Alexis smiles and nods.

The phone noise and talking seem to have encouraged Simon's struggle to open his eyes. His eyelids flutter, and his mouth twitches. The obvious relief in the room is accompanied by larger synchronized smiles as Simon's eyes continue fluttering until at last they burst open. With a questioning look, he turns his head toward Alexis and then Emma.

Even though everyone can see him, Alexis exclaims, "He's awake!" She presses the call button to the nurses' station.

"Where am I?" he finally asks.

"By God's grace, you will be all right," Alexis tells Simon. She caresses his face and then leans in and kisses his cheek. "You had us so worried."

Simon, dazed and half-awake, looks at Alexis. "Why am I here? Did I have a heart attack?"

"No, Dad," Emma blurts out. "They don't bandage your head if you had a heart attack." Simon lifts his hand to his head, feeling for the bandage. "Why is my head bandaged? Was I in a car accident?"

"No, honey," Alexis tells him. "You slipped in the shower on the loose tile."

"The one I said I would fix myself instead of calling the handyman?"

"The one and the same," Alexis tells him.

"But how did I get here?"

"After I left for work, I had forgotten my cell phone and came back to the house. I found you on the shower floor. Honey, It's a miracle. If I hadn't forgotten my phone, you could have been lying there all day, and we might have lost you."

"What is wrong with me?"

"The scan was normal, but you got a big bump on your head and a concussion. You have been out of it."

There's a knock on the hospital room door and a man in a lab coat enters. "Hello, Dr. Northstrum," he says. "You are quite the robotics man." Simon nods and attempts to smile. "I'm Dr. Reeves, your neurologist. The nurses told me you had regained consciousness. That's good. I have reviewed the scans we did when the paramedics brought you to the ER. Everything looks fine; we see no blood clots under your bump."

"When will I be able to go home?"

"I see no reason we can't release you now." Looking at Alexis, Dr. Reeves tells her, "I would suggest you keep him awake for the next twenty-four hours. It is easier to see any adverse reactions going on when he is awake." Addressing Simon, he says, "Your hat might not fit for a few days. The nurse will be in with your discharge papers in a few minutes." Dr. Reeves leaves the room.

Simon turns to Alexis and says, "I'm sorry I caused you so much worry. I'll fix that tile tomorrow."

"You'll do no such thing. I will personally call the handyman."

"Daddy, I was so worried," says Emma.

"Sorry to scare you, hon." She grabs his hand, and he nods toward Lennon. Simon then looks at Norm. "Thanks for coming, buddy," he tells him.

Alexis called me and said you were on the way to the ER, so I wanted to be here. I know you would do the same."

"Norm, I am sorry for the problems the Reliance program caused for you and JPL."

Norm stares at his friend with a questioning look. "Simon," he responds, what is a Reliance program?"

"You know, the software that helped reestablish communications with the rovers but infected computers globally."

"I have not looked at your new software yet, Simon," Norm tells him. He then turns to Alexis and says, "Simon might have been dreaming when he was out of it."

"Honey," Alexis tells her husband, "you aren't working at JPL right now."

"But I was working there, and then these weird things were happening with the rovers, computers, and cell phones. Five million died from unknown causes brought on by the Dominion."

"Dad, no one has died in any great numbers, but you might've been watching too much of *The Walking Dead*." She pokes him, knowing the show, to him, is mindless.

Norm adds, "It sounds like a good Spielberg movie with aliens killing people."

Simon turns to Alexis. "Was I imagining it?"

"We just need to get you home, hon, and let you get some rest and get healed."

Norm tells him, "There has not been a sabotage of any

communication anywhere, Simon. But what you're saying sounds like a remake of *The Day the Earth Stood Still*."

Simon's head falls back on the pillow. "But everything was so real."

"Sometimes dreams are like that," Alexis tells him. "And it takes a while to adjust to being awake if you have had a knock on the head."

A portly old black nurse in scrubs enters the room pushing a wheelchair. Her salt-and-pepper hair is in a bun with a pencil stabbed through it.

"My, my, my, this name is familiar," she says. "One of my babies has come home."

Alexis looks toward the voice, and a smile spreads across her face. "Thelma, is that you?" She turns to her husband and says, "Look, Simon. It's Thelma." Looking back to Thelma, she tells her, "I thought you retired."

"I did, for about a minute, but then I realized I was at home sitting in a chair, waiting to die. I decided I needed my babies back around me."

"You are still in maternity?" Alexis asks.

"Honey, I'll be there until they take me down to the morgue. I got to be close to my babies."

"You are not on this floor?"

"No, they needed a nurse to wheel you out, so they asked if I had a moment. My doctor says I need to take more steps for my health." She points to a pedometer on her waist. "They want me to wear this," she says with a laugh. "As if nurses don't get enough walking in. So anyway, I saw the name and wondered, 'Could it be one of my babies?'"

Thelma looks to Emma and says, "Are you the little one I met many years ago when my hair was a little darker?"

Alexis says, "Thelma, this is my daughter, Emma." To Emma, Alexis says, "Honey, Thelma was the nurse who first placed you in my arms after your delivery."

Thelma walks to Emma and brushes back her hair. "You're pretty like your momma." Emma smiles and thanks her. "I know you are a great kid," Thelma continues, "'cause you've got great parents. Don't forget that, sweetie."

She turns to Simon. "Well, well, Mr. Simon, worrying your family like this all because of an undone 'honey do' job, I hear. I guess you'll call the man next time." She smiles at Alexis and then hands her some papers. "Here you go. You'd better sign these release forms so we can get him out of here. Mr. Simon ain't in no condition to sign anything right now."

Alexis signs the forms, and Thelma tells him, "Your clothes are in the closet over there, so let's see if you can walk over to the closet, okay? First of all, let's get you up and moving and see how steady you are on your feet." She helps him push back the covers, and he swings his feet over the bed. He plants them on the cold tile floor, which he can feel even with his hospital socks on.

Thelma grabs each of Simon's forearms and helps him to stand. She backs away and encourages Simon to take steps with her help. Simon steps forward and shows no symptoms of dizziness. He makes his way a few more steps, reaching the closet. He politely pushes Thelma's hands away from him and assures her he will be fine.

Alexis asks Emma to give her father a few minutes to get dressed. Emma and Lennon leave the room. Norm stays to help with Simon if needed. Thelma says, "I'll be down here at the nurses' station. Push the call button when ready, and I'll wheel you out. Hospital policy." She leaves.

Simon tells Alexis he can dress himself. He does, and he then sits on the edge of the bed. "I can't wait to get out of here," he says. He then asks Alexis, "So I'm still unemployed?"

"Yes, dear."

"You're still at the funeral home?"

"Yes, I am."

Simon shakes his head and says, "It was the most amazing dream."

Norm, standing in the background, steps forward and says, "Simon, I would wait until later, but you both need good news right now. You will not be unemployed much longer. We want you back to help with the communications, and I've negotiated funding arrangements. You will have the same package you left with, but as an independent contractor, if it is okay with you."

"Are you kidding?" Simon replies. "I would love nothing more."

Alexis hugs Simon and mouths a thank-you to Norm. Alexis pushes the call button, and Thelma reenters shortly. Simon gets in the wheelchair and reaches out to shake Norm's hand and thank him on the way to the door as Thelma pushes him along. Emma and Lennon join Simon, Alexis, and Norm on the way out.

"We must make a small detour to the floor below," Thelma tells them. "They are doing Earl and Evie renovations, and I want to show you the changes." She presses the elevator button, and the doors slide open. The troupe boards the elevator, which stops on the next floor.

The doors open, and Alexis immediately notices the maternity sign.

"This is where you were born, Emma," Alexis tells her daughter. They move down the hall, coming to a large bronze statue of a woman standing behind a man with her arm draped around his shoulders. The man is a giant—about seven feet tall. He clutches a tiny infant in his large hands, almost shrouding the child in his palms. He holds the child in an encircling grasp against his chest and heart. The woman behind him looks over his shoulder at the child. The woman and man have loving, parental smiles carved into their faces.

Alexis says, "The statues are an addition."

"Yes," says Thelma. They are our Earl and Evie angels. We miss them here. All the upgrades are because of them.

"Earl and Evie?" asks Alexis.

"Earl Connery Hardin and his wife, Evie."

The mention of this man's name certainly catches Simon's attention.

Emma asks, "Wasn't that the attorney who represented all the scum and high-profile cases with celebrities and corrupt politicians? They discredited him, didn't they?"

Simon stares at the attorney's image as Thelma tells Emma, "Honey, don't judge a man by what you see on the news, because those stations might have an agenda. Martin Luther King Jr. said to judge him by the character of his soul." Thelma scans the group and continues. "Let me tell you about Earl and Evie and their selflessness." Simon's interest was high when he heard the name of Hardin, but now it is really piqued by the word "selflessness."

Thelma says, "Earl and Evie—a true love affair. Physically, I've not met a bigger man. He is what you might call a gentle giant. But he was a warrior in the courtroom, fighting for people and believing that every man and woman should woman should have their day. But, yes, it made him enemies."

Thelma pauses to admire the statue of the couple again. "They couldn't have children," she said. "So, at a young age, they both started down here, holding the babies in trouble. We call them the NICU kids. He was starting out as a lawyer, working long hours for no money. He would come in here bone tired, but he never missed a day, as he promised. The same with Evie. It must have been agonizing seeing the babies born and leave, but none with them. Then there were the days the troubled babies didn't make it. Earl would rail at God, but Evie would calm her giant." Thelma uses a finger to wipe her eyes. "Every loss ripped away part of his faith. As he progressed in his profession and the money got better, they would buy equipment for the hospital. It was things the nurses said we needed, but management refused, due to budgets. Yes, he represented some scum, but you never saw the news report on when he was down helping the poor or working for nothing—things that he did routinely. The little baby in his hands is Earl Junior."

The group looks up at the baby as Thelma goes on to say, "Let me tell you about that miracle child. The single mother was a drug-addicted woman who overdosed and died on the table. The baby was born premature and placed in the NICU with not much hope. But Earl and Evie had other ideas. Together, taking turns, they never left the child alone. Every minute of every day, one of them had a hand caressing the child. Earl's hand was so large it almost would not fit through the incubator opening, but he made it fit."

Emma has become mesmerized by Thelma's story. Thelma

continues: "I'm sure there were times their hands went to sleep, but there they stayed. The doctors tried everything known to medicine. Earl said he would sell everything if it would help. The staff called the little boy Earl Junior, which brought huge smiles to Earl and Evie. The day came when the doctors told Earl nothing more could be done, that the baby would not survive. This giant of a man broke into tears, asking why God hated them."

Now Emma wipes at her eyes as Thelma says, "There was Evie, caressing her grizzly bear, as she called him. She made him understand we are on God's time and they sent the baby to teach us. Earl and Evie then asked the doctors if they could hold the child outside the incubator, tubes, and machines. The doctors granted the request, and this was the day we saw a miracle. The statue is a representation of what occurred in that room."

Some others in the hospital hallway stop to listen as Thelma tells of the miracle. "We wrapped the child and placed him in Earl's arms. Evie wrapped herself around her husband. I don't know if they prayed; I wasn't close enough to hear. But I knew for sure the baby had passed when the doctor placed the infant in Earl's arms, because he looked at me and shook his head. Earl and Evie sat there with the little boy; it might have been ten minutes maybe. And then the doctor came to retrieve the baby."

Emma reaches down and grabs Lennon's hand, which surprises and thrills Lennon. He's never had the nerve to hold Emma's hand. But he realizes how meaningful this story is to Emma, knowing about the selflessness of her soul. Thelma says, "Earl asked the doctor for a little more time. Hesitantly, the doctor said okay. Earl continued holding him, gently caressing him and whispering into his little ear. And then the most amazing thing happened. There was a faint cry from within Earl's big hands. We all were breathless, waiting for another cry—and it came."

Simon looks up at Alexis, who looks down at him. Everyone is captivated, including the ones who have stopped in the hall to listen. Thelma continues. "The doctor, standing to the side to give Earl the few minutes he wanted, sprang to life and listened for a heartbeat, which came in rhythm. Grown men had teardrops spotting their clothes, but Earl's and Evie's eyes were rivers. I've never seen a grizzly bear cry tears of joy.

Seven days later, Earl Junior went home with them."

For the first time, Thelma notices the people who have stopped to listen. With a flick of the wrist, she waves them closer, and she continues. "I asked Earl later about what happened that day and how he saved the baby. He told me he didn't save the baby; the baby saved him. He said regardless of whether the child lived or died that day, something sent the baby's soul to him to teach him a lesson of learning selflessness and doing all we can without thought of reward.

The hallway crowd now moves even closer, circling Simon and his group, as Thelma says, "That day is branded in my mind—how I looked at a man's body and soul being enveloped and filled by grace and selflessness. It was a soul-to-soul connection. I'm no minister or physicist, but I have to believe that with God's grace Evie and Earl willed that child to life because they connected to their son physically and soulfully."

Not a listener is moving, but multiple eyes are moist. "We need more one-on-one personal connections," Thelma says. The son grew to be a fine young man. However, this story has a sad ending. Evie and Earl were on their way to see their son when their plane crashed. The hospital would not pay for the statue, because of Earl's publicity as an attorney. Hospital employees had the statue made with our money and other outside donations." Thelma clears her throat. "Before their deaths, you would not believe the multitude of people Evie and Earl helped, asking nothing in return. They lived by the 'Do for others what you would have others do for you' teaching, which Jesus described as the law of Moses and the prophets in a nutshell. The hospital may own this building, but the heart is right here with Earl and Evie."

Thelma then leads Simon and his group down the hall past the nursery window, everyone absorbing Thelma's story as they see the babies. Simon is recalling elements of his vivid dream—especially the

Sojourner talks and his own interaction with Earl Connery Hardin in the dream.

At the sound of special music coming over the hospital hallway speakers, Thelma smiles and announces, "Listen, everyone, a baby arrived. Music is played for each birth." While approaching the elevator that will take them to street level, a duty nurse pushes a clear bassinet holding a small baby swaddled in a blanket. Thelma stops the nurse so the troupe can see the baby. Thelma then reaches in and lifts the baby in her arms. "Girl?" Thelma asks. The nurse answers in the affirmative.

Alexis asks the duty nurse, "How old is she?"

"Born in the last hour," she answers.

"Simon," Alexis says, "look how tiny."

"Yes, and beautiful," Simon replies.

The duty nurse tells them, "The doctor said she came out laughing and giggling with a grin on her face, waving one hand. She has not stopped smiling since. Dr. Thompson said that in all his years of deliveries, every baby has come out crying, but not her. He said, and I quote him exactly, "This one is going to be a handful.""

"Isn't she pretty, Mom?" Emma says.

"So much promise," Simon responds to Emma, patting her hand.

Alexis asks the duty nurse, "What did they name her?"

The nurse says, "It's an unusual name—something historical, I guess. Sojo something."

Thelma reaches for the chart to find the name. "Sojourner," she reads aloud. "Don't see this name often."

It startles Simon, who stares at Thelma and Norm.

Norm blurts out, "How ironic. Simon here built a robot named 'Sojourner.'"

"Well, my! That is a coincidence," Thelma says. Noticing Simon's increased interest in Sojourner, she asks him, "Would you like to hold her?"

Simon looks at Thelma, then at Sojourner, and then up at Alexis, who says, "Go ahead, hon, take her. She won't break."

Thelma hands Sojourner to Simon. As he stares into her beautiful blue eyes, another song begins to play. Emma comments, "Dad, isn't that your favorite song from church?"

"Yeah, you're right, honey, 'Be Not Afraid.'"

Simon gets a curious look on his face and returns his gaze to the newborn. She is staring back at him with beautiful blue eyes, seemingly having a mischievous smile just for him. Her little fisted hand opens, and her arm begins waving as though she is leaving on a journey. An ever-so-faint childish laugh, a giggle, is heard as the nurse lifts her from Simon's arms, places her back in the bassinet, and wheels her away. Simon stares in disbelief with his mouth hanging open, followed by a calmness he hasn't experienced in quite a while.

Alexis looks at her husband and says, "You have the most peaceful look on your face, especially considering your accident."

"The music triggered a memory," Simon replies. "An old friend told me, 'Be not afraid; your faith will save you.' After today's experience, I know I'm on the right path." Everyone looks at him, and then at each other, questioningly. Simon leaves the hospital with a sense of peace that his soul is as it should be and he need not fear. He raises his eyes to the heavens and mumbles, "Thank you. I'm listening now."

The commander says unto mankind,
"Be Not Afraid. I await humanity's natural return
so we may reason how your life followed your
soul's benevolent story we wrote together."

ACKNOWLEDGMENTS

I would like to thank my family for their help in the project and their understanding when I asked a thousand times, "What do you think?" I thank the priests who tried to distance themselves when I asked continual questions on faith, and I am thankful I was not struck by lightning when doing so. I also thank the hundreds of patrons of grocery stores whom I pestered at the checkouts to see which test covers caught their eyes. I offer a special thank-you to all my advance readers who gave me insight to make the story better—especially Soni Davison. Finally, I give heartfelt thanks to Carl Mays for his excellent help in development.

ABOUT THE AUTHOR

John Milan Dudeff is a husband, father, grandfather, entrepreneur and former publisher and developer of a web-based student mentoring program. His first published writing was as a high school freshman when he was a winner of the New England United Nations Essay Award. Now, fifty years later, he has made time to finish and update a story he began writing several years ago. With a theme of benevolence in a world where "self" has infected society more than any virus or disease, he tells of one man's sacrifice to help many. The theme of benevolence holds true for any age and is the cure for a world so infected with "self."

Lightning Source UK Ltd.
Milton Keynes UK
UKHW041612240621
386092UK00001B/34

9 781489 734457